RISE OF THE BLADEMASTER

RISE OF THE BLADEMASTER

SWORDSONG SERIES
BOOK ONE

BRENT BATLA

gatekeeper press™
Columbus, Ohio

Rise of the Blademaster

Published by Gatekeeper Press
2167 Stringtown Rd, Suite 109
Columbus, OH 43123-2989
www.GatekeeperPress.com

The editorial work for this book is entirely the product of the author. Gatekeeper Press did not participate in and is not responsible for any aspect of this element.

Edited by: Pauline Harris Editorial
Cover art by: Helena Cnockaert
Map by: Taf Richards
Layout by: Gatekeeper Press

Library of Congress Control Number: 2021946506

ISBN (hardcover): 9780578926964
ISBN (paperback): 9780578946498
eISBN: 9780578926971

RiseoftheBlademaster.com

Contents

Acknowledgements

I would first and foremost like to thank my wife, Jessica (Evenstar), for her tireless patience and support, particularly during the incalculable hours that went in to the creation of this book. Thank you for your kindhearted enthusiasm when I would conclude a scene and excitedly geek out on you as I read it to you for the tenth time (after as many rewrites). Thank you for your understanding of my incessant drive to tell my story to the world. I truly could not have found a better soulmate to spend my life with.

I would also like to thank my friends Michael (Maugrim), Donnie (D'Jorn), Dan (Falcon), and Devin (Dante) for their deep, enduring friendship. I will always cherish our hours upon hours of sitting across from each other at the RPG table, telling stories, making fun of one another, and maybe occasionally getting in some actual gaming if any time remained. Thanks to each of you, this book memorializes many of those fond memories.

Thank you Troy (Nuich) and the entire Clark clan (Sondrax, Angelica, Et Al.) for letting me bounce so many different plot ideas off of you and helping me so much throughout this project.

The Epic of Alynthi

Part 1

Hear the bard as his song begins,
with a greatest tale of old.
An enchanting tune he weaves and spins,
a story that must be told.

In caverns deep, through shadowed halls,
unspeakable terror was wakened.
The ancient of evils awoke and stirred,
and foundation of world was shaken.

The nameless ones, both terrible and great
the lands they would consume.
Mankind would meet a terrible fate,
and all seemed surely doomed.

Through darkness deep and great despair,
the companions draw together.
A test that all of them would share,
they journey into the nether.

As shadow loomed across the land,
they set upon their quest.
Impossible task was nigh at hand,
to find the answers best.

For power was found through mortal test
by blade that had been bound.
The Age of Man would now stand up
to face the terror down.

INTRODUCTION

Dark Dreams

Adamar's heart skipped several beats, and his blood ran ice cold as a terrifying roar pierced the stillness of the thick, night air. He immediately recognized the terrible sound of the vile beasts, and the thought of their return after a long absence immediately filled him with dread. With trembling hands, he attempted to quietly put his book down on the end table, but missed it in his hasted panic. The book fell to the ground and struck with an alarmingly loud thud, that seemed to be amplified by a hollow echo throughout the house.

"You old fool!" he whispered to himself, upset at his clumsy and potentially deadly mistake. His dull eyes were wide with alarm, and his heart raced so quickly that he thought it might give out at any moment. Dark and sinister shadows flitted along the walls as the flames from his candles flickered and sputtered against the growing tide of darkness.

He grabbed his cane and quietly coaxed his venerable body up and out of his comfortable reading chair, but his legs did not want to cooperate. Every attempted movement seemed agonizingly slow and uncoordinated.

"My strength has finally failed me," he mumbled to himself in dismay.

Several more malevolent roars were followed by sounds of glass breaking and screaming as the terrible hunters ruthlessly sought their prey.

Just as he finished standing and stabilizing himself, there was a loud and violent strike against his sturdy oak door. As an added measure of security, he had installed a wooden draw beam, but he knew from the tremendous force of the blows that it would not take long for the beast to gain entry.

He shuffled over to a large, sturdy chest, but before he was even able to span the short distance, there were several more savage strikes against the door. Small fragments of wood splintered and fell into the entryway, and the beam creaked and groaned under the unrelenting pressure.

As he knelt next to the large, black, iron-strapped chest, his old bones and joints protested almost as loudly as did the door. He fumbled for a set of keys in his pocket, but they seemed to actively thwart any attempt of removal by catching every possible snag. After several frustrating moments, he finally managed to fish them out, but just as he freed them from the bonds of his pocket, he dropped them.

The black, iron skeleton keys hit the ground with a loud clang that was immediately followed by another frenzied onslaught against the door. He could hear the beast snarling in between the loud splintering sounds as it beat and ripped the wooden barrier into submission.

He shook his head in increasing ire at his lack of focus and dexterity.

"Slow is smooth, smooth is fast," he whispered, desperately trying to calm himself with his own military training catchphrase that he had told to countless others.

The chest had two separate locks, each requiring a different key. His hands continued to tremble so excessively that he found it extremely difficult to even place the key into the keyhole.

But as he followed his own advice and slowed down, he successfully inserted the key and heard the familiar click of the latch release as he turned it.

The wooden beam began to crack and splinter as the sturdy fibers continued to give way against the beast's tremendous strength.

"Just one more time, that's all I ask," he said as he quietly begged his hands to comply.

The second lock seemed to be easier than the first, and Adamar breathed a sigh of relief when he heard the release of the second latch.

"At least I will go down fighting."

He began to lift the lid but it felt impossibly heavy to his age-shriveled muscles. He had barely opened it halfway when his strength and grip failed, and it slammed shut with a loud crack that sounded like a clap of thunder had just struck the house.

"Have I lost so much strength that I can't even open the lid of my own secure chest? Am I to die two feet from my weapons?" he mused bitterly.

But his thoughts were interrupted by the small, trembling voice of a little girl calling to him from the upstairs bedroom.

"Anfadwé! Is that you? I'm scared!"

The fear in her voice was readily apparent, and it ignited within him a deep well of strength and fury that rivaled that of the beast's attempt to get through the door. With a sudden renewed fervor, Adamar grabbed ahold of the lid and flung it open, this time with surprising ease. The thick, iron hinges groaned in protest of the sudden wrath that had been imposed upon them, and the lid flew back so hard that it almost tipped the heavy chest over.

The ease with which it opened the second time confused him, but he did not waste any time considering it. He reached into the chest and grabbed his sword belt. The weathered leather was so old and cracked, and had been resting in the same position for so long, that it had become rigid and unwieldy.

The belt contained two scabbarded scimitars and felt far more cumbersome than he remembered.

"Lauriel, my dear, stay in your room. I will be right there," he instructed in as calm a voice as he could muster.

In his bygone days, he used both blades with equally devastating effect. But the only thing that he wielded now in his left hand was his cane. He withdrew a single blade and allowed the rest of the belt to fall to the ground.

The cold, gray steel had lost much of its luster but it was still enough to glint in the soft light of the candles. Like Adamar, the weapon appeared to be well beyond its days of glory.

"You will finally get the prey that you have long sought, but I am going to make you pay dearly before you do!" he shouted.

The shadows being cast by the candles were now playing tricks on his eyes. At the very corners of his vision, they would form into shapes that appeared as a massive four-armed beast with long, grasping claws. And when he would turn his head to look directly at them, they would scurry along the walls, staying just out of his direct line of vision. As he shuffled toward the stairs, he swung his scimitar at them several times but quickly realized that his attacks were an exercise in futility.

With his last remaining burst of strength and determination, he ascended the stairs that led to Lauriel's bedroom. As he reached the top step, the wooden draw beam splintered with a loud crack, and the entire door flew off its hinges. A dark, shadowy beast with red eyes emerged through the threshold and began to charge directly at the stairs.

Adamar entered the bedroom and slammed the door shut behind him, but it did nothing to quell the sound of the terrible beast drawing closer.

A small, blonde-haired elven girl stood in the center of the room, tightly clutching her treasured rag doll. She was trembling, but her intense, bright green eyes seemed strangely calm and focused, to the point that her stare was unnerving.

He attempted to turn and raise the scimitar to defend them, but his former surge of strength suddenly left him. The blade slipped from his weary grasp and crashed to the ground with a loud clang.

"Run, Lauriel! Jump out of the window!" he yelled.

Lauriel dropped her doll, but instead of following his directions and running away, she ran over to him and knelt down beside the scimitar to pick it up.

Before he could even speak a word of protest, she reached out and grabbed the weapon. But just as her hand wrapped around the pommel, it flared with a brilliant, blue-white glow that bathed the room in a radiance like that of a full moon on a cloudless night.

"Anfadwé! What do I do!?" she cried out in wide-eyed shock as she tried to hand the weapon back to him. But his arms would no longer move.

His face contorted in pain and anguish, but not because of his paralysis or impending doom. He suddenly saw the little girl as a fierce, grownup warrior that wielded the awakened blade in a deadly and familiar fighting stance. The sight of her carrying his burden caused him far worse agony than if the beast would have charged directly through the door and impaled him.

"No! Please no! It can't be ... Anyone but her ..." he cried in anguished sobs.

He dropped to his knees just as the door splintered open and a dark shadow overtook them. The elven warrior sprung toward the beast and launched into an intense whirlwind of attacks.

His eyes snapped open, and he sat bolt upright in his bed, choking for air. His heart pounded furiously, and he was drenched in a cold sweat.

As he looked around the familiar room, he was quickly reoriented, but the nightmare was so vivid that he still felt the urge to inspect his house to ensure that the horror hadn't followed him.

*   *   *   *

Adamar stood in the doorway of Lauriel's room and stared at her adoringly. The sight of her clutching her doll in her innocent slumber helped to calm him, but his heart continued to ache. Tears rolled down his cheeks as he quietly and repeatedly whispered the sentiments that he had expressed in his increasingly frequent recurring dream.

"Please do not let it be her … Anyone but her …"

CHAPTER ONE

Innocence Lost

yndril Forest was nestled quietly in the foothills of the majestic Emsré Mountains. The lofty peaks towered high above the land, creating a strikingly picturesque backdrop as their gleaming crown of pure white snow stood in stark contrast to the azure sky. The afternoon sun bathed the westward-facing peaks in brilliance as if the sun itself sought to highlight the splendor of the mountains. Crystalline streams meandered down from the alpine crags and into the foothills and valleys far below, providing a constant supply of life-giving water to the lush forest that had taken up residence before time immemorial.

It was this setting that the small community of woodland elves had chosen as the place for their remote settlement at least an age ago. But it was not only the breathtaking landscape and pure mountain streams that drew the elves' attention; the forest below the Emsré mountains was the unique home to giant Silverwood trees. The beautiful trees were extremely large, reaching high into the heavens as if mimicking the mountains' tall grandeur and majesty.

The sturdy branches and large leaves created a dense forest canopy, and the many seasons of fallen leaves created a soft, loamy blanket upon the forest floor below.

The trees were aptly named for their light-gray-colored bark that would reflect a silver color under the light of a full moon. According to legend, the first sapling was planted by the Goddess Kathele herself, and each of the Silverwood trees was considered sacred by the woodland elves. They named their settlement: Kelómé.

The wild and untamed land made it the ideal place for the elves. Unlike the humans, who mostly inhabited the hustling and bustling cities, the elves preferred to live in and with nature surrounding them, enjoying the solitude and sanctity of the forest. The remoteness of their community kept most outsiders away, providing a degree of insulation from the outside cares and troubles of the world, just as the elves intended. Many humans looked down upon the woodland elves with misguided prejudice, considering them wild and uncivilized. In reality, their communities were clean, orderly, and relatively harmonious.

Kelómé had not been completely cut off and isolated for quite some time. It had inadvertently become quite renowned for the highly sought after "Frostwine" that the elves produced, known as "Mhelekävin" in the elven tongue. As a labor of love, the first settlers had painstakingly turned an open forest glade into a vineyard of unparalleled beauty. Their affinity and steadfast passion for working with nature, coupled with the perfect location, produced bountiful harvests from the relatively small glade. The warm summer sun and the cool night air descending from the mountains created the perfect conditions for the grapes to sweeten and thrive. The dual influence resulted in a harmonious equilibrium that produced grapes of unparalleled quality. The now many-centuries-old vines would show their appreciation to the elves with every passing season.

It was about one hundred and fifty years ago when several casks of the wine had found their way into the distant human towns. A mere breath in the passing of time for the elves but several generations for humans. Once discovered, a thriving trading partnership rapidly developed between Kelómé and the remote human outpost town of Dailion, a twelve days' ride on horseback.

The journey was arduous and, at times, impossible when the spring snowmelt would turn the normally gentle mountain streams into mighty rivers that were much too dangerous to cross. There was no way to travel through the rough terrain with a wagon, and therefore the supply of Frostwine was very limited. This made it extremely rare and highly sought after throughout the realm. It became a status symbol for the richest of the human nobles to own a cask. The casks were easily recognizable as each one had a Silverwood tree, the symbol of Kelómé, lovingly emblazoned on the front. The elves were often urged to produce more and had been offered up to five hundred gold pieces per cask, more than a year's salary for the average laborer. The elves refused, choosing to only take what the vineyard would freely give and nothing more. They had a love of nature, not a love of gold.

* * * *

The sun was low on the horizon, and the fireflies were beginning to fill the forest with their yellow, otherworldly glow. Lauriel hurried to finish her chores, not because of her work ethic, but because she wanted to go play and explore. The elven children were assigned community chores based off of their age, and Lauriel had been assigned to vineyard duties because she was still a very young child. She hated it! She didn't understand why she could not be out learning how to track and hunt like her older brother. She was instead stuck at the vine trellis, mindlessly (and begrudgingly) tending to the grapes.

She had an uncharacteristic restlessness when it came to exploring the lands and couldn't wait until her next adventure. She'd gotten the trait from her father.

He would often take her and her brother on hikes through the forest, trying to find some new cave to explore or see how many forest animals they could encounter.

Her mother would shake her head and laugh when Lauriel would come back covered from head to toe in mud or with some new "pet" that she had befriended.

The vines were heavy with the large clusters of grapes and needed to be tied back so that the vine didn't break or bend to the ground. It was getting late in the season and the grapes would soon be harvested. The long summer nights were beginning to get earlier, and the slightest hint of chill was in the air.

The trees higher up on the mountain were just beginning to show a sprinkling of canary yellow, their first of many colors. It would not be long until the entire mountainside was ablaze in the full glory of the autumn splendor. Normally, grapes should have been harvested several weeks ago, but these grapes would stay on the vine until the first frost, making them particularly sweet and creating the appropriately named "Frostwine."

Lauriel worked until the last rays of sun dipped below the horizon and the distant mountains faded into a deep purple. It was her favorite time of the day, a "magical time" as she called it. It was that time of the day, just after dusk, when the wind in the trees would die down and everything would become still and quiet. The silvery moon would soon rise and bathe the forest in its glow, and all would seem right with the world. She sat down beside the trellis and closed her eyes for many long moments, enjoying the quiet solitude of her own pleasant thoughts.

Lauriel sat longer than she intended and was only brought back from her daydreams when she heard her mother's concerned voice in the distance calling for her to come home.

She peered up through the vines and saw the familiar glow of the starlight but was shocked to see that the silvery moon had already risen high in the sky above her.

Wow! I must have been daydreaming for hours! I'm going to be in big trouble …

She stood up but was mesmerized by the sight of the bright moon glowing through the grape leaves.

It looks so close!

As she refocused, she suddenly realized that she was not looking at the moon—something was glowing in the vines! Her highly inquisitive nature overtook any other thoughts of returning home; she had to investigate.

She crawled up on the trellis and inched closer to the illumination. As she did, she could hear a faint buzzing noise.

As stealthily as she could, she moved even closer. The buzzing continued to get louder. She came within a few feet of the object and could see that it was some sort of glowing ball of light, about the size of an apple.

If I can just get this one vine out of the way, I can grab it!

As carefully and quietly as she could, she slowly moved the large leaves out of the way.

There it is!

Some kind of buzzing, brightly glowing, round object floated just an arm's length above her.

She lunged for it, grabbing at it wildly.

Bzzzzzzing! The glow nimbly bolted away from her grasping hands and out from under the leaves, zooming right by her head. Normally sure footed, she tumbled off of the trellis, taking multiple bunches of the valuable grapes with her.

Bzzzzzzing!

Bzzzzzzing!

The glow darted around her head in rapid, concentric circles, staying playfully just out of her reach.

"A Will-o' Wisp!" Lauriel gasped.

She had never seen one before but had read enough about them to know that they were exceedingly rare.

Suddenly, it darted deeper into the woods, and Lauriel began to give chase, giggling lightheartedly as she ran after the whimsical illumination.

It continued its playful game for many minutes, drawing her deeper and deeper into the woods as she pursued it with singular focus. Suddenly, the Will-o' Wisp brought itself to a hover high above her head.

It was then that she got the strangest feeling. As she stared at it, still mesmerized by the experience, she felt as if it was doing the very same. She realized that it was not some mindless creature; it was sentient and purposeful.

Bzzzzzzing! The Will-o' Wisp was gone.

What was that all about? Did it just want to play? What was it doing here?

Lauriel's mind was so flooded with questions that she was oblivious to her present surroundings. She did not realize how far she had gone into the deep woods, and even in the elven realm, the evening woods were no place for a child.

She was suddenly drawn away from her thoughts and back to the present by strange noises in the distance. Her keen eyes were beginning to readjust from the bright ball and onto the darker woods beyond. She did not see any immediate danger but realized that she was deep in unfamiliar territory. She held her breath and listened intently.

She could hear the very faint sound of what she pictured in her mind to be many large animals clumsily crashing through the distant woods. She had an innate sense of direction, as did most of her kind, and she realized that the noises were coming from the direction of her village.

Her father had taught her how to move through the woods unheard and unseen, and she began to quietly make her way back home. Her footfalls were sure and silent as she skillfully traversed the forest floor with amazing dexterity for her age.

She quickly made her way back into familiar territory, but she could feel a growing sense that something was amiss. None of the familiar noises of the evening forest could be heard. There were no sounds of the familiar chirping crickets or hooting owls. Even the fireflies had hidden their illuminating beacons. It was as if the entire forest held its breath.

With growing concern, she proceeded onward until she heard a noise that made her stop dead in her tracks. Screams began to echo throughout the woods. They were quickly followed by the wail of the elven warning horn.

She began to run as fast as she could, foregoing her silent movement. "Ammé!" she called out to her mother in elvish. "Ammé!" She began to smell smoke and some other unnatural smell that she couldn't place.

As she neared, she could see the faint glow of a fire and could hear more and more screams. "Ammé!" she yelled frantically as tears began to stream down her face. "Fadwé! Nolthien!" she yelled for her father and brother. She quickly made her way back to the vineyard but it was almost unrecognizable. The carefully constructed trellises and well-tended vines had been torn to shreds as if a pack of wild boars had been living in them for weeks. Not a single trellis remained standing.

An icy cold chill took hold of her as she caught a brief glimpse of one of the terrible creatures that had descended upon her village. She was unable to move, paralyzed with fear from the scene that played out before her. As the creature came to a brief stop to find another prey, it was partially illuminated by the light from the numerous fires. Lauriel could see that it stood upright and was easily twice the size of the largest human.

It had a thick white mane of hair that began on the top of its head and continued down its broad back and onto its powerful shoulders. Its body was dark gray and it had glowing red eyes that made it appear like it had just come from the pits of hell. It had two terrifying sets of arms that rippled with powerful muscles.

The top set of arms were massive and ended in giant, fingerlike appendages that resembled razor-sharp claws. The lower set of arms had very much the same features, only smaller.

With the four-armed creatures, terrible dog-like monstrosities ran around like frenzied beasts. Lauriel was very young and inexperienced, but she knew that both of the creatures were not natural.

The four-armed beast that Lauriel observed suddenly found another mark as Ornthalas, a peaceful baker and grandfather-like figure to the small community, suddenly ran from his burning home.

Lauriel recognized him immediately and knew that he did not see the creature lying in wait to ambush. She tried to yell out to him but could not find her voice. "Reh Ornthalas, abacas da! (Mister Ornthalas, behind you!)" she said in a dry and barely audible whisper. "Abacas da!" she whispered as more tears streamed down her face. The creature immediately chased him down with incredible speed and seized a hold of him with its smaller, lower set of arms and claws. It raised its powerful upper arms overhead and came down upon him with enough force to split open a tree. The razor-sharp claws rent his frail body nearly in two while the second strike followed almost immediately after, disemboweling him. His blood splattered violently into the air, and his lifeless body crumpled to the ground with a loud thud as the creature quickly released him and moved on to find another.

It was then that Lauriel's legs failed her. She crashed down into the tangled heap of vines, unable to move. She could not bring herself to look onward at the many other horrors taking place.

She tried to cover herself in the vines just as a child would do with their blanket when afraid of the monsters in the night.

She lay silent and unmoving for several minutes while the screams lessened. It wasn't until she heard the distinct noise of something moving in her direction that she forced herself to peek through the twisted clump of vines covering her, and she immediately regretted it.

The vile creature was one of the dog-like aberrations that had come with the dark creatures moving around the village. The crash into the vines had drawn its attention away from its frenzied killing and toward the noise.

It was carrying something bloody in its mouth, and Lauriel did not want to know what it was. The "dog" had no fur and was a deathly pale gray with bulging yellow eyes that stuck out much like the eyes of a dragonfly. It had leathery, bat-like ears, much bigger than normal dog ears.

It walked like a dog but had a much bigger hunched back and huge front shoulders and legs that ended in large, bloody paws with equally large nails.

It looked deformed as the back half of the creature was much smaller in size and stature. Both the top and bottom sets of fangs, also dripping with blood, were way too big for the creature's mouth and protruded outward beyond its snarled lips.

It did not have a snout like other dogs, rather, a flat nose that the fangs protruded above from the mouth below. The aberration seemed to breathe frost out of its mouth as it exhaled.

The vile creature dropped the object in its mouth and stared straight in her direction, frost curling from its maw. A deep, hollow rumbling echoed from its unnaturally large chest cavity. It was unlike any dog growl she had ever heard; it was terrifyingly worse. The hollow sound seemed to pierce right through her soul.

Lauriel held her breath and tried desperately to blend into the vines and shadows. Her hand had come to rest on some grapes that had not yet been destroyed. She slowly squeezed them against her leg, crushing them on herself. She prayed to the Gods to protect her from the evil incarnate. She could see the creature trying to sniff with the open hole where a nose should be.

It seemed as if the creature could sense that there was a life form not far away, but had not yet picked it up with its other senses. After several moments, the creature, smelling nothing of interest other than grapes, turned and ran back toward the village.

After what felt like an eternity, the screams finally ended and the creatures drifted back into the shadows. A deathly silence fell upon the ruined village.

Lauriel had been too afraid to move from her spot, too weak and powerless to do anything. After many long hours of not hearing or seeing any movement, she pulled herself from her hiding place and walked on unsteady legs back into her village.

She could not even begin to grasp the unspeakable evil. In an instant, the innocence of youth no longer protected her.

The inner peace that comes from safety, security, and stability was suddenly shattered into a million pieces. She could not make any sense of it. The creatures did not even take anything, they only killed and destroyed.

In a daze, she walked from house to house, trying to find someone still alive; but the vile creatures had exterminated their prey with ruthless efficiency.

Scene after scene of unspeakable carnage played out with each house that she checked. Finally, she looked up and found herself standing in front of her home.

It was a gruesome attack. The creatures had no weapons, only huge claws that sliced and ripped apart their prey. Lauriel walked quietly back out and sat down on her front porch. The beautiful trees, the silvery trees that she had come to love, now reflected a new color in the light of the moon—blood red.

CHAPTER TWO

Vendëum Andúlari

The beautiful but deadly "singing blade" fighting style was a well-protected and jealously guarded secret among the elves. It was aptly named for the sonorous ringing sound that the scimitars or elven long-blades would make as they sliced through the air with great speed and precision.

The singing blade warriors—or *Andúlarium*, as they were known in the elven speech—used no shield and wore only light armor that did not impact their mobility. They relied upon complete freedom of movement, unparalleled dexterity, and a seemingly impenetrable blade-barrier as their defense. The fighting style involved fluid, circular motions that made the fighter fast, balanced, and deadly in all directions. It was the antithesis of many of the other fighting styles throughout the realms that involved large weapons, heavy armor, and brutish strength.

The *Andúlari* technique was rare even within the elven community. Many would seek to learn the ancient and deadly art, but very few would walk the long and narrow path to proficiency. Only after many years of relentless pursuit and determination could the finest of elven fighters achieve the lethal song with their weapons.

In order for an already skilled fighter to be considered for entry into the training, they had to be naturally ambidextrous. The fighting style used two lightweight and equal sized weapons in a dual-wielding technique, creating a beautiful exhibition of balance and symmetry. There was no single blade, shield, or "off hand;" both sides of the fighter were equally lethal, and equally defensive.

Those interested in joining the ranks of the *Andúlarium* would be put through many difficult physical challenges that tested their agility, dexterity, and natural coordination. Only after successful completion of all of them could the fighter begin their training.

One such renowned *Andúlari* fighter was Adamar Mithalvarin. Almost four hundred years had passed since his storied and distinguished service to the crown, but his legendary skill was still remembered by many of the elves that were now in their sunset years.

By the youthful elven age of 108, he became the youngest fighter in the long and honored history of the ancient art to complete the training and receive the coveted title *Andúlarium*.

In his 179th year, he was promoted to Captain of the King's Guard and granted the exceptionally rare title of "Grandmaster to the Singing Blades." It was a distinguished and respected designation, reserved only for those few that had demonstrated a full mastery of the *Andúlari* craft. He had fought in many of the famous battles that had been documented in the great libraries throughout the realms of Alynthi, and had earned tremendous recognition not only for his skill with his scimitars, but for his valor and bravery in battle.

His accomplishments reached a near unique pinnacle when, at the adult elven age of 253, he was bestowed the honorific title of *Vendëum Andúlari*, or most closely translated in the common speech as "Paragon of the Singing Blades." The title had only been awarded four times in the entire written and oral history of the elves, a span of epochs that stretched all the way back to the Age of Solace.

After his retirement from military service, he diligently taught the ancient elven fighting technique to those who would seek to learn it from him.

The art had become part of his sense of purpose, and he desperately wished to keep it alive by passing on his knowledge and skill to younger generations. For many decades, he was successful; High Elves, Wood Elves, Moon Elves, and even Sun Elves from the far distant land of Queth-Saldar would enthusiastically seek to be trained by the only living *Vendëum Andúlari*. But after a prolonged period of relative peace and stability, even the long memory of the elves began to fade and, after just a few hundred years, there were but a few that still practiced the art.

The very fighting style that had protected so many and survived countless battles, was now dying a slow death due to disinterest and complacency. Without even a single blade strike from an enemy, the beautiful art was in danger of extinction.

Hard Lessons

Lauriel quickly sprang back to her feet and scrambled to pick up her scimitars that were lying on the ground several feet away from her. In one fluid motion, she whirled around and immediately returned to her defensive-ready position. Her knuckles turned white as she gripped the scimitars with a death grip, determined not to lose them again.

Her blonde hair was a wild mess, and a small trickle of blood ran from her nose. Many bruises were appearing on her arms and hands from being on the receiving end of multiple strikes from the hard, wooden scimitars. Her bright green eyes locked onto Adamar in a steely-eyed stare, and her jaw clenched in resolute determination.

"Again!" Lauriel pleaded, raising her scimitars in another challenge.

Those intense eyes, Adamar thought to himself. He couldn't hold back a chuckle at the thought that even he became nervous when she would glare at him. He lowered his wooden training blades to his side, a signal that their training was over.

They had been practicing for over an hour, and Adamar, at his advanced age, had no choice but to call it a day. His 748-year-old body no longer freely accepted the rigors of many long hours of training in the secret elven art.

"We are done for the evening, my dear," he said in his customary gentle and soft spoken demeanor.

"AGAIN!" Lauriel insisted, her rising voice clearly revealing her frustration.

The old master knew that she was furious about being bested so many times and that she had no intention of ending the daily training. She was not even winded and would train for several more hours if allowed. She reminded him of himself in his younger days—driven, determined, and stubborn.

The final lesson of the evening would be a hard one for her, and it pained him greatly to have to do it, for he knew all too well what drove her. He subtly prepared his blades for the onslaught that he knew was about to ensue.

"Tomorro—"

As predicted, she lunged at him, attacking him with the fury of a rabid badger. Her strikes were quick and precise; but not practiced enough to bypass the master's defense. He parried the many attacks and then quickly took the offensive, striking back at her like a whirlwind. Their wooden blades clattered together in rapid succession, his blade meeting hers ten times in less than six seconds before she found herself on her back again, staring up at the evening sky. Her knuckles were bloody, but she had not lost her blades.

"You fight like some wild ravenous beast," Adamar said as he stood over her, his faded blue eyes never losing their warmth and compassion. "You must learn when to keep those emotions in check or it will be the death of you."

He sheathed the training blades and held out his heavily weathered hand to help her to her feet.

Lauriel, still glaring at him, begrudgingly took his hand and stood back up. "And for your final lesson this evening; you must listen to me when I tell you that we are through," he counseled.

"Those knuckles wouldn't hurt so bad if you would have just listened to me. Now ... go wash up."

Adamar carefully hid his proud smirk as he followed her into the small cottage. *She is getting much harder to beat, and nearing adulthood*, he thought to himself. She had parried, attempted to disarm, and counter attacked him with incredible speed and skill. Her grace and dexterity echoed his former perfection, and her unrivaled determination to master the art was truly beginning to show.

It won't be long now until she sets off on her own. The smirk slowly gave way to a look of sadness. He had never intended to adopt or raise a child at the age of a grandfather, but fate had other plans.

The quaint cottage on the outskirts of the village was humble but well kept. Rarely did there exist a space in the world that offered as much peace and tranquility as that found within the walls of Adamar's cozy dwelling. Everything was clean and orderly, a habit instilled in him throughout a lifetime of military service. The flickering light from the oil lamps illuminated his many service awards and accolades that tastefully adorned the walls and shelves. The comfortable furnishings and simple decorations were old fashioned but gave the space unique character—many of them having their own interesting stories on how or where he'd acquired them from far off lands.

The small cottage was equipped with a well-stocked kitchen, an adjoining dining room, a comfortable parlor with an inviting fireplace, and two small bedrooms. It was all the home that the two of them needed.

Adamar walked over to the far corner of the room and knelt down beside a sturdy, wood and iron chest that had been firmly affixed to the floor.

He opened the heavy lid and placed his training blades inside of it and then gently removed something much more deadly. The glint of steel caught in the firelight as he slid the beautiful scimitar from the scabbard. Its cold, hard edge appeared as sharp as it had been the day that it was forged. His face darkened as he stared at the blade in quiet introspection.

"The sting of your edge is of no consequence compared to the sting that you have placed in my heart and mind; you have cost me so much in this life, and now you cost me more than I can bear to give," he mumbled quietly to himself.

He had developed the habit of talking to himself from his many years of living a solitary life as a widower. He carefully sheathed the blade and placed it back in the chest. "Sometimes I wish that the burden of keeping you safe had never been tasked to me," he mused.

He closed the lid and locked the two heavy, iron locks. As he spoke a magic word of command, the locks and chest glowed subtly before quickly returning to their normal appearance. Not even a thief with the highest of skill would be able to pick the magical locks or get into the chest to steal the precious contents.

Adamar made his way over to the worn but comfortable fireside couch and slumped down on it wearily. He breathed a long sigh of relief, thankful that he was finally off of his feet. He tried to unlace his boots, but his aching hands and stiff fingers protested vehemently. It was becoming increasingly difficult for him to even grip the scimitar handles that he had mastered so long ago. He had been trying to hide it for quite some time but Lauriel had begun to notice his difficulties as well.

As he stared at the fire and let its warmth wash over his old bones, his thoughts drifted away to a scene that unfolded before him eighty years ago to the very day.

Out of the many horrors that he had observed throughout a lifetime of war and combat, the scenes of devastation and death in the small village were by far the worse that he had ever seen. The vivid pictures in his mind would forever haunt him.

"No child should ever see such things," he muttered to himself. A tear rolled down his face as he remembered how he'd run from house to house, seeing bodies and body parts stacked neatly upon the floors.

He had found Lauriel shivering under a bed in the back bedroom of her house, dirty, starving, and half-naked. She had been there for three weeks, a period of time that she did not at all remember.

All that she could say to him when he found her was, "Make it all go back to normal. Make it all go back to normal." Her bright green eyes stared right through him into some unknown and terrible place. Even though much of it had been destroyed, she had attempted to clean up the entire village.

In her fractured mental state, she had stacked each body and body part on the floor of the house that it belonged to, and had tried to place them back in order like some sick demonic puzzle. The most difficult memory for him was that of her family. She had reassembled them to be together—father, mother, and brother, all holding hands.

Adamar had come out of his retirement to rise up against what had become known among the elves as "The Decimation." Some type of hell spawned creatures had risen up from their vile place deep underground and waged war against a vast population of the surface-dwelling kingdoms throughout Alynthi. The forces were finally beaten back to Draxanarek'Vel, but at great cost.

An uneasiness still lingered upon the land because there was never any real conclusion or finality to the assault. The dark entities drifted away just as suddenly as they had appeared.

Adamar had not yet told Lauriel, but he had begun to hear rumors that the dark, malevolent force was beginning to return. Sadness crept over him as he knew that he would not be able to take a stand this time as he had so valiantly done before. He also knew that the realms were not ready to withstand another major attack. They had become fractured after the first incursion and were too embroiled in internal politics, petty squabbles, and territorial disputes to see the dark clouds forming again on the horizon.

Adamar nodded to himself and sighed reluctantly. "Yes, I do believe that it is time," he said quietly.

Many more tears welled up in his eyes as he struggled with the troubling thought, desperately trying to reach another conclusion.

"Time for what?" asked Lauriel as she came down the stairs. A piece of a small, bloody rag was stuck into her bruised nose.

"Damn her ears," Adamar muttered, this time even more quietly. He quickly wiped the tears from his eyes and cheeks while still facing away from her.

"Time for you to make a hungry, old elf dinner," he said, trying his best to sound cheerful after his troubled thoughts.

Lauriel filled the blackened kettle and walked over to the fireplace to hang it on the hook. She used the opportunity to face Adamar, but could only look down, embarrassed about her prior behavior.

"I'm sorry," she said. "I'm just tired of being weak and defenseless."

"Now, Lauriel," said Adamar, "we have been over this many times; you have been my finest student."

"But …" Lauriel interrupted.

Adamar continued, "I'm not just saying that because you are a daughter to me, shhhh …" he quieted Lauriel as she was about to speak again.

"You have finished your *Andúlari* training and will test for the title next week. You are even younger than I was when I completed the training! You are to compete in the Tournament of the Citadel in two weeks' time. That is where you will be able to test your skill against many other opponents. Should you win, you will be awarded with many opportunities. A skilled blade is valuable throughout the land these days."

"Do you think I can?" she asked.

"I have no doubt, my dear," he replied. His confidence in her helped to ease her racing mind. She desperately wanted to earn the long sought-after title, and she waited in nervous anticipation to compete in the tournament to prove herself.

"Besides, any sane enemy would flee from that glare of yours alone," he added with a smirk.

Lauriel made the same face at him that she'd made when she was lying on the ground, and they both burst into laughter that carried merrily throughout the house.

The lighthearted moment helped Adamar's troubled mind but it did not remove his troubling thoughts entirely.

As they sat at the small table and ate together just as they had done so many countless times before, Lauriel could tell that he carried a heavy burden. After many long moments, she finally broke the silence.

"Anfadwé, what is wrong?" she said, using the elven word for grandfather for greater emphasis. "You have been very quiet tonight and you have hardly touched your meal!"

Adamar looked at her with his kind eyes but he could not hide his inner turmoil. Immediately recognizing the serious nature of the ensuing conversation, Lauriel put down her utensils and looked at him intently as he began to speak.

"My dear daughter," he began and then paused to collect his thoughts. The silence was long and awkward and only intensified her anticipation.

"I must admit, there are many things that trouble me this evening; impossible decisions that must be made quickly. The burden of those decisions is mine alone to bear, and I am sorry that I cannot share them with you this evening, but I will soon enough."

Lauriel nodded in silence, knowing better than to pry.

Adamar continued, "However, there is one difficult subject that we must discuss tonight."

She had rarely heard his voice so serious. "Yes, Anfadwé, what is it?" she asked nervously.

Adamar knew that it would be a difficult conversation, and he had avoided it until now, but time had run out. He knew that it would bring back terrible memories but he felt it was something that should not be hidden from her.

She would hear soon enough, and he wanted her to hear it from him, in the safety and comfort of their home, not from some stranger.

He began, "You must understand that combat against another person holding a weapon is much different than fighting other ... things."

"Things?" replied Lauriel, not yet understanding where the conversation was heading.

Adamar paused again awkwardly and then decided that it was best to tell her in a frank and open manner. That method always seemed to work well for her. He began his second attempt. "The dark, four-armed creatures are emerging again, Lauriel."

Lauriel gripped the table firmly and began to shake as visions of the creatures flooded her mind.

Adamar reached out and put his hand over hers, giving her the time she needed to regain her composure. She closed her eyes and drew in a deep breath, fighting desperately to push away the panic that was creeping over her. After several moments, she nodded and looked back up at Adamar. "Please ... tell me everything."

With that, he began to tell her of the things that he had heard. He told her of the many hushed conversations and rumors of a dark and malevolent enemy beginning to rise back out of the Dark Elven kingdom of Draxanarek'Vel. He could see the struggle within her between panic and fury, and he paused again.

"I'm sorry, my daughter, but this is something that you must know." He was her grandfather and knew very well when to stop to comfort her.

She nodded silently, and he continued. He told her of his encounters with them and how powerful and dangerous they were, even to very skilled fighters. He told her of how they preferred to attack in groups and in coordination with their dog-like beasts. He also told her about the ways that they had learned how to defeat them. Lauriel sat quietly and listened to all that the *Vendëum Andúlari* had to say. When he was done, she quietly stood up from the table.

Her eyes were red and her lips pursed but she made no other expression.

"May I be excused?" she said.

"Yes of course, my dear, I'm sorry that I have burdened you with this knowledge," Adamar replied.

"Thank you for telling me," Lauriel said flatly as she walked to the front door of the cottage instead of her room.

"Where are you going?" Adamar asked.

"To train," she replied.

CHAPTER THREE

The Dance with the Blades

The private ceremony known as *Nöheo Andúlari* translated in the common speech to "The ceremony of the singing blades," took place in a small, open, forest glade less than an hour's walk from Adamar's cottage. It was traditionally held in the woodland elven realm of the Elderwood, at a sacred location known to the *Andúlarium* as Ravaryn glade, but Adamar was well past his days of long arduous journeys. It was also customary that all possible *Andúlarium* throughout the land would attend the ceremony, but only three of the eighteen were in attendance. After a lengthy private discussion in hushed tones that Lauriel could not quite hear, Adamar ordered the ceremony to continue, explaining to her that "urgent business is keeping the others from attending." Lauriel could tell by the concerned look on his face that there was more to the story than he was sharing.

Lauriel began the *Andúlari* movements, something that she affectionately called "The dance with the blades." The exhibition was designed to prove to the others in attendance that she had gained sufficient skill and proficiency in the art. Slowly, as the ceremony continued and the movements became faster, her blades began to ring as they sliced rapidly through the thick evening air.

The other three *Andúlarium* immediately joined her, each of them completing their well-practiced maneuvers in perfect synchronicity. The sound of the eight blades ringing together in pure harmonic resonance combined to form a resounding crescendo that heralded the return of the singing blade warriors.

The concentric and mirrored motions, coupled with the vibrant ringing of the blades was truly awe inspiring.

It was always Adamar's favorite part of the ceremony. He fought desperately to hold back his tears of pride as he watched his daughter complete the precise movements with flawless technique. Lauriel had never experienced anything like it, and for her, it was intoxicating.

As the demonstration came to an end, Adamar drew the two scimitars that were attached to his belt and motioned for Lauriel to take a knee. He placed the flat of each blade on her shoulders and began his speech very formally, intentionally removing any hint of bias. "Lauriel Valendril, under the heavens that grace us tonight and in the presence of all other *Andúlarium* here, I have personally witnessed your training and find you of sufficient skill to be considered worthy of title in this ancient art."

He looked around at the other *Andúlarium* and continued, "I ask all others that have just witnessed the demonstrated skills to consider carefully whether or not this candidate has proven themselves worthy to receive title. In the strict traditions of protecting the quality of our craft, and of your own free will and accord, please step forward and place your vote. The vote must be unanimous, and any down vote requires that the candidate return to training."

Lauriel's heart pounded wildly with nervous anticipation as each of the *Andúlarium* walked toward her. Without hesitation, each one placed both of their blades upon her shoulders, signaling a vote of acceptance.

"Very well," Adamar said, "the vote is unanimous." He paused briefly, attempting to maintain his formality and composure, but his watery eyes gave him away.

"Rise now, *Andúlarium*," Adamar instructed.

Lauriel stood slowly, her eyes also filling with tears. Hearing the title spoken for the first time filled her with a profound sense of joy and accomplishment, the likes of which she had never experienced in her young elven life of one hundred and seven years. She was now the youngest to ever receive the title.

Adamar cleared his throat and continued, "May your steps be swift, your strikes be true, and your protection of our ways unfaltering."

The other *Andúlarium* all spoke in unison, "So mote it be."

The saying was meant to formally end the ceremony and declare the title to be conferred, but they were all taken by surprise when Adamar continued.

"And one more thing Lauriel." His voice was now soft and much less formal.

He flipped his scimitars around and presented the pommels toward her. "I present to you the blades of my forefathers, may they serve you well," his voice broke briefly, "as they have served me … my daughter." His voice faltered.

Lauriel fully understood the significance of the moment, and the tears that she had tried so hard to hold back now ran freely down her cheeks.

The other *Andúlarium* were unable to hide their shock and stood with open mouths and wide-eyed stares. Adamar had possibly been one of the greatest *Andúlarium* of all time, and this final act signaled his permanent retirement.

Lauriel reached out slowly, and her hands closed reverently around the pommels as if they were ancient, holy relics. She held the blades up and stared at them in awe as the polished steel glimmered in the moonlight. The scimitars felt incredibly well-crafted and balanced compared to her other blades.

Adamar asked the other *Andúlarium* for a private moment with Lauriel and they quickly and respectfully complied. They each left in a separate direction and traveled well beyond the glade before setting up a watch to ensure that their privacy would be maintained.

"I ... I ..." Lauriel stammered. "Anfadwé, I can't! These are yours! You will need them to fight off the enemy!" she finally exclaimed as she tried to hand the blades back to him.

Adamar gently placed his hand to her cheek. "The sun is setting rapidly for me, Lauriel, but it is rising for you. You must now listen closely to what I am about to tell you."

Hearing the seriousness and strain in his voice, Lauriel immediately lowered the blades and focused on him intently.

Adamar began to speak in an earnest but hushed tone, his voice barely above a whisper. "There is something that you must know, something that I have kept secret for a very long time." He touched the blade that she held in her right hand. "I was the custodian and protector of this great blade, just as my father and grandfather before me. For almost an age, my family diligently performed our duty to keep this blade safe and hidden from the mortal realm. My duty became a great curse to me, my dear daughter, because I also have an obligation to allow this blade to be awakened by a new master if I feel that the time is right."

Adamar paused and looked down at the ground for several moments.

When he finally looked back up, Lauriel was startled by a look of intense grief etched upon his face. He had seen much in his life but it appeared that what he was trying to say was about to break him. He took a deep breath and continued, "I cannot deny that I believe the time is at hand for the blade to emerge, just as I cannot deny the possibility that you may be the one to awaken the blade and become the next Blademaster."

Lauriel stood and stared at him, her green eyes wide. She tried to speak but only one word came out. "Blademaster?"

Adamar's eyes began to well up with tears as he spoke again. "I have bitterly struggled with this decision to give you this blade, not because I believe you unworthy of it, but because I cannot bear the thought of placing this burden upon your shoulders, or losing you from something that I set in motion!

You must understand, the life of a Blademaster is fraught with constant peril and extreme danger; death lurks around every corner! Even the Bladerite itself is designed to kill anyone who attempts it if the blade does not find them worthy. You have been through much, and I have always tried to protect you ..." Adamar's emotions finally broke and he began to sob.

Adamar had always been the rock upon which Lauriel could stand. He knew exactly what to say to calm her down when she was angry or soothe her when she was sad, but the roles were suddenly reversed as she answered his question after quiet consideration.

"Anfadwé ..." she began, her soft voice immediately comforting him. "I'm honored that you think highly enough of me that you have shared with me the possibilities of this weapon, but it is not you that places me in harm's way. I have my own free will and choose my own path now. Besides, maybe you have given me just the tool that I need to protect myself and others from the approaching darkness."

Her eyes narrowed unconsciously as she spoke the last word, and Adamar could see the unquenched fire that burned deep within them. He knew that she had already made her decision but the simple yet profound statement had the immediate effect of helping to ease his intense inner turmoil. He knew that she was correct and that it was the right thing to do. In the blink of an eye, Lauriel seemed to pass from a child to an adult.

Adamar stepped forward and embraced Lauriel in a long and heartfelt hug.

It was the kind of hug that let her know he was deeply proud of her, but it was also the hug of acceptance.

"Well, I suppose you're right," Adamar finally conceded as he took a step back and wiped the tears from his eyes. He had many other words that he wanted to say but could find very few.

He quickly changed the subject and pointed to her other blade. "Oh, and this one … This is no less deadly. I think that you will really like it, but I will let you figure it out," he said cryptically with a wink.

Lauriel knew better than to question him on it. He was good at keeping secrets and she knew that she could not break him.

She nodded and smiled in understanding as she secured the scimitars and scabbards to her waist belt.

"These will never leave my side," she proclaimed.

Adamar looked at the completed warrior and nodded in approval, unable to say anything else. He simply turned and held out his arm to walk back with her.

"So, what is this Bladerite?" she asked as she joined him.

"It is something that I cannot walk you through, my dear, for the information is not privy to me. You must find the Bladerite Invocation, and where that is, I have no idea!"

"What? Where do I even begin to look for it!?" Lauriel exclaimed.

"I don't know, daughter; hopefully fate will show you the way."

As they left the grove, Lauriel happened to look back for one last glance. She glimpsed another unexpected audience member that was also leaving; a Will-o' Wisp.

CHAPTER FOUR

Amyrr

auriel stared at the many new and strange sights in wide-eyed wonderment as she slowly worked her way through the web of crowded and dirty streets. She was excited to be in a new and wholly foreign place for the first time, but she quickly began to understand why most of her kind rarely traveled to the human realms and why Adamar had chosen to remain at their inn instead of going with her to explore.

The bustling city of Amyrr was the absolute antithesis of her small elven community, and the vast differences were far greater than she had ever imagined. There was no room at all for nature or beauty, as every available space seemed to be filled by some type of unsightly wooden structure that had been built an uncomfortably close distance to the next. Every turn that she made led to another chaotic and noisy street packed with heckling merchants attempting to sell all manner of goods and supplies from the busy port. A constant undertone of simmering tension and impatience permeated the entire city.

Not long into her exploration, she began to notice that the human women were particularly unwelcoming toward her. Many of them would look her up and down with an open and unhidden look of distain, and whenever she would pass by several of them in a group, she could hear their venomous murmurs as they passed unfriendly judgement upon her, or their laughter at some joke that was obviously made at her expense. She found her exposure to the human men to be quite different but equally strange. Most of them would simply stare at her like she was from some other world, but several whistled or made comments when she walked by that would be considered rude and obnoxious in her culture.

But even though her first experiences were negative and she had found much to her dislike, just being in a new and different place full of sights, sounds, smells, and customs that were vastly different from her own was incredibly exciting. She couldn't wait to explore more, but the morning hours seemed to fly by in the blink of an eye, and the starting time for the Tournament of the Citadel drew near.

Friends

When Lauriel rounded the final street corner to the Citadel amphitheater, she was stopped in her tracks as she marveled at the unexpected beauty and grandiosity of the human crafted feat. A massive outer bailey made of a repeating series of open, white, marble arches encircled the entire amphitheater. It gleamed brightly in the mid-morning sun, welcoming spectators through the numerous magnificent spans that led to the seating areas beyond.

But as she passed through the gates and began to view the unexpectedly large seating area, cold spider-like fingers began to run up and down her spine as a sudden wave of nervousness assaulted her. She had never seen such a gathering in her entire life, and the thought of fighting in front of such a large crowd was terrifying.

The entire interior of the circular amphitheater had been carved deeply into the land like a manmade crater, with row upon row of tiered seats descending downward as they surrounded a large, open arena at the bottom.

The seating areas appeared large enough to hold many thousands of people, and many of them were already filled to capacity with raucous and excited spectators.

As she worked her way toward an open seat, she began to feel claustrophobic as she was swallowed by the crowd like a minnow in a large pond. Her breathing became rapid and shallow as her heart pounded increasingly harder in her chest. Part of her wanted to run as fast as she could, back to the solace of her peaceful forest, but there was another part of her that felt an energy and excitement like she had never before experienced—and even through her nervousness, it made her feel more alive than ever.

* * * *

By the time the opening parade full of music, dancing, colors, and costumes had concluded, Lauriel had completely forgotten about her nerves as she became caught up in the excitement of the spectacle. She fully immersed herself into the competition and culture as she cheered along with the crowd for her favored competitors in the axe throwing and archery competitions. She had become so lost in the moment that she was shocked when the high noon bells rang in signal of the midday lunch intermission.

The solo combat competitions were scheduled to begin after the midday break, and Lauriel had been assigned an opponent in the first fight bracket, a spot with lower attendance that was used for unknown competitors with little or no rank.

The later brackets were reserved for the more popular and higher ranked solo combatants, intentionally designed to continuously build upon the crowd's excitement and anticipation toward the pinnacle competition of the games—the heavy joust.

Her heart once again beat faster, and her stomach felt like it was tying itself into a knot as she made her way to the floor of the area and checked in to the ready room.

"Uhm, hello sir, is this where I check in?" Lauriel asked the attendant timidly.

"This room is for the competitors only," the attendant said gruffly and without even a single look from his table full of papers.

"I'm competing in the solo combat competition; my name is Lauriel Valendril."

The attendant looked up at her and gave a half-grunt, half-laugh as he answered, "Ahh, that's right; I did hear that we had a female competing this time."

She thought his greeting to be odd and relatively unfriendly, but his derogatory demeanor was lost to her naiveté and lack of exposure to such behavior.

"Choose your weapons, and wait over there," he ordered, pointing at a large rack of wooden weapons and then to a small waiting area near the entrance gate.

"You're up first, but you are almost an hour early," he said in irritation. "Good luck," he added with a laugh and a shake of his head as he went back to sorting the documents on the table.

This time, Lauriel picked up fully on his condescending mannerisms but paid no further attention to him, choosing instead to focus on the looming task at hand.

She took two wooden scimitars off the rack and went to her assigned place as instructed.

As she donned her light leather armor and prepared for the competition, her hands trembled, and doubts about her skills and readiness began to creep into her mind. She tried her best to calm her nerves, but it was one battle that she was already losing.

She looked through the wide bars of the entrance gate and desperately scanned the seats for Adamar. The long journey had been very difficult for him, and he had remained behind to rest, assuring her that he would arrive before the solo competition began. But what caught her eye instead was a female halfling that was already inside of the arena floor and walking in her direction.

Like others of her kind, she stood at a diminutive three feet tall. Her brown eyes reflected the wizened look of an adult, but her smooth childlike face made her look much younger than she actually was.

She had short brown hair that she wore in a bob, rosy cheeks, and was carrying a large bundle of bandages as she walked right past the gate that Lauriel stood behind.

"Hello!" Lauriel said, half expecting the same kind of rude response that she was becoming accustomed to. But something about the halfling's seemingly cheerful demeanor made her want to make her acquaintance.

"Oh, good heavens!" the halfling exclaimed as she jumped in startled surprise of the sudden and unexpected voice behind the gate. Her large bundle had blocked her view and she had not noticed Lauriel as she passed by.

She began to laugh at herself for almost throwing the entire stack of clean bandages in the air.

"Well, hello there!"

She smiled brightly at Lauriel and it had an immediate, calming effect on her, as if Adamar himself was standing right next to her offering his reassurance. It was the first truly warm and welcoming smile Lauriel had experienced in the city.

"I heard that a female was to compete today; are you up next?" the halfling asked excitedly.

Her friendly demeanor took Lauriel by surprise, and she stammered a response. "I ... Yes, I am."

"That's so awesome! Let me put these bandages away, and I'll be right back."

The halfling made her way to the injury room that was just next door and quickly returned to Lauriel.

"I'm sorry, where are my manners. I'm Nyx," she said as she held out her hand.

Lauriel shook her hand, and the friendly gesture put her even more at ease.

"I'm Lauriel, nice to meet you, Nyx."

"You are a long way from home! First time here?" Nyx asked.

"Yes, it is my first time to any city like this. But if I am not mistaken, you are a long way from home also; have you been here a while?

"Oh yes, I have been here for several years learning the healing arts at the Temple. I have worked several of these events, but this is the first where I'm the lead healer," Nyx replied.

"Well, no offense, but I sure hope I don't meet you again in that capacity," Lauriel quipped.

Nyx laughed. "Well, if you scare me like that again, I might not be around to help you anyway! I think my heart stopped!" Nyx joked. "You look a little nervous, are you okay?" she continued.

"I was fine until I saw you carrying all those bandages," Lauriel replied.

This time, they both began to laugh at each other's quick wit.

"Yes, I'm terribly nervous, to be honest with you. I could barely buckle the leather straps of my armor!" Lauriel admitted.

Nyx reached out and took both of Lauriel's hands in her own and looked at her intently. "I'm sure that you are going to do amazing. I'll be cheering for you since I won't be tending to a patient in the first round."

Nyx's matter-of-fact confidence and calming demeanor continued to ease Lauriel's apprehension.

"Thanks, Nyx! I appreciate that."

"Well, hey, I have to run, but since you are new to the city, I know a cool pub. Would you like to grab a drink later?" Nyx asked.

Lauriel nodded. "Sure! I would love to. Where?"

"There is a decent pub not far from the Citadel named the Foolish Faerie, meet a couple hours after sundown? That will give me time to get cleaned up after the tournament."

"Sure thing! See you there," Lauriel exclaimed, unable to hide her excitement at finally experiencing the town with someone who was actually friendly.

Foes

Lauriel stepped out from behind the gate and entered the large arena. Her heart felt like it was about to leap out of her chest as she made her way toward the starting circle.

She was greeted by a few cheers, but noticed that there were significantly more heckles and jeers that were spilling freely from the crowd, as well as many other rude comments about her body. Her eyes scanned desperately for Adamar, and she breathed a sigh of relief when she was finally able to locate him with only a few seconds to spare. He nodded and smiled confidently, and the calm reassurance that his presence brought helped her to refocus.

"You go, Lauriel! You've got this!" she heard Nyx yell from the doorway threshold of the injury room.

Five judges were seated in a section of the stands that had been made into an elevated observation platform. It provided an open and unobstructed view of the arena.

Each would raise a flag if any of them saw what they considered to be a "killing blow," and if all five judges raised their flags in acknowledgement of a strike, the battle was considered to be won.

Her opponent stepped out of the ready area on the opposing side, and his appearance drew a large cheer and enthusiastic round of applause. Lauriel could hear an increasing amount of demeaning and downright hostile comments directed at her from the raucous crowd.

The man wore a chainmail shirt and wielded a wooden longsword in his right hand. In his left, he held a buckler.

He proceeded to his starting circle which had been placed sixty feet away from hers on the opposing side. As soon as both opponents were set, the signaling horns sounded, and the crowd erupted in a loud roar.

Both Lauriel and her opponent closed the distance between themselves rapidly, stopping their approaches just short of each other's melee range.

Lauriel quickly set her scimitars into one of her defensive-ready positions and prepared for a highly skilled assault by her opponent.

But to her surprise, he stepped toward her without his weapon fully ready to strike.

Is he just toying with me? Is he joking? Is this some kind of trap he is trying to lure me into?

Lauriel's mind raced as she observed his advance into her threat range. She could not believe how open he was leaving himself, how slow he seemed to be, or how easy it was to read his intentions.

He might as well shout his next move!

Immediately as he stepped forward and began to draw his longsword back to take a full swing, Lauriel sprang into action. Her left scimitar hit his buckler with an intentionally distracting strike meant to remove his defense, and with a quick flip of her wrist, her second scimitar struck the man square in his wide-open neck with a shocking amount of speed and precision.

Whack!" The sound of the strike traveled over the noise of the crowd and could be heard throughout the entire arena.

"Ooohhhhh!" the crowd reacted.

She could distinctly hear Nyx's voice squeal with delight, "YEAH!"

The man staggered backward, dropping his sword as he grabbed his neck and shouted in pain. All five judges immediately raised their flags, and the ground officiant ordered a halt to the battle. A wave of silence washed over the entire amphitheater as all were stunned by the expediency of the encounter. The entire sequence of events from the starting signal to the strike took less than ten seconds.

The man began to turn bright red, and Lauriel felt genuinely terrible for him. She had not intended to embarrass or make a spectacle of him; she had just reacted with a simple technique from her many years of training.

She glanced up at Adamar and shrugged her shoulders, happy to have won, but disappointed that she had not even been able to fight. She could see that he was doing his very best to restrain his laugh, but there was no hiding his immense look of pride. He signaled for her to bow and she suddenly remembered her dueling etiquette that she had forgotten in her shock. She turned back to her opponent, crossed her scimitars, and respectfully bowed at him. He returned the acknowledgement with grace and elegance, but not dignity.

With the battle called, she left the arena for the day and moved into the next round without any dust, sweat, or bruises.

The Foolish Faerie

The tavern was filled to capacity, and the patrons seemed to be in high spirits. Along with the tournament came much drunken celebration throughout the entire town. Lauriel had never seen such a lively pub and thoroughly enjoyed the full immersion into the sociable human tradition.

She was glad to find a reprieve from the negative interactions that she had experienced throughout the city as her presence in the sea of bodies went largely unnoticed and unmolested.

Lauriel had arrived early for her meeting with Nyx and waited patiently for a table to open. After a time, a small table in the far corner vacated and she nimbly made her way through the crowd and sat down. She waited awkwardly for several minutes, hoping that someone would come by and take her order, but the barmaids did not seem to pay any attention to her whatsoever.

Whenever they would get near, she would try to call to them but they either did not hear her, or they were intentionally ignoring her, and after several attempts, she decided that they had no intention of taking her order.

The snub only helped to reconfirm her growing feelings of dislike toward the human women. But never one to be deterred from reaching her goal, even if it was to purchase a drink, she decided to go directly up to the bar to place her order.

As she approached, she watched as the bartender skillfully poured many pints, quickly and without overflowing a single drop. He was focused on the drinks but could tell that someone was standing at the bar ready to order.

"What'll it be?" he snapped hurriedly without looking up from his task.

"Uhm, I don't know. Do you have any elven wine?" she asked.

He began to laugh and looked up at the unfamiliar female voice with a different accent.

"Holy shit!" he blurted out.

Several men at the bar that had watched her approach began to laugh heartily.

Lauriel stepped back and looked quickly behind her to see what the fuss was about.

"Ha!" the bartender said as a deep shade of red began to creep across his face.

"Sorry about that. I … uh … wasn't expecting to see … uhh …"

Lauriel was completely unaware of it, but she was so captivatingly beautiful that even the enthralling lure of a Siren's call would pale in comparison to her own alluring appeal. Her modest upbringing in the remote forests, coupled with her intense focus on training, afforded her little opportunity to realize her own attractiveness. But her unassuming manner only served to enhance her qualities.

Her sunshine blonde hair fell to her shoulders and she often wore it pulled back into an athletic ponytail, allowing a smattering of golden locks to frame the sides of her youthfully radiant face. Her full lips had the slightest hint of seductiveness, but it was her bright green, almond-shaped eyes that were her most striking feature. They were captivating to the point that they could stop the world around her.

Her long hours of training every day had shaped her body into a lean, athletic-but-feminine build that was at the pinnacle of fitness. She wore tight clothes that accentuated every part of her body, not because she was trying to be provocative, but because she needed complete unhindered movement without anything flowing around her when she wielded her blades.

She had no idea that her outfit was so risqué to the other cultures.

He stared at her green eyes for several moments before speaking again.

"Yes, uh … what'll it be?"

"Your pint!" Lauriel exclaimed.

"Huh?" the bartender continued to stare at her, completely transfixed and oblivious to the rest of the world.

"Your pint!" she repeated. "It's overflowing!"

He was finally able to snap himself out of his mesmerization, and look back down. "Ahh, shit!"

The cheap and pungent smelling ale ran from the cask down the bar and had already made a large puddle on the floor. He shut off the tap and grabbed several rags.

Lauriel smiled brightly. "I'll just take two of whatever that is."

He leaned forward and beckoned her closer as he whispered, "Are you sure? This stuff is crap, but we have some good stuff down in the basement, something that you might find to your liking."

"Nah that's okay. Thank you though! I want to have what the locals have," she replied.

He slowly poured another pint and pushed both mugs toward her with a wink. "On the house."

"Wow, thank you!" she exclaimed.

She took the mugs of ale and tried her best not to spill any as she turned and made her way back to the small table.

Her tight outfit coupled with her naturally graceful elven gate was too much for him to even pretend to not gawk at. But no others noticed because they were openly and unabashedly staring at the exotic goddess as well.

When she sat down, several of the men at the bar began to playfully heckle him.

"Hell, I've been coming here for years and not gotten a drink 'on the house,' and she gets two!"

"Thomas, you're so ugly I'm going to start charging you double to make up for hers!" the bartender retorted.

"Well, if it keeps her here longer, I say give em all night!" the man next to him added as he slid a silver piece across the counter.

Lauriel had just taken her seat when she spotted Nyx's small frame navigating through the crowd in search of her.

"Nyx!" Lauriel yelled, but her voice barely traveled above the noise.

When Nyx turned in her direction, she waved her arms and tried again. "NYX!"

This time, the noise and commotion from the corner caught her attention. Nyx locked eyes with her and began to wave excitedly. Lauriel noticed that her permanently rosy cheeks seemed to accurately mirror her warm personality, and she was genuinely happy to see her friendly smile again.

"Hey again!" Nyx exclaimed as she approached the table and embraced Lauriel as if she were an old friend.

"I hope you haven't been waiting long!"

"Not long at all! I just got back to the table. And thanks again for the invite; it is so nice to meet with someone in this town that is actually friendly!" Lauriel replied and slid the second mug toward Nyx.

"Well, thanks for meeting—and the drink! And yes, unfortunately this town can be particularly unfriendly toward many races that are not their own. Anyway, so about today! That was so awesome! I told you that you would do well, I just didn't anticipate THAT well!"

Lauriel smiled shyly at Nyx's praise. "I really didn't mean to embarrass him. I was scared out of my wits that I would be the spectacle."

"I have never seen anyone win that quick! Where did you learn to fight like that!?" Nyx asked inquisitively.

"My grandfather taught me, but I didn't really even get to fight!"

Well, here is to your first win, and may you get the opportunity to actually fight next time!" Nyx said as she raised her glass.

Lauriel burst into laughter at Nyx's sincere but comical toast and clinked her mug against Nyx's.

"*Silára Éloth!*" Lauriel replied in Elven.

Nyx looked at her questioningly. "What does that mean?"

"To good friendships!" Lauriel translated.

Nyx's face lit up again. "To good friendships!"

Lauriel took a sip of the ale and immediately dry heaved at the foul taste. Her face winced and contorted uncontrollably into a look of disgust.

"Oh my goodness, that is terrible! How does anyone drink such a dreadful thing?" Lauriel exclaimed.

Nyx spit out the rest of her drink as Lauriel's response immediately struck her with a fit of laughter. "Locals affectionally refer to it as 'pond scum ale,' but it is cheap and plentiful!"

The watchful bartender was quick to abandon his post at the bar and bring Lauriel a glass of the finest and most expensive wine in the pub, an elven wine.

"Don't tell the owner … It's on the house also, we want to keep our customers," he said with a nervous smile and a painfully awkward linger.

"Wow, you have an interesting way of doing business," Lauriel replied, not fully understanding his enthrallment. "Thank you so much!" she said with a bright and innocent smile as she took the wine glass from him.

"Yes, thank you, Zander. My you're chivalrous this evening," Nyx said with a smirk.

The bartender's already red face seemed to grow several shades darker and he quickly turned and walked away.

"He is probably the nicest human that I have encountered since I have been here, but he sure does seem nervous," Lauriel observed.

Nyx laughed and shook her head but did not elaborate on her own observations.

Lauriel took a sip and held up the glass. "Ahh … now that's more like it!"

But Nyx noticed that the cheerful look on her face slowly began to change to one of reflective contemplation as she continued to stare at the glass in silence.

Nyx gently put her hand on Lauriel's arm. "Are you okay?"

Lauriel's pensive gaze went from the glass back to Nyx, and she forced a smile.

"Nyx, you said you have been here quite a while; do you miss your home?"

Nyx pondered the question for several moments before answering. "To be honest, I miss it terribly, but I am not ready to go back quite yet."

Lauriel looked at her expectantly.

"Nothing exciting ever really happens there; day in and day out it is the same routine, and the people seem perfectly content with it, which is fine, but I guess I have a bit more of a kindred spirit than normal. I felt restless there, like I was trapped in a cage."

"That's exactly how I feel!" Lauriel exclaimed, her eyes wide in amazement at how accurately Nyx had described the very same feelings that she was having.

Nyx nodded and continued, "I came here not just to learn and practice my healing, but in search of adventure. But what I have found is that even here I feel restless and still find myself wanting to go experience the wider world."

Lauriel looked back at her glass of wine, and her eyes began to well up with tears. "I want to do that too! But I feel so guilty for leaving those behind that may need me."

Nyx was just about to reply when a large man approached their table. He took a long drink and slammed his empty mug down on the table. The tall, muscular man had a massive, two-handed sword strapped across his broad back, and they could both tell that he was quite drunk.

He looked at Lauriel, and his eyes glided not-so-subtly down the length of her. "What are you doing with those schimmmitarsh, babe? Are they your husband's?"

"Well, that was rude, Eric," Nyx said as she shot a warning glance at Lauriel.

Lauriel had never experienced such a degree of sexism but gave his rude words the benefit of the doubt, dismissing them as either the ridiculous words of a drunken fool, or some cultural difference that she did not yet understand.

"These are MY scimitars. What do you think I'm doing with them?" Lauriel fired back at the drunkard.

The man laughed obnoxiously, and his dismissiveness became abundantly clear to her.

"Whosshh yer hot new friend, Nyxxss?"

Nyx rolled her eyes and subtly queued Lauriel in with her introduction. "Lauriel, this is Erik, the winner of the solo combat tournament for the last three years."

"Four after thisss one," he added.

He placed his large hand on Lauriel's shoulder but rested it in such a way that his fingers were uncomfortably close to the top of her breast. "Lemme buy you a drink, babe."

Lauriel squirmed away from his unwelcome touch.

"Thank you, but I'm fine."

"You shhhuure are. C'mon, I inshishth."

He tried to place his hand on her shoulder again but she ducked away from his grasp, nimbly standing up and moving around the table to create a barrier between them.

"I just want to sit here with my friend and enjoy a conversation! Is that too much to ask? Besides, why does everyone keep giving me drinks?" Lauriel questioned in frustration.

"Ha! Cause that hot ashhh of yorshh," the crude man replied.

Nyx's eyes narrowed, and her voice suddenly lost its pleasant qualities. "Okay, Eric, that's enough. You need to leave. NOW."

"Bish, I'm not talking to you," he said as he grabbed the wrist of her scolding hand in a viselike grip.

Lauriel's blood instantly boiled, and her hands slid from the table to her dagger. The pub was far too packed to draw her scimitars.

"Get your damn hands off her!" Lauriel yelled.

The drunken man noticed her move toward her weapon and yanked Nyx off of her chair. "Or what? Do it, bish, and see what happens."

Nyx shot Lauriel a stern warning look and subtly shook her head. Lauriel was shocked at just how composed Nyx seemed to be, and she relaxed her hand away from her blade.

"Eric, this is your last warning; let go of me right now," Nyx said calmly.

Lauriel looked around for help but there were no others that seemed to be willing to challenge the big man. Seeing none come forward, and following Nyx's cue to not draw her weapon, she decided to switch tactics.

Lauriel captured the man with her green eyes and walked around the table, stopping only when she stood directly in front of him. She put her hand up to his cheek and drew him near as she leaned in toward him. She found it interesting that he was seemingly powerless to resist her as he gladly followed her advance, puckering his lips and leaning in to meet hers. But at the last second, she dodged his lips and kissed him on the cheek. As she did, his eyes suddenly shot wide open and he let out a loud howl that echoed throughout the pub as she racked him hard with her knee. At the exact same time, Nyx had used the distraction to execute her plan. Lauriel would not have even noticed it if she were not standing so close, but just as Nyx whispered a few words, a faint red glow encompassed her unrestrained hand. She grasped the man's arm, and he howled again and recoiled as if he had just been bitten by a snake. He immediately collapsed to the ground, cursing and swearing as he held both his crotch and arm while writhing in pain.

"Thanks for the practice … babe," Lauriel said. The entire pub erupted into laughter, infuriating the man even more. He tried to kick her but she was able to nimbly dodge his drunken attempt. Nyx grabbed her hand and they disappeared into the crowd, promptly exiting the pub before Erik was able to stand.

They continued their escape for several blocks, giggling like innocent children playing hide and seek as they weaved in and out of crowds to ensure that the angry man was not able to follow them.

After they had cut through several random side streets and were sure that they were in the clear, they finally stopped and looked at each other for several seconds before bursting into a fit of laughter.

"I haven't had that much fun … in a long time!" Nyx said in a broken pant.

"Me either!" Lauriel exclaimed.

"His face when you said that to him—priceless!" Nyx added as she began another round of laughter at the fresh mental image.

"What did you do to him!?" Lauriel asked.

Nyx cocked her head to the side, and a questioning look drew across her face, but her coy smirk gave away any attempted look of innocence.

"What do you mean? I think that it was your knee square to his crotch that might have been the convincing factor to let go of me."

Lauriel laughed and shook her head. "Mm-hmm, and nothing at all to do with your gentle love pat?"

"Oh, that ..." Nyx smiled. "That was just a little added encouragement."

CHAPTER FIVE

Champion

auriel rushed to the gate of the ready room to see what the sudden chaos and pandemonium in the arena was about, but her view was blocked by the wall of competitors that had all gathered to watch the crazed barbarian in his third fight. Both of his previous opponents had to be carried out of the ring unconscious, and based on the shocked reactions of the crowd, something far worse was happening.

A string of cursing and swearing, the likes of which she had never before heard, echoed throughout the arena as nearly a dozen armed guards rushed the giant man to remove him from his opponent when he failed to heed the call to stop the battle.

By the time Lauriel was finally able to squeeze her way in and see what was happening, she witnessed a ghastly sight as the barbarian's critically injured opponent was rushed into the injury room. When she looked back out into the arena, the huge barbarian was in such a fit of rage that it took all of the guards to finally restrain him—yet he still continued to thrash about.

"What happened? What did I miss?" Lauriel asked.

She had finished her third battle and had just stepped back into the room to observe the other competitions when all hell broke loose in the arena.

She had won each of her matches handily and had slowly begun to earn the respect of most of the other skilled competitors. But it was not only her obvious skill in the competition that had won them over. The bias of the scoring judges had become readily apparent as each of her strikes were met with increasing scrutiny and hesitation. Her last battle only ended when her fourth lethal strike knocked her opponent's helm off and left them no choice but to acknowledge her win. Both she and her peers knew that she faced an increasingly uphill battle, and even those that she had bested found themselves rooting for her as she continued to move up the ladder.

"I think that crazy dude Dante just killed Tamenyr!" one of the men exclaimed as he quickly caught Lauriel up on what had just happened.

"The ground officiant ordered a reset after they began to grapple, and when Dante let him go and turned around to step back five paces, Tamenyr turned and hit him in the head. Dante lost his mind and ripped Tamenyr's helm off and beat him with it!"

"I'm just glad I didn't have to fight him," another said.

His comment was met with many nods of agreement.

Just then, Lauriel felt the sudden grasp of a strong hand around her waist and upper torso. She had been caught completely off guard as her attention was fully on the arena, and was grappled into a full restraint before she could even react. The hand grabbed her breast, and she heard a vaguely familiar voice as the man behind her began to speak.

"Next time you mess with my balls, make sure you are in the proper position, bitch."

He buckled her legs with his and forced her to her knees with his incredible strength, intentionally tearing her shirt and exposing her chest as she hit the ground.

Her eyes immediately reddened with tears of anger and embarrassment as she tried to get away from his strong grasp while covering herself. The other men quickly came to her rescue but

Erik, having already achieved his goal of humiliation, separated from her without any further resistance.

"Thanks for the practice ... babe." he scoffed as he exited the room.

* * * *

After several hours of walking the streets in a futile effort to calm down her anger and work through her shame, Lauriel arrived back at the room at the inn that she and Adamar were sharing. As she walked through the door, she hid both her torn shirt and her emotions from him. She wanted to ensure that Erik remained alive to participate further in the tournament. But even with her best attempt at concealment, he knew her far too well.

"What's wrong, my dear? You are back early this evening. I thought you were going out with your friend, Nyx?"

"I just had a rough day, and I wanted to get a good night's sleep before tomorrow," she replied.

She could immediately tell by the concerned look on his face that she had not convinced him. But instead of pressing, he nodded and tried to lighten the mood.

"Well, you're an adult now and make your own path, but I had not expected you to show back up so soon wearing another man's shirt."

She smiled and hugged him, and as she did, she was forced to use every bit of willpower within her to avoid bursting into tears.

"Long story, *Anfadwé*, better left for another day."

She released him, and before he could get another look at her, she quickly entered the washroom and closed the door.

Finale

The arena seating and observation areas were bursting with excited spectators that had crowded into the standing-room-only spaces until there was not a single space to be had. The vast crowd waited eagerly as the highly anticipated duel between an unranked, unheard of, female elf, and Eric, the unbeaten reigning champion, was finally at hand.

It was the largest crowd that the amphitheater had ever hosted, even more so than any previous heavy joust finale.

Lauriel had won her fourth match only after completely disarming her opponent with so many knuckle strikes that he could no longer hold his weapon; a tactic that she was forced to switch to when her killing blows went unacknowledged.

The time had finally come for her final battle, and she paced back and forth in the ready room, nervously awaiting her summons. The crowd suddenly erupted into a mixture of cheering and booing, and when she looked out into the arena, she could see her final challenger swaggering through the gate on the other side. Her eyes reddened, and she began to shake in silent fury.

"What's wrong, my dear? This is not like you to be so upset," Adamar questioned from her side.

He looked out into the arena at the man, and his eyes suddenly flared with a shocking intensity that she had never before seen as he quickly looked back at her. His hands went to the scimitars at his waist that he now held in safe keeping for her.

"Did this man hurt you in any way?"

Lauriel could see Adamar's jaw clench, and she intentionally downplayed her answer as she genuinely feared for the man's life.

"No, *Anfadwé*, only my dignity, and I intend to recover that right now."

Adamar seemed to accept her answer, and his hands relaxed off of the weapons.

"It is time, Mistress Lauriel." The gate attendant beckoned her forward.

"Any last advice, *Anfadwé*?" Lauriel asked.

Adamar looked back at her and placed his hand upon her shoulder. "You need no more instruction from me."

Lauriel nodded and took a long, deep breath, but her heart continued to pound wildly as she stepped back into the dusty arena for the final time. The crowd erupted into another round of loud cheers and boos as she entered. Just as she had won over her competitors, she had won a good portion of the crowd, but there were seemingly just as many that wanted to see the foreign female falter.

Her eyes locked on to her opponent who already stood at the ready on the opposite side. The mountain-of-a-man was protected by a nearly complete set of full plate armor. She tried to quickly size up her striking points as she walked, but could only find a few very narrow target areas that his armor did not cover.

He wielded a huge, two-handed sparring sword that looked to her like it was the size of a tree trunk, even from a distance. She knew that she could easily parry smaller and lighter weapons, but she couldn't help but wonder if her techniques would work against a weapon at least twice the size, or against a skilled opponent with such strength and reach.

Lauriel gripped the wooden scimitars in nervous anticipation as she entered her circle. The man across the arena raised the visor of his helm and winked at her, and just the brief sight of his face caused her blood to run hot.

Calm down, Lauriel. He is just trying to rattle you, don't give him the victory.

She reciprocated the gesture, blowing him a kiss and drawing much laughter from the crowd. Eric's face reddened, and he slammed his visor shut as the trumpeters raised their horns to signal the start of the battle.

And after what seemed like an eternity, the horns finally sounded and the crowd erupted again into a wild cheer as her opponent charged furiously at her.

Lauriel assumed her defensive-ready position but did not move, choosing instead to let the aggressive adversary continue his rapid move toward her.

And just as the behemoth drew near, she quickly shifted to an offset position to his straight line. The move made him alter his straight-line course and turn back toward her, but he was so encumbered by his armor that he lost most of his momentum.

He brought the giant sword up and swung it at her in a well-controlled and vicious swing, attempting to end the battle in the first few seconds, but her last second move caused him to miss by several feet. An audible gasp could be heard from the crowd.

Lauriel knew he was trying to make an example of her. He meant to show her, her proper place—and that was not here in the arena. The force of the swing, even with a wooden blade, would have killed her if it had hit her in the head, which was exactly where it was aimed. He wheeled around and swung again, but Lauriel quickly tumbled out of the way, not even trying to parry the vicious swing.

As the swing went over her head, she knew that it would take him a brief moment to return the large blade to a position to where he could attack again. It was now her turn for the offensive and she immediately lunged at him with a fury of blows from the wooden scimitars. *Thwack, whack, whack, clack, thwack, crack!* She spun around behind him. *Crack, whack, whack, crack!* Her left-handed scimitar broke, and the crowd cheered wildly.

One of the judges turned toward the other and nodded subtly, an unmistakably smug look on his face from the pride of his covert accomplishment in ensuring that she had a cracked blade.

Her *Andúlari* fighting style heavily depended on two blades for defense and symmetric balance, but she did not let the loss deter her.

Several of her strikes found armor, but there were also several that had found their way through any defense.

After nearly disarming him with a strike to his hand that obviously cracked several of his knuckles, Lauriel tumbled away and looked up at the judges, expecting to see a raised flag, but not a single one of the male judges had raised one.

She had hit the behemoth ten times and they had ruled them all non-lethal.

The man bellowed out as he charged back at her, jumping into the air and coming down with the sword with all his might, right where she was standing.

Good grief, that strike might have split a horse in two, even with the wooden blade!

She nimbly dodged out of the way and then counterattacked, this time at his helm. *Whack, whack, thwack!* She was only able to attack at half of her normal speed since the other blade had broken.

The man, somewhat disoriented from a mild concussion, took another wild swing at her but missed by several feet.

She counter-attacked yet again, sending three more strikes to his helmet, finally achieving her goal at dislodging it.

Lauriel had been carving him up like a dead tree, hitting him sixteen times and sending his helmet flying, but the judges had still not raised a single flag. The crowd began booing the abundantly obvious bias of the judges and chanting her name.

Lau ... ri ... el! Lau ... ri ... el!

The large man's face contorted with rage, and he charged at her again.

Almost immediately at the start of battle, when he attempted the first blow, Lauriel knew that she could best the clumsy fool if she was careful and fought like she had been taught. He was good, but he was just too slow with his heavy armor and huge sword.

This idiot may get lucky with a hit and win.

Her blood now boiled white hot, and she decided that she had no other choice but to change tactics.

As she dodged his next swing, she brought her scimitar upward into an arc that landed squarely in his groin.

"Oooffffff!" She could hear both him and the crowd exclaim. She let him pass by her as he stumbled forward, howling wildly.

She grabbed his head and leapt up onto him from behind, sitting on his shoulders and squeezing his head between her legs.

She let both his and her momentum continue forward as he stumbled with the sudden unexpected extra weight. She ducked as if diving into a pool of water but kept her legs wrapped tightly around his neck. The maneuver resulted in him doing an almost complete somersault and landing flat on his back.

Lauriel immediately pounced, and the series of events that quickly followed won over most of the remaining crowd that had been so adamantly opposed to her. His head was the only unprotected area, and she raised her scimitar to strike a final unquestionable blow, but she could tell that he was completely unguarded in his disorientation. She realized that the strike could truly harm the defenseless enemy and she withdrew her opportunity, choosing instead to gently place the blade on his exposed neck.

"Thanks for the practice, babe," she said with a wink.

The officiant called the battle after the flags were raised, but it was not Lauriel that was awarded. "Groin shots are strictly prohibited; you are hereby disqualified," the ground officiant ruled.

The crowd booed for many long minutes as Lauriel was escorted out of the arena and the big man was he was once again crowned "champion."

An old *Andúlarium* covered in a heavy, hooded cloak so as not to be seen smiled proudly and walked away.

Little Bird

Adamar had just finished packing the backpack when the door to their room burst open and a dusty, bruised, and distraught young elven woman stood in the threshold. Her hair was a wild mess, just like when she was a child, and the look of exasperation on her face clearly told the story of her experience in the arena without him even having to be there.

"Well, I lost …"

Adamar couldn't help but burst into laughter at the nostalgic sight; he had seen it countless times before.

His jovial reaction immediately disarmed her better than any of her opponents had been able to, and she began to laugh at the entertaining spectacle that she knew she had just unintentionally created for him. But he could immediately tell that something else weighed heavily on her mind, more so than the loss of the tournament.

He walked over to her and kissed her on the forehead.

"You did well, my dear, everyone knows who the real winner was, but what is really on your mind?" he asked as he handed her sword belt back to her.

She threw her arms around him and hugged him tightly for many long moments. Her eyes welled up with tears as she began her next heartfelt words.

"*Anfadwé*, I have realized something very important throughout all of this."

"And what is that, my dear?"

She stepped back and looked at him intently. Her green eyes captured him completely, just as they always had.

"Thank you for all of the effort you have put into me, not only in teaching me to fight, but for teaching me to be a good person. And …" Her eyes burned as she choked back her tears. "Thank you for taking me in and raising me as your own; there is no greater love."

He made no attempt at holding back his own torrent of tears that suddenly burst forth from his eyes.

He took her hand in his and was forced to sit for many long moments until he was able to regain his composure enough to speak. "I too have come to a conclusion, but it was one that I reached long ago. You have been my greatest and most worthwhile accomplishment in this life, my dear." He tried to continue but his voice faltered.

She hugged him again and then pulled back with a questioning look on her face. "What do you mean 'have been'? Aren't we going back home tomorrow?"

He had to avert his gaze so that his fortitude did not fail him. He desperately wished that she would go back with him, and he couldn't imagine his house without the joy of her in it. But he knew deep within his heart that the time had come for the little bird to leave the nest.

He cleared his throat and took a deep breath before beginning.

"Your skills were no doubt noticed by many, and you will have several opportunities afforded to you now. Choose one that appeals to your heart, and you will not go wrong."

Tears now spilled from her eyes, and she nodded in understanding, but the thought of leaving him caused her heart to ache terribly.

"But I can't just leave you now in your hour of need!" Lauriel cried.

Adamar placed his hand gently on her cheek. "I will be fine. You can't just live and die in that same village without experiencing what the world has to offer. I can see it in you; you were born to fly."

He smiled and moved his wrinkled hand to one of her scabbards. "You have the virtues, wisdom, skill, and means to protect yourself as you begin your own path that diverges now from mine. My greatest hope is that I have given you the wings, and my greatest distress is that it comes with this burden."

Lauriel looked down at the scabbard and put her hand on top of his. "It is a burden that I am honored to bear, *Anfadwé*."

Adamar stood up and hurriedly grabbed the backpack that he had packed and handed it to her before his resolve completely failed him.

"Here are your things, my dear daughter; your entire life stands open to you now. Please don't forget to check in on your old grandfather from time to time." He tried to make his last comment lighthearted but she could easily detect the longing sadness in his voice.

She took the pack from him with a clear understanding of the significance of the moment, and gave him another long hug. But this time it felt far too brief, and far too final.

"Goodbye for now, *Anfadwé*."

CHAPTER SIX

Companions

True to Adamar's wise words, Lauriel's skill at the Tournament of the Citadel was noticed by many, and before the sun had even reached its midday zenith, she had been offered several well-paying jobs. But one job in particular appealed to her natural desire to help others in need, and even though it did not pay as well as many of the others, she heeded Adamar's advice and let her heart chose instead of her dwindling coin pouch.

The commission required an armed escort to protect a supply wagon that was urgently needed by the small mining outpost of Conna, a seven-day journey from Amyrr. Several previous wagons had been ambushed before reaching the town, and Conna was beginning to run dangerously low on many vital supplies. Due to the increasingly dire situation, the merchant sought to hire a group with more courage and fighting skills than the average sellsword, and had approached Lauriel for the task.

"Excellent, Mistress Lauriel! Then we have a deal! I have one other that you will be working with, and I will wait to hear from you about this Nyx person," the merchant confirmed.

"Thank you so much! We will not let you down," Lauriel exclaimed as she shook the merchant's hand excitedly.

* * * *

"Nyx!" Lauriel exclaimed as she rounded the corner at a near sprint.

After a brief search of the Temple complex, she had found Nyx in the back courtyard area hanging laundry.

"Oh, good heavens!" Nyx shouted in surprise as the entire arm load of clean laundry went flying through the air.

Lauriel's eyes opened wide and she began to profusely apologize for the inadvertent scare that seemed to be becoming a habit. She ran over and helped Nyx pick up the pile of bedding that now littered the ground, but Nyx took the incident with good humor and it quickly turned into another shared laugh between them.

"Guess what?" Lauriel exclaimed. Before Nyx could even answer, she continued, "You know that talk we had about feeling a sense of adventure and wanting to go experience the wider world?"

"Yes, the one that got interrupted by Erik?" Nyx replied.

"Yes! Well, I have found one!" Lauriel declared.

Nyx looked at her questioningly.

"I got a job as a guard protecting a wagon load of supplies to some small town in desperate need of them."

Nyx's face immediately gave away her thoughts as her genuine smile slowly turned to one that was obviously forced.

"I'm so happy for you! That sounds like a fun adventure for such a great cause."

Lauriel continued after her intentional pause, "And … he said he would hire you as well!"

"Seriously!?" Nyx exclaimed, her face brightening with an uncontained look of excitement.

"Yes!"

"Oh my goodness! Seriously?" Nyx continued to question in disbelief.

Lauriel laughed at her apparent shock. "There is only one catch though."

"What's that?" Nyx asked.

"We have to leave first thing tomorrow morning."

Nyx stared at her and nodded slowly, contemplating the myriad of things that she would have to accomplish in the short amount of time that remained.

"So where are we going and how long will we be gone?"

"I think maybe a couple weeks?" Lauriel replied.

"Whew! Okay! No pub tonight; I have a lot to do here!"

She threw her arms around Lauriel. "This is so exciting! This is the opportunity that I have been looking for!"

"I know! I can't wait!" Lauriel said. "We are supposed to meet at Tirwen's Provisions just before dawn. I will go let him know that you have accepted!"

"Okay, see you then!" Nyx confirmed.

Both Lauriel and Nyx wasted no time in parting as they hastily sped off in their separate ways to prepare for their journey.

Dante

The bright moon had just dipped below the horizon when Lauriel and Nyx arrived at the merchant's shop in the dark hour before dawn. A large, heavy wagon packed full of provisions was already out front, and two men were hooking up the two large oxen that would pull the heavy load.

Lauriel could clearly see that one of them was the merchant, but she could not make out the other figure that was bent over, working on the other side of the oxen.

"Good morning. Mr. Tirwen," Lauriel said as they approached.

The merchant turned around and greeted the two cordially. "Ahh, Mistress Lauriel, good morning. I am assuming this is your friend, Nyx?"

Before Lauriel could make the introduction, the other man stood up, and both Lauriel and Nyx gasped in shock at the unexpected sight of their third colleague.

Dante, the huge barbarian that had been thrown in jail during the tournament, stared back at them.

As was the custom for many of the northernmost barbaric tribes, he wore several fur skins and a patchwork of hard leather armor. He was just as tall as Erik, her final opponent in the tournament, but was of considerably stockier build. His long, black hair fell just past his shoulders and looked as it were in a permanent state of wild disarray, mirroring the restless and unkempt nature of the large barbarian himself. His nervous, ice blue eyes darted back and forth, anxiously scanning for some unseen evil around every shadow. They matched the cold complexion of his light-colored skin, for the frigid northern tribal regions rarely saw sunlight.

His arms, shoulders, and face were covered in grotesque scars and long-healed burn marks. Lauriel could tell that they were not the kind of scars that had been received throughout many battles, nor did they look like some tribal ritual, but ones that had been placed on him with cruelty and malice.

Lauriel had only seen him from across the arena, but now that she stood much closer to him, she understood even more why no one wanted to fight him. His burly physique, unique physical features, and extremely large great axe made him appear as a mighty force to be reckoned with.

With his foul mouth and sudden rage issues, he would have been one of the last of the tournament competitors that she would have chosen as a traveling companion, and her initial reservations were laid bare with her inadvertent blurt of her next thought. "Aren't you supposed to be in jail?"

Dante looked at her, unsurprised. "Well, it's nice to fucking meet you too."

Nyx walked up to him and extended her hand. "Good morning, Dante, I'm Nyx. It's nice to meet you."

Her welcoming smile and warm greeting seemed to immediately disarm him, and Lauriel observed the very same look of surprise on his face that had been on her own when she first met Nyx. It was the feeling of being caught off guard by someone's kindness, after experiencing so much rudeness and downright hate. Lauriel suddenly felt ashamed of her reservations and rush to judgement.

He held his hand out and it was so large that Nyx's looked like a toddler's as they shook.

"I guess I owe you my thanks, and my life. If it weren't for you saving Tamynyr, I would be hanging from the gallows by now," Dante said.

"Dante has agreed to be a part of this escort in return for his bail that I posted. Part of our hurry is not only to get these much-needed supplies to Conna, but as part of the terms of his release, he must be out of the city by sunrise and never return," the merchant explained.

"Well, these people are assholes anyway. I have no intention of returning to this shitty city. Uhh, no offense," Dante said as he looked back at Tirwen.

Lauriel burst out laughing. "At least we have one thing in common; I agree!" Lauriel held out her hand. "I apologize, Dante. I have experienced far too many rude people here, and I never intended to be one of them. Please forgive me."

The look on Dante's face softened, and he held out his hand in greeting.

"Well, I have to say that I saw you fight with those fucking toothpicks of yours, and you seemed to do pretty decently."

"Thanks!? I think …" Lauriel replied.

Big Brother

The eclectic group of adventurers lumbered slowly but steadily down the dusty cart trail, urging the oxen ever onward with the heavily laden wagon of precious cargo. They had pressed hard for a good portion of the day, even skipping lunch in their enthusiasm to gain more distance.

Lauriel couldn't decide if it was the new inspiration and excitement of the adventure, the urge to get as far away from Amyrr as they could, or both, but they all seemed to be in unspoken agreement to continue onward without delay.

By late afternoon, they had made it all the way to the junction where they would turn off the main road and continue onto the smaller, northeasterly path that led to Conna.

"What do you think about stopping here for the night?" Lauriel asked as she studied the map.

"Wolfdancer creek is right over there and it's our last night in the relative safety of a well-traveled road."

"Looks good to me. Besides, I'm so hungry I could eat one of these fucking oxen," Dante bemoaned.

"In that case, I'll get some food going before we lose our draft animals and fail our quest before the first day is even over," Nyx said, drawing laughter from the others.

* * * *

The sun had just set when Dante returned from watering and securing the oxen for the night. Lauriel had already readied the camp, and Nyx was busily preparing their meal on the campfire.

"Well hell, are we all just going to each cook for ourselves tonight?" Dante questioned, clearly offended.

Nyx looked up at him, brows furrowed. "No, I'm cooking for all of us."

Dante's booming laugh seemed to echo throughout the light woods. "Ha! Is this a joke? Where is the rest of it?"

"The rest of what?" Nyx asked.

"The meal! One rabbit! Hell, I can eat that before we even start the meal! You make me hike all through lunch and we all three sit down for a tasty meal … of a SINGLE FUCKING RABBIT?"

Nyx's happy-go-lucky demeanor normally seemed to have a calming effect on Dante, but both her and Lauriel quickly learned that a ravenous barbarian with a meager dinner was not a good combination.

She looked at Lauriel for help, and Lauriel jumped into the discussion.

"Nyx, were you able to get any more fresh meat before we left?"

Nyx nodded and quickly retrieved the food that she had stashed in the wagon.

"Well, if you want to use it, I can hunt from here onward to supplement our rations."

Nyx nodded again and began to prepare the other meat, but neither of them were prepared for Dante's voracious appetite.

By the time that they had concluded the meal, both Lauriel and Nyx stared in shock at Dante, who seemed oblivious to their gaze. He was finally calm, but they had consumed their entire supply of fresh meat that Nyx had brought, with Dante eating four of the five rabbits.

"Well, I thought we packed enough for two weeks, but the way Dante eats, we won't even have any supplies left for the town!" Nyx whispered to Lauriel in a joking-but-serious manner.

Lauriel turned to look at the blissful barbarian just as he let out a loud and prolonged belch.

"Ahh, now that's fucking better."

Lauriel began to laugh. His crudeness matched perfectly with his foul-mouth. She looked back at Nyx. "Maybe I can kill a giant moose along the way; that should buy us a day or two."

The two began to giggle and it finally caught Dante's attention.

"What?" he questioned.

Lauriel immediately diverted the conversation. "Dante, I hope you saved some room, I brought a little something to celebrate our first night together on this adventure."

With their attention captured, Lauriel retrieved a small cask from the wagon.

"Is that …?" Nyx began.

"Pond Scum Ale!" Lauriel said proudly as she removed the keystone cap and bravely took a large drink.

Nyx erupted into a fit of laughter as Lauriel's face contorted and her eyes began to water as she choked back the mouthful of foul ale. Lauriel passed the cask to Nyx, and it looked like an entire wine barrel against her small frame.

But after she took a drink and passed it onward to Dante, it suddenly looked diminished when his large hand wrapped around it like it was only an oversized pint mug. Dante took a sip, and as soon as the first drop of liquid reached his tongue, his eyes lit up just like Lauriel's had when she had tasted the elven wine.

"This is amazing ale!" he exclaimed.

He tilted the cask up and proceeded to guzzle the remaining three pints, only stopping when there was not a single drop to be had.

* * * *

They were all in high spirits and beginning to share campfire stories with each other when another caravan crested the small rise and stopped a respectful distance from them.

"Good evening to the camp," one of the voices called.

Lauriel could see a total of four men escorting two wagons of goods.

"We come from Amyrr and had hoped to make it to the junction before nightfall, but we were a bit slower than anticipated. May we share the camp?"

It was customary for merchant caravans to merge into larger camps as there was safety in numbers, but it was polite to request to join.

Seeing no reason to deny the unassuming strangers, Lauriel and Nyx invited them to join before Dante could even protest.

"Damnit, I don't trust them. It's a little late to be plodding down the road," Dante said quietly as they approached.

"Good evening, and well met. I am Amrick, and these are my three sons. Thank you for your kindness."

Lauriel could immediately tell that the men were no fighters, and that there was probably no deception in the older man's story. Each of the other three bared some semblance to him.

But Dante was not so easily convinced. He watched hawkishly as the men prepared their camp, and when they led their mules to the water, he voiced his concerns. "These men keep staring in infatuation; I think they are up to no good."

Lauriel glanced over at them and caught all three of the younger men gawking, but it was a look from human men that she was becoming accustomed to.

Dante's brows furrowed when they began to whisper to each other and laugh.

"See!" he exclaimed.

Lauriel patted him on the knee. "Relax, Dante, I will protect you."

Nyx began another fit of laughter, and Dante's face reddened.

Without any support from his companions, Dante protested their joining in his own way. When the four had returned from hitching their mules, Dante waited until they had all just sat down around the campfire before drawing his huge battle axe.

He withdrew a whetstone from his bag and began to draw it slowly across the blade, creating a menacing grinding sound as his icy stare began to destroy any of their wills to stay and socialize.

His tactic of intimidation was immediately clear to Lauriel, and she was about to protest the frightening of the innocent merchants. But something about the big brother-like gesture made her think of her own brother that had been taken from her, and she instead found herself trying to hide her smile as the other men began to fidget about and discuss the many reasons that they should leave.

The Ties That Bind

The days had been long and uneventful, and the little group made relatively good progress for four more days.

There was something about the spending of long days together in the solitary wilderness, the sharing of meals after an exhausting day, and the telling of stories around the campfire at night that caused the group to bond rapidly.

It was the kind of deep bond born from trust, teamwork, and much uninterrupted time spent together. Each of them had to depend on each other to perform their duties, particularly during the night watch, and it was during Lauriel's watch on the fifth night that she was suddenly jolted out of her wistful thoughts of home when she heard a muffled yell.

She stood up and drew her weapons, but it was no enemy that she saw. Dante appeared to be having another fitful sleep, but this time seemed worse than his others. One hand was around his throat, and the other tightly clutched his dagger. The noise was enough to wake Nyx, and just as she sat up, Dante sprung to his feet, swinging at some unknown terror.

"Dante!" Lauriel cried, but he seemed to look right through her as he continued to swing and yell.

"DANTE!" Lauriel yelled.

He blinked several times, and recognition suddenly came back to his eyes. He wiped away his sweat and stowed his dagger.

"Do you have the nightmares often?" Lauriel asked quietly.

She didn't know what demons from his past haunted his dreams, but she could certainly empathize from her own recurring nightmares of the beasts that attacked her village.

Dante sat back down and seemed hesitant to answer. "Just a bad dream. I guess since I'm up, I'll take the watch."

Lauriel sat next to him and patted him on the shoulder. "I understand; I still have them too."

He looked at her with surprise, as if he completely unexpected a Woodland Elf to understand any type of hardship or affliction.

Nyx sat down next to him and took him by the hand. "We are always here to listen if you ever feel like sharing."

The invitation seemed to be all that was needed to tip the balance of his decision to share his story with them. They had already shared many laughs together, and they would also share a heartfelt cry as Dante began to tell them his story of a drunken father and the terrible abuse that had been the cause of his burns and scars. Tears streamed down Lauriel's face at the empathetic thought of him never being able to return home, even if it was for a much different reason than hers.

Lauriel noticed that even though he had suffered many abhorrent and unspeakable things, it did not break his spirit nor did he allow it to define him. She found his mental fortitude incredibly admirable and also found encouragement through his brutal honesty, openness, and ability to talk about it. She could see that telling his story seemed to free him from the dark bonds of it. Lauriel had never told her tragic childhood story to anyone, but it created in her a desperate desire to share it with them. But the iron wall of protection that she had built around herself was strong, and she repeatedly pushed away the urge to share her own story of tragedy with them.

"Dante," Lauriel said as soon he finished, "I'm going to give you a hug."

"What? I don't do fucking hugs!" he protested.

Nyx queued in on the moment and jumped in with Lauriel, "Dante, you're getting a hug."

He continued to belligerently protest, but both of them could tell it was an act. As they both hugged him tightly for several moments, he continued onward with his objections, but made no attempt to extract himself.

The Hour of Gold

The sixth day of the journey had been another tiring and uneventful day. They made good time again and were thankful that the weather had held out and given them a nice dry path that was free of mud.

The sun was just beginning to dip behind the horizon, and the sky was turning a brilliant crimson. The dramatic sunsets that had appeared repeatedly over the past several days indicated to Lauriel that a subtle change toward autumn was near.

The long summer was drawing to a close, and the leaves would soon ignite into their full glory. The days were already not as hot as they had been just one moon ago.

Lauriel often referred to the time of the day in her elven tongue as the "Anann Malthien" (Hour of Gold) because it seemed that everything, for a fleeting moment, was bathed in a peaceful radiant glow of gold.

"Even the foul-mouthed barbarian," Lauriel muttered and chuckled to herself as she glimpsed over at Dante lumbering steadily down the trail.

Her thoughts drifted wistfully away, back to those of her home and her fond memories of evenings just like this one. Very soon, her town would be decorated and made ready for the fall festival.

Smoke from the evening cooking fires would be lazily drifting from the quaint elven cottages, and the fireflies would soon transform the forest into a sight that looked like a fairy-tale drawing. Her throat constricted as she choked back the emotion and longing memories of a place that no longer existed.

She quickly dismissed the thought as she came back to her present reality, forcing the memory from her mind as she had learned to do so many times before. As she refocused on the road, her eyes were drawn quickly to something ahead. She couldn't quite make it out but it looked like two dead horses right in the middle of the cart path.

The wagon came to an abrupt halt as she drew her bow and notched an arrow in one smooth and fluid motion. She glanced at her companions with a look of concern and could see Dante already holding his great axe with a disturbingly enthusiastic look on his face.

Her heart raced, and she knew from her training that she had to remain calm. She would surely miss her mark with a shot that was too quickened, or from a slight tweak of the bow as she let loose.

The party stood fully ready for several long moments, watching, listening, waiting. They could see no signs of life, but the fact that no buzzards nor any other birds were to be found in the area made Lauriel uneasy. She had developed a sixth sense when in nature and could tell that something was amiss, but she knew she would have to get closer to investigate.

Dante and Nyx stayed with the wagon as Lauriel moved forward to scout ahead for any signs of danger. Her footfalls were silent, and her keen eyesight scanned every detail of the scene as she slowly proceeded down the path.

As she inched closer and closer, the overwhelming stench of the bloated horse carcasses told her that they had been there for several days, and as she began to gain a better view, she could see that several black-fletched crossbow bolts protruded from the carcasses that were still rigged as if they had been pulling a cart. She had never seen arrows like them; they looked crude and plain, exactly the opposite of any kind of elven arrow design.

There was no way to get the cart around the horses. Each side of the path had an embankment that rose by ten feet in elevation to dense brush and mixtures of small trees and light forest. They would have to move the heavy carcasses out of the way in order to continue onward.

As Dante and Nyx moved the cart closer, Lauriel pointed toward the ridgeline and began to whisper a warning to the others. "This is the perfect place for an ambu—"

Just then, she heard the snap of a twig, and she wheeled toward the noise, her bow smoothly and quickly arching back as the arrow slid back fully toward the bowstave. At the very same time, she heard the twang of several crossbows. She knew the sound well;

she had trained with them. Like most of her kind though, she preferred her longbow for ranged combat. The tremendous power of the longbow could send her sharp elven arrow through all but the toughest of armor.

Several large creatures suddenly burst from their well-hidden places behind the ridgeline and rushed down the embankment while others stepped forward and began to reload their crossbows for another shot.

"Fucking orcs!" Dante bellowed.

One of the bolts whizzed right by Lauriel's head and hit the wagon behind her with a loud thud, burying itself deep into the wood. She needed no reminder of what it would have done to her skull.

She reactively fired, doing precisely what she was trying not to do. She tweaked the bow as she loosed the arrow and missed wide by several feet.

"Damnit!" she muttered at her potentially deadly mistake.

Each of the orcs were slightly shorter than Dante, but they were even wider than his hulking build. They were a dark green color and had two small tusks protruding from their bottom jaws. Each one carried some various type of large weapon and were covered by a patchwork of armor affixed with spikes and skulls.

Lauriel spotted an orc that had just finished reloading his crossbow and was beginning to raise it for another shot. Her hand had already found another arrow, notched it, and was drawing back for another volley. It would be a difficult shot, she observed. He was only about fifty feet away, but he was uphill and partially in brush. She knew that she would only be able to get off one more shot before the other orcs charging at her would finish closing the distance.

"Steady ... Exhale ... Steady ... Loose!" She instinctively fell back to her many long hours of training, and the arrow zipped through the air, this time finding its intended target. *Thwack!* The arrow impaled deeply into the orc's head. His lifeless body slumped forward and crashed down the steep hill, landing with a heavy thud as it finally skidded to a stop at the bottom.

Five orcs burst onto the path and charged straight at them while three others continued to fire from the brush-covered ridgeline. They were being fired on from elevated and covered positions, and they were outnumbered.

How did I let this happen!? This is not good ... Lauriel thought to herself.

Just then, she caught a glimpse of Dante. He crashed headlong into the three orcs that had charged him, swinging his great axe as hard as he could. The orc nearest him tried to parry the vicious swing, but as strong as the orc was, it was to no avail. The monstrous axe came down with terrifying force, traveling right through the orc's parry, through his crude armor, and down into its shoulder, nearly amputating its right arm.

Dante allowed his momentum to carry him directly into the next orc and struck it squarely in the forehead with the steel-wrapped pommel. The strike temporarily stunned the orc and caused its knees to buckle, effectively removing him as an immediate threat.

The third orc managed to land a vicious blow to Dante's right side, slicing deeply across his lower ribcage with its crude longsword. The large gash partially exposed several rib bones, and a copious amount of blood immediately began to gush from the wound. Dante seemed to hardly notice any pain. Instead, the strike had the opposite effect on him. He glimpsed down at the wound and then back up at the orc that had caused it and began to laugh maniacally. The orc's eyes grew wide, and it began to back away from the melee.

I'm glad he is on my side! Lauriel thought.

The moment of pause was not good to her. A crossbow bolt hit her in the leg, only stopping as it hit bone. It felt like a red-hot iron spike had been pressed into her leg, and the force of it threw her slightly off balance.

She winced and let out a muffled yell at the sudden searing pain but had no time to let it slow her down as the other two orcs were nearing her.

She moved to the left of the path to engage the two orcs that were coming from that side, while Dante and Nyx moved farther to the right to engage the three orcs in that direction. Their movements and lack of communication unintentionally placed them dangerously far away from each other's help. They had never fought together and did not yet work well or communicate as a team.

She dropped the bow and in one fluid motion drew both scimitars. She was able to regain her balance just as the orcs engaged her, and she savagely attacked the closest one in a preemptive strike just as he began to raise his weapon. Her weapons were much lighter and faster and she used it to her advantage. She knew that she needed to end the battle quickly because there was no other help nearby with Nyx and Dante engaged with the other orcs.

The scimitars ripped through the air and toward their opponents with impressive speed. Both blades found their mark and cut deeply into the first orc, dropping him right where he stood before he even had a chance to complete his swing.

Lauriel had never fought orcs, but felt a brief sense of relief when she easily bypassed his defense and sliced through her first opponent. The remaining orc swung wildly at her, and she nimbly dodged his attack and quickly counter attacked. One scimitar strike was stopped by his crude armor but her second found its mark, opening a large wound diagonally across its broad chest.

The orc reeled from pain and shock at the surprisingly vicious, little, elven female. He was left with no choice other than attack or face two scimitars to his back. He lunged forward and swung his sword at her in a wide arc but was quickly disarmed by a well-practiced maneuver that sliced into his hand. The second blade fell quickly thereafter and nearly decapitated him.

Lauriel was just as surprised as the orc was; she had trained hard to learn how to fight but never knew if it would actually work in a real battle.

Nyx had assumed a defensive position on top of the wagon where she remained unharassed by the orcs; she did not have the armor or skill to engage in combat. The disengagement worked to help keep her out of immediate danger as Lauriel and Dante had quickly drawn all of their attention. Lauriel saw that she had evoked some sort of divine magical energy that enveloped the last orc as it turned to run away from the barbarian. A combination of her spell and his axe brought a swift end. Seeing the quick decimation of their numbers, the rest of the orcs began to flee.

With bloodlust still boiling within her, Lauriel picked up her longbow and began to run to the top of the hill in pursuit.

The pain in her leg was intense, but she pressed on, determined to exact a heavy toll on the attackers that had ambushed them and the many other innocent supply convoys.

She didn't want to get too far away from her group so she stopped at the top of the ridge and, even though the cover made it nearly impossible to hit them, she began to fire several rapid volleys at the orcs as they withdrew through the scattered trees and thick underbrush.

From her vantage point, Lauriel could see that the orcs would break into a large clearing on the hillside if they continued in the same direction. She estimated that it was a just over five hundred feet to the clearing, almost the maximum distance that she could send an arrow, and a near impossible shot at that range. As Lauriel was transfixed on the fleeing enemies, Dante and Nyx joined her.

They could see the orcs making their way through the rough terrain as they continued up the sloping hill in the direction of the clearing, just as she had hoped. As the first orc crashed into the distant clearing, Lauriel raised her bow at a high angle and pulled the bowstring back as far as it would go.

"What the fuck are you doing? Those orcs are long gone," Dante scoffed.

He was just beginning to feel the pain from the wound on his side, and his increasingly foul mood began to reflect it.

Lauriel smirked as she quickly settled the bow into position. She aimed for a point forty feet above the lead orc's head and twenty feet in front of him, trying to adjust for the distance and flight time while he moved forward. She had learned how to lead moving prey while hunting them but had never attempted any shot as far as this one. *Twang!* The bow let loose with impressive force.

The arrow zipped through the air, continuing upward to its apogee and then began to curve back down. Her calculation was perfect, and the orc stumbled forward as the arrow impaled its shoulder blade.

It did not kill him, but he would remember the painful sting of the small elf.

"Woah!" exclaimed Nyx.

Lauriel tried to hide her look of surprise, knowing that it took more luck than it did skill to make the shot. She could try the same shot ten more times and not hit the target once—but she hit the one that counted.

"Some fucking luck," mumbled Dante. He wasn't about to let her know that it was an impressive shot.

Lauriel had not noticed until now, and it seemed that Dante had not either, but both of them had crossbow bolts sticking out of their legs. The two hobbled back down the hill and sat on the wagon so that Nyx could inspect the wounds.

Nyx walked over to Lauriel and took a close look at the deeply embedded bolt.

"Let's see here," Nyx mumbled quietly.

Before Lauriel knew what she was up to, Nyx yanked the bolt out of her leg and quickly placed her hand over the bleeding hole that remained.

She almost passed out from the sudden excruciating pain, but a bright blue glow encircled Nyx's hand and Lauriel could feel a wave of relief wash over her. Her leg suddenly felt a warm sensation, and the pain immediately subsided.

When Nyx removed her hand, the wound was completely healed.

"What? How did you do that? It feels like it was never even there!" Lauriel closely inspected the place where the wound had been and to her amazement, not even the slightest hint of a scar remained. "Thank you, Nyx!" she exclaimed.

Nyx nodded, and her face beamed with pride.

"I know that I can't fight off enemies like each of you, but I can do my best to contribute to our well-being!"

She then walked over to Dante and began to tend to his many wounds.

His rage had begun to subside and as it did, the intensity of the pain grew to the point of terrible agony. She was able to remove the bolts from his leg and provide the same healing and sense of relief to him that she had Lauriel, but the puncture wounds were only a pin prick compared to the more significant open gash along his ribs. Lauriel came over to assist Nyx with the gruesome injury, doing exactly as she was told. The wound had opened wide during the fight and it would take all of Nyx's remaining healing ability help. But even then, she knew it would not be enough to fully heal the wound. The divine healing available to her was limited, and she had to rest, pray, and meditate to her goddess every morning in order to renew her abilities.

By the time Nyx had finished, Dante was in no more pain and even though his wound had not completely healed, he was in much better spirits. They could tell because his string of expletives had subsided to only the occasional colorful use of profanity.

Each of them needed time to rest and recover, but they decided that the time for celebrating their success would have to wait. They wanted to press on and get out of the dangerous area just in case the orcs returned with reinforcements.

* * * *

By the time they'd disconnected the wagon from the oxen and used them to pull the dead horses to the side of the path, the silver crescent moon had just begun to peek over the ridgeline.

After a short time of making slow but steady progress through the darkness, the companions decided that it would be safest to try to make it all the way to Conna. They feared that an attempt at camping anywhere short of the outpost would not be safe.

The journey became a long and exhausting slog, pushing them to their limits of endurance and patience. Nyx and Dante could see very little.

The fingernail sliver of moonlight was not enough to illuminate their path and they had to rely on Lauriel's elven Darkvision to identify hazards along the way. The oxen frequently protested their lack of sight and extra hard labor, only moving forward with Lauriel directly leading them by the reins.

The crescent moon had passed from one side of the sky to the other and the first rays of the morning sun were only a few hours away when they finally made it to the sleeping town. The modest inn was a welcome sight, and the thought of a warm safe place to stay quickened their weary steps. Lauriel knocked on the locked door several times and after many long moments, the heavy bolt slid from the latch and a sleepy-eyed innkeeper appeared in the darkened doorway.

Guests often arrived at late hours but it was rare for any to arrive in the early hours before dawn. He was visibly relieved to see that the supplies had made it to the small town and eagerly assisted them with safely stowing the shipment and stabling the oxen. He showed each of them to their quaint rooms, thanking them along the way for the successful delivery.

Lauriel took off her dusty traveling boots and sat down on the comfortable bed. She was exhausted and wanted nothing more than to bathe and rest; but she had to take a moment to revel in the great sense of accomplishment she felt from the successful completion of her job.

She quickly began to realize that it wasn't just the completion of a goal that she was so happy about, it was something much deeper than that. After several minutes of sitting in the stillness of the darkened room, quietly contemplating her thoughts, she came to a profound realization.

She had been part of something meaningful that had brought true relief and benefit to others, and with that very act, she felt something she'd never felt before—a true sense of purpose.

CHAPTER SEVEN

Dark Raiders

auriel was the first of her group to come downstairs for breakfast. She felt refreshed from the brief rest, but the soreness and aching muscles from the grueling push still lingered. The smell of frying eggs and potatoes filled the air and beckoned enticingly to her suddenly ravenous hunger. She chuckled at the thought of just how much food Dante would eat.

A warm and inviting fire crackled in the fireplace that was situated along the far wall in the common room, but it was the strange sight across from it that caught her attention. A High Elf sat on the edge of the comfortable couch and appeared to be intently studying the many maps, scrolls, and notebooks that were strewn about the coffee table in front of him.

Hmph, that's weird, what is a High Elf doing out here? she thought to herself as she began to pass through the room that led to the small breakfast area. It was extremely rare that a High Elf ventured so far from their realm, especially into a place so remote. She did not particularly care for High Elves because they always seemed to have a cold and aloof air about themselves toward their "uncivilized" Woodland Elf cousins.

The one at the couch had handsome features that were customary for many of his race, but he had strikingly unique lavender eyes.

His long, pure white hair suggested that he was wizened by many seasons, but his younger face indicated that he was about the same age as she.

He wore an ornate red robe as an outer garment that looked different from any other elven outfit that she had seen.

A short, round, red-haired waitress appeared from the kitchen doorway carrying several plates. She looked Lauriel up and down with the same disapproving glance that she had now come to expect as normal behavior from human females.

"Sit anywhere, what would you like?" the waitress said tersely.

The small breakfast area was only big enough for a few tables, and two rugged-looking men sat at one of them engaged in lively conversation.

"I'll take whatever you are making; it smells great," Lauriel replied, countering the waitress's seemingly judgmental attitude with kindness.

She took a seat at the larger table, assuming that the rest of her companions would eventually make their way down. While she waited for breakfast, her inquisitive nature couldn't help but try to figure out what the High Elf was doing. He looked to be concentrating deeply on the materials in front of him and seemed oblivious to the rest of the world.

Just after the waitress brought her food, Lauriel's attention was suddenly drawn away from the peculiar High Elf and to the two men sitting at the other table. She thought she had overheard one of them mention a small outpost nearby that had recently been attacked. She sat in silence and tried to listen in on the conversation, picking at her food to avoid the appearance of her eavesdropping. The man telling the story spoke in a hushed tone which piqued her interest even more, and as she focused all of her attention on what he was saying, her keen elven hearing was able to pick up his description of the attack.

"Dark Raiders they were, ripped them all to shreds."

She nearly choked on her food.

"No," said the other.

"I swear to yeh, that's what I heard, not even a fortnight ago."

Lauriel suddenly couldn't taste the food, a sudden vision of her peeking through the vines at the four-armed beast flashing through her mind.

She grabbed the table with both hands and took a deep breath to try to calm herself down. She remembered Adamar's council about a possible resurgence, but he had known exactly how to tell her. Hearing a story about a recent raid on a village by some sort of dark raiders ripping people to shreds brought vivid flashbacks to her mind.

"They had some kind of terrible dogs with bulging yellow eyes," the man continued in a barely audible whisper.

Lauriel began to shake as the flashbacks continued, this time seizing a firm hold of her. She saw the dog-like creature near the vineyard coming toward her, frost curling from its maw as the village burned behind it. It picked up her scent and began to run at her, and she quickly stood up to get away. She crashed into the table that the men were sitting at, knocking it over and spilling the contents all over the floor with a loud crash.

"Are ye okay, misses? Are ye okay?" One of the men reached out and tried to stabilize her. *Zing! Zing!* The man suddenly had two scimitars at his throat.

When he had reached for her, she saw it in her mind as one of the four-armed beasts reaching out to rip her apart. Luckily, at the very last second before decapitating him, she came back to reality. She dropped the scimitars in shock.

"I'm sorry! I'm so sorry!" she gasped.

The two men shrank back from her in a near panic, tripping over food and dishes as they tried desperately to distance themselves from the suddenly psychotic elf.

Hearing all of the dishes crashing, tables falling, and metal clanging on the floor, the waitress came running back out of the kitchen. "What the hell is going on here!?"

Lauriel tried to pull herself together and locked eyes with one of the men. "Tell me everything. What Dark Raiders?" she demanded.

The men continued to stumble backward toward the door, still in shock.

"Please!" Lauriel pleaded. "What are these Dark Raiders that you speak of?"

The man that had not been on the receiving end of the scimitars tried to answer. "I … I dunno, misses, it's just something that I heard. I … I haven't been there myself. It's not something that I made up, honest! They said some kind of beasts with four arms attacked them in the night. Huge, like giant men with red eyes. I swear to yeh, that's all I know!"

"They do not yet have names … for they are not from here," came a calm, matter-of-fact voice from behind her. She spun around to see the High Elf in red robes still sitting at the table, sipping his coffee as if nothing of interest had happened. She locked her piercing stare on him, hoping to immediately force the information from him. The tactic tended to work well for her but it did not seem to faze him.

While she was focused on the robed man, the other two used the opportunity to escape and ran out the door.

The waitress began to yell at Lauriel, "Those were good customers! You are going to pay for all of this mess AND clean it up!"

The High Elf remained sitting on the couch, unintimidated by her stare and smirking at the waitress's demands.

"Don't worry, Margaret, I'll take care of the bill," he said coolly.

He reached slowly over to a leather-bound notebook that was sitting on the table and began to flip through the pages.

"And please pardon my friend's clumsiness; it was an accident," he added.

The waitress stormed back into the kitchen, muttering something under her breath.

"Clumsy!" Lauriel scoffed, clearly offended. "I'll have you know—"

"This," the High Elf interrupted her, his hand pointed to a drawing in the notebook.

Lauriel followed his gaze to the page. It was a detailed drawing of the four-armed beast that might as well have been ripped straight from her mind.

The flood of memories began to reemerge, and Lauriel fought desperately to calm herself. She turned around and casually picked up her scimitars, sheathing them slowly and using the time to force the dark memory to the back of her mind.

"And how do you know of these?" she asked in as calm a voice as she could muster.

"I should ask you the same," he retorted.

He had a quiet confidence about him and seemed wise well beyond his years. His demeanor both frustrated Lauriel and helped to calm her at the same time. Her predisposed judgement of the High Elf seemed to be unfounded; he was neither cold nor snobbish.

His attention was drawn away from her piercing stare. "Those blades of yours, those are no ordinary blades."

Lauriel was unable to hide the shock on her face. "They were my … grandfather's," she stammered. "What of the vile creatures!?" she said sharply, trying to refocus the conversation and get the strange High Elf's attention off of her jealously guarded weapons.

He completely ignored her questioning. "May I see them?" He motioned for her to place them on the table.

It was not a response that she was expecting, nor was she used to being completely disregarded.

She normally wouldn't dream of letting anyone near her scimitars, especially to inspect them; but she felt oddly compelled to show them to the infuriating High Elf. She drew both of them from their sheaths and carefully laid them on the table in front of him.

He held his hand above them and mumbled several strange words that she could not understand, and both blades began to glow brightly.

Lauriel gasped. "What are you doing?"

She had seen some of the divine healing magic that Nyx could use, but the use of arcane magic was different, and exceedingly rare as well. She had heard of users of arcane magic but had never met one, nor seen its use up close.

"You're a Magic User!" she exclaimed.

"A wizard," he replied flatly with somewhat of an offensive tone, still intently focused on the blades. "Remarkable," he muttered.

"What!?"

"Do you not know what you carry?" He picked one of them up and carefully handed the blade back to her. "Very interesting indeed; it has very powerful magic that I cannot identify. And this one …" He held up the second. "May we never be enemies," he said with a smirk as he handed it back to her.

"What? You don't make any sense! What can you tell me about my blades?" Lauriel exclaimed, clearly frustrated. "And DAMNIT! TELL ME ABOUT THE VILE CREATURES!"

Nyx and Dante came down the stairs and walked into the common room just as Lauriel began her outburst. They had been awakened by the ruckus. By now, Nyx and Dante had learned that Lauriel could be pretty intense and impatient when she was focused on something. Dante would never show it, but he actually liked those qualities in her. When he got frustrated like that, someone usually had to be carried away unconscious.

"Shut the fuck up and let us enjoy breakfast in peace. It's barely dawn and you're already carrying on," Dante snapped at her.

He peered into the breakfast area. "And I suppose that's your disaster."

Lauriel was not used to being spoken to in such a manner but she secretly appreciated his bluntness. Only Dante could get away with calling her out "on her bullshit," as he called it. With Dante, you never had to guess how he felt about you or anything else.

Dante looked at the man in red robes balefully. "And who the fuck are you?" he snapped.

Nyx rolled her eyes and immediately interjected, "I'm sorry, sir, you'll have to forgive him. He gets cranky in the morning before breakfast, and he has only had a few hours' sleep."

The wizard smiled at Nyx. "No issue, my lady, I had hoped for nothing less. I am Eldrin Aeramiril, and I'm in need of a skilled group like yours."

Nyx looked at him with surprise. "How do you know that we are skilled?"

Taking another long and seemingly purposefully slow sip of coffee, Eldrin replied, "You." He pointed at Nyx. "Nyx Nymgul of Huatak, have the very rare gift of true clerical healing. You," he pointed at Dante, "Dante of … well, Dante from the Northern Umberlands, a barbarian with a notorious temper and skilled with great weapons. "And you," he pointed at Lauriel, "Lauriel Valendril, *Andúlarium*, and apparently keeper of two spectacular blades."

"How the fuck do you know that?" Dante said, stepping toward Eldrin menacingly.

The wizard did not appear the slightest bit intimidated by the hulking barbarian. He continued, "I cast a powerful scrying spell into this ancient crystal ball." A small, clear crystal ball the size of a large marble suddenly appeared in Eldrin's hand. "The Orb of Ful-Ashi-Tycus, forged by the Gods of magic themselves, and it was your faces, this place, and this very moment that was made apparent to me."

Nyx immediately began to laugh, but Dante stared at him with his mouth wide open. Lauriel was too flustered by him to pay any more attention.

"Well fuck," Dante exclaimed. "I guess in that case …"

Eldrin burst into laughter. "That, or my friend that hired you told me that I might find you here, although I didn't expect you here until later on today."

"We were ambushed and decided to push through the night," Nyx explained.

"Ahh yes, it is a dangerous route these days, that makes sense," replied Eldrin. "I am looking for a skilled group to help me with a very important task. My friend spoke very highly of your skills that were made evident during the Citadel Tournaments.

He suggested that you might be up to the challenge." Eldrin made no attempt to elaborate and instead began to pack his things into his backpack.

Dante quickly took the bait. "How much does it pay?"

Nyx elbowed him. "What is the task?"

Eldrin replied, "I have a very important errand that I need to run, and I am expecting one more this evening. If you can stay around until then, I will make everything clear, but it does involve the 'vial creatures,'" he admitted. As he finished his last word, he looked directly at Lauriel.

Lauriel's eyes opened wide as the term refocused her attention. She started to speak, but Eldrin immediately interrupted her.

"Until then," he looked back at Dante, "try to stay out of trouble." Eldrin tossed him the marble and picked up his backpack and an ornately carved staff. He then turned and walked over to the counter to pay for all of the meals.

The waitress was still clearly upset until he placed a small stack of silver coins on the counter.

"For the troubles and my clumsy friend," he said and walked out without another word. Lauriel's face grew red, and the waitress's eyes opened wide. The silver was more than enough to pay for the meals, any damages, and many weeks' worth of tips.

It wasn't until Nyx explained the wizard's joke to Dante that he finally understood. "The orb of Ful-Ashi-Tycus," Nyx repeated and then said the words much slower, sounding them out for him "The orb of full—a—-shit—icus."

"Aww hell!" he exclaimed, turning red in both anger and embarrassment. He threw the marble to the ground and it shattered into many pieces, and Nyx burst into a fit of laughter.

Lauriel sat at the table but neither laughed nor spoke. She was in her own world. She kept thinking about the beasts that Eldrin had shown her and how they had reemerged and attacked another town. She thought about the counsel that Adamar had given her. She was beginning to understand the reality. That these creatures really were reemerging and killing innocent people.

Part of her wanted to run to that town immediately, and the other part of her wanted to get as far away from it as possible.

Her mind continued to race, recounting every word from the confusing and exasperating High Elf wizard; *They do not yet have* names, for they are not from here," "it has very powerful magic," "May we never be enemies." After several minutes, Lauriel finally spoke, interrupting Nyx and Dante's conversation. "We need to help with this task."

Nyx and Dante immediately stopped talking, detecting the somber seriousness in her tone. Both could tell that she was struggling to get out her next words. Her eyes were red, and she began to speak quietly.

"There is something that I have to tell you. Something that I have never told anyone before. I couldn't even bring myself to tell you around the campfire, but it is something that you must know if we are going to continue on this path together. When I was a young child …" she began.

Lauriel quietly told them the story about her traumatic past, sparing no detail. The words flew out of her like a dam breaking from the onslaught of a flooded river. When she finished about an hour later, Nyx sat quietly with tears in her eyes and her hand holding tightly onto Lauriel's.

She didn't have to say anything, she just listened, which was precisely what Lauriel needed. Dante … almost gave Lauriel a hug. He fought desperately to hold back his tears and maintain his iron-tough facade.

Secretly, he made a silent oath to destroy as many of the creatures as possible to help one of his only friends exact revenge upon them. He patted Lauriel on the shoulder in understanding.

For Lauriel, finally sharing her story felt incredibly liberating. The little group that she had only known for just over a week had quickly and unexpectedly become like family. They would help her carry this burden that was no longer a dark and unspeakable secret. And as they sat huddled around the small breakfast table, they knew they were ready for another adventure, a real adventure.

CHAPTER EIGHT

Ruffians

It was early in the afternoon when Dante and Nyx made their way over to the general store to collect payment for the shipment they had just delivered. Lauriel had decided to enjoy a relaxing respite by the nearby fountain that had been built in the open town square. As she sat in the warmth of the sunlight and listened to the peaceful trickle of the running water, she saw a group of twelve armed men emerge from a large but dilapidated-looking keep that rested at the top of the hill overlooking the town.

They meandered down the short, dusty road that led straight into the town square, and the people that had been milling about the streets moments earlier seemed to disappear. Doors, windows, and businesses all closed, and the area quickly became a ghost town.

The men were all wearing black sashes around their waists and were obviously some kind of gang. Lauriel was confident but not stupid. She knew that no good could come out of the situation so she stood from the fountain and began to casually make her way across the square toward the general store that Nyx and Dante were in. She had only made it about halfway when she caught their attention.

"You there!" the man in the lead shouted.

"Uh oh," she muttered.

"Wow! Look at you, damn!" he continued, drawing raucous laughter from the other men around him.

Lauriel continued toward the store, acting like she had not heard them.

The group entered the other side of the square, and the man yelled out even louder, making it impossible for her to pretend not to hear.

"I said, you there! Where have you been all my life? I haven't seen you here before!"

Lauriel looked over at him and tried to speak loudly enough to get Dante's or Nyx's attention. "Just passing through; I'm not looking for any trouble."

"C'mon over here and sit on my lap, I mean have a little chat," the leader said, drawing even more obnoxious laughter from the men.

"I'm just kiddin with ya; but seriously, come over here," he demanded.

Lauriel had no choice but to comply. She didn't want to endanger people in the store by making a run for it so she turned toward the group and began to walk over to them. She immediately regretted her decision as each of them gawked lecherously at her as she approached. She began to hear their offensive mutterings as she got closer, "I bet that tight, little elven body of hers is tight everywhere." The group began to laugh again and the lewd sexual comments about every part of her body continued until she made it all the way to them.

The leader of the group waited until she walked up before he began to speak again. "Now obviously, you don't know the rules around here, so we'll give you a pass this time." He paused and looked her up and down, undressing her with his eyes and making no attempt at subtlety. "Well … on second thought, maybe just a good spankin," he added with an obnoxious wink. The unkempt group of men with him laughed and encircled her, drawing even closer.

The smell of their body odor coupled with stale alcohol was repulsive. She knew she was in a very bad situation; she could see it in their lust filled eyes that there was no way they were going to let her go.

She tried to take a step back but as soon as she did, one of the men behind her slapped her hard on the behind. *Smack!* She let out a startled gasp and tensed from the sudden sting.

"Damn, now that's a firm little ass," the man said.

Her blood boiled as she spun around to face him. As soon as she did, she was struck again on the behind by the man that was the leader. She was scared like a lone rabbit surrounded by a pack of wolves, but she was also cunning and calculating.

They are all a little bit drunk, not off balanced, but maybe a little slower to react. The leader is right-handed, and the other guy behind me is left, she observed.

Lauriel kept a calm outward demeanor and slowly turned back around to face the leader. Her mind raced as she desperately tried to come up with a strategy.

"No weapons in town, that's the rule. I'll take those," said the leader as he pointed to her scimitars. "Unless, of course, you want to show me where the rest of that tattoo of yours goes—we might be able to make an exception." He reached out and placed his finger on one of the tattooed vines on her lower abdomen and began to trace it downward to where it disappeared below the top of her pants.

She was emboldened by his demand. No matter how bad the situation was, she wasn't about to give them her scimitars. Without breaking eye contact, she slapped his hand away.

"Under whose orders? We came in yesterday and no one said anything about it."

The leader seemed genuinely shocked that she had the nerve to push back. The other men chuckled at him getting his hand slapped, and his face began to redden and contort with a look of fury. He swung his hand at her in an attempt to backhand slap her hard across the face, but her quick reflexes caused him to miss, which enraged him even more. "We run this town, little elf bitch; now I ain't gonna ask you again. Hand em over, each of em."

The same man behind her slapped her again on her behind, this time even harder and in the same spot as before. *SMACK!* "You herd em," he grunted.

The sting drew tears to her eyes and she fought hard not to make any noise in acknowledgement of the pain; she wasn't about to give him that satisfaction.

Lauriel felt oddly calm and clear headed. She knew she had two choices; give up her weapons and get raped, or fight and die. For her, the choice was clear.

She let out a defeated sigh and slowly reached down to remove her weapons. As she did, she intentionally but subtly pushed down on her sword belt which caused the top of her pants to move slightly lower, revealing a tantalizing fraction more of her tattoo. The move worked as planned; all of their attention was drawn away from her hands and scimitars. *Zing! Zing!* Both blades were out in a flash, causing the men to quickly take a step back. She pointed the razor-sharp end of each scimitar in opposite directions, one at the throat of the leader and the other at the man that had been striking her.

"Now ..." she said, locking her eyes back on the leader with a sudden intensity that startled him just as much as the blades. "You may get me in a rush, but I guarantee that I'm going to kill at least four of you. Who's it going to be?" She quickly spun around and looked at each of them, trying to keep moving in a circular motion to avoid getting grappled from behind.

The men paused for a split second, somewhat rattled by her cold confidence and matter-of-factness.

"Come get some steel!" bellowed a voice as Dante came crashing out of the supply store, breaking the door completely off of its hinges. The huge behemoth charged at them with his giant axe, his reddened face contorted in rage.

The sight of him caused the men to take their attention off of Lauriel and almost break ranks. They began to draw their weapons and it was exactly the additional distraction that Lauriel needed.

She immediately sprang to the offensive. She had learned from Adamar that in certain situations against many more opponents, violence of action could be used to devastating effect.

She swung the blade at the leader, and it quickly found its mark exactly where she intended. She meant to make an example of him and hopefully scare off the others. The words of Eldrin echoed in her mind as she struck him with the blade that he had handed back to her and said, "May we never be enemies."

The blade made a dreadful slicing noise, the likes of which she had not heard before as it ripped violently through the air and hit the leader precisely in the center of his exposed neck. It was not the ringing of the blade, but a different sound that was sinister and threatening. She could have sworn that she saw the blade turn a pitch-black color and red runes appeared to pulse with a faint glow right as it connected with her target. But she felt no resistance, no slowdown of the blade. It was the same feeling as if she had completely missed and sliced into nothing but thin air!

She unintentionally paused for a brief second, somewhat confused, but so did most of the others that had observed it. The leader was still standing in front of her with the same annoying smirk on his face.

Oh God, did I miss?

He blinked at her and tried to say something—and that is when his head rolled off his body. Blood spurted high into the air and the rest of his body fell backward and crashed to the ground.

His head fell directly at her feet, its eyes still open in a wide-eyed look of shock. The eyes appeared to blink once before they quickly drew to a close.

It was the first humanoid life that she had taken, and it had been far too easy. Her training and prior experience had not prepared her to understand the fragility of life against her determination to take it. And even though she was now fighting for her own, the feeling of being the one to snuff out another's was wretched. There was no sense of accomplishment or pride in her ability; she instead found it to be the exact opposite.

She immediately felt a sickening feeling in the pit of her stomach that made her want to vomit, and she second-guessed whether she had escalated too quickly. But she had no choice but to continue to press her attack as the others frantically sprang into action.

Her blade found the second target but the attack did not have quite as devastating of an effect. She used it as more of a repositioning attack, trying to avoid being flanked on all sides.

The men were shaken by the sight of her quick and deadly strikes but gained boldness from the pack-like mentality.

Lauriel's *Andúlari* fighting style was not some dainty ballerina dance. Every move had deadly purpose; to kill as quickly as possible while providing an impenetrable blade defense that was better than any armor. She dodged and parried, ducked and disarmed, just as she had been trained. She did well, but there were just too many opponents. One of their blades found its mark, and she felt searing pain race down her back as it sliced into her. It was quickly followed by another strike from a different direction that sliced deeply into her leg.

Dante crashed headlong into the foray, and several of the men's swords found their mark against him as well, but they seemed to have no effect on him. He grabbed one of them by the throat with one bare hand and crushed the life out of him while using him as a shield for another strike.

At the same time, one of the ruffian blades sliced across his back.

Dante dropped the limp body of his first victim and let out a sadistic laugh as he turned to face the man that had just attacked him. He brought his mighty axe right through the man's feeble attempt to parry and buried it deeply into his flank. Dante's second victim crumbled to the ground in a torrent of blood.

Still badly outnumbered and flanked on all sides, Lauriel and Dante slowly started to succumb to the numbered onslaught.

They were much better fighters but there were just too many opponents. The ground was becoming red and slippery with the spilled blood from both sides of the vicious foray; but Lauriel and Dante desperately fought on.

Lauriel knew that Nyx was close; she could feel wave after wave of the warm healing energy wash over her, each time renewing her vigor. She had just dropped her third victim when her heart sank.

"I can't heal anymore!" Nyx shouted.

They had together dropped six enemies, but they were still in a dire situation. *I'm going to die right here in this stupid little town*, Lauriel thought to herself as she fought to remain conscious. She knew that Dante, as crazed as he was, was also weakening from his significant injuries.

"Astak-ath-nurack," she could hear a strong, vaguely familiar voice carrying clearly on the wind. "Melath-nui-dragath!"

A small, orange ball streaked by her left shoulder and hovered momentarily in the center of the melee. The ball suddenly fractured as it detonated with a blinding flash. Lauriel immediately felt the violent concussion from the powerful blast wave that slammed into her. The force of it was so strong that it almost knocked her off her feet.

It was immediately followed by a rapidly expanding red-orange ball of searing flame that washed over all of them and continued expanding outward like a ripple in a glassy still pond.

To her amazement, the very spot that she was standing seemed to be protected from the heat and flames. She could see brief glimpses of her enemies through the translucent red and orange wall and unlike her, they were fully engulfed in the ball of fiery death.

Four of them were swatting at the air and grabbing their faces as they began to melt away while the other two writhed on the ground. Then, as suddenly as the conflagration had begun, all was quiet.

Eldrin stood not far from the courtyard, his staff clutched tightly in hand. Small bits of grass were still on fire, and the sandy ground around them had been melted into small, glassy clumps. The ruffians' remains were blackened and shriveled, some of them in a fetal position and some with their mouths still open in silent screams.

Remnants of their clothes still burned, and the stench of death and burnt flesh hung heavily upon the air.

The grotesque scene of carnage was a terrible sight to behold, but not a single finger of fire had burned Dante or Lauriel.

Dante passed out right where he stood, crashing heavily onto the blackened ground. His huge axe made a loud thud as it hit the ground beside him. Lauriel looked back at Eldrin, remembering his one and only request: "Try to stay out of trouble." She tried to go to Dante, but her legs were suddenly too weak to keep her standing and she slumped down onto the ground. Her arms and legs were covered in blood and she could not tell the extent of her injuries.

She could see the people coming back out of their shops, clapping their hands and cheering, but she could not hear any of it over the ringing in her ears from the concussive boom of the spell. The ground was still hot to the touch, but she didn't care. The world started to spin, and everything went dark.

*   *   *   *

Lauriel reached down to her side and did not feel her scimitars or scabbards. She bolted upright, and pain immediately wracked her body.

The room was spinning and she felt like someone had just hit her in the head with a bottle. She was disoriented and nothing at all looked familiar, except for Nyx. Nyx was standing beside her bed, trying to calm her down.

"Where are they?" Lauriel shouted.

"You are safe now, we won!" Nyx exclaimed.

"No! My scimitars! Where are they?" Lauriel shouted in a near panic.

"Ahh, Eldrin placed them in that chest over there in the corner. He put some kind of spell on it and said that no one could get into it," Nyx replied as she turned and pointed to it.

Lauriel stood up unsteadily and tried to make her way to the chest but quickly realized that she was still too dizzy to let go of the bed.

"Where is he?" she exclaimed.

"He said he would be back soon." Nyx paused and then began to laugh. "He also said that if you woke up worried about your scimitars to tell you that if he 'wanted to steal your scimitars, he would be long gone by now, so relax.'"

Lauriel's face reddened, and Nyx took her by the hand. "Rest, Lauriel. I have stabilized you to the best of my ability, but recovery takes some time."

Lauriel was slowly starting to come out of her fog, and the dizziness and disorientation was beginning to subside.

She looked around to find herself in a nondescript room with two beds and three chairs. Dante was sitting up in the other bed looking at her like she had lost her mind.

"I'm fucking alright, thanks for your concern," he said as soon as they made eye contact.

Lauriel suddenly felt ashamed. He had waded into battle without hesitation and faced almost certain death to help her.

"I … I'm sorry, Dante, I knew that you were okay. Thanks for—"

He interrupted, "Ahh fuck off, I couldn't let you go and get yourself killed."

The emotions of the incident quickly caught back up to her as her mind finally became clear.

Lauriel hugged Nyx in a long and meaningful embrace. "Thanks … truly …" She was unable to say anything else, but she didn't need to; Nyx understood.

When she was able to speak again, she continued, "Both of you are true friends, the likes of which I have never had."

Her words were sincere. She had never known such loyalty and friendship outside of her family. She walked over to Dante and gave him the biggest bear hug that she could. He protested the entire time but made no effort to stop her. Finally, he laughed at the feeble attempt and then hugged her back, squeezing any remaining words and breath out of her.

"I'm glad you're fast because you're sure as hell not strong," he said with a jest. "And give me a little warning next time you decide to fight twelve armed guys at once. What were you thinking?" he scolded her with brotherly affection.

The door opened, and Eldrin walked into the room. He looked at Lauriel and smiled. "Ahh, about time you joined us. We are running way behind!"

"Behind what?" Lauriel questioned.

He continued, again without answering her, "How are you feeling?"

She ignored him this time and continued, "Behind what!?"

He walked over to the chest and said a word of magic that caused it to open. He drew forth the blades and brought them to her. "There now, at least some of your questions have been answered." He smiled and turned to walk out.

Lauriel felt a wave of relief now that she had been reunited with her scimitars.

"Thanks!" Lauriel began awkwardly.

Eldrin paused with his back was still toward her.

She continued, "Thanks for saving us with your sorcerer magic."

He shook his head in disagreement and looked back at her. "I'm a WIZARD," he replied with a sharp correction, "and you're welcome; see you tonight."

As soon as Eldrin walked out, Nyx began to speak excitedly. "Oh yeah! About tonight—the town mayor has been by several times. He says that he wants to honor us this evening with a huge party and a symbolic 'town key!' Apparently, those ruffians showed up a few months ago and have been extorting the town, collecting 'protection taxes' and roughing up many of the citizens."

"Honor us!" Dante bellowed with laughter. "I'm starting to really like this town; these are my kind of people!" He pointed at Lauriel. "Hell, you've been here one day and have scared the shit out of two townspeople, destroyed a small café, caused the courtyard to nearly be burnt down, twelve people are dead, and they want to honor us! You really know how to make a fucking entrance, Lauriel!"

CHAPTER NINE

Nightfang and Isilmwé

The pub was packed so full that the crowd spilled out the front door and into the middle of the street. The ale flowed freely, and the mood was festive and cheerful. It seemed like the entire sleepy, little town had shown up for the celebration. The townspeople had all come out to show their gratitude for being rid of the miscreants and to celebrate the much-needed resupply.

The mayor, somewhat inebriated and in high spirits, had found a broomstick and had broken it in half to use as a prop for his theatrical reenactment. He climbed up on the table for the third time and pointed his "scimitars" at the crowd. "You may get me in a rush, but I guarantee that I'm going to kill at least four of you." Having seen the act previously, the crowd raised their mugs of ale in a toast and joined in cheerfully for the last line: "WHO'S IT GOING TO BE?" The crowd roared with laughter and applause, and Lauriel shook her head in embarrassment.

Just then, another one of the townspeople stood up on a table in the far corner of the room and raised a shovel above his head. "Come get some steel!" he shouted, trying his best to mimic Dante's booming voice. The crowd erupted again with laughter and used the opportunity for another toast.

Jexi

The party had been going strong for several hours when Eldrin returned with a strange new visitor.

"There they are over at the corner table." Eldrin pointed.

Her eyes locked onto them, and she took a step toward the table, but Eldrin stopped her.

"Jexi, please don't mess with them, we need them!" he begged.

Jexi shot a look at him that was a mixture of surprise and offense. "I wouldn't dream of it, brother."

She then unclasped her long, black, velvet robe, removed it, and tossed it at him as she began to make her way to the table.

He shook his head in frustration. "I should have known better than to say anything," he muttered to himself as she walked away.

She wore a sleek, form fitted cuirass that was low cut and fit more like a corset. It looked as if it had been made from glossy, jet-black dragon scales. She wore a matching but highly modified and form fitted Fauld piece around her waist that accentuated and covered the outside of her hips. Connected to it were layered tassets that were made from the same glossy black pieces. They formed a taper down to a point that rested on the outer portion of her mid thighs. It was open in the front and back, revealing a velvety black underskirt that concealed her legs. The underskirt had slits on the sides that ran all the way up her legs and were only covered by the tapered tassets of her armor.

She wore a choker with a ring in the front as if she had just slipped free from her masochistic bonds of some Demon Lord. Her dark red hair fell in tousled tresses to the middle of her back, giving her a sultry appearance. She had seductive, sapphire blue eyes that were accentuated by her dark eye shadow. Lauriel observed that she had both elven and human features.

"Half-Elf," Lauriel muttered.

"More like half-succubus, half grim reaper," Nyx added.

"The only thing she is missing is a whip!" Lauriel continued.

Both of them burst into laughter but Lauriel felt suddenly ashamed at her judgement as a picture flashed through her mind of a group of human women laughing at her as she walked by them.

"I'm sorry, let's not judge her," Lauriel added. "I have experienced far too much of that lately."

As Jexi walked toward them, the side armor plates accentuated every move of her shapely hips, and the high slit in her black underskirt tantalizingly revealed her legs as she walked. She exuded sensuality and confidence. She knew that she was being gawked at by nearly everyone in the room, and she enjoyed it.

She seemed to represent everything that Lauriel wasn't; she was dark and manipulative, and fully ready to exploit her attractiveness to any advantage. Jexi enjoyed the power of being able to control someone as she drove them crazy with lust, and she knew exactly how to accomplish that goal.

"Now THATS what I'm fucking talking about; half elf, half human, ALL woman," Dante blurted in his drunken state.

Lauriel rolled her eyes, and Nyx shook her head and laughed at him.

"Hi, I'm Dante," he said as she walked up to the table.

Without even a look in his direction, she walked right up to Lauriel and kissed her, turning to look at Dante as she did. Lauriel pulled away and was too shocked to speak or react.

"I do have a whip if you are that interested," the strange female said to Lauriel.

"What …? How did …" Lauriel stammered as her face turned an even brighter shade of red.

"Aww, fuck yeah!" said Dante.

Eldrin walked up to the table. "Lauriel, I see that you have met my half-sister. Dante, Nyx, meet Jexi."

Nyx reached out her hand to greet the strange new woman.

Instead of walking around the table, Jexi stepped in even closer to Lauriel and stood right in between her legs as she leaned over to shake Nyx's hand. Lauriel couldn't tell if she was messing with her, Dante, every man and woman in the room, or if she was serious. She didn't know whether she should be furious or amused. She sat … speechless.

Eldrin enjoyed seeing Lauriel's apparent discomfort and waited several moments before he spoke again. "Now that we are all here, I told you that I would answer a few questions, and I promise to do so." He raised his glass. "But this is not the place, and now is not the time. Let's enjoy our evening in your honor, for it may be the last celebration for a while." It was a strange and passively dubious toast, but they all raised their glasses.

The party finally ended, and the crowd began to dwindle. The small group sat at the table for many hours, laughing and sharing drinks until the wee hours of the morning. Jexi was the first to stand up to leave. She pushed her chair back and looked at Lauriel.

"Lauriel, are you coming to bed soon? I'm a bit cold," she said. Her sapphire eyes flickered and seemed to glow as they caught the light of the fire. "And maybe a little drunk if you want to take advantage of me."

Jexi had quickly learned that she could easily make Lauriel uncomfortable, and she relished and continually exploited that fact. Lauriel had never been exposed to such overtly seductive banter and still had no idea if Jexi was serious or if it was just her humor.

Jexi took a step backward and "accidentally" backed up into Dante's lap.

"Well, that settles it, I'm going to bed too," said Dante. "What room?"

Jexi didn't answer, her eyes still locked onto Lauriel's. Lauriel could see that Jexi already had full control of Dante.

"Are you sure you're not a succubus?" Lauriel blurted. She clasped her hands over her mouth. Her green eyes opened wide, and her face once again began to turn a bright shade red.

She didn't mean to verbally express what she was thinking but the alcohol seemed to have other plans. She slid her glass away from her toward the center of the table. Nyx, Dante, and Eldrin burst into laughter so hard that Nyx almost fell out of her chair. Jexi seemed to take immense pleasure at Lauriel's comment and subsequent embarrassment.

"Goodnight, Jexi. Meet at first light, near the fountain at the town square," Eldrin instructed.

Jexi nodded and turned to walk upstairs.

"And don't be late!" Eldrin added but appeared to already accept the inevitability.

One by one, the party dwindled down until the only two that remained were Lauriel and Eldrin. She found him unexpectedly easy to talk to, and the hours slipped by quickly as she sat transfixed in their enthralling conversation. The pub finally closed but she did not want the evening to end.

"Shall we move to the couch?" Eldrin asked.

Apparently, he did not either, she observed.

She nodded and he scooted it closer to the dwindling fire in the common room. It was the very same spot where she had first glimpsed him and judged him as cold and aloof. Now that she was beginning to get to know him, he'd turned out to be the exact opposite.

He was warm and engaging, and she found him mysteriously attractive and fascinating.

*   *   *   *

Eldrin's heart pounded wildly as they continued to engage in conversation. He could hardly concentrate on anything else as her eyes would dance when she laughed or when she would nervously twirl her hair.

He found even the sound of her voice to be as pleasant and attractive as the rest of her, and before long, he realized that there was no Charm spell in his inventory that could come close to achieving the intense allure that he'd begun to feel toward her.

She was by far the most physically attractive female he had ever seen, even more so than the many legendarily beautiful High Elven women that he had grown up around.

But it was not just her exotically beautiful physical characteristics that drove her attractiveness in his eyes. He could tell from her stories that she was individualistic, confident, and free spirited.

She seemed to be at ease with him on the comfortable couch in the common room and he could see her for who she truly was—a deeply caring, fun loving, and a loyal-to-a-fault companion.

He was ashamed at his snap judgement of her as some cold and unemotional killing machine that elven *Andúlarium* were often stereotyped as.

He desperately wanted to kiss her and had just worked up the nerve to try, but just before his attempt, they were interrupted by a great ruckus coming from upstairs. At first, they were alarmed. They could hear glass breaking and furniture moving around the floor followed by screaming and yelling. It didn't take too long to figure out that Dante had obviously found Jexi's room and she had let him in. They couldn't tell if she was killing him, he was killing her, or both. They discussed checking in on them and then decided against it.

* * * *

Having lost the perfect moment, Eldrin switched the topic and began to explain to Lauriel how he had recognized her scimitars even though they appeared mundane. "So, about those blades of yours; ever since I was a young child, I had this strange ability to sense magical energies, which is why I became a wizard."

"So, does that mean you are FINALLY going to tell me more about my scimitars, Sorcerer?" Lauriel asked with a flirtatious smile that drove him crazy. She had been around Jexi for one evening and had already begun to learn the art of seduction.

He looked at her with a suddenly serious look on his face and pointed to the scimitar on her left side. "Yes, I think it is the proper time ... That blade is known as ... maybe you should ask a sorcerer," he retorted.

She began to laugh and had to cover her mouth so that they would not wake up the other occupants. As he told her about her blades, he could see her wide-eyed excitement, so he went into great detail, telling her everything he could discover about them with his arcane magic.

"The blade you carry on your left hip is a vorpal scimitar. Meaning that it is the sharpest of blades known, and a nearly unique feat to create such a blade. When you strike at an enemy's neck, if you strike in just the right manner, it can instantly decapitate them."

"That happened with the ruffian leader! It makes sense now!" she exclaimed.

Eldrin replied, "Yes, as you know, it's quite a deadly weapon, and spectacularly rare. The spell of concealment must have been added to help protect it from those that would look upon it and covet it. When the blade is not concealed, it appears as black as the darkest night sky with glowing red runes that run down the length of it. A truly terrifying sight when wielded against someone in battle."

"Yes! I have seen that once too!" Lauriel exclaimed. She was now on the edge of her seat.

"How do I remove the concealment if I want to?"

"May I see it? I will have to truly study it carefully to fully identify its magical properties," Eldrin explained.

She drew the blade from the scabbard and placed it on the table.

The polished steel reflected off of the firelight and it looked to be a well-crafted but otherwise ordinary scimitar. Eldrin cast a spell on it, and the blade was suddenly revealed in its true form.

It turned pitch black, so dark that it seemed to absorb the dim light in the room. The faintly glowing red runes he had described began to appear on the blade, matching the look of the glowing red embers in the fireplace.

He closed his eyes and spoke several more words of magic as he gripped the blade. A perplexed look came across his face, and he reexamined the blade closely for several minutes. Finally, he held it out and spoke a single word, "Nuulz'rak." The blade instantly turned back in to a mundane-looking scimitar, and he handed it back to Lauriel.

"Well, that was unexpected."

"What is it!?" Lauriel asked anxiously.

"The runes and word of concealment are actually that of the Infernal tongue, a language that is only spoken in the hellish underworld!" Eldrin exclaimed. "I would love to hear the story about how you came to be in possession of such a rare item."

Lauriel looked at him with shock and alarm. "It was my grandfather's, I … I don't know where he got it from. I didn't think that it was some instrument of evil; he wouldn't have owned such a thing!"

Eldrin shook his head and tried to reassure her. "It is an inanimate object, so it's not something that is actively evil, cursed, nor are you some agent of evil for wielding it."

A visible look of relief washed over her. "Well, that's good to know. I'd hate for it to turn me into a succubus like your sister."

Eldrin burst into laughter so loud that it most certainly woke up several of the upstairs guests.

When he was finally able to pull himself together, he continued with the rest of what he had discovered.

"It has the most powerful enchantment magic that can be imbued in a blade. Its edge will never dull, which makes it particularly deadly and valuable beyond measure. And in answer to your original question, the phrase of un-concealment can be said in either Infernal or the common tongue: 'Swift death to my enemies.' I suspect that it was made that way to strike fear in the hearts of enemies that spoke the common speech instead of some garbled phrase in the Infernal language that very few could understand."

Lauriel stared at the blade with wide eyed wonderment. She then pointed it toward Eldrin and looked at him with a seductive squint. "Swift death to my enemies," she said playfully.

The blade again revealed its true form. Eldrin laughed and held his hands up in surrender. His keen perception of the arcane caused him to notice something that most would not. The blade did in fact seem to slightly darken the room. He couldn't tell if it was the pitch-black blade absorbing the light, or if it was casting a faint shadow throughout. Even more disturbingly, it also made the room slightly colder. The fire in the fireplace flickered and sputtered in protest. He made a mental note to try to do more research on the oddly sinister properties, but decided not to say anything about it to her.

"What will you name it? A blade that rare deserves a name," he asked.

"Hmm, I hadn't really thought about it," replied Lauriel.

Together, they sat and discussed many different names until Lauriel came up with one that she liked. "Nightfang."

"Nightfang it is," Eldrin replied.

"Well, now that we have settled that, may I see the other?" Eldrin asked.

"Nuulz'rak," Lauriel said wearily as she sheathed Nightfang back at her side. Eldrin made the same, unspoken observation. The relatively imperceptible shadow and coldness disappeared.

She then drew the other blade from her right hip and handed it to him.

Eldrin went through the same series of incantations and inspections but it took him twice as long as before. Lauriel could see another puzzled look on his face as he continued to inspect and cast spells.

"This blade is quite a different story. I don't know what it is but I feel a powerful and ancient magic, one that I don't quite understand."

He handed the weapon back to her. "I can only discover a single word—Isilmwé. And if memory serves me correctly ..." His voice trailed off in thought and the look on his face suddenly became serious.

"What!? What is it!?" Lauriel questioned.

"We need to do some research on this immediately," Eldrin said.

"There you go with riddles again," Lauriel joked, trying to pull him back from his sudden seriousness. "Where do we do that?"

Eldrin's mind appeared to be elsewhere and he did not seem to even hear her question.

"Eldrin!" Lauriel called even louder.

This time, her voice seemed to snap him out of his preoccupied thoughts and bring him back into focus.

"Ah, yes ... Sorry. The only place that I can think of is the Tower of Nemerse in Silenus. It is where I did much of my wizard study. It has a vast library and ..." His voice trailed off as he watched the enchanting sight of her sheathing the blade. The scene completely removed his mind from whatever thoughts had troubled it, and nothing else existed but her.

After a brief moment, they both realized the awkward pause and became embarrassed.

"Umm. Well, it's getting late and I need to go get ready for tomorrow," Eldrin said, cursing himself in his mind as the very words came out of his mouth.

"Yes, me too," said Lauriel, her face starting to flush. She stood up to leave. "Thanks for finally telling me about my weapons, Sorcerer!"

Eldrin smiled at her playful jest and could see that she had just opened one last opportunity to kiss her, and he wasn't about to miss out.

He stepped closer and drew her in nearer to him, desperately hoping that he was correct and that she would not reject his advance. His heart felt like it was about to leap out of his chest when she made no attempt to stop him.

He couldn't ever remember being more nervous.

How is this goddess even interested in me?

In the age of Magic, it was rumored that the most powerful wizards to have ever lived could cast a spell that briefly stopped time around them, and as their lips met for the first time, he found himself desperately wishing that he could cast it now.

When he began to slowly pull away, she locked her eyes back on his.

"I've been waiting for you to do that all night," she whispered.

He could see the hunger in her eyes, but with his last bit of willpower, he took her hand and kissed it, gambling that his restraint would only grow her interest and anticipation.

"Then my only regret is wasting so much time. Goodnight, *Írium Ælfen!*" he said, adding the polite elven compliment meaning, "beautiful female elf."

"Goodnight … Sorcerer."

With her final two words, she turned and walked up the stairs to her room.

CHAPTER TEN

Eldrin's Quest

The light of the new day had just begun to chase the shadows away, revealing the glistening early morning dew that had settled thickly upon the flora. The group had reassembled near the fountain at the town square as planned, with the exception of one. Jexi had not answered her door in the inn and was nowhere to be seen.

With the exception of a very disturbing smile, Dante looked terrible. He was even more pale than usual and had dark circles around his eyes. It was obvious from the numerous blood smatters that were soaking through the back of his shirt that he had received several injuries at some point throughout the night.

"Uhh, Nyx … since we are waiting, these scratches on my back hurt worse than that damn sword injury, could I get one of those handy heals of yours?"

Nyx looked up at him and shook her head. "I'm not going to waste my limited healing supporting your evening debauchery."

Eldrin and Lauriel burst into laughter, and Dante's face flushed with a mixture of embarrassment and ire.

Fifteen minutes had gone by when Jexi finally showed up to join them.

Much to Eldrin's consternation, she had no sense of urgency, nor any remorse for keeping all of them waiting.

Her red hair was a wild mess and she didn't appear to care.

She looked at Lauriel with a mischievous smirk. "Where were you? We waited up for you to join."

Lauriel didn't have a hard time imagining her standing there with horns, bat-like wings, a whip, and a flicking tail.

"Oh, that's right, you and Eldrin had an exciting evening of 'talking,'" she continued her quips.

Lauriel glanced at Eldrin with a bashful smirk, which seemed to immediately cease Jexi's banter.

Eldrin turned red and snapped back at her as he pointed to Dante.

"Do you even know his last name?"

She looked over at Dante and then back at Eldrin and shook her head.

"No …" She looked back at Dante.

"I actually didn't catch your first name."

"What the fuck?" Dante exclaimed, clearly offended.

Lauriel and Nyx laughed.

Eldrin knew that he would never get anywhere with his current line of interrogation, and changed the subject.

"Have any of you ever been teleported?"

Lauriel, Nyx, and Dante looked at each other in confusion.

"I ask because it can be a little unsettling the first few times. You will experience darkness and feel a sinking feeling; sort of like being in a dark closet of a boat that is catching a very large swell," he explained.

"That doesn't sound too bad." Nyx replied.

"We need to go outside of town, away from the view of other people. Teleportation magic is very rare and it can be quite disconcerting to the townspeople to see a group of people disappear," Eldrin instructed.

The group walked until they found a small forest clearing that appeared to be unoccupied, and when Eldrin was sure that no one else was watching, he reached into one of his many pouches and pulled out a handful of pure white sand.

"Please step inside the circle as soon as it's completed," he instructed.

He began to make a large circle with the sand, letting it slowly slip through his fingers as he said many strange words of magic.

The circle began to glow faintly and the group moved inside of it as instructed. As soon as Eldrin finished his strange words and gestures, everything went pitch black.

Eldrin's description was accurate, but the sinking feeling in Lauriel's stomach was far worse than she anticipated. She reached out to grab onto something but there was nothing to grab. Her feet were not on the ground and she floundered helplessly, a feeling that she hated. She spotted a tiny dot of light and tried to focus on it. She could see that it was moving toward her with incredible speed and getting larger as it approached her.

She was getting extremely nauseous as the combination of movement and her trying to focus on the dot proved to be too much. And then, as quickly as it had gone completely dark, all she could see was light.

It took a few moments for her eyes to adjust and when they did, she found that she was standing in a nondescript square room made of stone. She began to dry heave and tried to force herself not to vomit.

Nyx had already failed but Dante seemed to be completely unfazed.

"Well fuuuck me! That's the only way to go! Where the hell are we?" he asked enthusiastically.

"Welcome to the Grand Duchy of Silenus," Eldrin announced. "We are in the teleportation circle of the Tower of Nemerse."

Nyx started to regain her composure, but Lauriel still seemed to be a slight shade of her eye color as she continued her primal struggle against the nausea.

Eldrin led the group into a large foyer and introduced them to one of the newer wizards in training who ushered them to a private room with a large table.

"Breakfast will be served shortly," the apprentice wizard said. He excused himself politely and closed the door.

Once everyone was seated, Eldrin began without any further delay. "I promised to make everything clear to you. It has taken a few more days than anticipated, days that we do not have, but here is the story as I have come to know and understand it.

"Many years ago, the Dark Elves found an ancient magical device deep in their dark and sinister underground kingdom of Draxanarek'Vel." His face grew grim and solemn. "They discovered it quite by accident after a powerful earthquake caused a cave in that exposed a new and unexplored cavern. It took many years of magical study to learn and understand the ancient magics that had been bound up within the device. The Dark Sages of that vile realm concluded that the device was an artifact left over from the Age of Magic, created when the arcane magics were still wild and not bound as they are today. It was anchored to the bedrock and could not be removed or damaged by any means. They learned that the device contained within it a well of magical energy. They surmised that if they were able to somehow unlock it, their Magic Users could learn to tap into new arcane magic and harness the vast power as it existed in the ancient days.

"Seeking to further her realm, the Dark Queen ordered the device unlocked. But what they didn't know at the time was that the artifact had been created to open a rift to some other distant multiverse. It was a Nexial Gate, a portal to some unknown. When the sages finally learned the ritual magic required to activate and unlock it, a great rift appeared, and the denizens of the deep immediately began to spill forth into this realm.

"The Dark Elven kingdom fought with all resource but the foul creatures flowed from it like a tidal wave, spilling through their realm and up into the surface realms."

Lauriel gasped. "The Great Decimation," she said in a half whisper.

"Yes, Lauriel, that was the event, and those were the vile creatures you seek," Eldrin confirmed.

Nyx exchanged a concerned glance with Dante.

Eldrin continued, "After a time, and at great cost to Draxanarek'Vel, the sages were able to create a strong magic barrier that sealed the portal for a time, but they were unable to close it.

"With the recent return of the creatures, we can only conclude that the barrier must have finally succumbed to the power of the deep.

"I have been one of the many tasked with trying to figure out how to stop these creatures and seal off the portal. And as luck or fate would have it, Jexi may have stumbled upon some information that may help." Eldrin stopped and nodded at Jexi.

"I'm a warlock," Jexi said and paused. "The ... first of my kind."

Nyx, Lauriel, and Dante looked around the room at each other with a puzzled look.

"What the fuck is that?" asked Dante.

Jexi continued, "Well, just as Nyx draws her divine healing magic from her Goddess, and Eldrin has learned to channel his arcane magic, I draw my magic from a different ... source, a mixture of arcane and divine. I was kicked out of magic school because of it. According to the wizards," she added with obvious distain, "I practiced unknown magics. I learned things that I shouldn't have known, and conjured things that I shouldn't have been able to. But it was this very practice that provided me with the knowledge and understanding of 'reality shards.'"

"Reality shards?" Lauriel questioned.

Jexi looked around the room suspiciously, quieting her voice as if someone else were eavesdropping. She continued, "Reality shards were used by the gods during the creation of the planes to anchor and stabilize them, bringing them into order and existence. One shard was created for each plane, but for some unknown reason, one extra shard remained and was placed in the Plane of Discordance.

"We think that the shard itself, and nothing short of it, should be able to collapse the Nexial Gate that has been opened."

Eldrin spoke back up as Jexi finished, "We have tried in vain to convince the High Council of wizards to believe in or even accept the possibility that something like this exists, but we have been repeatedly ridiculed for presenting our 'ridiculous' idea. They flatly refuse to support our quest in any way. Instead, they bicker amongst themselves and have come up with no better alternatives.

"Unfortunately, in our case, traveling to a different plane of existence is no easy task. I have not been there myself and have very little knowledge about it; in fact, very few have. It is not wise to go to some place like that without a thorough understanding of it, which is why our quest has led us here. This building contains a vast library that should have something about the Plane of Discordance."

Eldrin paused, and his face darkened as he appeared to be choosing his next words very carefully. His unintentional expression coupled with his sudden hesitation had the effect of blanketing the room in an almost palpable layer of trepidation.

He continued, "All of the knowledge in the world does us no good if we can't actually get there. Going there requires certain magic that is very much more powerful than the Teleportation spell that we used to get here, and well beyond my capabilities. Jexi and I have been on a quest for months, trying to find a highly magical amulet that I think will allow us to travel there and back safely."

Dante said out loud what the others were thinking, interrupting Eldrin in his own colorful way, "What the fuck do you mean THINK? What happens if we try to get there and DON'T?"

"Well, if you plane travel to the wrong place, pretty much instant death," Jexi immediately interjected.

Dante seemed to weigh the options and shook his head in approval and full acceptance. "Fair enough."

Eldrin continued, "The good news is that if we can get a hold of it, we will have the ability to travel there."

"What's the bad news?" Lauriel asked.

Eldrin paused. "Well, it's a bit tough to get."

"What do you mean 'a bit tough to get?'"

Eldrin took a deep breath and continued, "To be very honest with you, we believe that it is in the possession of a Red Dragon named Malthrax."

Nyx, Dante, and Lauriel's jaws dropped open in an unhidden expression of shock.

"A dragon!?" Lauriel blurted. "I didn't even think they were real! How on earth do we fight a dragon?"

"You don't, if you want to live," Jexi said tersely. "But I am here to figure out where he might be, and just how we might survive such an encounter."

Eldrin began again. "I am asking each of you to help us on this very dangerous and difficult quest, and should you agree, you must understand that we will be in mortal danger through much of it."

"And just why the hell is it up to us to do this?" said Dante.

"Because if we want to try and save our lands, our friends, our families, and all of the innocent people of this realm, we will need to get the shard … and to get the shard, we need the amulet," Jexi snapped.

The sudden intensity of Jexi's scolding outburst took Lauriel by surprise.

She is not just some indifferent seductress as she portrays; she is genuinely concerned about others and not just herself, Lauriel observed

"Is that the only way?" Nyx asked quietly.

"I'm afraid that's the best plan that we could come up with," Eldrin replied.

Jexi nodded in confirmation.

"And you're not sure where the dragon is?" Nyx continued to question.

"That is correct, Nyx, we have run into many dead ends trying to figure out his whereabouts, but we are hoping to find some information here," replied Jexi.

"Well fuck it, it's better than guarding a damn wagon," Dante said enthusiastically, and without much other thought given. "I'm in!"

Lauriel had been quietly contemplating the gravity of the conversation, and the seemingly endless impossibilities of the task at hand before she spoke back up. "Well, if this has any chance of stopping the creatures and helping others, I'm in."

Nyx nodded in agreement. "I'm in."

"So, it looks like this task has somehow fallen to us; when do we leave?" Lauriel asked.

Eldrin looked directly at Lauriel. "We need to look for a book about your sword. This is probably our best chance to find something on it. I must also get the book that I am in search of. Jexi will try to learn more about Red Dragons and where Malthrax might be found. If the rest of you can stock up on supplies, we should be prepared to leave as soon as possible."

CHAPTER ELEVEN

Swordsong

Lauriel stood in the center of the large atrium and stared in awe at the endless rows of books that continued upward until they seemed to reach the heavens. The vast library was the tallest building that she had ever seen, far exceeding the height of even the tallest Silverpine trees from her home. She could hardly contain her excitement to find out more about her weapon, but Eldrin's discussion with the librarian was unexpectedly lengthy.

After what felt like hours, Eldrin finally came back to join her.

"Well, that was not easy." He rolled his eyes as he whispered.

"What's going on?" Lauriel asked quietly.

"The areas where we might be able to find the books are only available to wizards of certain rank, and off limits to the public. The librarian is a real stickler for the rules and it took quite a bit of convincing to let you in as a guest," Eldrin quietly explained.

The rigid-looking librarian removed a set of keys from her desk and motioned for them to follow her. Once they joined her, she escorted them across the main room and unlocked a sturdy door that led into a small, nondescript room.

She first turned to Eldrin. "She is to be supervised at all times."

Eldrin smiled and nodded in agreement. "Understood."

She then turned her stern gaze upon Lauriel, looking over her glasses and addressing her as if she were a child. "You are not to wander or disturb anything."

Lauriel was about to fire back when Eldrin quickly interrupted, "We will not stray a single step."

The librarian seemed to accept the reply and stepped back out of the room, closing the door behind her.

"Wow!" Lauriel exclaimed quietly.

"She obviously takes her job very seriously," Eldrin whispered.

They both shared a quiet laugh before Eldrin refocused their efforts.

He ushered Lauriel over to a wooden panel on the far wall that had many strange symbols burned into it.

"Remember the teleport?" he asked.

"NO! NOT AGAIN!" Lauriel whispered as loudly as possible, shaking her head in protest.

Eldrin started to trace a certain combination of symbols, and each one that he touched began to faintly glow as he spoke the corresponding words of magic. "This isn't as bad, trust me. It's just that in order to keep the area safe, there are no stairs that go there."

Lauriel opened her mouth to protest, and the room went dark. She felt the floor beneath her feet give way and she had the same brief sensation of falling in darkness, just like the previous teleport. Then, as quickly as it happened, she found herself standing in another room with the door standing wide open to more rows of books.

"See? Not that bad," Eldrin said with a smile. "I'll just be a moment; I think that I know right where to find this one. And whatever you do, don't 'wander' far from your chaperone," Eldrin joked.

"Well hurry back before I cause too much chaos or speak too loudly," Lauriel replied.

Eldrin laughed and quickly disappeared around the corner.

Lauriel took the opportunity to walk over to the window, and as soon as she drew near it, her eyes opened wide with a look of shock.

She was startled to see that they were very high up in the tower, when seconds ago they had just been on the ground floor.

"Woah!" she exclaimed as she took a step back and grabbed onto a nearby bookshelf to steady herself.

"Found it!" Eldrin's voice carried from around the corner.

Lauriel was all too happy to walk away from the large window and found him standing in a section labeled, "Planular Studies."

He held the brown leather book out for her to see, and she quietly spoke the title as she read it, "The Plane of Discordance."

She noticed that the book had very few pages, but had a unique motif embossed on the front cover, and she drew it closer to observe.

The symbol was made of a circle that had spikes all around it that pointed both inward and outward. The outward spikes each had a tip shaped like a jagged arrow, and Lauriel could see that the biggest ones were lined up like points on a compass. There were also smaller spikes in between the larger ones that looked like half-compass points. All of the outward spikes had sharp points on the opposite ends that went through the circle and pointed inward toward a dot in the center.

"What in the world is this?" she asked.

"This is the place that we are trying to find, and hopefully this book will serve as a guide," Eldrin explained.

He untied his backpack and carefully placed the book into it.

"Now, let's see if we can find something about your scimitar."

Eldrin led Lauriel up a small set of stairs that connected to another section.

They walked past several closed study rooms and multiple rows of books until they came to a section that was closed off by another sturdy door.

The title above the door read, "Artifacts and Relics." Eldrin withdrew an ornate key from one of the many pockets in his robe and unlocked the door.

"What book are we looking for? I'll help search for it," Lauriel offered excitedly, hoping to finally solve one of the mysteries about her weapons.

"That's the tough part. I know this answer doesn't make sense but I don't actually know what we are looking for, but I will know it when I see it," Eldrin replied.

"Um, yeah that doesn't make any sense at all. There are hundreds of books in here!"

Eldrin smiled and began a slow and methodical search while Lauriel restlessly began to wander throughout the rows. An hour passed when she finally heard Eldrin quietly exclaim, "I think I found it!"

She ran over to his row and found him standing on a small ladder retrieving a book from the very top of the library shelf.

"I think this is it!" he whispered excitedly.

They walked over to a grand table and sat down on the large, plush chairs that sat next to each other. Lauriel looked down at the dusty, black, leather-bound tome with nervous anticipation. Eldrin blew off the fine layer of dust, and she read the cover aloud, "Swords of Power by Sondrax the Black." He opened it with great care and began to carefully turn the pages as if it were some delicate treasure that would crumble at the slightest movement.

The old tome documented nine blades of power, and judging from the thickness of it, appeared to be extremely lengthy and detailed. Lauriel was fluent in many languages but she did not at all recognize the writing on the pages.

"What does it say?" she asked.

"It is written in elder draconic; this tome was meant to be read by very few."

Eldrin began to read the first page out loud:

Enchanted swords of ancient lords to wield the soul of fate,

lost in sleep for time untold, their masters call they wait.

Nine were forged to rend and mend the hearts and minds of men

through weal and woe and love and hate, they dream to reign again.

* * * *

Lauriel looked at Eldrin with a wide-eyed stare, her green eyes dancing with excitement. As he looked back at her, he completely forgot all about the book, the quest, and the rest of the world around him. In that moment, as in the night before, he saw in her a beautiful and innocent sense of wonder and adventure.

"Fascinating," he muttered.

"Eldrin!" she said in as loud of a whisper as she could. "What does it say?"

"Oh! Yes, sorry, I ... I was just ... contemplating the words of the poem."

He shook his head and continued, carefully turning through several pages until he stopped at a page with a single sentence:

The return of a Blade of Power is a harbinger of great change.

Eldrin did not read it out loud, nor express to Lauriel that the single sentence troubled him deeply. He continued slowly turning through the pages until he found a chapter titled, *Swords of Power—Chronicled*

He began to read the detailed description aloud:

"Sword #1—(Azurewrath) The Sword of Doom, Type: Longsword. Alignment: Chaotic Evil. Known Prime Properties:

Vampiric—As life is drained by the sword, it is transferred to the wielder."

He turned through many other pages, and finally stopped on one particular page, and his eyes lit up with excitement.

"Here it is!" he exclaimed loudly, completely forgetting to whisper.

Lauriel leaned forward on the edge of her chair.

Sword #8—(Isilmwé) The Sword of Dominion, Type: Scimitar. Alignment: Neutral Good. Elven only Moonblade. Known Prime Properties:

Sentient—Unknown degree of awareness.

Vorpal—Unmatched sharpness augmented by arcane enchantments.

Defender—Weapon has the ability to instantaneously produce an invisible barrier of magical force that helps to protect the wielder in the same manner as a small shield.

Description: Powerful magics guard this blade and ensure that it remains hidden. The magic makes the blade appear as a well-crafted but mundane scimitar but does not reveal its true nature unless the blade's master wills it to. In its true form, the blade is a gleaming silvery scimitar, appearing to glow like the light of the full silver moon. Upon close inspection of the blade in true form, the scimitar will have several glowing runes (see Arcana).

History: In the dark reaches of the past, when the foundations of the world were yet young and unstable, the Ancient Lords enslaved powerful entities from nine outer planes and compelled them to forge nine mighty artifacts: The Swords of Power. Thus, was Isilmwé, First Blade of the Elven Kingdoms, created. The forces of Neutrality sought to establish their balancing influence in the fledgling Prime Plane and it was gifted to the elves to help bring order from the chaos. It often remains obscure for an age until some event leads to its emergence. The blade has been passed down through the elves from time immemorial, each master conveying upon the blade untold powers.

Arcana: The Moonblade is intricately imbued with runes, each rune imbuing it with powerful arcane properties and a degree of sentience. Once the blade is bonded to its master (Blademaster), it can communicate by transmitting emotions, or sending a tingling sensation through the master's hand. The wielder must prove themselves to be of sufficient skill and power before the true potential of the blade can be used, referred to as the *Bladerite.

Swordsong fragment:

The blade awakes from deepened sleep

A master calls for it to keep

For test it proves a rightful heir

To wield a blade of power so rare

From Elven line they must be strong

And prove to them that they belong

The Swordsong has been lost but it is believed that the song contains verses that describe the Bladerite of each previous Blademaster, all the way back to the beginning.

*Bladerite: The Bladerite is the process of proving to the blade, and all previous masters associated with it, that the new wielder is worthy. To unlock the power of the blade, the wielder must go through many challenges, and failure of any of them results in death. Once *the Bladerite is started, the wielder must complete every step without stopping.*

Bladerite Invocation:

Gripping the blade, the wielder recites the following in Elven. (Caution, this is reportedly irrevocable.)

Awake Isilmwé, oh blade of power, a challenge you I give this hour.

I claim you now by Bladerite test and shall I fail, my soul doth rest.

So hear me now your masters call, and shall I pass to you in thrall.

"When do we start?" Lauriel asked as she jumped up from the chair excitedly.

Eldrin began to laugh, but as soon as he looked back up at her, he realized that she was dead serious.

"Oh! You're serious!"

He didn't have to say it to confirm; he just needed time to think of how to dissuade her from such a dangerous endeavor.

"Of course I am! I'm ready to do this! Where do we go?"

Her ambition was yet another attractive quality about her that he found both fascinating and frustrating at the same time.

"Did you miss the part about any failure results in death, or the special caution that it is irrevocable once you start?" he asked.

"I do not fear death," she said coldly.

Eldrin could tell that there was no lie in her statement.

He stood up from the chair and began to stammer as he tried to come up with another, more powerful dissuading response than possible death.

"I … It isn't …You should …"

"Is the great Sorcerer Eldrin afraid of a little magic ritual?" She smirked.

Eldrin stepped toward her and was finally able to collect his thoughts. His voice was clear and serious. "I just don't think it is a good idea ... You should prepare for something so powerful that can have such deadly consequences."

Lauriel took his hand in hers. "I have spent my whole life preparing for this! Besides, you of all people should understand, you have made it your life's quest to pursue the arcane."

Eldrin was frustrated by her logic, and that fact that he could not come up with a single rebuttal to it. He finally began to shake his head and express his exasperation at her hasty decision that he could clearly see would not be undone. "Damnit! You obstinate, impossible, impatient *Ælfen!*"

She laughed at his reaction, and the dancing of her eyes was the only response needed for her to render him incapable of putting up any further resistance. The entire world could fall away, and he wouldn't even notice, nor would he care as long as he could keep looking at her.

He placed his hand around her waist, drawing her closer as he began to kiss her supple lips. To his surprise, she not only reciprocated, but she leapt up on him and wrapped her legs tightly around his waist as she kissed him back with unbridled passion. She seemed like a caged lioness that had just been set free, and he was her fortunate prey.

Eldrin felt a synergy and intensity with her that he had never before felt, and he couldn't get enough of it.

They knocked over an entire bookshelf in the commotion as Eldrin pressed her up against it. The priceless, ancient tome was swept aside and crashed to the floor as Eldrin blindly cleared the desk with Lauriel still attached to him like another appendage.

"GET OUT! BOTH OF YOU!" an angry voice hissed from behind them.

* * * *

Eldrin lost all rights to the library indefinitely.

The stern librarian just wouldn't accept his "You said guests must be supervised at all times," and "I couldn't watch her any closer" arguments.

He had never seen Lauriel more embarrassed and thought that she had never been cuter. The deadly *Andúlarium* wouldn't even look at the scolding librarian.

Together, they walked down the road, both of them reflecting silently on what had just happened. They each knew that what they had shared was not some fling like Dante and Jexi, but much more significant, and it scared them.

Lauriel finally broke the silence. "By the way, where are we going?"

"Well, I know there is absolutely no convincing you otherwise, so we are headed to do the Bladerite," Eldrin replied.

CHAPTER TWELVE

Bladerite

The stars glimmered brilliantly against the backdrop of the clear night sky, and the full moon illuminated the druid's grove with a bright glow of comforting beauty. Lauriel clutched the scimitar tightly in her hand and nodded at Eldrin, ready to start. She had practiced saying the incantation several times until she got it perfect. She was amazed that Eldrin had not only remembered every word of it, but had remembered every single word that he had read from the tome. She waited anxiously for him to finish with his friend Gorian.

"Thank you for letting us do this here in the safety of your grove, my old friend," Eldrin said.

"It's an honor that such a substantial thing be done this night right here in Lanéthym Forest," Gorian replied. He looked up at the intense full moon and then back to Eldrin. "And from the looks of the heavens, no coincidence. It looks like the moon itself has asked for a front row seat."

Eldrin peered back up at the moon. "It does seem extraordinarily bright tonight."

"If she doesn't falter, a new Blademaster of an ancient power shall rise this very night!" Gorian said excitedly.

He took note of Eldrin's nervous, downward glance. "Ahh, she is more than that to you, isn't she, Eldrin?"

Eldrin did not speak, but simply nodded his head.

"Take heart, Eldrin, for the realm needs her now to rebalance. You know the evils that I speak of. The emergence of a Blade of Power during this time is no coincidence," Gorian said as he glanced back at Lauriel.

"Indeed," Eldrin replied. "One thing that I did not tell her was a sentence in the old tome that really stuck out to me: 'The return of a Blade of Power is often a harbinger of great change.'"

"Yes, but that does not have to be a bad thing," Gorian added. "There is something strange about her, both a power and an innocence, a pure soul but a deep scar, and something else …"

Eldrin raised his eyebrow and continued to listen intently.

"As you know, a druid's grove is sacred. I control everything in this grove. I know everything that comes here and everything that leaves. I can also stop just about anything from entering."

Eldrin nodded in understanding.

"There is a strange entity here tonight that I do not control, nor stop. It takes the form of a Will-o' Wisp, but it is no Wisp, Eldrin, it has immense power beyond my comprehension. I can tell that it means no harm and is here to observe … her. I…don't completely understand," said Gorian.

"Hmm, very strange indeed," Eldrin replied.

Lauriel was standing ready and obviously growing impatient.

"Are you two done yet? Are you ready?" she called to them.

"Yes, Lauriel, we will be right here the whole time," Eldrin said as they walked over to her in the open glade.

"Remember what we discussed. I don't know what you are going to go through, but according to the Swordsong fragment, you must prove your Elven line. That will be part of it."

Lauriel nodded impatiently. "Yes, we have been over this ten times!"

Gorian smirked at her impatience but said nothing.

"Whenever you are ready," said Eldrin. He stepped forward to kiss her but she had already closed her eyes and started the incantation, and knowing better than to interrupt, he slowly backed away to give her space.

With the bright moonlight shining down upon her in the open glade, she recited the words aloud, her voice unwavering as she did:

"Awake Isilmwé, oh blade of power, a challenge you I give this hour.

I claim you now by Bladerite test and shall I fail, my soul doth rest.

So hear me now, your masters call, and shall I pass to you in thrall."

As soon as the last word was spoken, there was a bright flash of the blade, and Lauriel disappeared.

Eldrin looked at Gorian with concern and began a spell to locate her, but it failed to find her.

Gorian closed his eyes for several seconds and concentrated.

"She is no longer in this place," he whispered.

Test of the Blademaster

Lauriel found herself standing in a cavernous, dark room that formed a large rectangle. Ten giant stone statues at least twenty feet tall stood in massive shadowy alcoves along the walls. The alcoves were evenly spaced and contained four statues on each of the long walls, and one statue on each shorter wall.

They each looked to have been created in the likenesses of a giant warrior in full armor, eternally gripping the pommel of a giant stone sword with the pointed end resting on the ground.

In the center of the room stood a two-foot-tall circular stone dais made of black obsidian.

She began to walk over to the dais and, against the backdrop of the otherwise silent chamber, each of her normally quiet footfalls sounded like heavy armor-plated boots stomping on stone. She tried to move as quietly as she could but winced at the sound of each step.

As she approached the dais, she looked down and saw that the surface of it was slightly concave and contained a small hole at the lowest point in the very center. Lauriel continued to investigate the room and found no doors, windows, or any other means of exit.

She walked back to the dais and stared at it for several moments, coming to the conclusion that the hole may be some type of drain.

"Well, this isn't like anything I expected," she muttered to herself.

It was then that she remembered the advice of Eldrin: *prove my elven line* … With scimitar in hand, she drug the sharp edge of the blade lightly across her forearm. Blood began to run down her arm as the blade sliced into her skin like warm butter. As the blood spilled from her arm and fell onto the surface of the dais, she heard a tremendous rumbling that sounded like an avalanche of rocks. It continued to intensify until it seemed to shake the very foundation of the great room. Suddenly, each of the giant stone statues animated and stepped out of their alcoves.

"Stone Golems!" Lauriel exclaimed.

They moved toward her, raising their massive swords into the air.

Lauriel glanced back down at the dais and saw that it had quite a bit of blood on it, and it was running toward the center hole, but no blood had yet made it down the drain. The statues took another step toward her, bringing themselves within striking range. They finished raising their swords high overhead and then paused, as if waiting to exact final judgement. Lauriel knew that there was no use in even trying to fight ten giant stone statues; her steel blades would have no effect whatsoever on rock. Unsure of what to do next, she did the only thing that she could think of and squeezed more blood from her arm as she held it closer to the drain.

It seemed like it took an eternity for the blood to finally drain into the hole on the dais, but as soon as the first drop entered, a soft white glow began to emanate from the far wall where the statue had been standing in the alcove. A large, open door manifested in the alcove, and one by one the statues lowered their weapons and formed two rows, each statue bowing toward the opposite, creating a giant archway that ended at the door.

As Lauriel stepped through, she entered another stone room that was much smaller. An elderly man clad in a thick cloak and leaning heavily on a gnarled staff suddenly appeared in the center. Lauriel jumped and took a step back at the sudden appearance His cloak was open just enough that she could see a very old-fashioned sword belt with two empty scabbards. The scabbards appeared weathered and cracked, like they had not been used or cared for in a very long time.

"Come forth, Lauriel Valendril, for I will see you to your next test," the old man beckoned.

She looked behind her and saw that no door remained, only a solid wall.

"There is no going back now." He smiled briefly and then turned and walked through the remaining door on the opposite side of the room.

Seeing no other choice but to follow the old man, she walked through the door and down a long, narrow corridor. They walked for what seemed like an eternity, each thump of the old man's staff on the stone floor grating against her nerves. She heard the sounds of battle getting closer and closer. Finally, they came to a closed door at the very end of the long hallway. The old man placed his hand on the knob and turned to her.

"There are no tricks here; you must prove your skill. Are you ready?" he asked.

Lauriel gripped her scimitars and nodded.

"You must make it to the exit on the other side of the arena. I will go first," he instructed.

The old man stepped through the door, and Lauriel followed immediately behind him.

"Behold!" he said in a booming voice that carried throughout the arena. The sounds of combat suddenly halted.

"I present to you Lauriel Valendril, *Andúlarium*, Daughter of the Woodland Realms. She carries with her, Isilmwé, Moonblade of Power, and Nightfang, a Vorpal Scimitar made by the Infernal Lords. Defeat her, and the blades of untold power are yours.

You need only keep her from getting to that tunnel," he said as he pointed to the tunnel on the far side. He then turned back to Lauriel, "Welcome to the Dark Elven realm of Draxanarek'Vel."

"WHAT!?" Lauriel gasped.

Without another word, the old man vanished.

Four Dark Elves stood in their combat training arena with their weapons drawn. They were lightly armored and wielded light blades much like her scimitars. She could immediately tell that they would have a similar fighting style to hers—speed and finesse. She eyed the tunnel on the opposite side but it was several hundred feet across and she knew that she would not be able to make it in a sprint.

The Dark Elves began to walk toward her, spreading out to flank her. As Lauriel moved into a defensive stance, she saw that her Moonblade now appeared in its true form, glowing brightly as if to hedge off the darkness of the evil realm.

She raised Nightfang into a threatening position and spoke the words of command, "Swift death to my enemies."

Lauriel suddenly stood as the balance between the light and dark. The blade turned pitch black and seemed to be doing the exact opposite of the Moonblade, devouring the darkness is if it was in its very element. Red runes flared down the length of the blade and glowed ominously.

Seeing the manifestation of the blades, the Dark Elves looked hesitant to fight her. But the blood feud between the Dark Elves and the surface elves ran deep. They were mortal enemies as far back as any history could remember, and the will to fight quickly returned. They coveted the blades intensely, each desiring to wield them for themselves. The spoils of battle, especially ones like these, would hold vast sway upon their standing in Draxanarek'Vel, and they simply could not allow such prizes to slip from their grasp, especially when presented to them in their realm.

All four of them sprang to attack her at once, and Lauriel immediately countered. Her blades sliced through the air and began to ring with a resonance that seemed amplified by the cavern. It echoed through the enclosed space and traveled far down the many tangled webs of corridors. The fight was so fast and furious that it also sounded like someone had dropped an entire weapon stand full of swords down a long, metal stairway. The sounds of the mortal combat with the *Andúlarium* drew many Dark Elf spectators into the stands of the arena, and within seconds, a large crowd had gathered to watch.

The Dark Elven fighters were fast and skilled, but so was she. She ducked and dodged, parried and viciously counter attacked her opponents at every opportunity. The fluid motion of the *Andúlari* fighting style helped to keep her opponents at bay, but her defense against eight other blades was not impenetrable. The arena floor grew red as the blood of all five of them began to cover the ground.

The one-versus-four battle was a deadly even match, and Lauriel knew that she had to do something quickly to turn the tide or she would not make it past her second test. She was starting to weaken from her injuries but she could tell that her enemies were beginning to falter as well.

A mental picture of one of her training sessions with Adamar flashed through her mind. She saw herself standing before him when she had refused to quit sparring after he had told her that they were finished. She remembered his flurry of blows that resulted in her quick defeat.

With renewed inspiration, she suddenly switched from her defensive style that afforded her maximal protection, to a violent offensive that threw all caution to the wind. Her opponents were caught by surprise at the unexpected burst of speed and intensity with which her strikes suddenly fell upon them. Each of them simply could not parry or dodge the bladed onslaught fast enough, and Lauriel felled two of them within seconds.

The death blow against her third enemy came again in epic fashion. In an odd, maniacal twist, the crowd gasped and cheered with delight as her strike with Nightfang quickly decapitated her third opponent in an oddly vicious sounding strike. They weren't necessarily cheering for her as their mortal enemy, but they appreciated true skill and battle prowess.

Before the head of her victim had even hit the ground, she wheeled around to face down her final opponent. The lone Dark Elf was covered in blood and had several deep gashes to both arms.

He was so injured that he could not lift his blades to defend himself. As she approached, he had no choice but to take a knee and drop his weapons in surrender.

The arena suddenly became noticeably colder, and the darkness intensified. A hush drew over the crowd like a suffocating blanket, and the only noise that could be heard was that of the crowd kneeling and bowing.

A lone voice broke the silence, "ALL HAIL THE DARK QUEEN!"

Lauriel watched as the dark entity walked out of the tunnel directly toward her. She was a Dark Elf with red eyes and long, flowing, white hair that looked partially spectral. She wore a crown of metal that had been so finely woven, that it looked like delicate but intricately spun spider webs. She was scantily clad with nothing but a sheer white gossamer gown that flowed around her. When she made it to the Dark Elf that had surrendered, she stopped and looked at Lauriel.

"Come finish what you started, woodland bitch."

It was not an ask; it was a command, and Lauriel felt an intense urge to do exactly as the queen commanded.

Lauriel walked closer to the kneeling Dark Elf and placed her scimitar against his neck. The Dark Elf looked up at her with calm, steady eyes, and exposed more of his neck.

"Do what you must," he said coldly.

Lauriel was surprised at the Dark Elf's calm and brave demeanor. She took a step back and moved her blade away from his neck.

"I will not, you have surrendered," she said.

The Dark Queen's eyes flared with an intense glowing red.

"How dare you defy me?" Her voice boomed throughout the arena.

"Do it now or you too shall die," she commanded.

Lauriel again fought off the intense urge to do exactly as the Dark Queen commanded. A cold shiver ran down her spine, and she began to shake as she spoke her next words.

"He has given up his swords; I will not."

Lauriel was suddenly slammed backward against a wooden post in the very center of the arena that had not been there moments ago.

She was wrapped so tightly in spider webs that she could hardly breathe. The Dark Queen held Nightfang in hand and the Moonblade rested at her feet.

"You surface elves and your rules," the Dark Queen hissed. "Down here, it is about power."

The Dark Elf's eyes suddenly opened wide, and Nightfang burst through his chest as the queen skewered him to the hilt. His eyes closed, and he sunk down in a pool of blood as she removed the blade from him. The Dark Queen walked up to Lauriel and pointed the bloody blade at her stomach. The cobwebs scurried out of the way of the queen's fury, leaving the area exposed.

"You come to MY realm and defy MY command! Yet, in the face of death you still refuse to kill the Dark Elf, your sworn enemy. Why would you do such a thing?" She slid the cobweb away from Lauriel's mouth with her long, black fingernails. Her mere touch sent another cold shiver down Lauriel's spine, but she also found the queen's power and majesty fascinating.

"I ... I don't know, I appreciated his skill and bravery. I was taught that it isn't right to kill someone, even a blood enemy, that has surrendered."

The queen stood for several moments with the point of the blade pressed against Lauriel. A small trickle of blood ran down her stomach.

Lauriel could hear the approach of someone from behind her, and by the sound of the slow, repeated thump on the ground, she could tell that it was the same old man that had ushered her into the arena. He came to a stop beside her and leaned on his staff.

"Thank you, Queen Seleniax, for allowing us to conduct the Bladerite. You know that it must be done in opposition."

"I shall hold you to your word, Terris," said the Dark Queen. "You will return the favor in due time if another opposing blade of power ever makes itself known."

"Yes, queen, of course, we will honor the ancient rites as they were agreed upon."

Lauriel was suddenly released from her bonds, and the queen handed her back the blade.

"You are skilled, pale one; if only you were mine. But you must hear me now for this is no part of your Bladerite. This affects us all, and we must set aside our opposition in this dark hour."

Lauriel looked at her intently and nodded in understanding.

The queen began again, "A nameless power has woken and rises to make war with our realm as well as yours. Its power is incomprehensible and eternal. If it makes it through the portal, no power here or in the heavens will be able to stop it. It is gathering strength as it manifests and summons its foul spawn. Each wave of them grows more numerous and powerful.

It is taking everything that we have to fight the entities coming through the portal, and we cannot hold them back for long. Every day, we lose ground. Every day, more of them get past our realm and wreak death and destruction in yours.

"I charge you, *Andúlarium*, if you complete your test and become the wielder of Isilmwé, you must rise up and help to meet this scourge upon us all."

Lauriel understood the significance of the request. In normal times, the queen would never stoop to ask for help from the surface, especially a surface elf.

This must be really dire!

Lauriel bowed respectfully to the Dark Queen. "Yes, Queen Seleniax, I accept this charge and will do everything in my power to help."

"Good … I will hold you to that," the queen said. She handed Lauriel a necklace made of fine silver that resembled a delicately crafted spider.

"This will allow you passage through the western gate into our realms. Toss it on the ground before the great gate."

Lauriel began to thank her but she was gone before she could say a single word.

She retrieved Isilmwé and continued through the arena exit with the old man. They walked down another long, stone corridor for quite some time when the old man broke finally broke the silence. "If you would have killed the Dark Elf that surrendered, you would have surely failed, and brought death upon yourself. You proved yourself to be of good moral character, a key trait that the blade requires; well done," he said.

"I am supposed to be impartial, but I had hoped that you would pass that trial of skill and character. If you finish, you will be the first female in the history of this blade to become Blademaster."

"Thank you, Mr. Terris, I hope that I don't let you down!" Lauriel replied. They shared a laugh together that temporarily broke the tension of the test.

"But … I'm not done yet?" Lauriel asked with a sound of concern in her voice. The old man smiled and didn't reply, and seeing that he would not answer, Lauriel changed the subject.

"Did Adamar go through these same tests?"

"No, Lauriel, he did not. He was the Bladewarden, keeper and custodian of the blade, not Master. He was charged with keeping the blade out of the wrong hands and hiding it away until the time came for a new master to rise and awaken the blade."

Lauriel nodded in understanding and continued down the corridor in silent contemplation.

The corridor ended in another small room that was about twenty-foot square. On the other side of the room there appeared to be a doorway that was shrouded in blackness.

The old man walked over to it and turned to her. "Good luck!" He smiled and then stepped into the blackness and was gone.

Lauriel, still weakened by the previous test, paused to catch her breath and strength. She had lost a lot of blood from the fight and knew that she could not survive another like it. She was also beginning to feel the weight and understand just how important that it was for a Blademaster to wake the blade, even if it was not her. But she desperately hoped to complete the test so that she could help stand up against the darkness and get her long-awaited revenge.

With a renewed sense of vigor and determination, she stepped through the darkness.

Lauriel was instantly blasted by an intense wave of heat that reminded her of opening the door to a baker's oven. It immediately began to leach the life out of her, and she knew that she could not survive long. She turned around, expecting to see the doorway that she had just passed through but there was nothing but solid stone.

She looked around to find that she was standing in a square stone alcove that was approximately twenty feet wide and twenty feet deep, with the far side open to a sheer cliff. The space had no other features except for a pile of sand by the far edge nearest the cliff.

A deep rumble rattled the very ground that she was standing on, and the stone wall on the side that she had just come through began to slowly move toward her.

The room is shrinking!

She tried her best to control her rising level of panic as she quickly searched for a way out. She ran to the far edge and looked down to see a river of molten lava several hundred feet below. The heat that rose up from the lava felt like a blast from a furnace. She could see across the divide to the other side, but the heat waves were so intense that it made it difficult to make out any detail. After a few seconds of concentrating, she could see a landing with a humanoid figure standing on it.

She determined that it was about thirty feet away but she couldn't find any kind of bridge, walkway, rope, or other means to span the chasm. She searched desperately for some hidden door or way to scale the cliff but found nothing.

The time that she spent searching was not kind to her. The rumbling continued, and the wall had moved about six feet closer to the edge. Her ears were beginning to blister, and every breath that she drew felt like it was slowly suffocating her.

She ran over to the pile of sand and began to dig through it. *Surely there must be some clue in the sand*, she thought to herself.

"Nothing!" she exclaimed bitterly. "What the hell am I supposed to do?" she yelled in frustration.

The wall was now only ten feet from her. She was in intense pain as she had endured just about as much heat as she could bear.

In desperation, she got down on her knees and started trying to feel if there was anything below the lip of the cliff. Suddenly, she hit something solid. *Something invisible!*

She didn't have any time to be excited; she felt like she was being cremated while still alive.

She had found something solid but invisible connected to the opening on her side but she couldn't tell where it went. She would burn to death before she slowly felt her way across it.

That's it! The sand!

She grabbed a large handful of sand and threw it in the direction that she thought the invisible surface went. Her heart leapt with joy as the sand that fell on the surface created a perfect outline of a two-foot-wide pathway that spanned the chasm below. She grabbed several handfuls, throwing the sand in front of her as fast as she could, each time farther and farther down the bridge path. She discovered a three-foot section right in the middle that was missing but she was easily able to jump over it. By the time she retrieved her last two handfuls, the wall was only two feet from the edge. As she got to the far edge of the walkway near the landing, she became dizzy and nearly passed out.

As she got close, she could see that the figure standing on the landing was the old man. He stood by another darkened door, casually smoking a pipe as if completely unaffected. Fearing that she would lose her balance while dizzy, she dropped to her hands and knees and crawled the last few feet of the bridge. As she made it to the landing, she had no time to hesitate or communicate with the old man—she had only seconds to live. With her last bit of strength and energy, she jumped up and sprinted through the darkened door.

* * * *

The air was cool and familiar, and Lauriel instantly felt a wave of relief even though the blistered burns were still causing her great pain.

She was standing back in the open glade with the silvery moon bathing her in its pure light. There was a note staked to the ground in front of her right where she had started. She took it and began to read. It was addressed to her and appeared to be hastily written.

The old man appeared next to her in the grove. "Congratulations, Lauriel Valendril! You have passed your final trial of wisdom and fortitude; Isilmwé is now yours to command.

"You have been gone for many days, and in your absence, much darkness has spilled into the land. You now have much responsibility and unfortunately that starts now. Rise now, Blademaster, take your weapons and defend the realms from this scourge."

Lauriel looked back down at the note: *Lauriel, Silenus is being attacked! Prepare yourself ... Vile Creatures.* She looked up with astonishment, and the old man was gone.

Now that she was refocused, she could hear faint screams coming from the town. Her blood ran ice cold as she thought about the vile creatures. She desperately fought off the urge to flee, but the screams of the dying drove her forward.

She was bloody, burned, and exhausted, but she sprinted toward the town as fast as she could, pushing herself far beyond any exertion that she had ever experienced.

When she rounded the final corner several minutes later, she saw a familiar sight. The four-armed beasts with their dog-like creatures were moving rapidly through town, destroying everyone and everything in their path. Her fear, and questions about whether she could face them again, was suddenly answered as it immediately gave way to unabated fury.

Her arrival caught the attention of one of the four-armed beasts and it charged at her. As soon as the two engaged, scimitars and claws erupted into a primal struggle for supremacy.

Her first strike fell with the ferocity of decades worth of planned vengeance, immediately amputating one of the creature's arms. It let out a loud roar and lashed at her with several vicious swipes.

But each one was met by the devastatingly keen edges of the finest blades that the realm could produce, and within seconds the creature fell to the ground as nothing more than a lump of putrid flesh.

It was not an easy fight—any given strike from the creature could easily extinguish the life of an enemy—but it did prove that they were not quite as indomitable as she had imagined.

Just then, she saw a large ball of fire encompass an area not too far from her. "Eldrin!" she shouted. She ran straight in the direction that it came from, but when she rounded the corner, she saw a site that made her heart sink. Several of the creatures had Eldrin and at least a dozen other hostages in their grip. The druid was lying in a pool of blood on the ground.

A cloaked and hooded figure the size of a large human stood in the center. Protruding from the darkness of the hood was a large beak that looked like that of a giant raven. In a strange whisper that she thought she heard in her mind, the figure spoke: *You will not stop us from emerging, for He is awakening. Surrender yourself and your blade and we will leave these pathetic creatures.*

Lauriel's mind raced as she tried to figure out the best course of action, and she pursued her best idea. She pointed the Moonblade at the cloaked figure. "I challenge you! If I win, you let them go."

The light of the Moonblade illuminated the creature's unusually large black eyes that had been hidden in the shadows of the hood. They were each about the size of a grapefruit and were so unnerving to look at that Lauriel subconsciously took a step backward.

One of the four armed creatures ripped one of the hostages in half in one fluid motion. The gruesome act reminded her of the scenes from her village, and tears began to stream down her face.

That is not how this works, she elf. Surrender or everyone dies.

Lauriel desperately tried to think of other options but could not come up with any that seemed feasible.

Unable to come up with another plan, she did something that she had not done since she was a child. She said a silent prayer to the Gods as she put down her weapons and raised her hands in surrender.

Please hear me, for whatever grace that you can extend to me, please do it now.

*   *   *   *

The town and everything else except the beaked figure faded away. She was standing back in the druid's grove with Eldrin and Gorian. Both looked startled at the sudden appearance of her and the strange creature, but the figure rapidly turned back into the old man before their eyes.

"Well done, Lauriel. You have faced up to your worst fears and you were willing give up that which is dear to you and sacrifice yourself in order to save other innocents that you didn't even know. You have passed the final trial of courage and valor. *Andúlarium* and sixth Blademaster of Isilmwé, Lauriel Valendril, you may now claim what is rightfully yours."

Lauriel walked over to the old man and he handed her the Moonblade. As she gripped it, it felt warm. She felt a surge of power and she suddenly understood the true properties of blade. She could feel an instant connection to the blade that transferred knowledge and emotion.

In a brief flash through her mind, she saw the entire history of the blade play out in seconds. She saw the creation of the blade, the previous five masters, one of them being Terris. She saw the significant battles, and the entire Swordsong.

Most importantly, she learned her obligation in wielding such an artifact. Lauriel stood trembling as she held out Isilmwé and looked at Terris. He winked at her in acknowledgement and disappeared.

The blade had heard its master's call, and both blade and master had awoken.

Swordsong of Lauriel Valendril

by Eldrin Aeramiril

With moon overhead and shining bright,
she begins the test of ancient Rite.
The blade she wields it tightly in hand
and down the path she slowly began.
And on this night she would not rest
for mortal a duel was deadly the test.

A trial so great that many would fail
but determined was she to surely prevail
through lethal combat with enemies old
with ancient blade of power untold
created by lords of distant past
the blade now wakes from sleep at last.

For she must bend it to her will
or she the blade would surely kill.
And if the blade should find her true,
it's power to her it would imbue.
So on she went into the night
her soul in balance through every plight.

The light flares bright and battle begins
her fury unleashed from somewhere within.
She wields her blades in deadly song
to prove her skill that she belong.
And dance she does in pale moonlight
her foes they reel at deadly sight.

Her determined pursuit she would not fail.
the Bladerite ends, she does prevail.
The blade now hers to freely draw
with power untold she stands in awe.
And humbled was she by blade so rare
accepting her solely as rightful heir.

The Wood Elf rises like legends of old
and begins her quest of tales untold.
And dragons will roar as she draws near
her Moonblade deadly they do so fear.
Now off to battle an ancient foe
her blade in hand she must now go.

CHAPTER THIRTEEN

Druid's Grove

orian ushered Lauriel and Eldrin to his house in the center of Lanéthym Forest. It was unlike anything that she had ever seen before. A giant Redwood tree rose high above all of the other trees in the forest. It was so large that it would have dwarfed even the majestic Silverwood trees from her homeland. Winding up the tree were stairs that ascended to a beautiful treehouse perched high above the forest canopy. The stairs and treehouse were so carefully crafted that they looked like a natural extension of the tree. The branches of the tree gently held the house in a loving embrace. When they reached the top, the view of the forest below was spectacular. The treehouse had a deck around it that afforded a full 360-degree view of the large forest glade and the lands far beyond. Lauriel wanted to enjoy the beautiful setting and the evening discussion about the quest, but she was so exhausted from the Bladerite that she had to rest and recover. Gorian had been able to use his druidic magic to help heal many of her wounds, but her body was still at the point of exhaustion. Lauriel had almost collapsed during the ascent up the stairs and Eldrin had to help her complete the climb.

* * * *

Eldrin and Gorian sat out on the large deck for many hours, enjoying their pipes in the evening tranquility of the grove; but it was hard for them to truly relax. Even in a place so far removed from the world's troubles, an uneasiness was beginning to grow in both of them. The portentous information that Lauriel had learned from the Dark Queen weighed heavily upon them.

"An existential threat is beginning to encompass the land, yet most of the unaffected surface realms sleep soundly in blissful ignorance this evening," Eldrin mused.

"Yes, Eldrin; I am afraid that they will all know soon enough. Hopefully it won't be too late," Gorian replied.

Eldrin discussed the quest with Gorian, explaining the need to go to the Plane of Discordance and how they would need to find the Amulet of the Planes to do so. He explained how he had found some evidence that the amulet could be found in Malthrax's Lair but had no luck finding any information on the dragon's location.

"Well, I might be able to help out with that, but it will take some time," Gorian offered. "As you know, a druid's domain covers a vast area. If there is a dragon in some area near one of my fellow druids, they would know about it. Give me a week to try and communicate with them and I'll see what I can find out. I will send the falcons, for they are the fastest."

"That will definitely help. We seem to keep running into dead ends," Eldrin replied.

The next morning, Lauriel woke up refreshed but not fully recovered from her many wounds. Gorian's limited healing had helped but it was not as focused and powerful as Nyx's. It was just enough though that Lauriel was able to make the short hike back with Eldrin to join up with the rest of the companions in Silenus.

While Eldrin and Lauriel were trying to find information at the library, the others had scattered throughout the town to gather the basic supplies that they would need for a long trip, as well as supplies to help them with their quest.

They had pooled all their spare money to buy the items that might help them survive an encounter with a Red Dragon. Dante was supposed to find a better Great Axe, Nyx was to buy magic potions, and Jexi was in search of information on Red Dragons.

Eldrin and Lauriel arrived back in town early and they decided to wait at the inn to let Lauriel get more rest. It wasn't until early afternoon that she felt well enough to get some food and drink from the pub below.

Nyx was the first to arrive. "Lauriel!" she shouted as she ran over and hugged her tightly, her face beaming with excitement. "You're still alive!" she exclaimed as she pulled back to get a better look. "Although from the looks of it, just barely!"

Lauriel was grateful for Nyx in her life, and equally happy to see her as well. It was rare to find someone that so genuinely cared for people. She hugged Nyx tightly but had to quickly let go as it began to cause pain.

Nyx took a careful look at the many wounds that Lauriel had received during the Bladerite test.

"Burns?"

"It's a long story! I'll tell you on the road," Lauriel promised.

"Well, it looks like it was pretty rough!" Nyx observed.

A soft blue glow encompassed Nyx's hand, and Lauriel immediately felt the warmth and relief that she had become accustomed to from Nyx's powerful healing spell. Lauriel immediately felt a surge of strength and vitality that completed her recovery.

"Ahh … thank you so much! I wish I could have taken you with me for some of that healing!" Lauriel exclaimed as she hugged Nyx again tightly.

Lauriel was about to speak again when she was interrupted by a gruff, booming voice behind her. "Well, do you know how to use that fucking toothpick yet?"

Lauriel turned and faced the barbarian who was taking up the entire doorway.

Feeling much more enthusiastic and in better spirits now that she was healed, she immediately responded. "Did you get rid of that piece of shit boat anchor of an axe you were carrying around?" With that statement, she finally got him to crack. He was surprised at her rare swearing that came so awkwardly to her. He grinned enthusiastically and dropped the sack of goods he was carrying as he ran up to her. He didn't even give her a chance to protest as he picked her up into a bear hug.

"Well; I'm glad you didn't die," he said.

She said nothing, completely unable to breathe.

As usual, Jexi was the last one of the group to show up.

"I see that you made it," she said as she walked up to the table. "Congratulations, Lauriel, I'm truly happy for you!" She gave Lauriel an inappropriately long and lingering hug and whispered into Lauriel's ear, intentionally loud enough for the others to hear, "This means that I still have a chance …"

Lauriel burst into laughter and shook her head. She was still unsure whether or not Jexi was serious, but she was beginning to get used to her quick wit and sense of humor.

Jexi released her and looked down at her sword belt. "Now, let's see this damn blade of yours that you almost got yourself killed for."

Lauriel looked around the bar and saw that it was getting crowded. "I think it might be best to get out of this town first, then I'll show it. How about you all?" Lauriel asked. "Did you get everything?"

"I got this sweet fucking axe!" Dante exclaimed as he grabbed the greataxe slung across his back and placed it across the table with a loud thud.

"They told me that it has the properties that you said to look for, Eldrin—magic AND an enchantment that makes the blade frost over as cold as ice." Dante said the command word to activate the enchantment and looked around proudly as the large blade of the axe frosted over.

"Great! I'm glad that you were able to find that; it will definitely help! How much did you get it for?" Eldrin asked.

"Uh, well ... I spent all of the money," Dante replied.

"What?" Lauriel gasped. "You had three hundred platinum and you spent all of it?"

"Please tell me you are joking," Eldrin probed, but he already knew the answer.

"Uh ... no, they told me it was on sale for one day only ... I thought it was a good deal and I didn't have time to wait and ask each of you. I didn't want to miss out on the sale," Dante explained.

Eldrin shook his head and rubbed his face with his hands in frustration. "It's nice but you shouldn't have had to pay more than two hundred!"

Dante's moment of proud elation was clearly over, and he was offended that they did not share his enthusiasm. "Uh, sorry!"

Nyx tried to help raise the mood. "Well, on the bright side, I was able to get three fly potions and five of fire resistance before he spent all of the money."

"Do they work against dragon fire?" Lauriel asked.

They all looked at each other in awkward silence. Finally, Jexi spoke up, "Well if they don't, we'll never know the difference!"

The joke drew no laughter from the others.

"A ... ny ... way ..." Jexi continued, "at least some of us didn't spend all of our money. I got what I needed for free. I was able to convince one of the Wizard School apprentices to find a book in the library for me since I don't have access to the 'wizards only' area."

She looked at Lauriel and Eldrin. "Speaking of libraries, I heard some rumor about wizard and a Woodland Elf fucking in the library. Have either of you heard anything about that?"

Lauriel and Eldrin turned bright red.

"What?" Lauriel exclaimed "But we weren't ..."

Dante did not catch on to Jexi's dead pan humor or subtle accusations, and he interrupted Lauriel with his outburst before she could finish.

"Fucking in the library! Who the fuck does that?" Dante shouted. His booming voice echoed throughout the room, and the pub suddenly got quiet. All of the patrons turned to stare at them.

Dante looked at Lauriel. "Damn, are you okay? You are awfully red."

Jexi paused for an uncomfortably long time and was silent as she seemed to relish in the awkwardness and embarrassment of Eldrin and Lauriel. "Well, anyway, I was quite surprised that he was able to find the specific book that I was looking for: *Councils on Dragons*."

She took the book out of her backpack and placed it on the table. The book had a black leather cover with an intricately embossed dragon adorning it. "I skimmed through it briefly, and it contains all kinds of descriptions about dragons. It's divided into two sections: Section one, *On Metallic Dragons*, and Section two, *On Chromatic Dragons*. I have started to read through the chromatic dragon section so I'll go over it with everyone along the way. Unfortunately, I've hit another dead end with trying to find any hint of Malthrax's location."

Eldrin, still embarrassed from Jexi's comment about the library, struck back, "So exactly how did you convince an apprentice wizard to do all that work for you for free, and risk getting kicked out of the Wizards' Academy by stealing a book for you sister?"

Jexi shrugged innocently and didn't answer.

Nyx broke out in laughter at his subtle accusation. Lauriel was still too embarrassed to engage in the conversation, and Dante simply sat with a look of confusion painted on his face.

Paths Less Traveled

One week of frustratingly little progress toward locating Malthrax's lair had gone by when the party received a carrier pigeon message from Gorian. He disliked coming into town so much that he requested that they meet him back in his grove. He had found "information that might be of interest to them."

Gorian met the party at the edge of the forest and ushered them back to the center of the grove. Lauriel had not noticed it the week before because of her exhaustion and near death from the Bladerite, but the grove teamed with an inordinate amount of natural woodland life. All manner of woodland creatures seemed drawn to the forest, and the grove had a sense of peace about it that reminded her of her homeland as a child. She felt the urge to stay and leave all of the dark troubles of the world behind.

As they came to the center, Dante, Nyx, and even Jexi were just as awestruck at the sight of the giant tree and treehouse as Lauriel had been.

They ascended the stairway and assembled in a small but comfortable parlor.

A large, detailed map was unfurled, covering the entire table.

"Well, we were able to narrow down the location to a region far from Silenus." Gorian tapped on the map on the far-left side.

Close inspection revealed the small mark and title: "Grand Duchy of Silenus." He then moved his finger all the way to the other side of the map and tapped on an area. "The Crimson Highlands," he said. "The area was once known as the Azure Highlands, which were said to be quite beautiful at one time. It once teamed with life and had lush rolling highland hills that would appear a bluish color in the distance.

"Over a period of several hundred years, the lush highlands slowly turned into a barren wasteland that was renamed for the red hue created by all of the small pools of lava that began bubbling to the surface.

I suspect that it might be from the corrupting regional influence of the dragon.

"A Red Dragon was said to have taken up residence in one of the many cavernous underground cave systems and had not been seen for hundreds of years—not because he is not active, but because everything with intelligence avoids the area and there is no real reason to travel to the remote area. It's a long shot, but there just aren't that many Red Dragons that we know of."

Eldrin leaned down to get a closer look at the area on the map that Gorian pointed out. "Hmm, that is very interesting, and our only viable lead." He looked back up at Gorian. "Does this map have many of the teleportation circles marked?"

"It should," Gorian replied as he pulled out two magnifying glasses and handed one of them to Eldrin.

"Like the one in the tower?" Lauriel asked.

"Yes, let's hope that we can find one close," Eldrin commented.

Dante pointed to the map where the Crimson Highlands were. "Why don't you just teleport us right here?"

"Good question, Dante. I am only able to teleport us to the teleportation circles. It is possible to teleport somewhere without them, but extremely dangerous unless you are intimately familiar with the place." Eldrin continue to expound, "There are a number of teleportation circles throughout the land, some of them quite ancient and even lost to memory. Most of them were created long ago during the Age of Magic. The circles have arcane properties that help focus the teleport and ensure that those intending to travel to them end up precisely at the teleportation circle that they mean to."

He drew a strange symbol on a piece of paper. "This is what we are looking for; it's the map symbol of an arcane teleportation circle. If it has the sigil sequence, I will be able to take us there."

"You will not find a map this detailed very often," Gorian said.

"The one downside is that it has so much information and detail, that it can be very difficult to find one small mark."

The group took turns looking over the map with the magnifying glasses, trying to find the closest symbol to the Crimson Highlands.

After half an hour of searching the map, the closest symbol they could find was in a place called Willowood Swamp, which was roughly two thirds of the way there. Luckily, the symbol also had the arcane spell sigils marked below it that were needed for the teleportation circle.

Lauriel's upbringing in the wilds provided her much insight into what they might expect based off of the map cartographer's detailed renderings. "That's still at least a three-week journey on foot, and if this map is correct, there are no towns or supply stops along the way. We will have to hunt to supplement our food, and if the Crimson Highlands are as sparse as they say, we'll really have to ration."

"And from the looks of it, getting there will be no easy task. Rivers, mountains, valleys, swamps, and forests lie between you and that dragon," Gorian observed.

"That is no accident on the dragon's part," Eldrin added.

Gorian nodded in agreement. "Well, tomorrow morning will come early, please stay here tonight as my honored guests."

The Steaming Grotto

The treehouse was not large, but it was accommodating enough for the companions to enjoy their last night of comfort for the foreseeable future. Gorian was a gracious host and provided a plentiful supply of food and fine wine to accompany his guests' stay.

Even though he ate almost four times more than anyone else, Dante remained unconvinced about the vegetarian meal and provided much entertaining banter back and forth with his host about the merits of meat over "eating fucking leaves."

After the meal, Eldrin pulled Gorian aside for a private word.

"Some of my fondest childhood memories are playing in the nearby hot springs when we would visit. It seems like just yesterday, doesn't it?"

Gorian smiled and shook his head. "Yes, those were good times. We had not a care in the world."

Eldrin continued, "I know it is a vital part of your grove, but if you don't mind …"

Gorian interrupted him before he could even finish. "Of course you can take her there."

Eldrin laughed and shook his head. "Is it that obvious?"

Gorian looked into the window and Eldrin followed his gaze just in time to observed Lauriel laughing lightheartedly with the others.

"Her smile brightens the room, and the great wizard cannot keep his eyes off of her," Gorian observed as if he were a narrating the scene.

Eldrin smiled and nodded.

Gorian placed his hand on Eldrin's shoulder. "I'll entertain the others."

As Eldrin hurriedly turned to retrieve Lauriel, Gorian added one last remark, "By the way, the springs are not the same as they once were, they are now the beating heart of Lanéthym Forest."

*   *   *   *

Lauriel's heart raced with an overwhelming excitement and anticipation that she had never before experienced with anyone else, as Eldrin held her by the hand and led her down the moonlit forest path.

His gentle yet secure grasp made her feel safe, desired, and cared for all at the same time, but it also brought to her mind the longing to have his hands all over her body.

"Not even a single clue?" Lauriel asked excitedly, trying her very best to break him.

Eldrin looked at her and smiled knowingly at her attempt. "You will see soon enough, *Ælfen*."

His sharp, lavender-eyed gaze coupled with his affectionate pet name caused the butterflies that already seemed to be flying in her stomach to rapidly multiply.

As they continued down the path, she found herself skipping like a little girl experiencing something for the first time. She began to think about their first kiss, and their blissful experience in the library, and the more that she let her thoughts race, the more she wanted to quickly reach their destination. She had never before felt such a desire to be so physically and emotionally connected with someone, and it was all new and exciting.

Her attention was suddenly drawn back to their surroundings when Eldrin stopped as the inconspicuous path that they had been on abruptly ended in dense vegetation.

She could hear the sound of moving water and could see that his eyes were alight with excitement.

"Okay, close your eyes. And no peaking!" Eldrin said quietly.

She nodded and complied with the playful game as he carefully led her through the dense leaves.

He stopped her and positioned her in front of him, placing his hands around her waist and drawing her near to him. His embrace was something that she felt she had always wanted but had never even known.

"Okay now," he whispered into her ear.

When she opened her eyes, her breath was taken away as she beheld the wondrous beauty, the likes of which she had never seen.

"Faeriefire Grotto," he breathed just above a whisper.

Steaming hot water poured from the mouth of a natural stone grotto that formed the backdrop of one of the purest and most unspoiled displays of nature that she had ever seen.

The crystalline water glimmered in the moonlight as it cascaded down a smooth rock formation and spilled into a natural pool of layered stones a short distance below.

To her amazement, it was not only the light of the moon that illuminated the grove, but an otherworldly blue-green glow that softly lit the pool from within. The luminance was just bright enough to highlight the constant steam that lazily rose into the heavens, giving the entire area a magical and mystifying ambience.

"The pool of radiance," Eldrin said.

"The flora that lives on the rocks under the surface of the water is called Faeriefire. It lives and thrives in the heat of the hot spring, and we believe that it is unique to this place."

"I didn't know that such marvelous places existed," Lauriel gasped in awe.

Eldrin led her to the water's edge, and her body tingled with excitement.

He drew her near and began to passionately kiss her. She immediately responded by wrapping her arms around his neck and returning the kiss with equal affection.

His lips moved slowly to her neck as he began to gently undress her, but he stopped before he had unlaced the first tie of her outfit.

"Is this okay with you?" he whispered.

She nodded in agreement, unable to get out anything more than a shy smile and a longing sigh.

They were soon inside the hot pool, and the rising steam seemed to become nature's own visual representative of the moment as their hands and lips continued to explore the new and exciting wonders of each other.

* * * *

The heavenly beauty of the grotto paled in comparison to the fairytale scene that played out before Eldrin's eyes.

The impossibly beautiful Woodland Elf looked like a deific forest nymph as she laid before him on the soft carpet of green grass that surrounded the radiant pool.

He could feel her body tremble slightly as she stared up at him with nervous anticipation.

"You, Lauriel Valendril, one who fears nothing, not even death, tremble?"

Lauriel suddenly looked shy. "This … is my first time; I don't know what to do."

Eldrin was again transfixed by her green eyes. The entire world could fall away, and he wouldn't even notice, nor would he care.

She did not have to say it, but Eldrin understood the significance of the moment. It wasn't just her first time, but it was the first time since childhood that she had let herself be completely vulnerable.

He kissed her again and whispered, "I don't either, but I'm sure that we will figure it out ... *Ælfen.*"

She seemed to relax at his reassuring words and gentle touch. She pulled him closer with her legs and whispered into his ear, "Good ... Sorcerer."

CHAPTER FOURTEEN

Willowood Swamp

The next morning, the party awoke early and readied for their journey. "I'm sorry that I will not be able to complete this task with you. I must stay and ready the grove. I have received word that the enemy is on the move and the hammer will fall hard here very soon," Gorian advised.

He handed a small, golden acorn to Nyx. "Please take this for your journey; I hope that it will help you along the way."

The gold was so pure that it was slightly transparent when held up to the light. Nyx inspected it closely and to her surprise, she could see a very tiny tree suspended within the gold inside of the acorn.

"If your journey becomes too taxing and you find yourselves in need of solace along the way, throw it upon the ground. It can only be used once so do so sparingly," Gorian instructed.

The companions descended from the lofty treehouse, spiraling around the tree many times, each step bringing them closer and closer to the ground. And when they finally got to the bottom, they were shocked by the sight that beheld them. The glade was full of the many forest animals that inhabited it.

"They can sense the subtle change upon the air and have assembled to stand in support, bidding each of you well on your quest," Gorian explained.

Timber wolves stood next to rabbits, all in harmony against the common threat. The scene was so moving that all of the companions were brought to tears. They all knew that these most innocent and majestic of woodland creatures would not be spared from the spreading darkness.

One of the large timber wolves walked forward and stopped just a few feet from Dante. The wolf had a thick, black, fur coat that changed to gray around its mouth. It had bright and intelligent hazel eyes that stared up at him intently.

It sat down in front of him, ceding his authority over the others to Dante. The wolf could see his many terrible scars and thought that he must be the greatest of warriors among men. Dante knelt down on one knee and held his hand out to the wolf. The wolf stood and began to lick his hand. Sensing the acceptance of the big man, he moved even closer and began to lick Dante's face as a sign of trust, acceptance, and respect. Lauriel stood speechless, knowing how uniquely rare the moment was.

"This is Midnight, and he is Alpha," Gorian said quietly. "He recognizes your strength, and wishes you well on behalf of all creatures here."

Midnight sat down and placed his large front paw on top of Dante's foot. He then raised his head toward the heavens and let out a mighty howl that echoed throughout the forest. To the amazement of everyone, it was not only the other wolves that answered him, but all of the animals in the glade began to call out in any way that they could. The rallying cry affected each of the companions deeply; they realized that they were not only fighting for their fellow man, but for all inhabitants of the realm.

Once all of the animals had slowly faded back into the forest, Eldrin reached into one of his spell component pouches and drew out the pure white sand, just as he had done before. After he created the circle, the group gathered inside of it and Eldrin began the strange words of magic.

* * * *

The teleport was not as bad as Lauriel and Nyx had remembered. The two were beginning to get use to the feeling and were learning how to deal with it, but for some unknown reason, Dante never seemed affected at all.

The teleportation circle that they suddenly found themselves standing on was made of many large flagstones that had been carefully placed on the ground to form a large circle. Just outside of the circle were eight very large stones that stood at least fifteen feet tall and were evenly spaced.

Lauriel looked at them in awe; she had spent a lot of time in nature, and it was difficult to fathom how the stones were even moved there in the first place. With her natural directional sense, she noticed that the four stones were lined up perfectly with the cardinal points—north, south, east, and west, with the other stones placed at the half cardinal points. They were heavily covered in moss and vines and had obviously been there a very long time. A few of them appeared to be leaning forward slightly from sinking into the wet ground over time.

The flagstone circle was on slightly higher ground than everything else around them and was the only thing that was dry. Just outside of the circle was a murky swamp that continued as far as they could see in every direction. The swamp had a rotten smell from the stagnant, green, scum-covered water. They immediately started swatting at the many large flies that were already harassing the new and tasty dinner that had just arrived.

"Welcome to Willowood Swamp," Eldrin said rather unenthusiastically.

The party set out through the muck with eager purpose, but the swamp quickly had a very demoralizing effect.

Every step through the stagnant water became a struggle against the sticky mud below, and every minute that they spent in the foul place brought with it more mosquito bites.

By the time the first hour passed, even Nyx had succumbed to a rare moment of complaint. "At this rate, the war will be over and we won't even know about it!"

She had been forced to use her divine magic several times to neutralize the poison from multiple snake bites.

Dante could see that she was having a terrible time navigating the swamp because of her small stature and decided to scoop her up and place her on his shoulders. The heartwarming sight of the big man helping the small halfling was the only positive experience for any of them.

After several hours of slogging, and with still no end in sight, Eldrin stopped his waterlogged companions.

"I hate to use any of my spells frivolously; I like to save them for when we really need them. But I'm about sick of this water. I think that it's time to see if I can find some dry ground."

They nodded in enthusiastic agreement, but Jexi's eyes narrowed slightly as he spoke.

He's oddly chipper for such a dispiriting place. What are you hiding, brother?

"How will you do that?" Lauriel asked.

Jexi's eyes opened wide in sudden understanding.

Ahh ha!

She just couldn't help herself. "You two seem to be full of cheerful energy. You must have had a great night's sleep at Gorian's."

Lauriel and Eldrin both flushed but were let immediately off the hook by Dante.

"Man, I barely slept a wink on that hard fucking tree bed."

Eldrin led the conversation back to the original subject. "I will be right back."

He began to speak his strange words of magic, and when he concluded, he slowly levitated above the swamp. Nyx, Dante, and Lauriel gasped at the strange sight, and Jexi rolled her eyes.

She knew the spell was a simple one that was taught to the younger apprentice wizards, but the others had never seen anything like it.

Eldrin continued to rise up in the air until he was far above the trees, and once there, he relayed to them what he saw.

"We are only about a mile away from a small rise. If we alter our course slightly to the northeast, we will intersect it."

The spell had a short duration, and he lowered himself to the ground.

Lauriel took the lead through the swamp and headed in the direction that Eldrin had instructed. Her natural agility and athleticism helped her navigate the swamp with considerably more ease than the others.

"Slow down, Lauriel, some of us didn't get laid last night," Jexi continued with her increasingly brutal assault.

Lauriel attempted the same tactic as Eldrin—avoidance. "At the speed we're traveling, it should take us about an hour to get to the rise. Since it's already early in the afternoon, we may want to get there and make camp well before nightfall. We need plenty of time to find dry firewood and kindling to keep the many swamp denizens at bay. It is already full of dangerous creatures, but will be far more dangerous after dark."

Nyx—Cleric of Corinne

As the party approached the rise, they found it was encircled by an area of water that was much deeper, and seeing no other good way to the higher ground but to travel through, Lauriel waded into the foul-smelling muck. She had made it halfway through when the water suddenly rippled outward in several directions.

"Lauriel!" Eldrin yelled.

A five-headed monstrosity rose up out of the water, sending waves rippling throughout the swamp. Its top side was a green color just like the swamp scum, and it had a cream underside that resembled the underbelly of a giant serpent.

Each massive head and neck had a similar appearance to the embossed dragon on Jexi's book, but it also had distinct serpentine features as well. Its gaping maw had large teeth meant to ensnare and swallow its unfortunate prey. It had large spines that ran from the top of its head down the center of each of its long necks.

The spines were covered in moss and scum from the swamp. Each of the heads and necks connected to a single large body with four powerful legs that propelled it through the water. It reared back its heads and lunged at them, attacking all five of them at the same time.

"Hydra!" Jexi yelled.

Lauriel was waist deep in water and unable to use any of her dexterity and combat maneuverability to dodge out of the way of the monster. One of the heads lunged at her, catching her left shoulder and clamping down on it with near bone crushing force. Its teeth penetrated her skin deeply, and warm blood began to run freely down her side. In one fluid motion, it yanked her out of the water and violently shook her. The second and third head attacked Dante.

He had not had the chance to drop Nyx, and she took the brunt of the second head's attack. The hydra snapped her up in its jaws and, sensing that she was the right size, attempted to swallow her whole.

It would have succeeded if one of its large fangs had not caught part of her leather armor. Dante was able to duck out of the way of the third head as it snapped its powerful jaws shut right where his head had been moments before.

The fourth head lunged at Eldrin, but just as it snapped at him, a shimmering force that appeared in a likeness as that of a translucent blue half-hemispherical shield instantaneously manifested directly in front of him, forming an area of protection that was just large enough to deflect the creature's head.

The fifth and final head attacked Jexi. It lunged at her, catching the armor on the side of her hip which absorbed much of the bite. She reacted by shouting a single word of magic, "Kira-snyl!" The hydra's head and neck erupted into flames that looked like they came straight out of the pits of hell.

The sudden eruption caused it to reel backward, letting go of Jexi and dropping Lauriel and Nyx back into the water. The flames only lasted a few seconds but left obvious burn wounds on the hydra's head and neck. It was clearly susceptible to fire.

Even though the puncture wounds on her right shoulder caused her severe pain, Lauriel did not waste any time attempting to attack the creature after splashing back into the water. She struck the creature with the Moonblade, allowing it to take its true appearance. The blade flashed brightly for a split second as if announcing to the world that it had arrived. It sliced deeply into the hydra's leg with her first attack, drawing a loud hiss and an immediate counterattack from one of the heads. She was able to duck away from the hydra's lunge, feeling the blade move with her in perfect counterbalance harmony.

The attack completely missed her, and she used the opportunity to counter-attack the head and neck as it was near her. Both blades cut deeply into the creature, causing the head to slump down and crash into the water as the life drained from it. She could hear Eldrin and Jexi saying words of magic but couldn't see Nyx.

Dante brought his greataxe down in a mighty swing that would have ended the battle for any normal creature. It struck the neck of the hydra's head that had been attacking him. The hydra counter-attacked, its mouth clamping down violently on his leg. But before the head could lift him off the ground, Dante finished his attack by burying the greataxe deeply in the center of its skull, causing it to release his leg as another one of the heads slumped into the water. In a blind rage, Dante continued to press his brutal offensive, swinging his axe furiously at the creature's torso.

Eldrin did not waste a single moment exploiting the creature's weakness as six rays of fire sprung from his outstretched hands and streaked toward the beast. Lauriel could feel the searing heat from them as they traveled over her head and slammed into the hydra's upper torso just below the necks.

Five of the rays found their mark, catching its skin on fire where each ray hit. The monster reeled back, and another one of the heads crashed into the water.

Jexi finished her spell as the monster was still reeling from Eldrin's fiery assault. Giant spectral chains manifested in the air around it and began to wrap around the beast's heads, necks, and torso in several directions.

Within a few seconds, the glowing chains bound and constricted the hydra so tightly that it couldn't move at all. It couldn't even hiss at them. One end of the chain extended into Jexi's hand as if she held a small, submissive puppy on a leash. "There now, nothing quite like being restrained," she quipped.

Her ribald humor and blasé attitude never seemed to change, even in battle.

Eldrin observed that the chains were not physical but made up of some type of magical force. It had the same effect as his "Hold

Monster" spell, but all of her spells had her own special flare and style. She didn't have the broad and diverse spell abilities that Eldrin had, but the ones that she did have seemed particularly potent and focused.

Lauriel wasn't sure what was more disturbing, the huge hydra standing motionless, doing nothing but blinking at them, or observing Jexi's bliss as she held fast the creature with her spell.

"This won't last long!" Jexi yelled at the temporarily motionless party.

Lauriel and Dante quickly resumed their attacks on the motionless creature, to devastating effect.

Between Lauriel's unabated scimitar onslaught, Dante's greataxe, and another fiery spell from Eldrin, the remaining two heads of the hydra crashed down heavily into the water.

It wasn't good enough for Dante. He kept chopping at the beast furiously with just as many cuss words flying out of his mouth as there was blood flying from the dead creature.

"Where is Nyx!?" Eldrin shouted.

They suddenly realized that there was no time for group celebration.

"She fell near me by the other leg. I thought she swam out!" Lauriel exclaimed.

"No, I didn't see her after that!" Jexi said.

Lauriel immediately dove down into the water where she had seen Nyx fall. She could not see anything in the murky, bloody swamp and was becoming increasingly desperate as she searched around blindly. It was then that she felt a strange and unexpected sensation. A sense of peace and calm washed over her, and she suddenly knew exactly where to go. She swam blindly but in a straight line to Nyx and found her still trapped under the hydra's giant, scaly foot. Its dead weight was pressing her into the mud on the bottom.

Nyx had been trapped for well over a minute and grabbed onto Lauriel's hand frantically. Lauriel pulled with all her might but Nyx didn't budge. Nyx's grasp began to weaken and then went limp as she lost consciousness. Lauriel surfaced. "HELP! SHE'S TRAPPED RIGHT HERE!"

"Nyx!" Dante roared. His face was distraught, and his eyes were red and full of tears.

He crashed through the water furiously, making it to Lauriel with incredible speed. They each took a deep breath and dove down into the dark water. Lauriel quickly guided him to Nyx's location. It was only seven feet deep but not being able to stand greatly hindered their leverage.

He grabbed the hydra's huge leg and began to lift with all of his might, slowly sinking into the mud on the bottom of the pond. Lauriel could hear his distressed yell as it traveled through the water. She could feel the impossibly heavy creature begin to rotate slowly as he continued his herculean effort, and she frantically pulled at Nyx with all of the strength and determination in her.

* * * *

The party sat on the dry ground of the rise for several minutes, silently reflecting on the close call.

They were not long into their quest, and the experience was a brutal reminder of just how difficult and dangerous the rest of it might be.

Nyx had been pulled out just in time, regaining consciousness shortly after Lauriel and Dante got her to the rise. Ten more seconds and she would have never made it out of the swamp. Her near death took away any elation of a great victory against the hydra.

Dante finally broke the pensiveness in an eloquent summary of what all of them were thinking.

"I can't wait to get out of this fucking swamp."

The statement did not even draw any laughs or feedback, only quiet head nods in full agreement.

* * * *

It wasn't until everyone was warm and dry from Lauriel's fire that the gloom that hung over the group finally began to lift. The campfire had the effect that Lauriel intended, hedging away the dreariness of the swamp and giving the party a needed morale boost. Nyx finally broke the long silence as she walked over to Dante and gave him a big hug. "Thank you for saving me."

He tried to hide the tears in his eyes, but the sight of the big man brought to tears by five words from the small halfling was enough for all of them to join him.

She went next to Lauriel and embraced her.

"Well, I guess my prayers were answered," Nyx said.

"What do you mean?" Lauriel asked.

Nyx replied, "I didn't know what else to do. I was quickly running out of air and so I prayed to my Goddess Corinne that someone would be shown where to find me."

More tears welled up in Lauriel's eyes, and goosebumps appeared on her skin as she recalled the clear and unexplained feeling of being led to Nyx.

She looked at Nyx and tried to speak but could only get out three words. "She was listening …"

CHAPTER FIFTEEN

The Will-o' Wisp

fter two more grueling days, the party finally made it through the swamp. They were waterlogged, demoralized, and exhausted, but the mood quickly changed once they were on dry ground and making good progress. They were now beginning to traverse through a lightly forested area, and Lauriel was fully in her element. She navigated them toward their destination with great ease, pushing hard over the next seven days to make up for their lost time in the swamp. But with each passing day, the sense of urgency grew ever more persistent in their minds.

As the party sat around the small campfire and rested from another long day of travel, Jexi pulled out the book on dragons that she had acquired and began to read sections of it aloud. Lauriel, Dante, and Nyx had never seen or heard of a live dragon outside of fairy tales, and they all listened intently.

Jexi flipped to Section two of the book that detailed "Chromatic Dragons" and began to read: "Chromatic Dragons are most commonly known to be White, Black, Green, Blue, and Red. Each dragon type has their own specific type of breath weapon and abilities."

She skimmed further through the section, reading aloud only the important points. "Just the mere site of a dragon can cause one to flee in uncontrolled panic."

"Ha!" Dante interrupted. "I ain't running like a little bitch!"

Jexi slowly rose to her feet and kept reading while Lauriel and Nyx gave him the evil eye. Eldrin shook his head.

"Uh-oh," he mumbled.

Without missing a beat, Jexi switched casually from reading the book in the common speech, to speaking in some strange language as she began to stare directly at Dante.

"Uh … present company excluded, I didn't mean—" before Dante could finish, Jexi completed her spell and Dante was suddenly encircled by floating, translucent green skulls that began to whirl around him. His eyes grew wide as he looked at Jexi with a look of horror on his face. He fell backward off the log that he was sitting on and desperately tried to get away from her as if she were some demonic Pit Fiend. He tried to run twice and stumbled, unable to get his legs under him. Finally, after the third attempt, he was able to stand and ran as far away from Jexi as he could.

Jexi sat back down and continued as if nothing happened. "Ahh, here we go. Chapter five of Section two, Red Dragons."

"Wait! What did you do to him!? I've never seen him scared of anything!" Lauriel questioned nervously.

Jexi couldn't hold her laugh any longer as she told the group what she had done. "It's one of my specialties, a warlock Fear spell. It's sort of like a wizard Fear spell, but much more focused and much more intense. I would hate to be on the receiving end of it," she concluded with a smirk.

"How long will it last?" Lauriel asked.

"Probably a minute or so, we'll see how far he can run during that time," Jexi replied.

"Oh my goodness he's going to be pissed!" said Nyx, a look of both concern and amusement was on her face.

Jexi continued, "A Red Dragon is terribly covetous and vain. It is the fiercest and most cunning of all Chromatic Dragons."

"Of all the dragons, it had to be a red one," Nyx mumbled.

"Their breath weapon is fire, and it becomes more and more powerful with age, and by the time they reach the height of their power, they are able to melt solid stone." Jexi put the book down. "How old is this dragon, Eldrin?"

"I'm not sure, but we believe that he is about 350 to 450 years old," he replied.

Jexi flipped through several more pages. "According to this, he is at least a mature adult." She sighed and closed the book. "Well, enough of that tonight. There is plenty more to learn along the way. I know it is overwhelming, but the more we learn, the better chance we have to beat this thing."

Lauriel tried to rally the group morale after Jexi's words fell upon them like a portent of doom. "I just have to believe that we can! Remember how much is at stake here. For some reason, this great task has fallen to us."

* * * *

The wilds were a dangerous place, and it was important for the safety and survival of the group that someone stay awake and keep a watch out for things that could come lurking through the night. It was three hours past midnight when Lauriel woke up fully rested and ready to take her turn for the last night watch that would continue until the first rays of sunlight began to dance across the clear morning sky.

She walked over to the log by the fire that Dante was sitting on and patted him on the shoulder, letting him know that she was ready to relieve him.

He was still fuming at Jexi's Fear spell, and the entire group was guilty by association.

Without a word or glance in her direction, he stood up and went back to his bedroll. Lauriel knew that he was embarrassed more than anything, and she did not take the snub with offense.

She had only been on watch for a little less than an hour when her heart skipped a beat at the familiar sight from her childhood. A Will-o' Wisp came down from high in the tree where it had been camouflaged against the starry backdrop. It hovered in between the trees just outside of the camp, and she could hear the faint but unmistakable buzzing sound. She somehow instantly knew that it was the very same one that she had chased so long ago.

She stood up and walked toward it, following it into the nearby woods as it withdrew from her in the same playful manner that it had done when it led her away from certain slaughter. They did not travel far before Lauriel stopped. "If you are leading me away from danger again, I thank you, but I will not leave my group. What is it that you want of me?"

The Wisp stopped, hovering five feet above the ground. She heard a clear, melodic voice in her mind.

That is exactly why I choose you, Lauriel. Your loyalty and dedication to those around you. You are willing to protect them above all else, even at your own peril. The voice paused briefly before continuing, *You called to me once, in the vineyard as the creature looked for you. Do you remember?*

The scene flashed through Lauriel's mind like a dreaded nightmare. She could see herself lying under the grapevines as the dog-like aberration sniffed for her. She could see her lips moving in silent prayer, praying desperately that she would not be found. Her heart pounded wildly at the memory as she tried to choke back the emotion before responding.

"I do, but I don't recall anyone coming to help me save the village."

The Wisp started to expand and reform, taking on a vague humanoid shape that appeared to be made of softly glowing light.

A feeling of peace and warmth radiated outward from the figure, instantly snuffing out any fear and emotions that were invoked from the memory.

She could now hear the calm, melodic voice out loud as the entity continued to speak to her. "You did precisely what you needed to do to live, Lauriel. That was not your fight—not yet anyway."

The statement from the glowing entity had an immediate and profound effect upon Lauriel. She had never been able to come to terms with her inaction that night, and the guilt still weighed heavily upon her after all this time. The entity's statement carried with it a certain authority, and it somehow lifted the great burden of guilt from her.

Lauriel suddenly understood what she had so long struggled with. Doing nothing WAS the right decision for her at that time. She had desperately sought forgiveness for her inaction but it was not forgiveness that she needed. It was acceptance of the fact that she didn't cause the slaughter, nor could she have done anything at all to prevent it.

"You called to me again, in the last fight of your Bladerite, when the blade seemed lost. Do you remember that also?" the voice asked.

"I do remember, but again, you did not show yourself to me," Lauriel replied.

"I did hear you, Lauriel, but the Bladerite was your test, not something for me to cheapen by intervening."

Lauriel suddenly felt ashamed for even bringing up such a petty insignificance to the marvelous entity.

The glowing figure continued to take form and manifested into a woman of singular grace and beauty. She had flowing auburn hair and elven-like facial features, but she was much taller than any elf. She wore green scale armor that looked like it had been made from transparent emeralds, and a brightly glowing mace that pulsated with sublime power rested at the side of her hip. She wore an intricately crafted golden circlet on her head that was accentuated by clear green stones that also glowed. Her piercing green eyes matched that of her armor and reflected the infinite years of wisdom. Her power and authority rippled outward from her as if claiming dominion upon all lesser beings.

Lauriel could immediately feel the numinous presence radiating from her and knew that she was no mortal. She unwittingly took a knee and bowed deeply in reverence and respect.

"Who ARE you?" she gasped.

The entity's voice was now clear and authoritative. "I am Kathele, Goddess of Elfkind and the Fey. The time has come for champions of the mortal realms to rise up and protect those that are weak and defenseless from the coming darkness. You have called upon me, Lauriel Valendril, and I have heard you.

"I call upon you now, Blademaster, *Andúlarium*, and Daughter of the Woodland realm, the realm that I created. You shall seek vengeance against these abominations for the terrible things that they have done to you and your kind. They cannot be allowed to continue, for they are not of this realm and surely seek to destroy it. You shall smite down those creatures that rise against you, exacting my divine retribution upon them. As my champion, you must stop them before it is too late, even at the cost of your own life, for the path that I offer you is exceedingly perilous and not even I can guarantee your safety." The Goddess continued, "This task is up to mortals, for the Gods can only empower them to help themselves. Only if the Nameless One makes it through the Nexial Gate can we intervene, but it would be to the destruction of all things, ourselves included."

Lauriel stood in awe, trying to understand all that she had just been told.

The Goddess stepped toward Lauriel. "If this is the path that you choose, Lauriel Valendril, you must do so of your own free will. What say you, Blademaster?"

Lauriel stammered, trying to find her words. "I ... I ... This is exactly what I choose! Yes! I want nothing more than this!"

The Goddess smiled warmly at Lauriel's enthusiasm. "Very well, woodland daughter."

She drew her mace and it crackled with an eldritch energy that Lauriel could not even comprehend. The Goddess touched it to Lauriel's shoulder, and she suddenly felt the divine connection to the Goddess, with no veil remaining between them.

"Go forth, my champion, fulfill your destiny and become what you were meant to be. But remember, with great power comes great responsibility."

* * * *

The connection with her Goddess afforded her several new abilities that she knew and understood immediately. She gained an ability to channel a fragment of the Goddess's wrathful energy into her attacks, infusing her weapons with devastating eldritch power that she could unleash upon her opponents as she struck them.

She also learned how to draw upon the divine power of the Goddess to heal and cast several divine spells that could aid her in battle against her enemies. The healing abilities were just like Nyx's divine magic, but much more limited. Nyx was a true Cleric and well-practiced at drawing upon her own Goddess's power, and Lauriel was not.

The Goddess placed her hand on Lauriel's shoulder. "Power is earned, not freely given, and through practice and devotion, you will learn to draw increasing power to heal your allies and smite your enemies. But until then, you will only be able to wield a small amount."

Lauriel nodded in revered silence and understanding.

"Go now, and finish your quest. Your path is narrow and fraught with danger, and the slightest misstep could end your journey in this world.

But that very path that you and your companions travel may very well be the last beacon of hope that is needed now in the realms of mortals."

The Goddess disappeared, and Lauriel stood alone in the dark forest until the break of dawn, contemplating all that had happened.

She replayed each word that the Goddess had told her over and over in her mind. She had many conflicting feelings that she tried to sort through. She felt a sense of peace that she had never known since her childhood. She now had freedom from her past, from her guilt, from her traumas. She felt the enormous pressure and importance of their quest, which weighed upon her now more than ever. She also felt the spark of power that was beginning to turn into an inferno. No longer was she too weak and powerless to help make a true difference.

As the first rays of sunlight crept across the sky, she walked back into the encampment, forever and profoundly changed.

CHAPTER SIXTEEN

A Wing and a Prayer

Eldrin was usually the first one to wake and greet the person assigned to the watch duties. He used the quiet time to study his newly acquired book on the Plane of Discord and to memorize his spells. He had a vast number of spells that he could choose from, but his magic was limited; so he had to choose wisely which ones to prepare for the day.

He took pride in his uncanny ability to always have the perfect spell for the occasion, and he was quite renowned in the various wizard circles for it. Some were convinced that he had the supernatural ability of foresight.

"Good morning, *Ælfen*," Eldrin whispered as he stood to greet her.

She was returning from the nearby woods, and he immediately noticed the glimmer in her eyes and the lighthearted spring in her step as she approached him.

With only a tantalizing smirk as a forewarning, she leapt up on him just like she had done in the library and began to passionately kiss him. But even in the moment, Eldrin could sense something was different about her. She had a certain ease and relaxation, but he also felt a new and inexplicable energy from her that he did not understand.

"I don't know how else to describe it, but you have a lighthearted and carefree look about you this morning ... an extra spring in your step, but something else is different that I cannot place," Eldrin said quietly.

"I guess I just woke up thankful to be part of this quest. Now … let's go kill a dragon," Lauriel said.

Eldrin was too smart to buy into the answer, but he let it go. He knew it was not the time to pry even though his curiosity was getting the best of him.

The rest of the party began to wake up and discuss the day's agenda over breakfast. Dante had time to cool down and seemed to have completely forgotten that he was mad at the group. The only thing he was upset about was the meager rations.

"You going to eat that?" he asked Lauriel.

Lauriel smiled and passed him the remainder of her breakfast as she began to brief the group about the expected journey.

"Based off of a rough sketch of Gorian's map, we should come across a large river very soon and cross into the Hinterlands beyond it. The light forested area will slowly turn more mountainous and rockier over the next week of travel. Once past the Hinterlands, there will be significantly less opportunity to hunt for food; so we will be even more reliant on our rations from that point forward."

The party took stock and determined that they had enough rations to last another week if they were careful. They only needed enough food to get there, and Eldrin would teleport them back to the Tower of Silenus teleportation circle.

Lauriel began the twelfth day of their journey in high spirits. She was light on her feet, and the party struggled to keep up with her. They were encouraged by her newfound zeal and determination but were quickly fatigued by the grueling pace. Still, they pushed onward to the point of exhaustion. With each passing day, the sense of urgency and weight upon their shoulders continued to grow.

They had no news from the outside world and could only guess how bad it was getting as the "vile creatures" spilled through the Nexial Gate in ever increasing numbers and power.

By midday, the party stood upon the banks of the Darmansk river, one of the last named features on Gorian's map. Beyond it lay the Hinterlands, the gateway to the Crimson Highlands. The river was much larger than they had anticipated, at least one hundred feet across at the narrowest point. The water was deep and roared past them with incredible power, making it far too dangerous to cross on foot.

"Well, this is just as good of a place to practice as any," Eldrin said. "I'm going to cast a Fly spell on us. I have to use a lot of my spell energy for the day to make all of us fly at the same time, so we won't be able to do this very often. Lauriel and Dante, each of you need to take the opportunity to practice so you know how to move yourselves through the air when you drink the fly potion before the dragon fight. Flying is a little disorienting at first, and my spell only lasts ten minutes, so make absolutely sure that you are down before the spell runs out."

"How do we know when it is about to run out?" Nyx asked.

"You will feel the energy starting to fade and will have one minute before it goes away completely, so make certain that you are down in time!" Eldrin stressed his point again.

After receiving nods of understanding, he continued, "Okay, let's have a little fun!"

As he finished casting his spell, it felt like the weight of the world suddenly fell away from them, and with it, their worries and cares.

They flew around awkwardly, laughing like children at a playground. Neither Nyx, Dante, nor Lauriel had ever experienced flying before. The feeling of the wind rushing by them as they flew effortlessly through the air was exhilarating. Lauriel and Nyx caught on quickly and learned how to control their movements. Dante was a bit slower and eventually caught on, but only after he had smashed into three trees.

Jexi had used her own warlock magic to fly, but in typical spectacle, her spell had yet another unique and maleficent twist away from the wizard's arcane Fly spell.

When she finished her incantation, huge dark red spectral wings suddenly sprung from her back, casting a baleful shadow on the ground as they slowly waved back and forth. Their demonic-like form appeared to give her the same ability to fly but also gave her a sinister, fiendish appearance that she was obviously proud of. The sudden site of her shocked the other companions and dismayed Nyx, but they had learned to expect nothing less.

Lauriel drew her scimitars and began to dance in the air with them, laughing lightheartedly as she did. The sight of her carefree moment was too much for Eldrin and he flew up next to her. "What do you think, *Ælfen*?"

"It's wonnnnderful!" she exclaimed as she turned in a slowly rotating backflip while sheathing her blades.

He took her by the hand and pulled her close. "You have mastered this quite quickly! I bet you have never done this ..." He pulled her even closer and continued the rotation as he began to kiss her. She held onto him tightly and whispered into his ear, "There are a few other things I would like to try while doing this ..."

Eldrin almost choked as he tried to find his words. "Well ... uh ... I do have an Invisibility spell," he said in a half-joking, half-serious stammer. He had no idea if Lauriel was serious or flirting with him.

As if right on cue, they could hear Jexi in the background. "Get a room!"

Lauriel laughed and looked at Jexi while still holding tightly onto Eldrin. "Something tells me that she could still see us." She kissed Eldrin briefly and then leapt off of him in another slowly rotating backflip.

The ten minutes seemed to go by in the blink of an eye, and when the spell's duration ended, the party stood on the eastern bank of the Darmansk river—with one notable exception.

Dante had become so distracted that he had forgotten to fly over and was forced to crash land into the water ten feet from the western bank as he tried to make it over just as the spell wore off. He was barely able to make it back to the bank without being swept away by the powerful current. Clearly exasperated, Eldrin was forced to use even more of his limited daily well of magic energy to bring him back.

Once they both got over the eastern bank, it did not take long for Eldrin to cool down as they all shared a laugh at Dante's expense. He was soaking wet and had a bloody nose from flying into the trees. It looked like he had been in a fist fight that had tumbled into the water. Even with his bruised face and ego, Dante stood with a broad smile on his face that warmed everyone's hearts.

The companions were all in high spirits and decided to take a break for lunch.

"Are you sure we can't do that again?" Lauriel asked enthusiastically. She had asked in such an unintentionally cute way that Eldrin had almost no willpower to resist the request.

"Well, I would love to but I need to make sure to save enough magic to fight off a random hydra or whatever else stands between us and that God forsaken dragon." He looked directly at Dante. "I have already had to use way more than I intended to."

Dante sat and ate his lunch in blissful ignorance. He looked up at Eldrin's accusatory stare. "Huh? Are you going to eat the rest of your lunch?" Dante asked as he pointed at the remainder of Eldrin's uneaten food, clearly oblivious to the conversation.

They all couldn't help but share another laugh at his expense.

Lauriel looked back at Eldrin and sighed, a subtle mischievous smirk on her face as she tried to change his mind.

"Well, your loss."

"You have been spending way too much time with Jexi," Eldrin teased.

Jexi looked up with an innocent look of shock on her face. "Whatever do you mean, brother?"

They continued their lighthearted banter until they set out again in earnest after their brief lunch break. The lowlands slowly began to fall away as they continued eastward into the Hinterlands.

They gained in elevation with each passing hour and could feel a chill in the air that they had not felt at any point in their journey. The night would be very cold, but they had packed appropriately, each of them bringing heavy cloaks to use if needed. It was autumn and the leaves on the trees were in full glory. They lit up the landscape with brilliant yellows, oranges, and fiery reds. The colors blanketed hill after hill and created strikingly beautiful scenery, the likes of which many of them had never seen. Lauriel loved being in the untamed wilderness. It was unmarred by humans and very much like the wilds that she grew up exploring. It was hard to fathom that they would soon pass from such beauty and serenity to a land suffering from the corruption of such a terrible presence.

The day passed quickly, and the sky began to turn a deep purple as the sun sunk well below the tall hills on the horizon. The quickly gathering evening was quiet and peaceful, but they each had a feeling like it was the calm before a storm.

The party drew around the warm campfire, and Jexi pulled out her book. She knew that hearing about the power of dragons had a demoralizing effect, but they were closer now and needed to finish learning all they could in order to come up with a plan.

"I have read through this several times while it was my turn for watch so I'll spare you the intricate details and read a few things that I found important. Red Dragons are highly intelligent and can cast arcane spells."

Eldrin's eyes opened wide. "What spells do they have access to?"

"Unfortunately, it doesn't say," Jexi replied. She continued, "Normal weapons will not pierce through the tough dragon scales; they must have magic properties that augment their power."

Dante interrupted, "Well thank the Gods we got this axe that y'all were bitching about before we left. I'd be fucked!"

Jexi rolled her eyes and continued on, "However, even the most powerful blades have a difficult time piercing a dragon's tough scales." Lauriel drew her blades in cold confidence and held them up to the light of the fire. "That may be true, but I wonder if that applies to two Vorpal blades?"

"For the sake of all of us, let's hope all of them can find their way through," Eldrin replied.

"We will find out soon enough," Jexi added.

After listening intently to all that Jexi had to read about dragons, the party set watches and went to sleep.

* * * *

The night was cold, and it was Jexi's turn for the watch. She placed another log on the fire and looked around at the sleeping group. Dante almost always had a fitful sleep, but it was Nyx that caught her attention. She began to thrash around and cry out in unintelligible words. Jexi walked over and shook her out of the night terror. Nyx awoke suddenly and began to shake, tears rolling down her face. "That is not the first time that you have had that dream, is it?" Jexi asked.

"No," Nyx replied, burying her head in her hands and sobbing quietly.

"Tell me about it."

Nyx shook her head. "It's just a bad dream."

"Dreams can be a powerful premonition or message. Please … share it with me, even if it is unpleasant," Jexi coaxed.

"Well, I'll try."

"I've had the dream three times now. The first time was when we were in the swamp. It was after we fought the hydra and I just thought that it was a reaction to my near drowning. The next time was after we were in the forest again. It was the night that you first read to us about Red Dragons.

"Again, I thought that it had to do with my worry about that. The third time was tonight. You did read about dragons, but I don't know what it is.

It feels much more real than a terrible nightmare!" Her eyes again welled up with tears. "I wish it would just go away; it is so scary!"

"Describe it to me. I know that it is difficult but tell me every detail," Jexi urged.

"Well … I am in a shadowy room that is very dark. I cannot see very well, but I know that the room is massive. I am scared out of my wits and want to run but can't move a muscle. Suddenly, I see something move. Dark, shadowy wings rise up in front of me and blot out any remaining light. They are huge and take up my entire sight. Suddenly the room seems small, and I feel trapped and claustrophobic. It is terrifying, Jexi! That's when I wake up. What do you think it means?"

Jexi pondered for several moments. "Did you die in the dream?"

"No I didn't, it ends there every time," Nyx replied.

"Dreams can be difficult to decipher, but if you had the same dream three times, I do not believe it is coincidence. I would consider it a premonition or a warning. We just need to figure out the meaning. Deep down in your soul, what do you feel that it means?" Jexi asked.

Nyx looked down at the ground and spoke in a hushed tone. "I have had a sick feeling in the pit of my stomach ever since we teleported to the swamp. I feel like something bad is going to happen and I don't know what.

"I have prayed repeatedly that if it is to be, let it be me. I'm so scared!" She burst into tears and looked back down.

Nyx's self-sacrificing statement shook Jexi to the core. Never before had she experienced such selfless concern for the well-being of others. Her respect and admiration of Nyx was high but grew with each passing moment. Jexi hugged Nyx and tried to comfort her. "We choose our own paths in this world and they are not predestined. Even if this dream is a premonition that the path we are on will lead us to experience something terrible, I would have rather lived with purpose and died trying to help than died not having tried at all."

Nyx found Jexi's statement equally profound and awe inspiring. It was then that she could finally see Jexi's true character. Beneath her exterior facade of a carefree and apathetic spirit, rested an unbelievably strong, determined, brave, and caring soul.

It gave Nyx hope, for as long as there were still people like Jexi in the realm, they still had a chance against the darkness. The two sat and talked until sunrise, each having a newfound respect and understanding of one another.

*   *   *   *

The next morning, the party set out toward the Highlands. It became increasingly difficult to make good time as the party had to navigate around jagged crags and steep ravines.

It was around mid-morning when Lauriel crested the rise just ahead of the group. It opened into a large mesa with beautiful views in all directions. But it was not the views that caught her immediate attention—an aerie of griffons had made the mesa their home.

Lauriel had heard of them in elven legends but had never seen one. They were both majestic and frightening, with heads and wings like that of giant eagles, pure white as new snow. Their muscular bodies were golden in color and resembled large lions. Lauriel guessed they were around eight feet long.

There were six adults and five smaller griffons that appeared to be adolescents. The smaller ones were all feeding on a deer that had been brought to them. Each of the griffons had razor sharp talons and an equally formidable beak.

Lauriel froze, hoping not to startle them, but it was too late. One of them saw her at the same time that she saw them and let out a loud warning cry. *SCREECH!*

All six of the adults quickly darted to the edge of the aerie, placing themselves as a phalanx in between the intruders and the adolescents.

The rest of the party topped the rise just in time to see the griffons line up in formation. Seeing more intruders, the convocation of griffons erupted into a cacophony of shrieks and aggressive stomps and wing flaps. Lauriel took a step forward and raised her hands away from her weapons.

"We mean no harm," she said in elvish.

One of the griffons cautiously stepped forward toward Lauriel. The sight of the majestic beast standing nobly on the hilltop brought a childhood bedtime story about a griffon and an elven princess to her mind. She could remember it vividly, just as Adamar had told her ...

Many centuries ago, when the princess was still a very young girl, she wandered off and got hopelessly lost in the woods. She was so small and left so little trace of her passing, that not even the best elven rangers could find her. As she wandered aimlessly, she stumbled upon a griffon resting in a small glade. She was terribly frightened by the creature and thought to run when she suddenly heard a female voice in her mind, "What are you doing here, child?"

She replied to the creature in the same mind-to-mind communication. "I am lost and can't find my way back home." A tear welled up in her eye and ran down her cheek. "I'm scared, can you please help me?"

The griffon, having lost a small fledgling herself, was immediately drawn to the young elven princess. "I will help you, child, for you are pure and do not carry the evil intents of the world with you."

The magnificent griffon stooped low and allowed the princess to climb upon its broad back. "Hold on tightly to my mane, and I will take you home. I know where your village is." The griffon swiftly flew her directly back to her village and landed in the very center of the main village crossroads. The elven king and queen were so relieved and thankful to the griffon that they actively sought to protect the griffons from all other races that would enslave them. The griffons of the area formed a mutual trust with the elves.

From time to time, the griffon that rescued the princess would show back up in the village and take her for long rides. They spent many hours together and formed a strong bond with one another. Many generations went by and both princess and griffon faded from this world. The Gods, seeing the deep bond between them, allowed both to pass together into the afterlife where they enjoy many adventures together.

It wasn't until Lauriel was much older that Adamar told her the rest of the story about the griffons. The childhood bedtime tale was only part of the story. The full recounting was one of tragedy that he did not want her to hear as a child.

As time continued onward, the griffons were forced to move farther and farther away from civilizations as the elves slowly lost power to protect them.

They became more and more prized by many of the other races and were hunted relentlessly until most of them were caught and enslaved. They were used like beasts of burden, forced to fly men and goods to and fro. The griffons were a proud species and refused to reproduce in captivity, even to the point of death. They would not allow their children to live out the same lives of enslavement. Slowly, most of the griffons died out, and it became almost impossible to find any in the wild.

Any griffons that remained stayed far away from civilizations and were extremely hostile toward them. However, as legend has it, griffons still remember their storied past with the elves and will help them in rare and dire circumstances.

Lauriel walked toward the griffon and stopped at a non-threatening distance, thirty feet away. She decided to try to communicate with the griffon in the same mind-to-mind way that she had heard during her bedtime stories.

A direct and honest question worked for the princess, so Lauriel asked in the same manner, *We are in desperate need of assistance, can you please help us?*

The griffon sat back upon its powerful rear legs into an upright and seated position. Lauriel knew that it was an obvious signal that meant to show a non-threatening position as well. Lauriel waited several moments and was about to ask again out loud when she heard the reply in her mind. *What is it that you need, woodland being?*

Lauriel replied, *We must get to the Lair of Malthrax in the Crimson Highlands with all haste. It is a matter of grave importance.*

She heard the voice again in her mind, this time almost immediately. *We do not cross into the realm of Malthrax.* There was a brief pause and then a change of tone. *Nor do we help humans*, the Griffon replied as it peered steely eyed at Dante.

It caught Dante's eye and let out a loud shriek and beat its wings angrily. Dante's hands instinctively went to his weapon that was strapped to his back.

"Do NOT draw your weapons!" Lauriel said sternly. Dante heard the serious tone in Lauriel's voice and did as instructed, but not without protest.

"That fucking Bird Lion looks like he wants to eat me!"

And now you see why we don't work with humans, said the griffon. Lauriel couldn't help but laugh, the griffon had a point.

My name is Lauriel, by what name do you go by? Lauriel asked the griffon.

I am Kanarus, he replied.

Well met, Lauriel said. She continued, *When I was a little girl, I was told a story about a griffon that rescued an elven princess. It was the beginning of many generations of goodwill between the elves and your kind.*

By way of this quest that we are on, we seek to help all beings in this realm, including yourself. The shadow will not stop at our borders. The human that is with me is of pure heart, and we need him to help us with our quest.

Kanarus was impressed by Lauriel's knowledge of history. He also found no deceit in her story, nor disingenuous intent. *I too know the story of the elven princess and the friendships that were forged in the bygone days. It is a song of remembrance that we sing still to this day. And I have also heard rumors of this dark scourge upon the land from our avian friends whose wings and songs travel far.*

So shall it be just as in the days of our forefathers that we will help you as equals, not as slaves. We will carry your group to the edge of Malthrax's domain but we will go no farther. But we have one request in return ... Kanarus added.

Thank you for your willingness to help! exclaimed Lauriel. *What is your request? We will honor it if at all possible.*

We wish to be free again to roam with the wind, unconfined and unbound, forever rid of the constant threat of arrow or enslavement. Not just us, but all griffons throughout the realms, for this is our land too, Kanarus stated. Lauriel could detect the wistful longing even in the mind-to-mind speech.

Four of the adult griffons stepped forward and joined Kanarus. Lauriel looked back at the rest of the party with tears in her eyes. "They have agreed to take us to the edge of the Highlands, under one condition ... They wish to fly free throughout the realms, free of hunting, enslavement, or harassment."

She turned back to face the griffons. "I swear that I will do anything and everything within my power to make that happen."

"And I," Eldrin immediately and sincerely proclaimed. Both Jexi and Nyx also swore the same.

Lauriel could see Dante about to protest and quickly interrupted him, "Dante, you should understand that this is a unique honor for them to agree to take you. They do not interact with humans."

"Humans!" he snorted. "What do you mean humans? We are out in the middle of nowhere and we come across some prejudice." Suddenly, no sound came from his mouth even though his lips continued to move. Jexi finished her spell and tried her best to contain her smile as they began to approach the griffons.

The griffons could see what she had done and flapped their wings and shrieked with apparent humor. Dante's face became red and even though he made no sound, they counted a string of at least eight swear words from his silent rant. Dante was the last to approach, but he decided that it would be better than walking for another week.

After the party had taken up riding positions, the griffons leapt into the sky. Their majestic wings carried them skyward with each powerful stroke. Each of the companions had enjoyed their time flying with Eldrin's magical Fly spell but this was much different. They were unrestrained by the constant reminder that the Fly spell would run out soon.

The griffons were much faster and could fly great distances. They watched in amazement as the ground passed rapidly beneath them. They covered an entire day's hike in less than one hour flying.

The view was breathtaking, and the terrain was wild and beautiful. They crossed many rocky gorges, mesas, hills, small rivers, and forested valleys, each uniquely beautiful. There was all manner of wildlife that they could see from their vantage point: elk, moose, deer, bear, fox, and wolves were just a few of the notable creatures that passed below them.

Eldrin had used a spell that allowed each of the party to communicate mind-to-mind, and all of them could now converse freely with the griffons. They continued their flight eastward until just after midday when they spotted a large herd of deer crossing an open field.

Kanarus instructed them to hold on tightly and led the griffon formation into a sudden steep dive.

The companions held on tightly as instructed and quickly reached a speed that they never thought possible. The velocity of the wind buffeting them was even more intense than the wind from a powerful storm. It caused a constant stream of tears to flow from their narrowly squinting eyes that they fought to keep open so they could observe the awe-inspiring hunt.

The griffons folded their wings back into a sleek, arrow-like shape, causing them to drop out of the heavens like a bolt of lightning. The herd spotted the griffons at the last second, but it was too late to even react. The griffons cut through them, instantly culling the herd as they each gripped a separate prey tightly with their razor-sharp talons. They used their speed and momentum to pull back up into a steep climb and then dropped them from a lethal height.

The seemingly effortless hunt made for a plentiful lunch. The griffons needed to consume large amounts of food for their long flights.

Let this be a lesson for when you cross into the realm of Malthrax, said Kanarus to all of them, *you will be the deer if you are not careful.*

The lesson was wise, and they all took note.

To everyone's surprise, including the other griffons, Dante had not only convinced his griffon to talk to him, but they had engaged in lively conversation and were quickly befriending one another. Much to the griffon's surprise and fascination, Dante disliked most humans even more so than he. Dante had learned that the griffon he was riding was one of the warriors or "protectors," as the griffons called them, tasked with fighting away enemies. It was in that common bond that Dante found the most unlikely of friends. The griffon was missing several feathers, and his beak had several large scars that he proudly displayed as a badge of honor.

After a quick but filling lunch, they continued eastward toward the Highlands. Over the next three hours, they continued over the wild and untamed landscape until they finally saw large mountains looming in the distance.

What should have been beautiful snowcapped peaks ringed by dense thriving forest below turned out to be the exact opposite.

The mountains stood dark and foreboding with no customary snowcapped rises. It looked like the mountains themselves were dead remnants of a once great land.

The treeless landscape was blackened and dead from constant lava pockets bubbling to the surface, giving the entire area a red hue. The foul smell of sulphur grew stronger and stronger as they drew closer. The griffons landed, and Kanarus spoke, *This is as far as we can take you. As you could see from above, the mountains are not a far journey on foot from here. I wish you luck in your quest, and may we sing songs of your success in the future. A success that we had the privilege to be a small part of.*

Lauriel hugged the Griffon. *You have helped us greatly, thank you so much for all that you have done.*

Thank you, and may the bond between the elves and griffons be reforged as it was in the days of old, Eldrin said.

Jexi and Nyx bid their griffons a fond farewell, but it was Dante that had the most difficult time saying goodbye.

I truly hope to see you again, my friend, he said wistfully as he gave the griffon a pat on the neck.

Likewise, when this is all said and done, we shall have many great adventures together! the griffon replied.

With the final word of farewell, the griffons leapt into the air and began their journey back home.

The daylight hours grew shorter, and Lauriel knew that the night would be clear and bitterly cold. The terrain was rocky, and the trees in the area were stunted and gnarled. They were on the front lines of the struggle between the thriving nature of the Hinterlands and the creeping doom of the Highlands. The party found a small rocky ravine to make camp in.

They would have to make a good-sized campfire in order to survive the night, and the slopes of the ravine would hide it sufficiently enough so that it would not be a beacon in the night for the dragon.

There were many small fires and bubbling pockets of lava in the Highlands, but they did not want to take any chances of being seen if the dragon happened to be out hunting along the perimeter of his vast domain.

There was little rest, and the night seemed to drag on endlessly. The griffon's analogy of the deer weighed constantly in their minds as they were now the prey waiting to be slaughtered in the open field. The nervousness created an almost palpable sense of foreboding that hung thickly in the air. Every crackle of the fire or rustle of trees in the wind awakened them with a start. About three hours before sunrise, Eldrin gave up any hope of being able to rest. It was Lauriel's turn for the watch and he could see her with his keen elven sight sitting in the darkness at the top of the ridge. He walked over to join her and found her wrapped heavily in a thick fur cloak but still shivering.

"No warmth of the fire?" Eldrin whispered.

Lauriel shook her head. "I was hoping to get a glimpse of him."

"Anything?"

"Nothing at all; not even a field mouse ventures out into the darkness," Lauriel replied. "I have figured something out this night, Eldrin." He could see the pensive look on her face as she continued, "I am not scared of death, but I am terrified of failure. The pressure of all of this seems to be upon us, but what happens to all of the innocent people if we are not able to complete this quest?"

Eldrin sat next to her and put his arm around her, silently contemplating his answer for several moments. "I too feel the weight of this growing upon our shoulders. We don't have news from the outside world but something inside me can feel it. The darkness sweeps across the land even now. Yet for some reason, it is our little group that has been drawn together to help find a way to push the darkness back through the portal from where it came, before it is too late.

"I too am terrified of the thought of failing, but when I find myself in doubt, there is one thing that gives me great comfort throughout all of this." Eldrin took Lauriel by the hand and stood up with her.

"And what is that?" she asked.

He turned her around to face the campsite and raised his hand in a gesture to her and the others. "I would rather be with no other group than ours throughout all of this. Each of us have our own unique skills and abilities that we bring to the table, and combined as one, we are strong. Our paths have led us together in this moment and if there is any group that can complete this quest, it is ours."

Lauriel stood and quietly contemplated Eldrin's words. She nodded in agreement. "Yes, Eldrin, I couldn't agree more."

The two sat back down on the ridge and continued in quiet conversation, and after a time, Eldrin circled back around to his previous observations.

"So, when are you going to tell me what happened to you in the woods a few nights ago?"

Lauriel smirked at him and replied, "Well, I would, but I rather enjoy torturing you with not knowing; you will see soon enough."

Her statement was accurate; Eldrin had a never-ending thirst for knowledge, and not knowing something was equivalent to torture for him.

Lauriel was about to continue when both of their hearts seemed to stop. A shadow rose from the mountains in the distance. It was terrible to behold, and it sent ice running through their veins, even at a great distance.

Both of them scrambled down from the ridge like roaches running for cover from a light. Lauriel quickly doused the fire while Eldrin woke the group to make sure that they were completely silent.

"What is it?" Nyx whispered.

"The dragon. It's out hunting, and it's headed in this direction!" Eldrin whispered.

"It can see in complete darkness. We must hide!" Jexi instructed quietly.

"I can make us invisible," Eldrin whispered.

"He can see that too!" Jexi replied in a quiet but earnest tone.

The party quickly cleared the campsite and hid in the small alcoves formed by the rocky outcroppings on the side of the ravine.

Just as they did, they began to hear a slow and steady, *whoosh ... whoosh ... whoosh ...* as the huge dragon wings cut effortlessly through the thick, night air.

The sound grew louder and equally more terrifying with each moment. *Whoosh ... whoosh ... whoosh ...*

The dragon passed within a thousand yards of them to the north but they remained hidden from his sharp gaze.

He could smell the campfire but it was not unusual for wood to burn here. The malaise of the Highlands slowly and unrelentingly continued to creep into the Hinterlands, each new pocket of lava consuming more of the precious few trees in its path. There was another interesting smell on the air but it was very faint. Lauriel peered through a small rock crevice and could see the dark shadow suddenly bank in their direction. As the dragon began to turn, its giant wings and body blocked out the light of the moon. The giant beast became outlined like a solar eclipse as the moon shone behind him.

"He is on to us!" Lauriel whispered a warning of her observations.

He began to follow the mysterious smell in the air. Lauriel drew an arrow slowly and quietly from her quiver beside her, but the arrow was so insignificant compared to the size of the dragon that she felt foolish for even readying it. Even the best shot would be of no more consequence to him than a mosquito bite.

SCREECH! The group could hear the sudden outburst of the distinct sound of griffons! Two griffons dove down from somewhere high in the clear night sky and passed by the dragon like a bolt of lightning. The surprised dragon wheeled sharply in their direction.

The griffons banked so hard that feathers could be seen flying from their tails and wings. They used their speed and momentum to turn hard away from the dragon, leading him in the opposite direction of the group. The night sky was illuminated by a burst of fire so large and bright that it made Eldrin's Fireball spell look like a small candle.

Even at that great distance, they could feel the heat radiate into the night sky. The dragon was not as fast, nor could he maneuver as sharply as the griffons, but his deadly breath weapon made up the difference.

Another jet of flames ripped through the heavens and caught up to the griffon flying rearguard, enveloping him in flames. A dying screech could be heard that sickened each of them. The griffon fell from the heavens in a flaming ball of fire, and they could hear a sickening crash and thud as it smashed through the trees and slammed to the ground. The dragon quickly pursued its prey to the spot that it had fallen, and within seconds, launched himself back into the heavens, turning eastward toward his lair. In his huge claws could be seen the limp body of a griffon.

Lauriel could see the unmistakable scars on the griffon's nose with her sharp eyes, and could hear a strange language traveling on the whisper of the wind.

"What did he say?" Lauriel whispered to Eldrin after the dragon was no longer seen.

Eldrin hung his head. "He spoke in ancient draconic, something about a 'rare and tasty little treat.'"

Eldrin turned to the group. "There was no way that we would have had even a remote chance against him in the open skies with no cover, and they knew that."

"That was one of the bravest things I have ever seen," Jexi added, her eyes shimmering with tears.

"What griffon?" Dante demanded.

Lauriel hung her head, and Dante's eyes welled up with tears. Seeing Lauriel's reaction, he knew the answer, but he had to hear it from her. "What griffon did you see, Lauriel?" he asked desperately.

"I'm sorry, Dante, it was yours, the one with the large scars on his beak."

Dante began to wipe the many tears from his eyes and cheeks, which caused all of them to cry at the sight of his anguish. Dante did not make friends easily, but the ones that he did befriend, he cared for greatly. After a few moments, he stood up, grabbed his items, and without a word began walking eastward toward the mountain.

"Where are you going? It's still hours before dawn!" Nyx called.

"To kill a fucking dragon," he blurted tersely. "Besides, I can see these pools of lava better at night, and the dragon is done hunting and back in his lair now."

The idea made sense; they would not have to worry about the dragon overhead if they left immediately, and the dark shadow of a mountain in the distance was an easy landmark to follow, even in the dark of night. The group quickly picked up their items and caught up to Dante, each walking in mournful silence as they slipped silently and unnoticed into the Highlands.

"The last charge of the griffons was heroic and inspiring. Their act must be chronicled, so that it is never forgotten," Eldrin observed.

They all nodded and quietly began discussing a poem of remembrance while they made their way toward the dragon's lair.

The Last Charge of the Griffons

Soaring high up in the heavens,
the moonlight shines down bright,
the griffons fly out together
keeping watch throughout the night.

The cares of the world below them
and the weight upon their wings,
the quest is but a narrow path
the fate of all now clings.

So on into the night they soar
as sentries of ancient past,
the dragon now leaves his dreadful lair,
a glimpse of him at last.

And dread throughout the land is felt
the peril for all severe,
the griffons they see the allies plight
as shadow and death draws near.

And with not a moment wasted,
the griffons tuck their wings.
They dive directly at the dragon,
a warning call they sing.

Great peril do they place themselves
to save the fated quest.
They dive right beside the dragon
and bank sharply to the west.

Attention drawn they hurry to
the safety of the night.
The dragon breathes his deadly flame
and the heavens do ignite.

A star falls from the moonlit sky
and crashes to the ground.
Great sacrifice this night was made
by bravest of griffon around.

And sing he does upon the wind
with family he thought once lost
for fly they do in heavens great
the gates he now has crossed.

CHAPTER SEVENTEEN

Malthrax

ante's rage-driven decision to push forward into the darkness turned out to be very fortuitous to the group. If they had waited until daybreak to cross on foot as they had planned, they would almost certainly have experienced disaster. They discovered that there were not only a multitude of lava pools that could be seen, but there were also innumerable hidden pools that bubbled just beneath a very thin surface crust. Only in the darkness could they see the faint glow that emanated from them.

The landscape looked both foreboding and primordial. Jagged black rocks, some of them as large as a house, littered the scorched ground in all directions. Many of the lava pools were very small, but a few of the larger ones they passed were the size of small lakes. The heat was so intense that they had to travel long distances out of the way to avoid coming near the pools. The pungent smell of Sulphur hung thick in the air and made it difficult to breathe.

As they continued their trek toward the mountain, they saw numerous unexpected monsters that inhabited the area. There were five fire imps, two fire elementals, a large fire worm, and two hellhounds that they counted along the way.

Jexi desperately wanted to try and use one of her powerful spells to "make one of the hellhounds her pet" but could not guarantee that it would be successful. The group decided that it would be better to not chance it and avoid everything at all costs. They did not want to draw any attention to themselves, nor use any of their magic or spells to get to the dragon's lair, so they took great care to hide or keep their distance from them.

*   *   *   *

Even with the many delays and detours, the companions made it all the way to the base of the blackened and desolate mountain just as the first rays of dawn began to creep over it. They huddled close together and began to quietly discuss their next move behind the cover of a giant igneous boulder that had come to rest at the base of the mountain.

"There may be no obvious entrance or gaping hole in the top of the mountain as you would think. Dragons often used magical means to enter their lair. It adds a layer of protection from ambush," Jexi whispered.

"If we can just find a small fissure, I have a spell that I have prepared that can help scout the interior," Eldrin said quietly.

"Okay, I'll go see what I can find," Lauriel whispered. "This is a rough and dangerous climb so there is no sense in all of us wandering aimlessly up the side of this thing. Besides, the more time and movement we have on the mountainside, the more chance we have of attracting attention."

The others nodded in agreement, and Lauriel quickly and quietly scurried up the steep slope. The rest of the group tried to keep as low of a profile as possible, hoping that their presence would continue to be unnoticed by all of the foul creatures that inhabited the land.

After two uncomfortably long hours, Lauriel finally rejoined the group. She was out of breath and had several minor cuts and scrapes on her arms and legs.

"I found a fissure that looks like it opens up into a larger cave. It might be a little tight for Dante but it is the only thing that I can find that looked promising. It is only about halfway up the mountain but the climb to get there is very dangerous. It is full of steep areas and sharp rocks that are prone to giving way without warning. I have done a lot of climbing and it was difficult for me," Lauriel warned as she pointed to her wounds.

The others looked at each other with concern. They knew that if the climb was difficult for Lauriel, the most dexterous of all of them, it would be almost impossible for everyone to make the ascent safely.

"I really hate to waste a lot of spell energy that could be used against the dragon, but I think in this case, we have no other options. It's more important that we get there uninjured and unnoticed," Eldrin concluded, his voice barely above a whisper as he spoke.

"I will cast fly on us, just like before."

The others nodded in agreement; it was the safest way forward.

As soon as Eldrin finished his spell, Lauriel led the quick and silent flight to the fissure that she had found. The opening was four feet high and slightly less than two feet wide. There was just enough space around it for the group to huddle together closely.

Dante looked at the opening and then back at Lauriel with a look of bemusement. "What the fuck do you mean 'might be a little tight for Dante.'? My axe will barely fit through that!" he grumbled. He had luckily remembered to whisper, but even his whisper was inordinately loud and immediately drew sharp but silent rebukes from the others.

"Okay, I'm going to use a spell that will save us a lot of time, but I'll need complete uninterrupted concentration in order to scout as much as I can," Eldrin quietly instructed.

The others nodded in understanding, and Eldrin began another spell. When he finished, a disturbing and unexpected scene unfolded.

A disembodied, floating eye about the size of a grapefruit manifested at the mouth of the fissure. He was able to mentally move the eye and could see what it was seeing, even in near total darkness.

"That's fucked up," Dante whispered.

Eldrin began to move the eye through the labyrinth of tunnels throughout the cave, systematically searching each passage in an attempt to locate one that led to the dragon's lair.

After almost an hour of exploring the cave system, and right before the spell ended, Eldrin found an area that opened up into a large, dark cavern. Even though the eye could normally see through darkness, the darkness in the cavern was impenetrable.

"That has to be it," Eldrin muttered.

"Did you see him!?" Lauriel whispered excitedly.

"No, but I think I know where he is. His lair is protected by a magical darkness that I couldn't see through. There was a labyrinth of tunnels, but I know how to get back to that area now."

"Okay let's talk strategy," Jexi whispered. "I've read the entire book on dragons, and I have a little bit better understanding of them now. I've been working on a plan to try and maximize our chances against him."

"Let's hear it," Eldrin urged. All of them had come to highly respect Jexi's prowess. If there was a weakness to exploit, she would find it.

In a hushed but earnest conversation, Jexi began to lay out her strategy to the group. "His most devastating attack is his dragon's breath, and he will try to catch us all in it at the same time. As soon as we engage him, we should try to spread out so he can't get all of us. The fire resistance potions should work to a certain extent but I'm not sure how well, so try to avoid the fire as best as possible." She turned to Nyx. "Nyx, if you see that one of us is going to get hit directly by the dragon's breath, immediately use your most powerful healing spell to heal that person.

I'll try to lead off by restraining him just like the hydra; hopefully that will take away his physical attacks for a short amount of time. Lauriel and Dante, if you can flank him, that will make him spread out his attacks and give you some advantage. You will need it because his dragon scales give him an incredible amount of protection from weapons, far more than even full plate armor."

She looked at Eldrin. "Eldrin, I would suggest that you try to maximize whatever damage you can do to him with your spells as quickly as possible without holding anything back."

She glanced around at the group. "Any questions?"

"Do you think that we can sneak in and gain the element of surprise?" Lauriel asked.

"I'm not sure, but it's worth a shot." Jexi replied.

With Jexi done with her briefing, Eldrin pulled out a piece of parchment and a quill ink pen and began to draw the direct path to the large cavern.

"There is a small alcove that is just a few minutes' walk from the main cavern." He marked the place on the map with X. "We should be able to stop here and prepare for the battle by drinking our potions and casting any defensive spells that we can. It should be far enough from the cavern that the dragon will not hear us. If things go south, let's try to make it back to this area and I will try to teleport us out. Just beware, any distraction during that spell can be disastrous."

They all looked at each other for reassurance but the brief moment of hesitation allowed fear and doubt to creep in. Lauriel broke the silence, her eyes were driven, determined, and ambitious as she whispered a rallying call to the others, "Okay, let's do this! This is up to us, and we WILL succeed!"

With that, they each nodded and crawled into the cave entrance.

The cave floor was covered in dust and rock debris. No creature had come through the area for a very long time.

As expected, Dante had a very difficult time getting through the opening and was only able to make it through with assistance from the others.

There were several other narrow points that he had to be helped through in the first one hundred feet, but after the short distance, the fissure opened up wide enough for even Dante to stand comfortably.

Dante turned around and looked back toward the entrance and raged in as silent of a whisper as he could muster, "Fuck this cave, and fuck that dragon."

He was scraped, bruised, and already furious. The rest of the companions carefully hid their smiles as they nodded in agreement.

The group followed the path in complete silence all the way to the alcove that Eldrin had identified. Nyx carefully opened her backpack as quietly as she could and passed out the fire resistance potions.

"These should last one hour, so go ahead and take them now. I'm not sure how long the magic resistance will hold against dragon's fire though," she whispered.

She then pulled two flying potions from her pack and handed them to Lauriel and Dante. "These only last ten minutes so drink these in case the dragon takes flight. We will need to hurry as soon as you do."

Jexi quietly cast several spells in preparation for battle. Suddenly, a scantily clad female succubus appeared and stood right beside Jexi.

Jexi held her finger to her lips and then whispered to the fiend, "Welcome back to my service, Moridana; you are not to mess with any of my friends that are here."

"Yessss, mistress," Moridana hissed in a whispered reply.

She looked at Lauriel with her seductive gaze, her tail flicked back and forth excitedly. "Just one?"

"I mean it," said Jexi.

"What is this vile demon going to do to a dragon?" Nyx demanded in protest. Her whispering voice began to shake in anger as she continued, "Her being here is an affront to everything that I stand for. Besides, I doubt a dragon will fall for any of her evil tricks."

Moridana looked at Nyx and winked as she blew her a kiss. In a rare role reversal, it was Dante that had to hold Nyx back and help calm her down.

Jexi cast another spell on Moridana. "This spell gives you the ability to attack with an ice breath weapon just like a very young White Dragon. It should be effective against a creature of fire. Try to use it on the dragon's head."

"Dragon?" whispered Moridana. "You continue to make powerful enemies, mistress. You do know that if I am killed in this fight, I simply go back to my own plane of existence. It's not quite the same for you."

Jexi did not answer but looked at Nyx instead, "And that is why she is here."

"A sacrificial lamb," hissed Moridana. "I love it."

Lauriel used one of her newly learned divine spells, and a faintly shimmering field of force appeared to briefly surround her and then disappear.

Eldrin's eyebrows raised as he observed Lauriel's spell preparation for battle. "Well, you are just full of surprises, aren't you?"

Nyx recognized the spell and looked at Lauriel, wide eyed and confused. "You have learned a Divine Shield spell?"

Lauriel looked at them, smirked, and without saying a word, turned around and walked silently toward the lair. She peered around the corner and into the darkness of the cavern. The steam and heat from the lava tube created an eerie fog that encompassed the entire area. She could normally see very well in the darkness with her natural elven Darkvision, but she could not see into the cavern. Just as Eldrin had observed with his spell, some type of unnatural darkness obscured the cavern from her view.

"Why don't you quit sneaking around like a bunch of little rats and join me for dinner," a booming voice said as the darkness suddenly lifted.

She could now see the entire cavern very well, and the sight that she beheld caused the blood to drain from her face. She had to fight with every ounce of her mental fortitude to keep from running.

"Oh … shit …" she muttered.

Lauriel was not prone to swearing, and when the rest of the group heard her reaction to the voice, it fell upon them like a portent of doom. They had never seen Lauriel even hesitate to engage an opponent.

Lauriel clenched her jaw and regained her composure, refusing to be paralyzed by inaction. She drew her scimitars, and Isilmwé began to glow in the cavern like a radiant star. Lauriel said a quick silent prayer to Kathele, and she could feel her newfound connection to the Goddess.

The dragon seemed delighted that the small elf had the courage to face him. "Ha!" the dragon snorted. "I'm going to enjoy keeping those blades of yours." He raised his claw and pointed at a large pile of weapons and armor in the far corner of the cavern. "You fools always come dressed in your best, and those will be a nice little addition to my collection."

Lauriel felt a shiver run down her spine and once again had to fight the urge to run.

The huge dragon's deep crimson scales covered him from head to toe and glistened in the steam of the cavern. Each scale created a nearly impenetrable surface that was harder than full plate armor. A single nail on his claw was half the size of Lauriel's entire body.

Her incredibly powerful scimitars suddenly felt small and insubstantial compared to him. She began to doubt that she could find even a single place to get through his armor. The hydra they had fought was impressive, but she could tell immediately that it wouldn't have lasted more than a few seconds against the magnificent and terrifying dragon.

"You think that you can sneak into my lair like a bunch of rats without me noticing?" the dragon scoffed as he began to stand, a move that seemed to shake the very foundation of the cavern itself.

His tail unfurled and swept effortlessly through the piles of gold and gems, splashing them throughout the room like water.

His tail muscles alone were stronger than all of them combined. Lauriel observed that she would need to do her best to avoid it or surely be crushed.

She had learned from Adamar how to quickly size up opponents, but the power of this dragon went well beyond her comprehension.

"Little rats ..." he said with a patronizing sneer, "why don't the rest of you quit hiding and join us for the party?"

Seeing that the plan to sneak in and gain the initiative had been foiled, the rest of the group stepped around the corner and joined Lauriel. The others all had to desperately fight off the urge to run, but the sight of the dragon was just too much for Nyx. Without saying a word, she turned and ran back down the cave just as Dante had done when Jexi had cast her Fear spell against him. The dragon seemed delighted that his presence had caused her to flee.

"Perhaps I should destroy you now while your healer runs in fear. After all, it would be awfully difficult to win a battle without getting healed."

The dragon sat back on his rear legs, towering above them and making them feel painfully insignificant. "But what is the fun in that? Let's wait, shall we?"

He brought his head down low, peering at each of them. It was so large that he could easily swallow any of them. The two main horns on the top of his head were twice as long as Dante's great axe, and every single tooth looked as sharp as Lauriel's blades.

He appeared to smile at their clear discomfort at the mere sight of him. A ring of smoke puffed out of his nostrils as he spoke. "So what possession of mine brings you all the way out here to try to steal it from me?"

Eldrin stepped forward right next to Lauriel and spoke up, "We seek an amulet that we are in dire need of. Would you be willing to trade?" He touched Lauriel's hand as if to hold it. Lauriel could hear Eldrin's voice in her mind. "Take this and drop it at the dragon's feet within the next sixty seconds then move away quickly." He slipped a freezing cold sphere the size of a marble into her hand and she gripped both it and the scimitar at the same time.

The dragon immediately replied, "Why would I trade when I can have the amulet AND all of the precious little things that you brought with you?" Nyx slowly entered the cavern and joined the others, out of breath and as pale as a ghost.

"Ahh, I see that you have found your courage, little one. I think I'll eat you first as an appetizer." The dragon stood back up. He was many times the size of the hydra.

It wasn't just his enormous presence that was terrifying, but his confidence shook them as well. It reminded Lauriel of a cat toying with a mouse that could not escape.

The cat could easily kill the mouse but wanted to have fun toying with it first. Jexi's book description of Red Dragons proved to be dead on. He was intelligent, cunning, and egotistical.

"Let's see, a magic user, two fighters, a healer, and some kind of witch with a succubus, if I'm not mistaken. I'm not sure why you brought her," he said as he pointed to Jexi, "but what a delightful little group you have assembled here to defeat me. I'm a little offended that you didn't bring more."

Jexi stepped forward and initiated the pre-scripted battle plan. "I'm a warlock!" she yelled as she began to cast the same chain spell that she had effectively used on the hydra. The spectral chains suddenly whirled around the dragon and began to wrap around him. "Now!" shouted Lauriel.

Dante and Lauriel charged at the dragon, trying to cover the one hundred feet between them as rapidly as they could.

Nyx sprinted away from the group as they all tried to scatter in different directions in preparation for the dragon's dreaded breath weapon attack.

As expected, the dragon inhaled quickly and then released a violent stream of flames that instantly heated the entire cavern. The plan was effective as Malthrax was not able to catch all of them together in the flames. Lauriel knew all too well the effects of searing heat from her Bladerite experience and sought to avoid the flames at all costs. She was prepared for the attack and used one of her new divine spells to avoid it.

The spell instantaneously caused her to disappear from where she had been standing and suddenly reappear behind the dragon, untouched by the flames and flanking him. Dante was not as lucky. He received the full fury of the dragon's breath. He was completely enveloped in the white-hot jet that turned part of the rocky cavern floor into lava. He could feel the magic of the fire protection potion hedging the heat and flames but quickly realized that he had relied too heavily upon its protection. His skin began to blister and slough off in large sections, but Nyx was apparently nearby and following the plan as he could feel a very powerful healing spell wash over him at the same time.

The dragon's fire also caught Eldrin and Jexi, but not as directly as it had Dante, and the combination of the potion and their fire resistance spells were able to ward off the effects of the attack.

Eldrin began to unleash his most powerful spell against the dragon, one that he called "Empowered Disintegration." It was such a powerful spell that he could only cast it once per day. The magical energies involved were too taxing upon him to attempt it again.

As the strands of magic gathered around him, a bright green glow began to encircle his hands; and that is when their plan completely collapsed.

Just as Eldrin pointed his hands toward the dragon, intending to send the deadly spell hurtling toward him, the dragon used his own magical abilities to cancel out the spell.

Jexi had warned the group that the dragon could have innate spell casting abilities, but they did not think he had the more advanced arcane ability to counter-spell.

Eldrin's eyes opened wide in shock and disbelief; he had lost his most powerful attack and any advantage that he had hoped to gain from it.

Malthrax looked directly at Jexi and let out a booming laugh that echoed throughout the immense cavern. The force chains that encircled him suddenly shattered into tiny fragments and winked out of existence.

"Interesting spell, witch, but I don't think I will allow myself to be restrained today," he said with a malevolent sneer. "I had hoped for a little more of a challenge!"

Nyx had to maneuver dangerously close to the dragon so that she could heal Dante, but the dragon saw her attempt and backhanded her with his incredibly huge claw, knocking her over fifty feet through the air and into the cavern wall. She smashed into it with a sickening thud.

Dante brought his axe down upon the dragon twice with as much force as he could muster.

The first hit glanced off of the thick dragon scale, but the second found its mark. The icy blade cracked one of the scales but it did not appear to do any significant damage.

Lauriel knew that her attacks had to land, and she tried desperately to turn the tide of battle. She attacked the dragon with all of the ferocity and skill in her. She wanted to inflict as much pain as she could, hoping to draw his attention to her and away from the rest of her party. She no longer felt any fear at all from Malthrax's presence; she would fight Demogorgon himself if it meant protecting her group.

She found a position just to the left of the dragon's left leg that afforded her some protection against his giant tail.

Each gleaming scale reminded her of a finely polished shield.

She decided to take aim at the places where the scales came together, hoping to catch a weaker area in the armor, and she was surprised when her first two attacks penetrated the seam.

Isilmwé cut into the side of the dragon's leg, and Nightfang quickly found the same mark, both drawing blood. Her next two attacks glanced off of his thick scales, but she had proven that he was not completely invincible. It may have had the same effect upon him as an ant, but it was a start. Lauriel held off calling down her Goddess's wrathful energy, waiting for the perfect hit to use it. She could only use it a few times per day and wanted to make them count.

* * * *

Jexi decided to try her most powerful spell as well. She called the spell "Soul Shatter." She saw the dragon counter-spell Eldrin's spell and knew that he could not do it again immediately. She also knew that the dragon's spell abilities were not limitless and hoped that he would run out quickly.

"Melath-nuak-arwes-tverseth … nolos-versek-kirenath!"

A dark shadowy bolt of negative energy shot from her outstretched hand and struck the dragon in the chest. Blood spurted from his eyes and began to seep from under his thick scales. The attack seemed to be the most successful annoyance to him so far, and the party braced themselves for the vicious counterattack.

Blood and Fury

Malthrax was not some dumb brute. He was as intelligent as Eldrin, as cunning as Jexi, as vicious as Lauriel, and as deadly as Dante. Immediately after Jexi finished her spell, he unleashed the trap that he had prepared.

A whirlwind of small daggers rose up from the pile of treasure and encircled Dante, cutting him as they freely spun around him.

It was not a powerful spell like Eldrin's; each dagger that sliced into Dante seemed to have little effect on him. Dante was enraged and barely even felt them.

That's odd, of all the damage he can do to us by attacking us with his claws, tail, bite, and breath weapon, and he chooses a minor spell? Eldrin thought to himself.

To his sudden horror, he realized that Malthrax had a far more sinister plan in store. He started to yell as he got a glimpse if it, but it was already too late.

The dragon had some type of small transparent cube in his clutches that he hurled directly at Dante. Dante was too focused on his attacks to even notice. Eldrin could feel the extremely powerful magic energy radiating outward from the cube.

"Dante, run!" he yelled.

As the cube landed at Dante's feet, it instantaneously expanded into a ten-foot transparent cube. Eldrin recognized it as a cubical force cage, and he knew that nothing could get in or out of the prison. No spell in his vast repertoire could dispel or remove the cube, and there was nothing that he knew of that could damage it.

Dante was trapped inside, and the blades that were trapped with him continued to spin around him. His blood began to splatter upon the walls, and they could see him yelling, but not even sound traveled through the force. It created such a horrible spectacle that the battle temporarily halted. The dragon paused to admire his handiwork, and the rest of the party looked on in horror.

"Eldrin! Do something!" Lauriel pleaded.

Malthrax let out a great roar, "Embrace the inevitability, scum, for I have given you a front row seat. How dare you challenge me?"

Nyx, had almost been knocked out from slamming up against the cavern wall. She fought to regain her senses and was still groggy when the cube had trapped Dante.

She suddenly regained a clear head as she realized the dire situation. She tried to heal him, but the spell was wasted as it too would not pass through the cube.

"Dante!" she cried in terrible anguish.

Eldrin quickly weighed his options and found none of them to be great. The dragon had set up the terrible chess game, and he had been several moves ahead of them.

Eldrin knew that he could not do anything about the cube, so he decided to use the brief pause to try and help Lauriel be more effective since they were down one attacker and at a severe disadvantage.

He cast a Haste spell on her which had the effect of doubling her speed, attacks, and made her even harder to hit. He had already decided that if something didn't turn quickly, his next spell would be to teleport them out. There was no guarantee though that the dragon wouldn't try to counter-spell his teleport.

Jexi's succubus flew near the dragon and used her frost breath that Jexi's spell had given her. The magic of the spell was powerful, and the dragon's head was blasted with freezing cold as she exhaled. He reeled his head backward out of the icy cloud and shook the ice off of himself, clearly annoyed.

He swatted her like a fly, and she was unable to avoid the attack. He caught her squarely with his massive claw and slammed her to the ground. The life was knocked out of her as soon as she hit the ground, but he stomped heavily on her to make a point to the others. Blood and tissue oozed from under the claw.

*   *   *   *

Tears streamed down Lauriel's face as she continued her solo melee attack against the dragon. She could see the horror of Dante's plight out of the corner of her eye.

She had the distinct metallic taste in her mouth as her throat constricted and she began to breathe rapidly. She continued with her so far unsuccessful plan of trying to draw the dragon's attention to her, hoping that it would give Eldrin and Jexi time to figure out some way to save Dante.

Lauriel decided that it was now or never. She would use every possible skill, maneuver, and Divine Smite that she had during her next string of attacks. She whispered another quick prayer to her newfound deity: "If this is to be my last, please give whatever grace you have for me, that I may bring this dragon with me into the afterlife … amen."

Her eyes flared as she finished the last word, and the world around her seemed to slow as she launched into her next series of attacks.

She had learned an ability from Adamar called Surge of Violence. The ability allowed her to momentarily harness a sudden and intense burst of energy to ferociously attack an enemy twice as fast as she normally could. But it came with a cost. It was extremely taxing, and she could not do it more than once per day.

Her surge, battle maneuvers, *Andúlari* movements, and Eldrin's Haste spell made her suddenly appear like a whirlwind of blades.

She was now four times faster than normal, and the blades began to ring with a clear, steady resonance, much louder than she had ever heard before. The ringing and the dreadful slicing sound of the vorpal blades echoed off of the cavern walls.

The Moonblade pulsed with light as it appeared eager to strike down another opponent. But it was not the specter of the whirling blades, nor the noise of the *Andúlarium* that drew the most attention. Lauriel became encircled in glowing, crackling energy that she had called down from her Goddess.

Her strikes fell upon the dragon in a flurry of devastating blows that were quick, accurate, and full of divine wrath. She struck at the dragon twelve times in six seconds.

His thick scales protected him from a portion of the onslaught, but eight of her rapid string of attacks found their marks, and she released all of the divine energy into three of the hits when she felt the scimitars bite deeply into the dragon.

The others could hear her screaming above the ringing as she struck him, "You will pay for what you have done!"

Blood gushed from the sudden, massive, gaping wound in the dragon's leg. Malthrax reeled away from her, staggering backward through the piles of treasure as he realized that he had greatly underestimated the small female elf. He had simply paid no attention to her at all, choosing to focus on what he considered to be higher threats.

She had cut his rear left leg so badly that he could no longer put his full weight on it, greatly slowing his movement. It also took away his deadly tail attack as he now had to use it for balance. He had never experienced such a devastating attack from any enemy with a blade.

Fire and Death

The transparent cube was now covered in Dante's blood from the inside and the splattered blood of Malthrax on the outside.

Nothing could be seen from within the cube except the faint glimpse of blades still whirling around in their silent hell.

Jexi caused her Soul Shatter spell to pulse again, and blood began to pour from his gaping leg wound and seep from under his crimson scales. Between Lauriel and Jexi's attacks, so much blood had been spilled that small rivulets began to form and flow through the piles of gold coins upon the floor.

The dragon was observant and saw that both Jexi and Eldrin had used a quick reaction spell at the beginning of the fight to protect themselves against his deadly breath weapon.

He was cunning and knew that if he could trick them into using a different quick reaction spell, they wouldn't have time to cast their fire protection spells before he breathed upon them again. His breath weapon was his most deadly attack and so he carefully laid his trap.

Instead of attacking Lauriel with his full wrath as all of them expected, he lunged foreword and lashed out at Jexi and Eldrin with his giant front claws. As he did, he discreetly maneuvered into position. They fell for his trick and were forced to immediately used their shield spells to avoid getting ripped in half. Their spells helped to protect them, but he was still able to knock both of them onto the ground near Lauriel.

Jexi's powerful Soul Shatter spell ended as she lost concentration when she hit the ground hard, and the dragon could feel the surge of life come back into him as the necromantic spell lifted.

The claw attacks were not meant to be lethal but effectively grouped them into a position where he could get all of them with his deadly fire. His scheme worked just as he had planned. They were all grouped together, he was in position, and he knew that they would not have time to cast another spell before he unleashed his devastating strike.

Jexi, Eldrin, and Lauriel realized the trap as it was too late. The jet of flames roared toward them, turning the piles of gold into molten liquid that ran in every direction.

Lauriel was still moving so fast that she was able to tumble out of the direct line of the fire at the last second, but Jexi and Eldrin were not as lucky. They were not able to get out of the direct line of fire and experienced the full fury of the dragon's breath. And even with the fire resistance potion still in effect, their skin blistered and burned to the point of turning black in the more exposed areas. Their outer garments were magical and withstood the inferno, but all other non-magical items burned or melted off of them.

"Eldrin! Jexi!" Lauriel screamed in a near panic as they both collapsed to the ground.

Their senses were completely overcome by an all-encompassing, excruciating pain. Their lungs had been seared by inhaling the super-heated environment and they began to gasp for air like fish out of water.

Nyx was farther away from the blast and was able to move out of the path of the direct flames, but as soon as they died down, she immediately realized that she had a terrible decision to make. She could only heal one at a time and they were both in such bad shape that she feared whichever one she did not heal first would succumb to their terrible injuries.

She knew that Eldrin was the only one able to teleport them out and so she decided to heal him first. But in order to deliver her most powerful healing spell, she would have to place herself in harm's way to physically touch him. Without a moment's hesitation, she began to run to him as fast as she could.

Lauriel was chosen for *Andúlari* training not only for her physical skills but also her mental prowess. She was ready to come back at the dragon with another bladed onslaught, but she was not so tunnel visioned that she didn't see Nyx trying to get to Eldrin, or Jexi in desperate need of healing also.

She knew that she had few chances left to do as much damage as she could to the dragon, but the others were in dire need of her help.

She used her speed to turn back toward the dragon on a path that would hopefully draw his attention away from the others.

Her plan worked as the dragon suddenly turned his head and body to defend himself from the surprisingly painful blades of the small elf. As he did, it gave Nyx the brief opportunity to close the distance to Eldrin.

Nyx reached out to him, and a bright blue light flashed and surrounded him, and when it subsided, many of his burn injuries appeared to have been healed, and he was once again able to take a full breath. Nyx helped him to his feet but there was no time for thanks.

"Run to the rally point!" Eldrin said in a hoarse whisper.

Instead of attacking the dragon as expected, Lauriel ducked behind his injured leg and dropped the cold sphere that Eldrin had given her right as she made it to Jexi.

A blue radiance flared and encircled Jexi as Lauriel used every bit of her new divine healing magic on her. It wasn't as powerful as Nyx's spell, but it was enough to stabilize her breathing and heal some of her horrific burns.

"Let's go!" Lauriel shouted as she helped Jexi stand.

She had no idea what the cold sphere was, but it had been almost sixty seconds and she knew that she did not want to be anywhere near it when the time expired. But even with her divine healing, Jexi was still moving far too slowly to escape the wrath of the dragon or get any distance from the sphere.

Eldrin shouted at Jexi and Lauriel with the little remaining voice that he had. "Run! Now!"

Lauriel knew not to take the time to question or hesitate, but she would not leave Jexi.

"Go! I'll be okay," Jexi said.

Lauriel nodded and sprinted to the far corner of the cavern where Nyx had gone, narrowly avoiding another vicious swipe of the dragon's claw.

Jexi spoke a single word of magic, and a shadowy doorway that only she could see appeared directly in front of her. Right before she stepped through, she peered back at the dragon and saw his huge claw about to come down on top of her.

Nyx and Lauriel gasped as they saw the dragon's claw come down right where Jexi was standing. The force of the attack shook the cavern as his claw smashed through the pile of gold. They knew that any living creature under it would have been crushed into oblivion, and as they looked on in horror, they suddenly realized that Jexi was standing right behind them. She had used her Dimensional

Step spell just in the nick of time. She had a calm, collected look as if nothing in particular had happened.

A great blast shook the cavern as the bound magical energy of Eldrin's spell released. The freezing, marble-sized sphere that Lauriel had dropped near the dragon suddenly and violently detonated, sending thousands of tiny razor-sharp ice shards outward at incredible speed, slicing through anything in their path.

The spell formed a huge icy ball that temporarily enveloped the dragon and then vanished out of existence as quickly is it appeared. The attack temporarily disoriented him, and he began to reel backward from the sudden pain of the icy needles.

Seeing a glimmer of opportunity, Eldrin turned from heading to the rally point and unleashed his last effort at harming the dragon.

"Agarath-nolosekk-ondivious!"

A bolt of lightning raced from his outstretched hands and struck the dragon squarely in the chest.

The cavern flashed with blinding light followed by a deafening boom that shook the cavern. The bolt was so powerful that the group could feel the tingling remnants of energy as it traveled through the dragon and into the pile of gold that they were standing on.

Lauriel did not wait for the dragon's reaction and furiously charged back at him with an anger that even Dante would be proud of. She could feel the effects of the Haste spell beginning to wear off and knew that she would not be able to move or attack as fast for much longer.

She jumped into the air and could feel the effects of the fly potion surround her as she flew straight toward the dragon's head. The Moonblade again appeared to gleam in eager anticipation of the next strikes.

He now had a tremendous respect for the keen blades and the skilled fighter that wielded them. They had caused gaping wounds to his legs, and he was none too thrilled that they were now aimed at his head. His breath weapon had not yet recovered so he decided to attack her with his claws to keep her at bay.

To the others, it almost looked comical as she flew around him like an annoying fly, dodging his swats as he became more and more infuriated. Finally, the fly landed and dealt a mighty sting as she brought her blades down in two vicious attacks.

She struck the dragon's snout just below his eye with Isilmwé, cracking the protective scale and creating yet another open wound. The attack was followed by a spin maneuver that moved her quickly to the right, just out of the maw of the dragon as he snapped ferociously at her. What happened next was both devastating to the dragon and surprising to Lauriel.

She brought Nightfang down upon the exact same wound that had just been opened.

A sickening crack echoed through the cavern as the vorpal blade sliced deeply into his face and was only stopped by the thick skull bones. Blood poured from him, and he frantically tried to get away.

The rapid combination of all of the powerful spells and melee attacks not only severely injured the dragon, but genuinely shocked him. He had never felt his own mortality and had rarely experienced opponents that could even slightly hurt him.

He unfurled his giant wings and tried to leap into the air, but his back legs were too injured to give him the power that he needed.

The dragon used a wing buffet attack that was so rare it was not even chronicled in Jexi's book. Lauriel was unable to avoid the entire wing like she had been able to avoid his claw, and the thick, leathery wing batted her to the ground so hard that it snapped her wrist.

The pain was excruciating, and she could no longer grip Nightfang or use her left hand. The sudden burst of wind from the large wings sent gold, gemstones, bones, and any other loose debris in the cavern flying.

Eldrin, Nyx, and Jexi were in the middle of casting more spells and had to fight to remain concentrated as they were buffeted by the wind and debris.

The wing buffet helped the dragon gain a little distance from the attackers but it was too late. Eldrin and Jexi finished their next round of destructive magic spells, and the dragon crashed down upon the cavern floor and struggled to regain his footing.

Lauriel picked herself up and quickly reengaged him, hacking at him with her one good arm. He lashed out with one last feeble attempt to crush her, but he was now far too weak and moving too slowly.

Finally, the dragon's head crashed down heavily upon the ground. His glossy, red eyes suddenly lost their luster, and his cavernous chest stopped rising. The great Malthrax had been defeated.

A sudden wave of lethargy washed over Lauriel, and she collapsed on the ground, unable to stand. The Haste spell and her Surge of Violence did not come without consequence.

She'd burned through an entire day's worth of energy in just a few minutes and it had pushed her body well beyond exhaustion. Her heart felt like it was about to leap out of her chest, and she found herself breathing so rapidly that she became lightheaded. She realized that if the battle had lasted any longer, not only could she not carry on fighting, but she would have been so weak that she couldn't even defend herself. She learned that she would have to work even harder to prepare herself to use such augmentations in future battles.

With the dragon now dead, Jexi and Eldrin tried in vain for many minutes to figure out how to open the force prison that held Dante. It was still so covered in blood on the inside that they could only see the occasional whirl of a bloody blade.

Nyx tried to keep busy by tending to Lauriel's broken wrist. A sharp dagger of pain shot through Lauriel's arm as Nyx suddenly set her wrist into place. Lauriel yelled out and bit her lip so hard that it drew blood, but Nyx's healing magic quickly washed over her, healing the injury and removing the pain.

After five more frustrating minutes, the magic of both the whirling blades and the cubical prison of force suddenly and silently expired. The cube reverted back to its original size, and the blades fell to the ground.

What they saw next would haunt them for the rest of their lives. Each of them had seen many terrible things, but the butchery before them was by far the most gruesome.

CHAPTER EIGHTEEN

Upon Lofty Winds

The force prison turned back into a perfectly clean translucent cube that was four inches on each side. It gleamed as it sat squarely on top of a bloody pile of gore, sinew, bones, and a magic greataxe that had not been damaged by the mundane blades. At first glance, none of them could comprehend what they were looking at. They had each prepared themselves to see a terrible sight, but expected to see an intact body of Dante. It wasn't until Jexi went over to take a closer inspection that they began to realize the horror. Jexi took the cube and tossed it to Eldrin, and then quickly took off her half-burned cloak and laid it over the pile.

Jexi had an iron constitution and was used to experimenting with many disturbing things, but she could not keep from vomiting. She turned away with tears in her eyes and walked over to the far corner of the cavern, away from everyone else. She stood facing the wall with her back toward the group, trying to regain her composure.

Nyx was in such a state of shock that she kept asking in a quiet, innocent voice, "Where is Dante?"

Each time she said it, it was like a small dagger to their hearts. Whenever anyone would try to answer, she would repeatedly reply, "NO! That's not Dante, where is he?"

Lauriel was overcome by many emotions. She had tried desperately throughout the battle to draw the attention of the dragon onto herself and protect her beloved friends that had become her family. That plan had not gone as intended and she felt an overwhelming sense of guilt because of it. She also felt a sense of grief like she had not felt since losing her family. Dante had quickly become her big brother.

The two emotions seized hold of her strongly, and before she was even able to make it over to Eldrin, she collapsed onto her knees and burst into tears, weeping bitterly over the loss.

Eldrin ran to her and held her tightly, and they were soon joined by Jexi. Nyx finally came to terms with the reality and joined the others, sobbing so hard that she began to dry heave. Together as one, they all huddled and held each other tightly.

Many hours went by before they were able to pull themselves together enough to make rational decisions. The grief-stricken companions decided that it would be best to rest and recover before they began the search for the amulet. The search could take hours, and they were all in much need of rest. They did not want to stay in the room with Dante's remains and decided to rest for the evening back in the alcove where they had prepared for battle.

The night went by slowly as each of them woke up several times reliving the horror of Dante's demise. The scenes kept playing over and over in each of their minds, and even though Malthrax was dead, he still seemed to enact revenge upon them from the grave.

The next morning, the party slowly and unenthusiastically filed back into the cavern.

It was quite the opposite of what Lauriel had pictured days before when she imagined the party blissfully swimming through the piles of gold and joyfully stuffing priceless treasure into their belongings as they laughed and danced on the corpse of a dead dragon.

Instead, the group quietly and somberly helped dig out treasure that Eldrin identified as magical, and after a solid hour of meticulous hunting, they found their costly prize.

The amulet was circular and looked to be made of pure platinum that was highly polished to a mirror-like finish. It had an outer ring that had strange writing carefully carved into it. Inside the outer ring, the amulet had a series of smaller and smaller geometric shapes that converged in the center. Each of the outer shapes contained a different sigil. It was warm to the touch and attached to a strong but slender platinum chain.

It was intricate and beautiful, but the sight of it turned Lauriel's stomach, continually reminding her of the heavy cost that they had paid to gain possession of it.

They each removed all of the contents of their packs and began to fill them with the many magical items that the dragon had collected, hoping that they might help them with their quest. They took as much as they could because they had no idea if they would ever be able to make it back to claim the rest of the hoard, and there was no guarantee that any of it would be there when they had time to make it back. With the dragon now dead, all manner of creatures would soon return to the area and come lurking.

It was a terribly difficult thing to do, but it was something that the companions all agreed had be done. They tied their cloaks together to form a large square of material and scooped Dante's remains into it with a shield that they turned into a makeshift shovel.

The four of them each took a corner and slowly made their way out to the entrance of the cave system.

As they stepped out into the light of the day and their eyes adjusted to the brightness, they found that the land had already begun to change. The pools of lava that had turned the area into a barren wasteland had already begun to sink back into the earth, and the foreboding feeling of doom was gone.

The companions found a high hilltop with a long, westward facing slope that looked out over the Highlands as if standing watch. Each day it would warm in the afternoon sun and catch the last streams of light as it slowly sunk below the horizon. The companions dug a shallow grave and assembled many rocks to give Dante a proper burial. They placed his remains in it and began to scoop the dirt back in, and as they did, Lauriel began to sing an ancient elven lament to a fallen warrior. It was a deep honor in her culture for it was rarely sung for anyone not of elven blood, and reserved only for those that died as heroes:

Upon Lofty Winds

Upon lofty winds,
through radiant sky doth soar,
a soul deserving honor,
a most fearless warrior.
His legacy will live on,
in my heart and thine,
inspiring us through our journeys,
for his blood protected yours and mine.
We honor his bravery,
as we wish him farewell,
our lives now are changed,
and his story we will tell.
Goodbye our dear friend,
as you soar far away.
We must carry on
but we will see you again someday.

As Lauriel finished her song, Nyx was overcome by a strange urge. She reached into her pocket and pulled out the acorn that Gorian had given her and cast it upon the ground right where Dante had been buried.

To their amazement, a carpet of lush grass rippled outward in all directions and quickly blanketed the scorched and barren hillside. The spark of life suddenly returned to the Highlands, and the grove continued marching outward, slowly reclaiming the land that had been stolen. It would take a very long time to recover, but the Highlands would slowly become the Azure Highlands again.

A lone tree sprung up and grew at an incredible rate, reaching maturity in less than ten minutes. The tree produced all manner of fruit, the quality of which none of them had ever seen.

Each piece was lush and renewed their vigor and spirits. The area had the same sense of peace and tranquility that they had experienced in Gorian's grove.

After a time of resting and reflection, the somber mood lightened and the companions laughed heartily as they shared fond memories and stories of their all-too-brief friendship with Dante. Lauriel had tried to talk like him and reenact several of her favorite moments, but the curse words spilled awkwardly from her and they laughed at her feeble attempt.

Before they left, they shared a drink together in his honor, and Eldrin proposed a toast: "Dante, beneath your crude exterior we found one of the most loyal friends and companions that anyone could ever ask for. Your life has been snuffed out far too soon and will truly be missed."

Eldrin had just finished the words when they suddenly heard the distinct sound of a griffon's call. It sounded far distant and only carried lightly on the wind, but it was undeniable.

It caused all of them to look up, but there was no Griffon. And that was when, for a fleeting moment, each of them saw a shadow of a soaring griffon briefly pass by them and disappear. The griffon appeared to be carrying a large rider.

CHAPTER NINETEEN

Charge of the Centarum

The companions decided that the safest place to return with their bags full of priceless treasure would be Gorian's grove. They knew that they could trust Gorian with keeping it safe. Druids had no use for such items and no desire for worldly wealth or possessions. The grove was well protected and would make a good place to store anything that they would not need to take with them on their continued quest.

The group assembled back inside of the cavern and stood in somber silence, eagerly awaiting Eldrin's teleport. The dragon's lair was a constant reminder of the deadly cost of the battle, and every moment inside of it tormented them. Although it was still full of many valuable treasures, they knew they would never come back to it. Reliving the horrible memories that returning to the site would bring made any thoughts of coming back reprehensible.

Eldrin was very familiar with Gorian's grove and comfortable with teleporting the group directly to it. He began to cast his Teleportation spell, and they all stepped forward into the circle. As the words of magic began to flow, a tear rolled down Lauriel's cheek. She began to laugh and cry at the same time. She laughed at she thought of how Dante was completely unaffected by the teleportation travel.

She laughed at the memories of his crude jokes, foul mouth, and beaming smile. She laughed at Jexi's warlock Fear spell on him, and she cried because she already missed her loyal friend terribly. Without saying a word, Nyx and Jexi knew exactly what she was thinking, and they both began to laugh and cry along with her.

The Grove

As the companions arrived in the inner grove near Gorian's tree house, they were immediately set upon by centaurs from many directions. Before they could even draw their weapons or cast a spell, the half-man, half-horse beings charged toward them with tremendous speed and formed a ring around the party. The half-men that formed the upper torso had large, muscular arms that leveled large, sharp spears at them. Lauriel quickly counted eight of them and knew that this was not the time to fight. She took her hands off the handles of her scimitars that were still sheathed at her side and held them up to show no hostile intent.

"Who comes here?" the centaur holding the spear at Eldrin shouted.

Eldrin replied, "I am Eldrin Aeramiril, a longtime friend of Gorian. These are my companions, and we are welcome here."

"The Forestmaster has not told us of expected visitors," the centaur snapped. "Some sort of dark malevolent creatures attack us. You must wait here until we can confirm that your presence is welcome here."

It was dusk, and the stars were beginning to shine brightly in the sky above them. Lauriel looked around at her surroundings and noticed that the forest was vastly different than it had been when they left. It now appeared dark and ominous; the feeling of peaceful serenity was replaced by a sense of danger and foreboding. A thick and seemingly impenetrable barrier of large, thorny vines encompassed the entire treed area just outside the glade.

Beyond the vines and deeper into the forest, gnarled roots now protruded above the surface of the dirt, branching out from every tree in all directions and forming a thick, tangled web that was nearly impossible to navigate through with any sure footing.

She was amazed at the transformation; it looked like the entire forest had determined to keep enemies out.

One of the centaurs galloped away to alert Gorian.

"What creatures do you speak of?" Eldrin asked.

The lead centaur replied, "Some large beasts with four arms and some type of hell-spawned, demon dogs. They attacked Silenus two nights ago and now that it has almost fallen, some of their attention has been drawn here."

A chill ran down Lauriel's spine.

"Have you killed any?" she asked, abruptly inserting herself into the conversation.

"They have not made it here yet, woodland daughter. The forest provides a difficult and deadly resistance. We wait for them here as instructed. We are the centarum; the last line of defense," the centaur declared proudly.

"And the town?" she continued her abrupt questioning.

"The town was well defended with both steel from the army and magic from the school of magic, both sides have suffered heavy losses but I'm afraid the defenses of Silenus have almost collapsed under the onslaught. The town has fallen back to the stronghold, the last defense. The creatures continue to attack relentlessly," the centaur briefed.

Their conversation was interrupted by the screech of a majestic, golden eagle. The eagle was giant, much larger than any other eagle. It was not quite as large as the griffons but looked just as formidable. It flew toward them with great speed and just before it landed near the party, it rotated and used its large, powerful wings to rapidly slow down.

The sudden gust of wind buffeted the area, sending small debris flying and creating a large cloud of dust.

As the dust settled, Gorian stood where the eagle had just landed. His druidic abilities allowed him to take many animal forms, but the giant eagle was one of the fastest, and most majestic.

"We must hurry! Silenus is about to fall!" he shouted.

The centarum broke the encirclement and raised their spears to allow the party to pass.

"There is not much time!" he exclaimed. His eyes suddenly widened and his jaw clenched. "Dante?" he asked solemnly.

Eldrin shook his head; a sudden look of sadness drew across his face. Gorian needed no more explanation. He nodded in understanding. "I'm so sorry …"

"We will mourn him properly when we have time, but that will be later. How can we help?" Eldrin asked.

"Many of the innocent townspeople are taking shelter in the cellar below the stronghold. I don't think they will hold up much longer, we must leave quickly!" Gorian advised. His great sense of urgency was apparent to all of them.

"We need to rid ourselves of the many important things we have carried from the dragon's lair. May we store them here?" Eldrin asked.

Gorian nodded; he knew that the loot could be priceless and needed protection. "Place your gear at the foot of the steps and I will have it taken to the treehouse," he replied.

The party immediately did as instructed, placing their backpacks at the foot of the giant tree.

"Centarum, we must ride with haste. These are my allies, see them to battle," Gorian ordered.

Five of the centaurs came over to each one of them and allowed the party to mount. They did so and took no time to ask any questions.

Once assembled, the group charged straight toward the wall of thorns just outside the grove. The centaur that Lauriel was riding was the first to rapidly approach the wall. She only had time to raise her arms instinctively to cover her face and shout one word before they hit the thorny barrier, "No!"

But just as the centaur got to the wall of thorns, the vines drew to the side and allowed them to pass.

The thorns, brambles, grasping roots, and forest inhabitants all allowed them to pass through without delay, ensuring that the way was not blocked. Lauriel was amazed at the forest's ability to defend itself from enemy attack.

The party traveled with great speed toward nearby Silenus, and just as they were about to exit Gorian's forest domain, they spotted several of the creatures that had broken off their attack on the town. There were eight of the large, four armed creatures that Eldrin and Lauriel had given the name *abraxoth*, and four of the dog-like creatures that they had given the name of *gwillinix*. The two new words were made up of parts of elven words that roughly translated to "other world creature" for abraxoth and "hounds of hell" for the gwillinix.

They were less than two hundred feet away and closing the distance rapidly. The time of reckoning had finally arrived for Lauriel. These were the same type of "vile creatures" that had killed her family and friends, ruined the innocence of her childhood, and haunted her dreams. She had trained her entire life for this very moment, and now she finally faced them in the field of battle. There was no fear in her, only focus, determination, and fury. No question remained in her mind whether or not she could face them.

As the centarum charged forward, Lauriel pointed out to her centaur the abraxoth that appeared to be the leader. It had a thick, white mane of hair and was the largest one in the formation.

Lauriel cast her Divine Shield spell and drew her weapons. She could hear the now familiar sounds of spell casting as Gorian, Jexi, and Eldrin simultaneously began to unleash a preemptive offensive onslaught. She could also hear Nyx's prayer of blessing upon them as they charged.

The enemy formation quickly formed into a semi-circular phalanx in the open field beyond the forest and prepared to receive the charge.

Gorian was the first of the group to finish casting a spell, and as he said the final word, roots sprung up from the ground around the abraxoth formation. The roots grasped at them in all directions and appeared to hold them firmly in place.

In one fluid motion, Gorian leapt off the centaur and turned into a giant dire wolf while in midair. The dire wolf landed sure-footedly on the ground and with a vicious snarl, began to charge at the formation.

Jexi was the next one to finish her spell. A floating, shadowy orb manifested from her outstretched palm and streaked toward the abraxoth formation. It traveled directly into the center of them where it appeared to hover for less than a second. The abraxoths looked at the orb and immediately began to try to get away from it but they were held fast by the roots. An explosion of shadows encircled them, covering them in darkness. The darkness lifted as quickly as it appeared, and dark, shadowy flames appeared to be burning each of them. It reminded Lauriel of Eldrin's Fireball spell. The beast flailed wildly as they tried to free themselves and stop the dark flames from burning them.

Eldrin was the next one to finish his spell. He timed the spell perfectly so that the magic would manifest just as they broke through the forest and into the clearing. As they exited the forest less than fifty feet from the abraxoth formation, the spears that the centaurs were holding began to grow into heavy lances.

The centaurs were very strong and able to quickly adjust to the new weight of the large weapon, and the charge of the centarum suddenly became an open field, full, heavy cavalry charge.

The only sound remaining was that of the thunder of hooves charging forward, gathering speed over the open ground with each stride.

The centarum had just finished leveling and steadying the lances when they crashed full speed into the enemy formation. The violence of the engagement was a stunning sight to behold. As the centarum hit the formation, a powerful, bone crushing impact occurred as four of the five lances found their targets. A loud splintering sound thundered across the glade as bone and lance fragmented from the tremendous force of the impact.

Three of the large abraxoths were catapulted off their feet and flew backward in the air several feet before crashing onto the ground with a loud thud.

Their bodies tumbled across the ground, and the sharp crack of snapping bones could be heard until the large lumps of burned and bloody fur skidded to a stop in a cloud of dust. Fur, skin, and one of the beast's feet still remained at the site of the impact where the grasping roots had tightly bound the creatures.

The fourth abraxoth was completely skewered all the way up to the vamplate of the lance by the centaur that carried Nyx. The centaur had too much momentum to stop without throwing off Nyx and was forced to release the lance and continue past the beast. As he did, the beast took a wild swipe at the centaur but missed by several feet. The mortally wounded beast let out a hollow, unnatural sounding roar that sent chills throughout the group. The roar seemed to be that of rage and malevolence, not pain. It grasped the large lance with its two giant clawed hands as well as its other two-man size hands and began to pull at the lance as it continued to roar. The lance slowly slid from the beast, and a fountain of blood gushed from the gaping wound.

The large hole had been plugged so tightly by the lance, that it did not bleed until the beast began to remove it.

With its last bit of strength, it removed the last foot of the lance and fell to the ground in a pool of blood, finally succumbing to the gruesome injury.

The heavy mounted charge was a spectacular success and had the effect of immediately evening out the field of battle, but all did not go perfectly as planned. As Lauriel and the centaur that she was riding charged at the leader, they did not realize that he had broken free from his entanglement.

At the very last second, he sidestepped the lance and batted it downward. The move caused the centaur to drop the lance and lose some of his balance and momentum. The creature took full advantage of the moment and viciously struck the centaur with his other large claw. The sharp claw ripped a gaping wound in the centaur's chest and sent Lauriel tumbling.

The dismount was sudden and violent. As she tumbled through the air, she tried desperately to tuck into a position to roll immediately as she hit the ground.

She knew that rolling would distribute some of the impact instead of hitting the ground with a sudden stop. Her quick actions worked but not as well as she had hoped. She managed to hit and roll, but the impact was still so hard that it knocked the breath out of her and sent her weapons flying several feet in opposite directions. The tumble disoriented her but it worked to prevent a much more serious injury.

Before she came to a stop, the beast had torn the centaur into multiple gory pieces, and sensing no life left in him, set its next task to destroying the rider that had just tumbled past his reach.

Lauriel looked up from the ground and could see the trees against the backdrop of the evening sky. She was lying flat on her back and briefly could not remember how she got there.

She reached for her scimitars and could not feel their familiar presence at her side, and a wave of panic washed over her as she could not remember where they were. She heard a distant voice calling to her.

"Lauriel! Get up!"

She tried to focus on the voice but was still dazed.

"What? Where are my scimitars?" she said groggily.

"LAURIEL, MOVE!" shouted the voice, this time much clearer in her head.

The urgency of the voice suddenly brought Lauriel back to her senses. She recognized the voice as Nyx's. Just then, she heard heavy footfalls approaching her from her left side and she was now fully aware of her dire situation. She instinctively rolled to the right, away from the sound of the heavy footfalls, and as she did, she could hear a loud "thud" as the beast's claw struck the ground where she had just been lying.

The ferocity and power of the attack would have had the same result on her as it did on the centaur she had been riding. The claw dug deeply into the ground, and dirt and rocks pelted her.

The beast let out a malevolent roar and raised his two large claws to strike again. Lauriel sprung to her feet and barely dodged the beast's second claw attack.

Just when she thought that her situation could not get any worse as she faced the abraxoth leader unarmed, two gwillinix sprung to attack her. They fought as a team and attacked her from opposite directions. She was well practiced in fighting multiple opponents in different directions but her *Andúlari* movements involved using her blades as part of the defense.

She was not able to avoid the onslaught and felt the incredible power of the creature's bite, followed immediately by searing pain in her calf. It felt like several nails had been driven into her leg at the same time and then held in place with a vice. She could also feel the creature's icy breath beginning to freeze her leg.

As she tried to get away from the creature's grasp, the second dog-like creature latched onto her other leg with the very same consequences. They began to pull in opposite directions, keeping her off balance and held in place as the abraxoth charged up to her. She could feel the warm blood against her ice-cold skin as the sharp fangs tore into her and held her with crushing force.

The entire sequence of events from the dismount to the creatures attacking her seemed like an eternity, but in reality, it was only seconds. In that time, Gorian had engaged one of the abraxoths in his dire wolf form and did not see her plight as he was locked in mortal combat. Nyx had seen the entire event unfold and shouted the warning that brought Lauriel back to her senses, but it happened so quickly that she was not able to return all the way back to assist her.

She and the centaur were only able to get turned back around to head toward Lauriel when one of the other abraxoths and gwillinix engaged them, preventing their return.

Nyx was the only one that Lauriel could immediately see, and she knew that she would not be able to help her out of the dire situation. She heard the many sounds of combat followed by a deafening thunderclap that rumbled throughout the grove and shook the trees beyond.

She did not hear him but assumed that it was one of Eldrin's spells. She could hear Jexi's voice faintly on the wind but could not tell where she was or how she was faring.

The pain from the two gwillinix attacking her was excruciating, but it paled in comparison to the despair that washed over her.

She had trained so hard, bent on exacting final vengeance on the creatures, and she found it bitterly ironic that she would not even get to take one swing at them. The abraxoth leader grabbed her by both arms with both of his human sized hands. She was unable to maneuver out of his grasp with the gwillinix pulling at her and keeping her off balance.

She was easily overpowered and left defenseless in a spread-eagle position. He raised his other set of arms with his huge claws above his head and let out another hollow roar.

The centaur that Eldrin was riding dropped the shattered remains of the heavy lance and veered to the right in order to avoid another abraxoth and gwillinix that had not been caught in the roots. As they did, Eldrin heard a sudden commotion to his left. He glanced back just in time to see Lauriel de-horsed. He saw her hit the ground but lost her in the commotion and clouds of dust as his centaur tried to gain distance from the creatures pursuing them. Eldrin was surprised at their incredible speed. They were not able to chase down the centaur over the open ground, but they were just as fast as he was.

Eldrin saw that the group had separated away from each other after the charge, scattering in different directions to avoid the remaining abraxoths. He knew from previous experience that separating during a fight was not to their advantage. He was well skilled but it was very dangerous for him to fight such a vicious enemy in solo combat. He decided to use a powerful spell on the pursuing abraxoth, hoping to end the battle quickly since he was dangerously far away from the others.

He could cast many spells, but the magic energies involved in casting his most powerful spells, or "big spells" as he referred to them, were very taxing both mentally and physically, and he could only use them a few times per day.

He began the incantation for a difficult Chain Lightning spell that could target several enemies. It was a much more powerful version of a wizard's standard Lightning Bolt spell and a different variation of the one that he had used against Malthrax. The spell was difficult and he had to maintain complete concentration while casting it; one single mistake and the spell would not manifest.

He knew that it would be no easy feat while clinging to a galloping centaur with his legs so that he could use his hands for the intricate somatic components that were needed to form the powerful spell.

He would have to turn around at the last moment to face the pursuing abraxoth to deliver the spell.

"Doriath nos traxus, menelthos graja dollos, archen terrax galthonis." The primal elemental magic began to flow through him, and his hands glowed a bright white from the powerful evocation.

"Narthrex alchadeum darras nalcor antedum." He formed the bright white glow into a ball of crackling energy. As he began the last phrase, he turned around to face the abraxoth as the centaur continued to maintain the distance.

"Gradja eveloss!" he shouted as he finished the spell and stuck out his hands toward the creature.

The ball of crackling energy suddenly flashed, illuminating the area with such intense white light that it temporarily blinded anyone that had been looking.

It turned into a blue-white bolt of jagged lightning that arced and immediately struck the abraxoth square in the chest. It then arced from the abraxoth to the gwillinix next to it. A thunderclap followed that was so intense, it blew several of the thorny vines off the trees that were now over one hundred feet away, and temporarily deafened everything within thirty feet of them.

Even with his eyes closed at the instant that the spell manifested, the vision of a jagged lightning bolt imprinted on Eldrin's vision for several moments. He could see it every time that he blinked. As he looked back toward the creatures, both abraxoth and gwillinix lay dead in smoking piles upon the ground before the thunderclap had even finished echoing through the forest.

Eldrin felt the familiar wave of lethargy wash over him from the use of a powerful spell, but he was relieved to see that it had killed the vile creatures.

They had learned that these creatures were very difficult and dangerous to fight but not indomitable.

His relief instantly turned to horror as he turned his gaze to witness the lead abraxoth raise his large claws above his head in a death strike that would surely rip Lauriel apart. She stood defenseless, and Eldrin, having just finished a spell, did not have time to say a single word.

The beast's blow landed heavily with a sickening hollow thud followed by the sound of ripping flesh as the claw tore into his opponent. It left a massive mortal gaping wound that not even Nyx could heal with her most potent healing spell. The dire wolf let out a loud yelp and was knocked to the ground ten feet away. As it hit the ground and rolled, it created a cloud of dust, and as it skidded to a stop, the dire wolf morphed back into Gorian. He stood up from the cloud of dust, with bloody scratches on his face and side. The abraxoth charged at him but was suddenly met by something very unexpected. Gorian changed into a strange primal creature made of earth and stone. It was two feet taller than the large abraxoth and much wider. It had large, club-like, stony arms and massive hands formed of jagged stones. Its legs, torso, and large head were made of large clumps of earth and spiked rock. It plodded toward the abraxoth like a walking hill, meeting its charge head on.

The abraxoth lashed out at the earthen creature, striking it twice with its large deadly claws. The claws struck the hard rock surface of the creature with tremendous force, knocking a few small chunks of rock and dirt loose but otherwise seemed to have little effect.

Jexi was the closest one to the earthen creature and could hear a slow, deep rumble coming from the hole where its mouth should be. It sounded to her like its form of laughter. She wanted to watch the interesting battle but her attention was quickly drawn away to other pressing needs.

The earthen creature counter attacked the abraxoth. It raised its large, club-like arms and pummeled the beast with its stony hands and unnatural strength.

*   *   *   *

The beast staggered backward from the powerful blow, suddenly realizing that it had finally met an adversary in the realm that it could not immediately dominate or overpower. The lumbering earthen monster wasted no time. It grabbed the abraxoth and, using its several-thousand-pound weight advantage, slammed it to the ground and fell directly on top of it.

"*Drakerzyys Nohelë Xavarath!*" Jexi shouted. Her words were spoken as fast as possible, and the sound of her concerned shout carried above the noise of the battle, echoing clearly and distinctly throughout the glade.

Lauriel stared steely-eyed at the abraxoth in complete silence, never breaking eye contact with him nor making a single sound no matter how bad the pain was from the gwillinix attack. She refused to give him any satisfaction by closing her eyes and cowering down to him, or yelling out in pain.

She could tell that that the beast's hollow roar was meant to draw attention to himself so that he could make an example out of her to the others in her group.

Neither he nor Lauriel realized it, but he had already drawn the full attention of one member of the group.

Lauriel heard the quickened words on the wind from somewhere far behind her: *"Drakerzyys Nohelë Xavarath!"* The abraxoth and both gwillinix were suddenly encircled by floating, green, translucent skulls. Lauriel immediately recognized it as the same spell that Jexi had used on Dante. She could see the abraxoth's red eyes widen, and he immediately released her. He turned back toward Silenus and began to run at full speed.

One of the gwillinix repeatedly let out a hollow but higher pitched yelp as it tucked its leathery, bat-like ears down and ran after the Abraxoth with its hairless tail between its legs.

The other gwillinix seemed to shake off the effects of the warlock Fear spell and clamped down even harder on Lauriel's leg, pulling at her to keep her off balance.

She was not prepared for the sudden release from the other gwillinix and lost her footing from the pull. She fell to the ground, and the gwillinix began to pull her farther away from the group.

She reached out for something to grab onto and suddenly felt a warm, familiar presence in her hand. She did not have to look; she knew exactly what it was although she did not understand how it came to her. Isilmwé flashed as she quickly struck out at the beast, skewering it directly through the chest in one fluid motion. The vice-like grip of the beast immediately loosened, and it let out a hollow but feeble yelp as it collapsed to the ground.

Its bulging, yellow eyes stared unblinking at her and quickly began to lose their luster as the life drained from it. Lauriel watched as the cold frost from his last breath exited the vile creature.

Shaken

Lauriel was shocked when she quickly surveyed the field of battle only to find a large, earthen and stone creature slowly pummeling an abraxoth to death. The abraxoth was incredibly strong, but not strong enough to move the small hill off of itself, and it was oddly satisfying to see the beast killed in such a gruesome manner— much as it had done to many others. The rest of the battle had ended quickly as the remaining abraxoth and gwillinix near Nyx disengaged and ran to follow their fleeing leader.

Lauriel tried to stand but collapsed as a sudden wave of intense pain washed over her from the terrible wounds that the two gwillinix had caused to her legs. She reached down only to find that both of her legs were icy cold and had no feeling at all of her hand being on top of either of them.

Without delay, she closed her eyes and began to speak her words of divine healing magic that she had come to know from her Goddess, and a blue glow encircled her hand.

As the blue radiance washed over her calf, she could immediately feel the same familiar surge of vitality course through her that she had become accustomed to when Nyx healed her. When it subsided, the wound was closed and her leg warmed to the touch. But her healing spell was not as focused or powerful as Nyx's, and the injury to her other leg remained.

* * * *

Nyx arrived at Lauriel's side just as Lauriel's healing spell concluded. "Very good!" she exclaimed in a hoarse whisper. Tears spilled down her cheeks and she was doing her very best that she could to choke back her emotions so that she could focus on her task of healing. She had seen the entire event play out in front of her but had been unable to help Lauriel out of the dire situation. For a brief moment, she was sure she was watching Lauriel's last breath, and the incident had shaken her to the core.

She had to clear her eyes several times as she inspected the gruesome wound to Lauriel's other leg. The bites had made many large puncture wounds that penetrated deeply into Lauriel's calf. It bled very little because the blood and tissue had been frozen from the creature's icy breath.

A large area around the wound showed signs of severe frostbite, and Nyx knew that in the absence of divine healing, the flesh would die and fester, and her leg would almost surely end up needing to be amputated.

"These creatures inflict such terrible wounds!" Nyx gasped.

She reached down and placed her hand gently on Lauriel's mauled leg and spoke her words of divine magic.

When the spell concluded and Lauriel's wounds were healed, she helped her to stand. She looked up at Lauriel's tear-filled eyes and threw her arms around her as if she would never again let go of her friend. But she was not at all prepared for the response she received back from Lauriel.

"I am so thankful for you; you are the sister that I never had," Lauriel said as she tightly embraced her.

Nyx was instantly blinded with tears, and she was so overcome that she was only able to give a single word reply.

"Faataa."

It was the colloquial halfling language term that translated to "same to you."

Lauriel took Nyx's hand in hers. "I lived to fight another day because of my new family. It was your warning that brought me out of the daze just in time … thank you."

* * * *

Jexi was the next to arrive at Lauriel's side. The near-death experience was just beginning to sink in, and she knew that it was Jexi's spell that had just saved her life.

"Jexi," Lauriel began. Her eyes shimmered as she tried to find the words to thank her, but there was nothing in the common or elven tongue that seemed adequate. She instead hugged her tightly, and the embrace meant more to Jexi than any spoken words.

"I'm happy to have been able to return the favor," Jexi said.

But ever true to form, she slid her hand down Lauriel's back and onto her butt. "I mean … I really couldn't let you die before I had the chance."

The flippant comment drew laughter from all of them and provided some brief but needed comic relief. Jexi quickly looked away and let go of Lauriel, acting like her attention had been drawn elsewhere.

"Ahh, here is Nightfang."

She began to walk over to retrieve the scimitar that was partially impaled into the ground some distance from them. Jexi hid it well, but Lauriel got a brief glimpse of her tear-filled eyes as she pulled away. She could immediately see right through Jexi's facade.

* * * *

Lauriel was shaken by what had just happened, but her thoughts were drawn elsewhere as Eldrin quickly approached. His red, glistening eyes were full of compassion, and she could easily see the genuine look of concern that radiated from his pale face.

"Are you okay, *Ælfen*?" His voice trembled as he embraced her.

She clutched him tightly, and a warm, safe feeling washed over her.

"I am now," she whispered.

Their first talk on the couch by the fireplace now seemed like a lifetime ago, and her affection for him had only grown since that time. But she had long been haunted by an emotional wall of protection that she had built in the aftermath of the tragic losses of those she loved, and she had been reticent to allow herself to completely fall for someone that could so easily be taken from her. But after seeing his reaction to the incident and feeling the love and warmth in his embrace, her mind finally accepted what her heart had been telling her for some time, and her last barriers of resistance crumbled.

"Eldrin ... I—"

Lauriel's expression was suddenly interrupted by several large rumbles that came from the direction of Silenus.

Gorian had turned back into his regular form but remained standing on top of the bloody remains of the smashed and mangled abraxoth corpse.

"I hate to break this up, but we must hurry, there is still a town that desperately needs our help."

With the moment gone and her courage to say what she had wanted to now failing her, Lauriel smiled, nodded in agreement, and quickly gathered her things

CHAPTER TWENTY

Vile Creatures

auriel quickly walked over to the fallen centaur that she had been riding. They were in a hurry to get to Silenus, but she wanted to ensure that his courageous death in battle was properly recognized. His broken and mangled upper torso was a hideous reminder of the danger that they faced with each encounter. She knelt down beside him and gently placed her hand on his shoulder.

"I'm sorry, my friend," her voice quivered as she spoke, "you were one of the bravest that I have known."

She was quickly joined by Gorian and the other remaining centarum. "He was indeed a brave warrior," Gorian echoed. His eyes were filled with tears, and he had to pause briefly before he was able to finish. "May he now run free in the great forest beyond."

One of the centarum stepped forward and began to speak in a husky and declarative voice. "As soon as we can make it back here, we will take him for a proper burial; a hero's burial." All of the other centarum stomped the ground with their front hooves, signaling their agreement. The dull thuds of their powerful strikes echoed throughout the glade.

The other companions joined Lauriel and knelt down around him and paid their respects to the brave warrior who, without any hesitation, had charged headlong into battle against a terrible and unknown enemy.

He had paid the ultimate sacrifice but was posthumously victorious as his enemy was driven away from the grove that he was determined to protect.

They had to cut short the somber reflection, knowing that the town desperately needed their help. The companions re-mounted the centaurs and turned toward Silenus, now one short. Lauriel joined with Nyx but the centaur was not at all encumbered by the two riders; both of them together did not even equal the weight of a heavy rider or single armored warrior.

The new moon was now rising, and the tiny sliver of silvery light only illuminated the forest enough to cause it to look especially dark and sinister. Shadows flitted amongst the trees with every movement of the leaves. Gorian looked around nervously, continually scouting the forest. He knew that there were several more of the abraxoth scout groups making their way through the outer forested areas around the city in an attempt to round up and exterminate those that were trying to flee the terror. The abraxoths did not want to capture and enslave; they only wanted to kill.

As they raced toward the city with Gorian leading the way, he suddenly veered off the path and onto an obscure game trail. He looked back at the companions and spoke in quick, hushed tones that were only loud enough to rise above the noise of the surprisingly quiet gallop. "I know a secret way into the stronghold; hopefully the enemy has not found it yet."

The rest of the centarum followed the narrow trail that led through the dense forest and they quickly made their way to a small stream. Gorian turned upstream and continued following it for several minutes until the right bank of the river began to rise sharply with the steep terrain that formed a large hill.

He brought them to an abrupt stop near a portion of the bank that had heavy foliage that grew down to the life-giving waters of the small stream.

Lauriel could tell from her natural direction sense that Silenus was not far away in the direction of the hill. Gorian dismounted and ran over to the right bank and began to search.

He had not frequented this area, especially after dark, so the secret way remained hidden to him until he could locate it. The darkness and shadows from the small amount of moonlight made the entrance even more difficult to find, but after a few minutes of searching, Gorian pulled aside several vines, that made up part of the thick foliage and revealed a four-foot round stone opening that peaked out inconspicuously from the steep embankment. A small but steady trickle of water flowed through the stone opening and into the stream below. The stones were covered in moss and slime from the constant dampness around them, blending perfectly with flora of the hill. The thick foliage had completely camouflaged the opening.

"This is a very old aqueduct that is used to divert excess water from a natural spring within the inner city walls. A secret exit from the cellar below the stronghold connects to it," Gorian whispered.

The rest of the group dismounted and quietly thanked the centarum for their aid. Gorian entered the dark, stone tunnel.

"Watch your step, the wet moss makes it very slippery," he cautioned as he disappeared into the darkness.

One by one, the rest of the companions entered the cramped stone tunnel behind him, and everyone but Nyx was forced to hunch over into an awkward and uncomfortable position. They were immediately beset upon by the all-encompassing odor of dankness and decay. The entire tunnel was damp, and water dripped from the ceiling as it slowly seeped into the stone tunnel from the mountain of earth above.

But it was the entire bottom surface of the aqueduct that presented the biggest problem for them. It was covered in a slimy moss that made each and every step incredibly difficult.

As they pressed deeper into the hillside, every few feet seemed to bring them into an ever-increasing amount of the slippery moss, and all of them slipped and fell numerous times as the journey became more and more precarious.

They traveled for what seemed like several frustrating and painful hours before they finally came to a stop at a spot in the tunnel that had a heavy iron handle attached to the ceiling. Upon closer inspection, they could see that the handle marked a well-crafted stone that could be removed.

"I was here when this was built long ago, but there are few that now remember this escape," Gorian whispered.

He grabbed the handle and began to push against the stone. Dust began to fall into the tunnel as the stone began to break free from its resting place. Soft candlelight began to spill into the dark cave through the crack, and with it, the muffled cries of young children.

With one final push, Gorian heaved the stone up and out of the way. He peered through the hole when suddenly several broom sticks came down hard on top of his head, and he was forced to duck back into the tunnel.

"GO AWAY, EVIL THINGS!" a voice shouted from above.

"You'll not have our children no matter the cost," another scared but determined voice yelled.

"We are here to help you! We are not the evil creatures!" Gorian yelled up through the hole, making sure to stay well away from it.

There was a brief muffled conversation, and then a female voice from the cellar above called back down to them. "Hurry then, we don't have much time!" One by one, the party exited the aqueduct through the escape hole and filed into the cellar. They found twenty-five women tending to over one hundred children and elderly.

They were crammed into a space that normally would not be comfortable for even fifty.

The air was heavy, and a palpable sense of sheer terror could be felt throughout the room.

The party was covered in mud, slime, and bloody scrapes as they emerged through the hole and stepped into the room. The moldy stench of the aqueduct carried with them.

The younger children began to cry hysterically at the new sight. To them, it looked like swamp monsters had just emerged through the floor.

The women did their best to console them, but it was not until Nyx knelt down beside them to show that she was not a monster that they began to settle down.

The escape had been well hidden and appeared to be one of the many flagstone floor pieces until it was moved out of the way.

"Good heavens, where did you come from? We had no idea that was even there!" one of the women exclaimed as she brought them a small amount of water and a few hand towels to clean themselves off.

They happily obliged and quickly cleaned themselves of the foul-smelling slime while Gorian explained the aqueduct and how to escape into the woods through it. It was a remarkable escape system but, in this case, the companions knew any attempt at escaping through the pipe would be fruitless. The gwillinix would track them down in the pipe, and they would never even make it to the woods. And even in the off chance that some of them did make it to the woods, they would be hunted down quickly and mercilessly.

Seeing the scared women and children awoke a flame in Lauriel that began to grow into an unquenched inferno. It reached its pinnacle when she walked over to one of the women holding the hand of a small girl that looked like she was about six years old. The little girl had blonde hair and bright green eyes. She reminded Lauriel of her terrified self as a child.

She was shaking uncontrollably, and her eyes were so red and swollen from crying that they could shed no more tears.

Lauriel knelt down, and the young girl, seeing her scimitars, immediately ran up to her and threw her arms around her neck and held on as tightly as she could.

Lauriel gently held her until the girl was able to calm down enough to whisper something in her ear that she was not at all prepared for. "Please save my mommy and my brother and my sister. My brother is out fighting the monsters."

Lauriel's heart melted at the small girl's selfless request, and she fought desperately to maintain her calm and collected composure so she didn't scare the children with tears.

Lauriel began to shake as she looked at the girl and then her mother.

"I swear to you by the Gods as my witness, no harm will come to you or any of these children tonight," she declared.

The woman could see Lauriel's green eyes flash with the same fearless fury as that of a mother bear protecting her cubs. The look was so shocking that she could only stare back at Lauriel in wide-eyed wonderment. Lauriel's words carried throughout the room, and her matter-of-fact confidence gave the refugees a sliver of hope and courage, the only sense of reassurance they had experienced since the attack had begun two days prior.

Eldrin and Jexi exchanged a worried glance, not only because they were concerned about making a promise they did not know they could keep, but because Eldrin could hear the same determined voice from Lauriel that he did when she set her mind to complete the Bladerite—no matter the danger to herself. They both knew that Lauriel meant what she said; she would stop the creatures or die trying, and no force in Alynthi would hold her back. Likewise, the other companions would never abandon the women and children, their stand against the darkness would happen here and now.

Lauriel stood up and unwittingly stepped fully into her role as Blademaster to a Blade of Power.

She slowly drew her scimitars with calm assurance. The Moonblade bathed the room in a soft, blue-white light that had an immediate calming effect on the women and children. Her companions could feel the sudden, strong desire to follow the Blademaster as she took full command of the situation.

Eldrin suddenly understood the deeper significance of the moment. He had been so close to Lauriel the he had been blinded to the events that had shaped her path.

Lauriel wielded Isilmwé, a representation of all forces in the realm that were good and lawful. She also wielded Nightfang, a representation of all forces in the realm that represented chaos and evil. She stood in the balance of the two, a counter-point representing a unifying neutrality, and as the Blademaster, she was in a unique position to unite the two.

Eldrin recalled that the blade of power had been called a "Sword of Dominion" in the ancient tome, and he now understood what it meant. Those that observed the Blademaster wielding it, good or evil, would be compelled to follow her. They would not follow her against their will, but would have a strong desire to stand with her, even at great peril to themselves. He himself could feel it and would stop at nothing to help her. The rise of the Blademaster was not just the rise of a powerful warrior wielding an ancient blade of power as he had thought, but the rise of someone that could unite the realms into a unified stand against the darkness from the otherworld that poured through the portal. Eldrin felt foolish for being so focused on the quest that he could not see what was manifesting right in front of him.

"How could I have missed that?" Eldrin mused. He knew that Lauriel did not yet understand the full significance of her role.

"Gorian," Lauriel said calmly, "should they get past us, see to it that these women and children safely escape through the aqueducts. Try to at least get the stone back in place and disguised to buy them time."

"Yes, Lauriel," Gorian found himself answering without question.

"May the Gods be with you tonight," one of the ladies quietly spoke, her eyes still open wide in awe.

Lauriel called down the divine wrathful energy from her Goddess, and her arms and scimitars were suddenly surrounded by scintillating energies that further illuminated the room.

"They are with all of us," Lauriel answered as she turned and walked up the stone stairway that led to the room above.

Eldrin, Jexi, Gorian, and Nyx quickly followed her up and through the hatch that led into the small antechamber.

The small room had an open door that led into a large kitchen. From there, an open archway led directly to the Great Hall, the largest room inside the stronghold.

The party entered the Great Hall and briefly observed the magnificent grandeur of the room. It was beautifully crafted with wooden knot work and timbers. The splendor of the hall was known throughout the kingdom, and it was frequently used by visiting nobles for royal ceremonies and large feasts. The walls were decorated by large tapestries of great battles.

The room had a tall, heavy timber ceiling and was surrounded by a second-floor balcony that allowed many onlookers to observe the royal festivities. Banners of the great houses hung from the heavy timbers in a grand display of the power of the kingdom. Most of the large tables and furnishings of the room had been pushed hastily against the heavy, wooden, double doors that provided the main entry into the room, opposite to where they entered. The doors were barred by a heavy timber log, and several of the heavy tables had been turned on their side and placed into covered firing positions away from the door.

Six remaining soldiers crouched behind them with crossbows at the ready. Heavy blows upon the door echoed throughout the hall, and the distinct sound of cracking wood could be heard with each strike.

Near the archway stood eight remaining elite guards surrounding the grand duke and duchess. They were known as the "Golden Company" and were widely renowned and respected for their skill and dedication. Many of the guards were bloodied and suffered terrible wounds. Several pieces of their heavy, full plate armor had been torn off, and their signature golden capes had been ripped into shreds. Two of the loyal men struggled to remain standing, unable to even lift their swords, but they stood as a protective barrier nonetheless.

All of them were surprised to see the companions enter the room through the antechamber near them.

"Who comes here?" barked the captain of the guard threateningly.

"Gorian!" exclaimed the duke. His eyebrows raised, and his tense face lightened as the look of recognition dawned on his face. "It is okay, Stephen, they are allies," the duke quickly explained, his voice choked with emotion.

The companions and the elite guard had no time for introduction or pleasantries. They immediately joined forces and readied for the enemy. The heavy pounding on the doors continued, and pieces of it splintered inward as it finally began to succumb to the unrelenting force.

Nyx used a powerful healing spell that provided a small amount of healing to every one of the guards. The two men who struggled to stand seemed to be renewed to the point that they could once again lift their swords.

As she faced the doors, Lauriel was oblivious to everything else around her. She could hear the voice of her Goddess's instructions clearly echoing in her mind: *You shall seek vengeance against these abominations for the terrible things that they have done to you and your kind …*

Visions of the scared, little girl hiding in the cellar below flashed through her mind as she walked toward the doors at the far end of the room.

"What the hell is she doing?" the captain gasped as she broke from their ranks and moved into a forward position.

"Swift death to my enemies," she sneered, her jaw clenched in tense anticipation. The guards stared at her in shock as she moved boldly toward the enemy. One of her blades bathed the room in a peaceful, radiant glow while the other seemed to cast a shadow of impending doom. She held her swords at the ready. It was not her standard "defensive ready" position, but her aggressive "offensive attack." She would meet the brutality of the vile creatures with violence, their strength with her skill and dexterity, and their deadly claws with the sharpest blades known to mankind.

Eldrin knew that the time had come and cast his Haste spell on her. She was so focused that she did not notice the effects as the arcane magic washed over her.

"Please don't be alarmed, I'm about to change into something that may frighten you; just know that it is still me," Gorian said quickly as he looked intently at the guards and royals.

They nodded, trying to understand, but they were still shocked and frightened as he changed into his earth elemental form. He turned and followed Lauriel to the doors, his heavy footfalls echoing loudly throughout the room.

The doors shuddered heavily, and a loud cracking noise could be heard as the heavy timber log that barred them began to crack.

The captain lowered his visor, and all of the guards followed suit. "Men, it has been an honor to fight at your side. Let us at least die with dignity, as fighting men. Let's give them hell!"

He raised his sword in final salute and prepared for the onslaught.

With one final push, the doors burst open as the heavy timber log splintered and gave way. Tables, chairs, and pieces of door scattered wildly as fifteen abraxoths and five gwillinix burst into the room.

Lauriel and the earth elemental immediately charged at the abraxoth formation.

Witnessing the direct charge of the Blademaster awoke the primal warrior spirit within the Golden Company formation, and they let out a bellowing war cry as all of them charged valiantly with Lauriel. Eldrin was amazed at the blade's profound effect; even the duke and duchess charged with them. They were fully rallied and would follow her at all costs.

It had been ninety-seven years, and two hundred thirty-three days since the attack on her village when Lauriel finally struck her first abraxoth. The first strike carried with it all of the pent-up vengeance and fury within her. Her *Andúlari* movements were swift, and the dreadful slicing sound of her blades instantaneously turned into a clear ringing that echoed throughout the Great Hall.

The sound of thunder echoed throughout as Lauriel released the wrathful energy from her Goddess as her first strike fell with deadly accuracy and timing. The lead abraxoth was immediately fallen before it even had a chance to raise its deadly claws. It slumped to the ground, its vile head falling next to it.

The voice in her head continued as she immediately pressed the attack to the next enemy. *You shall smite down those creatures that rise against you, exacting my divine retribution upon them.* She could also hear the voice of the little girl, *Please save my mommy and my little sister.*

Her second strike ripped violently across the upper torso of the next abraxoth standing just to the left of where the first had been. The room shook again in a thunderous crescendo of energy as she called down the same wrath from her Goddess.

Lauriel was quickly becoming a conduit, learning how to safely channel more and more of the Goddess's energy through her attacks.

Five more blade-strikes landed upon the creature in quick succession as Lauriel systematically dismembered it. Three of the creature's arms were completely severed, and one hung mutilated at its side before it slumped to the ground in a pool of blood and tattered fur.

The speed of her blades slung the creature's blood all the way to the banners hanging from the large ceiling rafters twenty-five feet above.

The final voice that Lauriel heard in her mind was that of Adamar and his wise words of instructions to her when she fought too wildly: *You must learn when to keep that in check or it will be the death of you.*

She immediately stopped pressing the attack and began to maneuver defensively, giving time for the others to catch up and engage the remaining enemies.

The third abraxoth attempted to decisively end her reign of terror against them with two vicious swipes with his large claws, but she was moving so fast that its attack seemed oddly slow to her, and she was able to easily dodge and roll past them.

The earth elemental crashed head long into the third abraxoth at a full run, catching it off guard just as it missed Lauriel.

The earthen juggernaut had so much momentum that it careened straight into the stone wall immediately to the left of the doorway, its grappled enemy leading the way. There was a tremendous shudder throughout the hall as part of the wall crumbled, creating a small avalanche of stone and a newly enlarged doorway. Blood and gore splattered high on the wall as the monster was smashed almost flat in between the two mountains of stone. It reminded Eldrin of a hammer striking molten metal against an anvil.

Six men fired crossbow bolts from their forward crouched positions behind the tables.

Many of the bolts hit but did not seem to slow the creatures down in any meaningful way. The gwillinix charged at the men with the crossbows, quickly hurdling the tables between them.

Jexi began one of her warlock incantations she had learned for use against multiple enemies at the same time.

"*Avas nalthios graxethas.*"

She placed her two thumbs together and held her arms fingers upward in a fan pattern, and darkness began to gather around her hands.

"*Neriak andothas!*"

As she spoke the final words of the spell, she threw her hands downward in front of her, and the darkness moved quickly toward five of the abraxoths in a snakelike movement, encircling each of their heads. The darkness coalesced into five black, shadowy crowns that sat on the head of each abraxoth target.

Jexi winked at them and waved goodbye as she could feel the spell successfully take hold. The abraxoths with the crowns suddenly turned against the other abraxoths and began to attack them.

The other unsuspecting abraxoths were caught flat footed by the sudden attacks from their allies and suffered quick and devastating injuries.

Waves of blood began to splash onto the floor and quickly covered the entire far end of the Great Hall. Jexi's control spell lasted only ten seconds, but it was long enough to cause four of the abraxoths to inflict mortal wounds on each other.

The elite guard, now inspired and following the charge of the Blademaster, crashed head long into the chaotic abraxoth foray. Blades and claws fought furiously for the contested hall. Three guards fell heroically in the furious struggle but not before another two abraxoths were hacked down.

Lauriel was able to get a glimpse of the hallway through the newly widened doorway and could see at least six more abraxoths running down the long hall to join the battle. The hallway was wide, but the creatures were so large that they could only fit single file. She knew that if she could delay the lead in the hallway, the others would not be able to attack or flank her, nor could they continue to pour unchecked into the room. In the confusion of battle, she was able to slip by the original formation and into the hallway.

Eldrin's spell shook the Great Hall to the point that it knocked several of the banners from the rafters. Bits of sand and dust fell from the ceiling as the blinding white lightning bolt jumped from creature to creature, each time creating a deafening thunderclap. The lightning bolt arced six times in less than a second, and when the spell ended, four of the remaining abraxoths and one gwillinix lay smoldering on the ground.

"For Silenus!" the duchess cried.

The lone remaining abraxoth's eyes narrowed as it felt a small but painful sting in its back as the duchess jabbed her dirk into the creature with as much strength as she could muster. It spun around to see what annoyance had caused the small injury. The remaining four gwillinix disengaged from their near complete mauling of the crossbowmen and began to charge at the duchess.

The duke leapt upon the abraxoth's back and began to furiously stab it in its head and neck, trying desperately to draw its attention off of his wife.

His blade was joined by a flurry of blade strikes from the Golden Company, and the monster was cut down in all directions before it had the chance to counter-attack.

The gwillinix were fast and leapt at the duchess just as the abraxoth was being engaged.

They savagely attacked her like a pack of wolves attacking a wounded deer. They were not trying to hold her in place like they had Lauriel, but were instead trying to kill their prey as quickly as possible.

The crushing force from the beast's powerful jaws snapped several bones in her arms, hands, and legs. Blood began to freely pour from her many wounds, joining with the other pools of blood that were already covering the ground. Her screams of terror and pain echoed throughout the halls, sending cold chills down the allies' spines. One of the beasts ripped her arm away from her face, and the other quickly moved in to rip out her soft and unprotected throat.

The attack happened so quickly, that the other warriors near her did not even have time to turn around to help her. It was Nyx that saw the horror unfolding and immediately cast one of her spells on the duchess. She was suddenly enveloped in a bright, blue-white light that caused the creatures to recoil. As they did, one of the dog-like beasts was snatched up and held fast by the mountain of rock. The rock creature began to beat the other gwillinix with it, using it as a blunt but deadly weapon.

Each strike caused a bone crushing thud to echo throughout the room as the dead body of the grappled gwillinix crushed the life out of the others, slamming into them with tremendous force. When Gorian got through with his rampage, four very mangled and dead gwillinix corpses lay around his stony feet.

As the last of the beasts fell, there was a brief moment of pause as both the companions and the elite guard quickly surveyed the room to see who had fallen during the chaos of battle. Blood, corpses, and debris littered the floor of the Great Hall in an apocalyptic scene of complete carnage.

The room had been partially destroyed and was in such a state of devastation and disorder that it made the grand room seem diminished from its once mighty grandeur. Littered across the floor were the scattered remains of three elite guards, four crossbowmen, fifteen abraxoths, and five gwillinix.

The Duchess

A sudden, anguished cry echoed throughout the room, breaking the momentary lull. As Nyx's spell of hedging protection ended, the blue light that had been enveloping the duchess faded, revealing yet another gruesome sight. The duchess's mangled and lifeless remains laid in a twisted heap upon the floor. She was covered in bright red blood that stood in stark contrast to her ghost white skin.

The blood of the creatures intermixed on the floor with the massive amount of blood that she had lost and created a thick, hideous pool around her. Her eyes were closed, but her mouth gaped open in a silent scream. The duke ran to the duchess, desperately attempting to join her side as he slipped wildly through the blood. He fell to his hands and knees and frantically clawed his way to her.

The captain ripped off his helm and threw it to the ground with a loud crash, bellowing out in grief at the scene of the fallen duchess. He had been fully committed to protecting them with his life, and her death was his failure. It was a personal affront to his position that he so proudly and dutifully held.

Nyx quickly made her way to the duke and duchess's side and knelt down beside them, checking to see if there was any sign of life that remained in her.

"Please help her!" cried the duke.

Tears streamed down his cheeks, and his face was wracked with anguish.

Nyx had just started to shake her head when she suddenly gasped in astonishment. She could feel the faintest beat of the duchess's quickly slowing heart.

"She's still alive!" she cried.

She immediately began her healing spell, and the hulking earth elemental suddenly turned back into Gorian as he quickly knelt down at the fallen noble's feet. He was forced to change back because he was not able to use his druidic healing magic in his other forms.

Blue light flared almost immediately from Nyx's and Gorian's outstretched hands, and the duchess was bathed in the divine radiance of their combined healing spells.

The duchess's eyes opened wide, and she began to gasp and sputter, trying desperately to fill her lungs back with the breath of life that had already left them.

The combined healing spells helped to bring her from the very brink of death, stabilizing her and closing many of the terrible wounds. When she finally caught her breath, she cried out in agony as she became reoriented and realized that her last thoughts were not some terrible nightmare; they were true. Untold death and destruction had befallen their city.

"By the Gods! I have never seen such healing!" the captain cried.

His face was suddenly transformed from that of darkness and despair to one of light and hope.

The duke threw his arms around the duchess and they held each other in a firm embrace. He was unable to speak, but tears of joy flowed freely from his eyes.

Avatar of Vengeance

At the same time that the duchess regained consciousness, Eldrin and Jexi began to run toward the hallway, and the rest of the group quickly realized that there was no time to celebrate the saved life, or mourn the dead. The sounds of furious battle echoed down the hallway and spilled through the newly made large opening of the Great Hall. The guards quickly wiped the blood off their swords with the tattered remnants of their golden capes and charged into the hallway.

The carnage that greeted them was another extension of the hellish landscape of the stronghold.

The much narrower hallway floor was completely covered in blood, and clumps of fur and blood dripped nightmarishly from the walls and ceilings.

Large chunks of meat, severed limbs, and gore littered the ground around the corpses of several vile creatures that had all been sliced to varying degrees of dismemberment. The air was thick, and the smell of iron and death filled their nostrils.

The many torches that lined the hallway illuminated the fine droplets of blood that hung oppressively in the air, causing the entire length of the corridor to be bathed in a faint, pink hue.

They filed into the hallway just in time to witness the Blademaster's next killing blow of the only enemy that remained in the stronghold. As it fell, Lauriel kicked it in the head and muttered something inaudible as if to conclude some final grievance against him. They realized that the felled abraxoth appeared to be no other than the one that had almost killed her during the charge of the centarum.

With the last enemy inside the stronghold now dead, a sudden and complete silence blanketed the area. No enemies remained alive in the stronghold, and no sounds of battle raged throughout.

Lauriel turned back toward the Great Hall and looked up to find the group standing in the hallway staring silently at her. The mouths of the elite guards gaped in awe, and a look of shock and admiration was etched on their faces.

Lauriel had single handedly sliced through six abraxoths and three gwillinix. She was covered in blood from head to toe but did not seem to be suffering from any significant injuries.

The captain took a knee and was quickly joined by the other guards.

"Your skill and bravery is remarkable, my lady. I would gladly follow you into the gates of hell if needed," the captain proclaimed.

"And I!" The other guards shouted their affirmation one by one until all of them had joined in their commitment.

Lauriel nodded politely and awkwardly to the captain and the guards, somewhat embarrassed at his deference.

Adamar had also been a captain, and she held his rank and years of service and dedication in high regard; she was but a civilian.

The soldiers of the Golden Company had been truly inspired by her skill and bravery, but she was still unaware of the effect that she had on them with wielding Isilmwé as the Blademaster.

The adrenaline, emotions, and Eldrin's Haste spell wore off simultaneously, and an intense wave of lethargy washed over her, just as it had after the dragon fight. She was forced to lean heavily against the wall and hold herself up with her hands so that she would not collapse onto the cobblestone floor. She tried to reply to the captain but could only speak in broken sentences in between her heavy gasps for air. "Thank you for the kind words ... and the commitment to help ... I may well take you up on that before this is all said and done ..."

As she took a moment to catch her breath, the magnitude and significance of the entire day began to set in, and she was overcome by a complex mixture of emotions. She had gone from burying a dear friend, to a near death experience, to finally getting her revenge while saving many others, all in a very brief amount of time. The weight of the lives of the refugees in the cellar was now off of her shoulders, and the realization of their successful rescue was such a joy and relief to her that it manifested as a sudden and unabated stream of tears. She dropped her scimitars to the ground and slid down against the wall into a seated position, covering her face with her shaking hands.

She had kept her promise to the refugees in the cellar. The young, green-eyed girl would live and be able to hug her "mommy and sister" again, one small example of many joyous celebrations that would happen throughout the city. But the feelings of joy and relief were also mixed with the finality of a lifelong pursuit, exacting vengeance against the "vile creatures." Her relentless training and determination had finally come to fruition against her mortal enemy, and she had performed well, just as she had been taught by her dear grandfather, Adamar.

She knew that he would be proud of her, and she suddenly realized that she desperately missed him. She missed the peace and stability of what seemed like a previous life with him. Her departure had only seemed to lead her down a trail of death, destruction, and dark events that had led up to this moment.

She struggled with the wave of many emotions but there was one ever-present burden that weighed increasingly heavily upon her; she knew that what they had accomplished in such a desperate struggle was but a single ripple in a pond, and the thought of what remained was overwhelming. She did not yet know the full extent of her role as Blademaster, but she was beginning to feel the crushing weight of it.

Eldrin, Jexi, and Nyx sunk down beside her and wrapped their comforting arms around her. The companions had shared and experienced enough together that they fully understood her reaction. Their warm embrace brought her comfort in the knowledge that she was not alone; she had friends by her side that she had come to love. She knew she could not shoulder the burden that she felt alone, nor did she have to; it was being shared equally by all of them.

The Golden Company quietly filed back into the Great Hall and began to clean up so that the children could be brought out of the cellar without being exposed to such a horrible display of death. The duke and duchess joined them in a show of determination to rebuild the devastated city. One by one, the companions filed back into the Great Hall and helped clean up the carnage.

Lauriel was the last one to emerge from the hallway. She had needed some extra time alone so that she could reflect, regain her composure, and clean herself off. She was finally able to calm herself down enough to realize that the victory they had just experienced was monumental. They had stopped the enemy from killing the entire town, and made them pay dearly for their atrocities.

As she rounded the corner and stood in the doorway, the sense of relief that she felt was immediately evident on her radiant face. Her bright eyes gleamed, and her jaw was no longer tensed with the stress of imminent mortal combat. Her sheathed scimitars hung on their belt around her hips, no longer drawn menacingly.

Eldrin couldn't help but openly admire the beautiful elven Blademaster as she stood in the doorway and observed the room with a look of shock as if it was the first time that she had seen it.

"Stunning," he said absentmindedly.

He loved the brief moments when he could see her free of her troubles and cares.

As her eyes scanned the room, they came to meet Eldrin's. She smiled sheepishly at him, suddenly embarrassed at her rampaging warpath of destruction.

The men of the Golden Company stood up and began to clap, applauding her performance in admiration. They were fully committed to her and stood ready to carry out any command that she would give them. The duke, also under the heavy influence of the controlling presence from Blademaster's sword, had already offered their service to whatever end was needed in order to bring an end to the creatures.

Lauriel was becoming uncomfortable with the attention and was about to say something when the moment was suddenly broken up by Jexi.

"Good grief, and you all thought that I was the demented one; look at this place, you crazy bitch!" Jexi jested playfully from across the room.

Jexi could immediately see that her familiarity and lack of deference to Lauriel made the guards very uncomfortable, so she of course continued. She leaned over to the captain and began talking to him in a quiet voice, but spoke intentionally loud enough that the other guards near him could hear her.

"I'm just upset that my spell didn't create the most chaos in this battle—my crazy lover did!"

He turned bright red, unable to respond, and upon seeing his obvious discomfort, Jexi continued again, escalating her rhetoric even more. "You think that was crazy, you should see her in bed! I still have nail marks down my back that not even Nyx could heal."

All he could do was look at her pleadingly, his eyes and face begging her to stop her current one-way conversation with him. Both Lauriel and Jexi were two of the most beautiful women that he had ever seen and his sense of duty and professionalism could only hold out so long. Jexi appeared to get as much satisfaction out of his discomfort as she did winning the battle.

"Good job, love!" she shouted across the room to Lauriel, her eyes still locked onto the captain's.

Lauriel had not been paying attention to what Jexi was saying and only heard her last statement directed at her.

"Thanks, love!" Lauriel immediately responded, unwittingly playing into Jexi's psychological torture of the Golden Company.

"I hope you saved some energy for tonight," Jexi continued.

Lauriel thought the statement was odd and knew that she had missed something, but she quickly came to the conclusion that they were talking about a party or celebration of the great victory.

"Well … I'm exhausted but I wouldn't miss out on that."

Now all of the men stood even more wide eyed and speechless. Eldrin shook his head and burst into laughter that he was no longer able to contain, and Nyx began to giggle like a little girl.

Jexi's eyebrows flashed. "See what I mean? Insatiable!"

She turned quickly to hide her smile by walking away. She almost kept up the ruse without breaking until Lauriel figured out what she was doing and began to laugh. Once Lauriel started, Jexi burst into laughter that brought her to tears.

"Damn, sister, that's just not right," Eldrin said, still shaking his head and chuckling quietly at her as she walked by.

He knew though that the comic relief that Jexi often provided after a battle was very much intentional. It helped to provide an avenue for the companions to defuse the stress and anxiety that accompanied the brutal, life-threatening affair.

The group cleaned the Great Hall for almost an hour before it was presentable enough to let the townspeople out of their hiding place in the cellar.

Gorian had a very handy spell that he used several times to create enough water to wash the thick blood off of most of the surfaces. Once they were satisfied with the degree of clean up, they opened the doors to the cellar, and the duchess herself spoke, "You can come out now; the enemy has been defeated!"

A great cheer came up from the darkness, and the children burst out of the opening. The companions exchanged worried glances about the duchess's choice of wording but it was quickly lost to the exuberance of the moment. The blonde girl immediately found Lauriel and leapt into her outstretched arms.

"I knew that you would save us!" she exclaimed excitedly as she hugged her tightly and kissed her on the cheek.

It was then that Lauriel realized that if the little girl's life was the only life that she would have ever saved, even at the cost of sacrificing her own, she would have done it without hesitation. The brief interaction with the little girl had a profound and lasting impact on Lauriel. Her pursuit of the vile creatures that had started as a self-serving goal of vengeance, had grown into something infinitely more substantial. She would pursue the creatures to any end, not for herself, but for all.

CHAPTER TWENTY-ONE

The Bells of Silenus

The stars gleamed brilliantly in the darkness of the pre-dawn sky above Silenus, but there were none of them that could be seen by its weary inhabitants. Silvery white smoke climbed high into the chill night air and spread out in a thick, cloud-like blanket that hung oppressively over the entire city. The numerous glowing piles of red-hot embers from the remnants of the once proud structures reflected dramatically off of the looming veil, creating an eerie orange luminance throughout the city that seemed to further highlight the devastation.

The acrid smell of death and destruction permeated every corner, and a wraithlike haze of smoke wafted slowly throughout the empty city streets, seeking to burn the eyes and constrict the throat of anyone who dared emerge. With the lone exception of the occasional crackle and pop of wood as it protested being consumed by fire, all was still and silent.

The incursion had brought with it a level of destruction to the city that had not been seen in recent memory. The incredible power of the creatures and their propensity for destruction by fire had laid waste to many of the wooden structures outside of the castle walls.

The stone castle had faired far better but it had turned out to be a bane for the townspeople.

Most of them had run into the castle for safety, just as they were supposed to do in the event of an attack, but it did not provide the protection they had expected. To their horror, the four-armed creatures were able to easily scale the walls in every direction.

They quickly overwhelmed the outer castle defenses and once inside, began to exterminate their prey with brutal efficiency as the trapped inhabitants frantically scattered like mice.

But all was not lost in Silenus. Like a phoenix rising from the ashes, the companions, Golden Company, duke, and duchess emerged out of the smoky shadows of the shattered causeway and into the cool night air of the main castle courtyard that seemed to have escaped much of the death and destruction. With them, the large group of jubilant yet anxious residents that had sought shelter in the cellar followed closely behind.

Lauriel came to know the little girl that had appealed to her in the cellar as "Mira." Mira held onto Lauriel's hand tightly, skipping light heartedly as they went. In her other hand, she fiercely wielded a broken piece of wood as her "sword, just like Miss Lauriel's." Lauriel laughed adoringly as Mira emerged from the causeway and into the courtyard, holding her sword high with and a proud and victorious look on her face, as if she alone had stopped the incursion.

As the spark of life began to spill back into the courtyard, the bells throughout the city rang steadily and enthusiastically, emphatically proclaiming a hard-fought victory. Cheers could be heard carrying throughout the castle as the relieved residents began to emerge from their many hiding places. The main courtyard filled as separated families desperately sought to reunify with each other.

Mira's face brightened, and her eyes danced with joy when she spotted her brother in the crowd. She quickly ran to him and jumped up into his arms, wrapping her arms so tightly around his neck that he could hardly breathe.

Lauriel couldn't be happier witnessing their reunification, but it was also a small dagger to her heart.

She had not been so lucky to be able to hug her brother, and knew all too well the pain that many of the townspeople were about to experience as some of those who had been separated would not be so lucky as Mira.

There was both joyous celebration and heart-wrenching agony as some families were reunited while others were not, but it was very soon that the "Miracle of Silenus" was fully realized. To everyone's astonishment, most of the families were successfully reunited, and the toll of death was not as high as expected. One of the few remaining men that had stayed outside to fight with the impromptu militia gave a firsthand account of how that miracle came to be. As he stood up on a broken wagon and began to tell his story, the crowd drew to a hush:

"Please! Hear my story for it is one that shall never be forgotten! This is my testimony and account ... The four-armed demons quickly scaled the outer castle walls, just as easily as if there had been ladders! The garrison defending the walls stood bravely, never leaving their post and buying valuable time for all of us. But they were quickly overrun by the unexpected nature of the attack, and all of them fell as brave heroes. The demons carried with them in their other arms the vile demon hounds, and once inside, they let them loose, and they began to hunt like a wolf pack does a trapped sheep. As the demons began their bloodthirsty killing, the remaining soldiers fought valiantly, heroically placing themselves in between the demons and the townspeople. Many men of fighting age joined with them as a militia, but the demons quickly decimated anything in their path. The brave heroes died, but their sacrifice gave many of you the necessary time to hide yourselves in any crack or crevice that you could find.

"The wizards had safely locked themselves inside of the Tower of Nemerse and had placed some kind of magic that turned the doors and lower windows into solid stone!

Any creature that tried to scale the tower was met with a thunderous bolt of lightning. From their high vantage point, they could see the desperate plight begin to unfold as the soldiers quickly fell. The wizards could not sit back and watch the murders, and they poured out of the safety of their impenetrable fortress and waded into the battle.

"They raised the portcullis and lured a large mass of the demons away from the castle with an illusion that looked like many people running out of the gates. The demons pursued the illusion and fell into the wizards' trap. The wizards attacked them with a fury of elements such as this world has never seen! Fire, ice, earth, wind, and lightning shook the very foundations of the tower as their magic slammed into the demons. They killed scores of them, but alas, even the powerful wizards finally succumbed to the darkness, for there were too many. At least two hundred of these foul demons attacked Silenus, and they did not seem to care that they were suffering catastrophic losses. They pushed forward into the wizards, finally overrunning them and their tower. I have not seen any of them since.

"We have long been wary of the mystical wizards, shunning them for their odd and mysterious ways and in many cases treating them with suspicion and even outright distain. But it was them that sacrificed themselves in the streets right alongside our soldiers. Now the streets beyond the castle walls run red with rivers of blood from the demons and the brave souls that opposed them, yet here we stand! So you see, my fellow townspeople, tonight is not only a story of loss and devastation, but one of bravery and sacrifice, and I believe our finest hour!"

The crowd that had stood and listened in stunned silence suddenly erupted into cheering and the shouting of many blessings and ovations to the "Heroes of Silenus." Unbeknownst to the others,

Eldrin quietly slipped away from the joyous celebration and began to hastily make his way to the tower.

The duke understood that in a time of such tragedy, formal recognition of the heroic efforts of the soldiers, militia, wizards, and the unexpected companions would be good for the people.

Most of the crowd had not yet realized the presence of the royals until he climbed up next to the man on the broken remains of the wagon. The crowd again drew to a hush as they waited with excited anticipation for his address. He first shook the man's hand and thanked him for his stunning account, assuring him that it would never be forgotten.

He grasped the man's hand with his own and, turning to the crowd, held it up high in a sign of victory. "To our finest hour!"

As the crowd erupted into another round of cheering, the bedraggled soldiers of the Golden Company moved forward and formally assembled into a heart-wrenchingly depleted rank. They snapped rigidly to attention at the captain's orders, and as they did, the crowd quieted back down to watch the ensuing protocol. As was their custom and tradition, the captain ordered the soldiers to salute the royals. The scene that ensued caused audible gasps followed by quiet sobs to ripple throughout the crowd.

Many of the Golden Company had sustained such injuries that they could not fully salute, though they tried their best nonetheless. The duchess began to weep at the sight of the loyal men and slowly made her way to the captain. She gently placed her hand on his arm that was desperately trying to maintain the salute. She gently drew it downward and then, in a dramatic act of veneration, saluted the soldiers and began to speak to them in a quiet, choked voice:

"Captain Stephen Drägo and valiant Golden Company, it is us that should be saluting you this evening."

The duke, companions, and the entire crowd saluted the Golden Company, and there was no dry eye among them as a reverent silence washed over the courtyard.

Tower of Nemerse

Eldrin stood helplessly in front of the smoking remains of the Tower of Nemerse. The sickening smell of burning flesh carried heavily upon the thick, night air.

Unchecked tears spilled from his reddened eyes and ran down his ashen face until finally splashing upon the parched ground. The interior of the tower had collapsed and formed a burning heap of death and debris that was at least twenty feet tall.

The exterior stone structure of the tower remained intact, forming a giant natural chimney that continuously belched black smoke high into the air as the contents slowly burned to ash.

The powerful spells of magic that had protected the tower and library for many hundreds of years had eventually succumbed to the unrelenting fire as the wizards' protective magic waned during the attack. Eldrin observed that the wizards had put up a fierce resistance as the blackened and scorched area in a large radius around the tower was littered with layers of abraxoth and gwillinix corpses, just as the man on the wagon had described.

After sustaining heavy losses, the creatures had finally overwhelmed the wizards, and the mutilated remains of his friends and colleagues were scattered throughout the outdoor arena of death and destruction. Eldrin moved sullenly around the tower grounds and began the grim task of identifying and counting the bodies of his friends and colleagues. As he did, his overwhelming grief and sense of loss turned into a deep, seething anger. The creatures had to be stopped at all costs, and as quickly as possible.

He had found fifteen wizard corpses when he was startled by a sudden presence near him. He looked up, and his eyes were met by a green captivating gaze that instantly transported his mind far away from the terrible field of death.

They shielded him from the rest of the world, holding him in a state of blissful oblivion where no other thoughts, cares, or emotions clouded his mind other than the singularity of her. Her eyes glistened with tears of understanding and a shared burden of his pain and anger. He felt his heart pound like it may leap out of his chest as Lauriel walked up to him and wrapped her arms around him in a loving embrace.

Together, they silently observed one of the greatest tragedies that had struck the realm in at least an age. In less than two hours, fully one half of all wizards throughout Alynthi, as well as the greatest repository of knowledge that had ever been assembled, were lost.

After several moments, Lauriel broke the silence. "Ni vas ornthé (I'm so sorry), Eldrin."

Her words were few but they overflowed with true compassion and understanding. The simple, heartfelt statement helped to immediately calm and refocus him on the looming task at hand.

He turned to her and took both of her hands in his and looked deeply into her eyes. In a sudden reversal, it was now her that stood transfixed by his newly hawkish gaze. She marveled as his eyes suddenly seemed to burn with the arcane power and determination of the magi.

"I'm so glad that I have you here with me, *Ælfen*. Thank you," he said as he kissed her. "Now, let's go finish this."

One Banner

Lauriel and Eldrin returned just as the duke and duchess finished properly recognizing both the living and fallen soldiers.

The duke's eyes lit up, and he turned his attention to the companions, introducing each of them to the enthusiastic crowd. He regaled the citizens with a colorful and accurate description of their timely arrival in the Great Hall and spoke eloquently of their heroic skills.

The crowd was captivated by the picture that he painted of magic and steel, healing and destruction, and unflinching bravery. They cheered wildly as he described the inspiring charge of the Blademaster that caused even the duchess to charge headlong into combat. They vicariously sought their vengeance as they pictured the one petite elven female systematically dismembering the terrible demons in a deadly flurry of blade-strikes.

As he drew his story to a close, the duke turned from the crowd and faced the companions. "What each of you have given us this evening is nothing short of our lives and our city, and for that we can never repay you." The crowd clapped and cheered loudly in appreciation, continuing to shout blessings and thanksgivings to all involved.

Stepping down from the wagon, the duke finished his address to the companions. "We will never forget each of your contributions. From this day forward, each of you will have an honored seat at our table. I know that it has been a long night, but please follow me to the palace so that you can clean up and we can further discuss what has happened here." As he finished, Lauriel could see an earnest look on his face that he was unsuccessfully trying to hide.

Together, they slowly made their way to the palace, stopping many dozens of times to meet with the enthusiastic citizens, or to mourn with those less fortunate that had lost loved ones. With each passing moment, the sense of urgency grew in each of their minds, and the weight of their quest upon their shoulders. They knew that the same tragedies were being replicated all over Alynthi as the vile creatures continued to spread their tendrils over the land. They also knew that almost no other city was as well fortified or prepared for such a terrible raid and would fare far worse. This fact was not lost to the duke as his face began to grow increasingly apprehensive as he unconsciously quickened his pace.

He was sincerely concerned about the rest of the kingdoms but had also concluded that it would only be a matter of time before another wave of the creatures would make their way back to Silenus to finish what they had started.

A foreboding, deep crimson dawn was beginning to creep over the early morning sky when they finally made it into the private royal chambers of the castle. The duchess showed them to a comfortable sitting room that was attached to a beautiful, ornate bath chamber where several castle workers were already pouring hot water into the large basin.

"Please feel free to use our private chambers," the duchess said.

As the companions rotated through the bath chambers one by one, beginning with Lauriel, the duke joined with the rest of them in the sitting room and began in earnest, not waiting for the entire group to be present.

"Gorian, it has been a long time, my friend. I can't thank you and your brave group enough for everything that you have done here, but I am still trying to make sense of all of this. This is not over, is it?" he asked bluntly, quickly cutting short the formalities and expecting an equally straightforward answer.

"No, this is just the beginning," Gorian replied frankly.

The duke's face darkened, and he looked down at the floor, trying to hide his worry. "That's what I was afraid of," he mumbled quietly.

He looked back up at Gorian, grave concern etched upon his face. "What do you know of these terrible creatures? How can we defeat them?"

Gorian's deep connection with nature provided him a level of insight that was not fully perceptible to the others. He could feel deep within him that the land itself was crying out under the strain of the unnatural beings spilling into it, disrupting and destroying the harmonious balance. He could feel the countless innocent forest creatures' primal fear as they fled from the darkness.

Gorian began a very abridged debriefing. "I have felt this darkness growing for many moons, but I did not fully understand the extent of it until I met with my friends in what has turned out to be a very fortuitous meeting," he said as he gestured at the rest of the companions. "They recently found that the creatures are coming through an ancient portal that was discovered in the darkness of Draxanarek'Vel."

The duke's face contorted with disgust at the mere mention of the dark realm. "Of course it would be them to bring this scourge upon us!"

Gorian continued, "We have named the four-armed creatures abraxoth and the dog-like creatures gwillinix. They come through with increasing numbers and power, and I'm afraid that this destruction will continue to happen throughout the realm with increasing frequency and devastation until the portal is closed."

"Or there is no life left to oppose them," Jexi added dubiously.

The duchess's face turned pale.

Gorian continued, "My friends have discovered a possible way to close it, but their journey will be terribly difficult."

"What can we do to help?" the duke asked earnestly.

"I'm afraid it is something that you will not like," Gorian replied. "While they go retrieve the shard that has the power to close the portal, you will have to unify all of the fractured realms and join with Draxanarek'Vel to give us a chance to get to it."

The duke's face contorted as if a terrible taste had suddenly entered his mouth. He shook his head in opposition. "I don't see how the realms could be united with Draxanarek'Vel; they have always been mortally opposed. Even our own realms are fractured, fighting separately for their own lands. The dwarves protect their own, the elves theirs, and so on and so forth throughout the whole of Alynthi. Our armies would not leave their own lands and people to fight beside our mortal enemies in such a foreign and vile place."

Eldrin interjected, "Draxanarek'Vel has suffered greatly, so much so that the Dark Queen herself has reached out for an alliance; an act that is unique in our history. And to your point about a united army, I believe that it is our only hope to get close enough. It will be difficult to convince all of the armies to leave their lands and join under one banner, but if you can get them together, they will follow her ... the Blademaster." Eldrin paused dramatically before continuing, "You yourself have seen the unifying power."

The duchess nodded eagerly in agreement and placed her hand on the duke's arm, gently urging him to consider. He looked at Eldrin keenly for several moments. Finally, he spoke. "I must say that I have never seen men rallied like that before. Nor have I ever felt such a strong command presence from anyone. How is that possible?"

"She wields the most powerful blade ever created by the elven kingdoms, and with it, power and responsibility that she still does not fully comprehend. As you have experienced, those that see her wield it are strongly compelled to follow her," Eldrin said.

As if on cue, Lauriel emerged from the bath chamber, hastily fixing her damp golden hair into her signature athletic ponytail as she walked over to the comfortable chair. She sat down quietly, trying to avoid any distraction to the conversation.

But her entrance had the unintended opposite effect; the room grew silent as all eyes turned upon her. She suddenly felt incredibly awkward as she realized that she was the focus of attention. The duchess had given her a fine, green, silk robe to wear while her clothes were being washed. It was of elven make but Lauriel had never owned such fine elven garments, nor had she felt any cloth that comfortable against her skin. The robe was so comely on her that it looked as if it had been created specifically for the woodland elf, so much so that the duchess inadvertently found herself telling Lauriel that she must keep it for herself.

Her green eyes shimmered in the firelight as they reflected both the color of the robe and the morale boost that a clean hot bath brought with it. The soak had provided a relaxing and much needed respite, temporarily washing away the many worries that she carried with her. Her high spirits manifested on her radiant face and it helped to bring a glimmer of hope into the room with her.

Isilmwé

"I apologize, my lady, but we have been so busy and distracted that I'm afraid we have not properly introduced ourselves. I am Duke Dunric Arkayz, and this is my lovely wife, Duchess Faelyn."

The sudden formality of the introduction caused Lauriel to stand and curtsy awkwardly. "My name is Lauriel Valendril. Well met, Lord Duke and Duchess Faelyn." Her gesture looked so awkward and unnatural coming from her that it caused the other companions to chuckle. They tried their best to suppress the noise and hide their amused smirks but it was to no avail. Lauriel's face blushed red with embarrassment.

The Woodland Elves had similar monarchical structures, but the more formal outward acknowledgement of royalty was primarily a human tradition.

The duke was a gentleman and immediately came to her rescue. "Well done, Lady Valendril, first among elves in this court." His voice grew apprehensive as he quickly switched back to his inquiry.

"We have just been discussing the current situation at hand, and I'm afraid that I must have a very real and difficult conversation with you, so please forgive the frank manner of the subject."

Lauriel nodded at him politely.

He began in earnest. "I have learned of your quest and understand that it is necessary to clear a way to this 'portal' for you, yet you must see this from my eyes.

"To do so requires the summoning and unification of all of the available armies throughout Alynthi and Draxanarek'Vel, something that has never been done in any known history. They will be expected to put all of their differences aside and dutifully follow you, a Woodland Elf of no station, military background, nor known to the realm until now. You have emerged out of the remote wilds with an ancestral blade of elven design and require an unquestionable commitment from each of these soldiers to place themselves in great peril in order to escort you to the equivalent of the gates of hell. Even if you make it, how can we be sure that this plan will work? Again, forgive me for my blunt questioning.

"I have seen your unmatched skills and felt the unquestionable power of the blade, but this is a stretch for my mind. Even now, such a short time has passed since your valiant charge in the hallway, and fear and doubt have already crept back into my mind, clouding the inspiring feelings that I felt."

Lauriel gently took her blade that had been leaning against her chair and brought it over to the duke. She kept it sheathed and held it out to him, bidding him to behold it. He took it from her gingerly and slowly removed it from the sheath like it was an ancient museum relic. To his surprise, it looked like a well-crafted elven scimitar, but was otherwise unremarkable.

It appeared nothing like the blade that he saw her wielding, and the sight of it carried with it no particular desire or inspiration.

"It is true, Lord Duke, everything that you have expressed is accurate and of great concern. I long sought vengeance against these vile creatures for the murder of my friends, family, and village; but I never expected it would lead to the crushing weight that is now upon our shoulders," Lauriel said as she gestured around the room at her companions. "I have no station, no nobility, and no training or experience in military things, and to be honest, I don't know or understand why anyone would follow or help me under those circumstances that you so accurately describe.

"In answer to your question, I don't know if the plan will work, but I don't see any other options. I can tell you one thing that I am sure of though ..." She paused and walked back over to the duke and grasped the scimitar by the pommel. It was then that all of them together observed the Blademaster intentionally use the blade to sway those to her cause. Isilmwé flared with a radiant light, transforming into its fully unmasked blade form that illuminated the room with brilliance and encouragement. Just as the blade changed in the blink of an eye, Lauriel also seemed to be transformed from a beautiful but unassuming Woodland Elf, to that of one of the greatest leaders among men.

"One way or another, I'm going to get to that portal and seal it, or die trying. The more that help us get to it, the better our chances," Lauriel declared.

There was no question left in the duke's mind, and he suddenly felt foolish for even questioning her. The duchess looked on with admiration. "This is no simple magic trick," she uttered.

The duke rose from his chair. "And you shall get there under a unified banner."

CHAPTER TWENTY-TWO

Divided We Fall

It was a bright morning by the time the companions finished meeting with the duke. They held the key to the Plane of Discordance in their hands and were eager to get going on their quest as soon as possible, but they were in no shape to leave immediately. They were completely exhausted and needed time to rest and recover from the long night. A brief delay would not only give them time to rest, but it would give Eldrin the time he needed to finish reading the manual about the Plane of Discord and identify several of the magic items that they took from Malthrax's lair, so they decided to reassemble at dusk.

Gorian politely declined the invitation to stay and returned to check on his grove. When he arrived, he found it completely intact. It had been spared from the main assault and had only experienced a glancing blow. The centarum, as well as the rest of the forest's predators, had successfully hunted down the few remaining marauders that plagued them.

As Gorian climbed up to his lofty treehouse, he could see the light, wispy smoke that still rose from several of the stubborn fires that continued to smolder on the outskirts of Silenus.

But it was not the smoke that drew his attention, it was the now blackened husk of the Tower of Nemerse that loomed over the city like a giant desecrated headstone.

He always hated the imposing structure but shook his head in disgust at the tragic loss. Completely exhausted, he closed his shutters, crawled into his plush bed, and soon fell fast asleep.

*   *   *   *

It seemed like only minutes had gone by when he was awakened with a start by the sound of knocking. Visitors to his outer forest domain were not uncommon, but no visitor was permitted entry into the grove without his explicit approval. He closed his eyes and concentrated for a moment to determine who the uninvited intruder was. The knocking on the door began again, this time even harder.

"Jexi?" Gorian called. "What are you doing here?"

"Open the damn door, you solitary, paranoid, tree hugger, we are running out of time."

He opened the door and stared at her with a look of shock on his face. Somehow, she had slipped by all of his forest defenses, including the centarum.

He walked by her and peered over the edge of the deck to find an even more disturbing site. A succubus stood in the center of a ring of centarum that were not pointing weapons at her, but staring at her in captivated inaction as she performed a striptease for them.

"You really need better security; that was way too easy," she jested. "Anyway, Eldrin is awake and almost done studying his book. He asked me to gather the items so he can study them next."

Gorian could not hide the perturbed look on his face as he spoke. "My forest keeps out almost a dozen of the terrible creatures, and you just waltz in here unchecked?"

She couldn't tell who he was angrier at, her or the centarum. "Yeah, pretty much; but in our defense I think we helped with that."

Gorian shook his head and walked back into the treehouse to retrieve the items. He already knew better than to keep questioning her; he would only receive more frustrating half-answers.

He returned shortly with several of their backpacks and began to help her equip them. He could quickly see that there was no way that she could carry all of the equipment. "As much as I hate going to town, I'll help you with these," he offered.

He went back a second time to retrieve the rest of the backpacks and came back with Dante's axe in hand.

Jexi's eyes filled with tears at the sight of it. "Please don't bother with the axe, we don't need anything else demoralizing."

Gorian nodded in understanding and quietly leaned it against the wall as he prepared to leave.

"There is something that I need to ask you, the real reason why I came in private." Jexi spoke in such a serious tone that it caught Gorian completely off guard; he had never seen her so earnest.

Gorian looked directly at her with his eyebrows raised and nodded in acknowledgement.

"You pride yourself on being a force of balance, truly neutral and free of prejudice in all things … yes?"

"Yes, I do," he replied.

"Then you must convince the duke to expand his outreach far beyond only summoning the available fighting forces of the human, dwarven, and elven kingdoms; it will not be enough. He won't like it any more than joining forces with Draxanarek'Vel, but he must remove himself from predisposed prejudice and form an alliance with all of the other races throughout this realm that have been mortal enemies throughout all history.

"He must get help from the orcs, goblins, hobgoblins, minotaur, and any others that will join the field of battle. This is a threat to them too, and if we stay divided, we will all fall."

Gorian stared off into the distance, lost in his own thoughts. He slowly nodded in agreement, and his eyes soon refocused. "You are very wise, Jexi. There are few that can put away their differences and think the way you do. I will set about to do that very task, but even if they do join, it will be difficult to join them as one force under one command."

"It will," Jexi replied. "But get them to the field of battle and they will follow the Blademaster."

Priceless Treasure

Eldrin closed the manual and stared at it in quiet contemplation. Reading through it had only served to heighten his apprehension, not relieve it as he had hoped. He had studied about general planular travel, but he could never remember reading a book that made less sense. It seemed to have been a long rambling codex that was written by someone who had gone mad, and it was frustratingly the only relevant information that they could find on the odd place. *Why the hell did this damn shard have to be in the Plane of Discordance? If it was the Plane of Hell, at least we would know what to expect.*

His troubled thoughts were interrupted by a knock at his door.

"Come in," he answered.

Jexi and Gorian entered the room appearing to have just robbed all of the magic shops throughout Alynthi. Both of them wore two backpacks, one on their back and one on their front, and Gorian carried the fifth.

"Ahh, thanks for bringing those," Eldrin said as he stood to help them unload their burden.

"We seem to have run out of time," Jexi said as she pointed to the window. The sun was rapidly diving for the horizon.

"Yes, that book took much longer to read than I anticipated, and after reading it, I don't think we should delay any longer. I'll just choose a couple of items before we go."

They emptied the priceless contents of the backpacks on the floor. The dragon had amassed a spectacular treasure trove that was better than any magic shop, but every item was a reminder of a life that had been eradicated.

Eldrin observed the pile carefully before choosing two items to identify; the rest would have to wait. He picked up a pair of brown leather bracers with an embossed, delicate, golden leaf pattern, and a black, smooth polished ring that had a thin red inlay encircling it.

Jexi looked at Eldrin inquisitively. "That is interesting, brother; the first thing that you chose was a gift for her. You truly are smitten by her, aren't you?"

Eldrin had not even realized what he had done. He glanced up at her with a sudden look of embarrassment but he could see that she had not said it in jest. It was simply a genuine observation.

"Yes, I guess I am," he replied thoughtfully.

"I'm happy for you, brother. She is a good woman," Jexi said in a unique moment of endorsement.

"Yes, my friend, I have to agree with Jexi; you have found a good one," Gorian added.

Eldrin looked down at the ground and then back up at them with concern. "The more I care for her, the harder it is for me to observe her at the tip of the spear, and the more guilty I feel for recruiting her for this quest."

"It was no accident that she is here with us. We would not be here if you had chosen any other. But you cannot let your feelings cloud your decisions, brother."

Eldrin quickly changed the subject. "Gorian, are you coming with us?"

Gorian glanced at Jexi and then back at Eldrin. "I think that my services would be more beneficial if I stay. I will try to assemble more help for the push into Draxanarek'Vel and work on organizing a coordinated resistance throughout the realm so that you encounter as few of those creatures within that dark place as possible. The more reinforcements that they send out into all of Alynthi, the less of them that stand in your way of the portal. It will take time to pull that off, and I think that we will need all of the help we can get."

Eldrin nodded in agreement. "We will surely miss your skills, but I think you are right; to get to the portal we will need all of the help we can muster and the fewest number of those creatures in our way as possible. I do have one request before you go though."

"What is that?" Gorian asked.

"One of the few wizards left of my order will be here tomorrow. He can also identify the rest of these things." Eldrin motioned to the items on the floor. "As much as it pains me to give these powerful magic items away, they do us no good locked up and unused, especially if they can help us with the upcoming battle. Would you please see that they are distributed properly?"

Jexi winced at the thought of giving all of their hard-fought items away, but she made no objection; she knew Eldrin was right.

Gorian nodded and gathered the items back into the backpacks with Jexi's help.

Blinding Strike

The dark orange twilight was just fading into a deep purple when Eldrin met the rest of the companions downstairs in the private castle ward. Lauriel had been discussing details of the remaining quest with and Captain Drägo and the duke.

"So, we will see you and everyone that you can rally very soon, on the plain of Hycor at the western gate of Draxanarek'Vel," Lauriel confirmed.

The duke nodded. "Yes we have a lot of work to do while you are gone." He turned to look at Eldrin as he entered the room. "Did you get it figured out?"

Eldrin nodded. "Yes, Lord Duke, as much as I can with the limited information that we have. I think that we are as ready as we will ever be."

"Very well, it looks like the time has come then," Duke Arkayz concluded.

He walked to each of the companions and shook their hands in appreciation, offering a private but sincere blessing and farewell to each of them.

When the duke finished, Eldrin walked over to Lauriel. "There is one thing that you should have before we go." He handed the leather bracers to her, unable to hide the proud and excited look on his face.

Her face lit up at the unexpected present. "Wow, they are beautiful! Thank you!" she said as she threw her arms around him.

"I saw these in the dragon's hoard and I thought you may like them; and now that I have had a chance to identify their magical properties, I think you might like them even more."

Lauriel looked up at him, her green eyes glittering with excitement. She quickly began to unlace her well-worn but mundane leather bracers.

He let the anticipation build until she had them completely laced them up. "These are Bracers of Blinding Strike. Three times per day you can use them to cast the same Haste spell on yourself that I have cast on you previously. You will no longer need my spell to double your speed."

"May the Gods have mercy upon your opponents in the afterlife," the duke joked.

Lauriel beamed with excitement, ready to try out her new complement.

CHAPTER TWENTY-THREE

The Plane of Discordance

The companions assembled in a close circle, just as they had become accustomed to doing when they were about to teleport. Eldrin pulled a supple leather pouch from one of the inner pockets of his robe and untied the thong that held its priceless contents securely inside. As he did, he prepared the others for their journey.

"As you all know, I don't have any firsthand knowledge or experience to share with you about traveling to another plane. But from what I have been able to read and understand, it can be very disorienting, even more so than teleportation."

Lauriel and Nyx let out an audible groan.

Eldrin smiled and continued, "You should know that the Plane of Discordance is described as particularly peculiar and difficult. Not many have been there and there was very little intelligible information in the manual on what to expect, but I was able to find a few tidbits that may help."

He pulled the amulet from the leather pouch by its delicate chain and it began to pendulate back and forth in celebration of its newfound freedom. Its highly polished platinum surface gleamed brilliantly as it caught the torchlight.

Eldrin placed the amulet on display in the palm of his outstretched hand and continued his instructions.

"Because of the two reality shards there, the Plane of Discordance has two opposing realities that constantly seek to establish themselves while destroying the other. This creates an instability in that the realities never fully form past their prime elemental states, a condition which has been described as the elemental chaos."

As Lauriel observed the amulet lying so serenely in the palm of his hand, her attention was drawn fully to it instead of Eldrin's instructions. She couldn't help but think of the how many lives rested on such an insignificant trinket. She found the device to be both incredibly beautiful and inspiring, yet morbidly repulsive at the same time. Having such a thing in their possession gave them a glimmer of hope that their quest could progress, but it was also a dark reminder of the blood and death that had purchased it. She found it bitterly ironic that many of the lives that depended on the amulet would never know or appreciate its true cost. The musing made her think of Dante, and how much she missed him.

He should be standing right here with us, she thought wistfully.

"Lauriel!" Eldrin called out.

The rumination had caused her to miss most of his instruction. She tore her gaze from the amulet and looked back up at Eldrin's troubled face.

"Yes?" she answered.

"Do you have any questions?"

Against her better judgement, she shook her head no. She was embarrassed by her inattention and captivation of the amulet.

He seemed unconvinced and was about to speak again when Nyx asked him another question.

"So we just concentrate to move?"

"Yes, if you are in the pocket of incorporeality," Eldrin answered.

He looked back around at the group for one last check, and one by one, each of them nodded that they were ready.

"Okay, we better not waste any more time. Here we go!" Eldrin said, unsuccessfully trying to hide his apprehension.

Jexi, Nyx, and Lauriel placed their hand on top of Eldrin's, and he began the command words to activate the magical device.

A bright flash emanated from under the concealment of their hands, and the world that they knew instantly faded away.

Existential Dread

Did the amulet fail? Am I dead? Am I a spirit? Lauriel's mind raced to understand her current state of existence, or lack thereof, but the abstract reality that she now seemed to occupy was so mind-bendingly disorienting, that any rational answers eluded her.

Her only perception was that of an all-encompassing silver radiance that had no discernible sky or ground, up or down, left or right. The absence of any kind of focal point against an infinite silvery void made it impossible to gain any sense of movement, direction, or spacial orientation.

Something has gone terribly wrong with the magic!

As she desperately tried to make sense of her confounding situation, her thoughts were drawn to Eldrin. She began to wish she had paid much closer attention to his instructions.

Is he still near? Is he stuck in this bewildering space too? Certainly he will know what to do.

"Eldrin!" she tried to call out to him, but there was no noise whatsoever, only infinite and absolute silence. The absence of sound was so complete that it could drive those trapped within it mad in a very short amount of time.

She became increasingly desperate and tried to reach out to where she had last seen him standing. But when she did, she realized that she did not have any awareness or sensation of her own body, only a vague feeling of weightlessness.

I'm dead! she gasped.

She began to despair.

This miserable existence of an afterlife was not at all what I was taught or envisioned. Was Fadwé wrong? Will I never see Ammé, Nolthien, or Dante? Is this all there is?

The notion quickly led her away from trying to work rationally through her problem and down the dark rabbit trail of her own existential dread.

All of that time and effort and I didn't even get to finish the one quest that made a difference, she thought sullenly.

She thought again about her beloved companions and the impossible challenge that they still faced.

"I just can't go like this! I HAVE to be there with them!" she yelled angrily, but the attempt only made her further realize the maddening silence.

"Kathele!" she cried out in anguish to her Goddess.

She suddenly had a thought enter her mind that brought her back from the deep pit of despair.

Think Lauriel, what did they say?

She tried to remember her last lucid thoughts and found it easy to focus on them because no other stimuli affected her attention, and it was the only part of her that seemed to still exist. She remembered everything up to the point of the amulet's activation, including Nyx's seemingly odd question; "So we just concentrate to move?" She then remembered Eldrin's equally strange answer that had not made any sense at the time, "Yes, if you are in the pocket of incorporeality."

That's it! I'm incorporeal!

She began to create a picture in her mind of her ghostlike self, floating in an infinite sea of silvery ether.

She concentrated on moving herself forward, even though she had no idea which way forward actually was, and she began to feel a sensation of movement through the space, much like the feeling that she had when flying.

It's working!

She continued the ethereal movement until she came to an opaque, shimmering wall. The observation of anything other than disorienting silver was a welcome site, but it did nothing to help her gain her bearings. As she faced it, the wall continued out of her sight to the left and right as well as up and down.

Lauriel pictured in her mind the motion of reaching out to touch the wall, and she immediately felt her first sensation of touch. The wall felt slightly warm, and she could immediately tell that it was not at all solid. She passed her hand through it and could immediately feel her hand and fingers!

Well, I guess I have to take a leap of faith here.

She began her forward movement and traversed right through the opaque wall, and as soon as she broke through the outer plane of the wall, she felt like a veil had been lifted as she transitioned from a spirit-like form to her regular corporeal body. Her mind was immediately inundated with sudden but familiar feelings of touch, sight, hearing, taste, and smell. She took a deep breath and could feel the air filling her lungs. It was the kind of deep inhalation that one takes after breaching the surface of the water after almost drowning. But as soon as her eyes brought her surroundings into focus, she immediately felt the urge to retreat back into the relative comfort and safety of the incorporeality.

* * * *

Jexi exited the pocket of incorporeality and took several moments to survey her new reality, and the more that she observed her strange and wholly foreign surroundings, the more of a fantastic and terrifying new place that she found it to be.

The earthen landscape that stretched out before her seemed to be in a constant state of ebb and flow, forming mountains in the distance that would quickly rise to an impossible height, only to collapse into a crevasse of equal depths moments later.

The stony ground beneath her feet slowly undulated as it lapped up against the shimmering barrier of the pocket of incorporeality, moving oddly like a high tide of thick water against a shoreline.

She knew that traveling alone in such a strange place was an extremely dangerous endeavor, and she waited anxiously for several minutes for the rest of her companions. But after none of them materialized, she reached the conclusion that they could have exited at any point in the massive hemispherical pocket that Eldrin had described as a "bubble," and she would have to search for them.

I'll just fly around the barrier to see if I can find them and maybe get a better view of the surroundings.

Dark red spectral wings sprung from her back, and she traveled upward along the slowly but continuously curving surface of the barrier. But after only a few hundred feet of movement, she felt a strange and unnerving sensation. The wind against her skin began to feel like thick, viscous liquid, and before she could even turn around, she was captured in the atmospheric quagmire like a tiny fly trapped in an ocean of honey. Terrifying feelings of suffocation and claustrophobia began to wash over her.

Oh shit! Keep calm, Jexi. Think through this.

She closed her eyes and attempted to calm herself, but it wasn't until she drew in a deep and unlabored breath that she began to feel a sense of relief. The ability to breathe the thick atmosphere without difficulty felt counterintuitive, but once she learned that she was not being smothered by it, the feelings of panic quickly subsided and she began to look around for a solution to extract herself from the situation.

I wonder if I can use my Dimensional Step spell to get back to the ground, or if that method of travel is too dangerous here?

As she pondered how to get out of her dilemma, she had the sudden and unmistakable realization that she was not alone.

She looked around and could see no other lifeforms, but she felt so sure of the sentient presence near her that she couldn't help but call to it.

"Hello?"

Less than ten feet from her, the air coalesced into a small gray cloud, and a breathy whisper carried lightly upon the wind.

"Outsider ... visit ... rare."

Jexi had done rudimentary studies on elementals, but this was something far different. She could only reconcile it in her mind as some sort of primordial living air being that seemed to be ubiquitous, and as far as she was concerned, omnipotent. She was not afraid of it, quickly surmising that if it was hostile, she would already be dead. It appeared to her to be more curious about her arrival and passage.

It seemed that fate smiled upon her in the chance meeting with the entity in one of strangest and most random places possible. All students of the school of magic were required to learn three languages during their studies, and before her expulsion from the school, Jexi happened to learn primordial speech to a semi-conversational fluency. While the others took Dwarven, Elven, Under-common, or some other useful dialect, Jexi had chosen one of the rarest and most difficult.

"Well met, I ... Jexi ... no harm," Jexi whispered back into the wind, responding as best as she could in the odd language.

Jexi suddenly felt the emotions of the living air that she found herself enveloped within, and it put her even more at ease. The air immediately began to feel less restraining, and her claustrophobic feeling continued to diminish.

The unmistakable emotions of excitement mixed with a lonely eagerness to converse came to her along with another breathy whisper that sounded like a slow exhalation of air traveling upon the wind.

The entity spoke, this time in Primordial.

"Etheriani ... name ... no ... harm ... if ... not ... you ... harm."

"No ... harm," Jexi replied.

Jexi's mind raced as she tried to make her best attempt at finding diplomacy with the strange being. She quickly settled on finding something that they both might have in common.

She had few elemental spells compared to her brother Eldrin, but she did happen to have a minor cantrip spell that could cause a small clap of thunder.

Maybe if I show some knowledge or mastery of elements, I can win its trust, she considered to herself.

She was about to show off her spell, but reconsidered just before she did.

Or, maybe it will have the opposite effect and trigger it to kill me.

Once again using her best attempt at Primordial, she decided to first ask for permission.

"I thunder can make too, I may?" Her speech was slightly jumbled and it took her considerable time, but she felt the living air seemed to understand and even appreciate her attempt.

The cloud began to move around and rumble like a small thunderhead, but the noise was continuous, and it contained no lightning. Jexi felt the emotions of eager anticipation of the entity as it once again spoke simply.

"Yes."

"Drazzgoulath!" she shouted the single word to evoke her simple spell.

A single clap of thunder cracked around them, but as it did, it continued to amplify and propagate until it reached an incomprehensible level of power and sonic energy. Jexi was somehow protected from the noise that should have instantly killed her by the entity's protective swaddle of air.

The strange occurrence went far beyond any understanding of even the most potent spell attack as the thunderclap seemed to shake and reverberate throughout the entirety of the infinite plane.

She felt that the living air was immensely pleased and excited, but she detected other feelings that she was not at all prepared for, awe and reverence.

"Welcome ... Thunder ... Goddess ... Jexi."

* * * *

Eldrin gasped as he got a clear view of his surroundings after he exited the bubble at the very top. The baffling book that he had read many times in preparation now made much more sense to him, and it also came nowhere close to capturing the full extent of the elemental chaos and the inhospitable anathema that awaited them.

From the high vantage point, he could see that the barrier of incorporeality, the singular, one-way point of entrance into the plane, was a large hemisphere shape that spanned several thousand feet in diameter. The entirety of it rested upon a city-sized chunk of land that was slowly floating amongst innumerable others in an infinite, endless void.

Several thousand yards past the bubble, Eldrin could see a river flowing across the landscape in the distance, but it contained no water. The river was instead made of lightning, continuously and instantaneously changing its banks.

When it reached the edge, it cascaded like a waterfall of light into the void, creating a crackling and thundering cloud of illuminated mist at some indeterminable point below.

Beyond the floating earth-berg that he now found himself inhabiting, he observed an increasingly chaotic and mind-bending display of elements that all orbited around a swirling maelstrom in the very center, the very point that they needed to reach.

An entire ocean of liquid fire was suspended in the void, unbound by any shores. He could see mountains of ice, thunderclouds made of fire, and giant storms made of earth instead of water. All of the elements were in a constant state of growth, change, or destruction.

The book had described the pocket of incorporeality as orbiting in the "outer perimeter," a relatively safe area at the far fringes of the maelstrom that was far away from most of the chaos. Eldrin now understood that, in order to get closer, they would have to find a way to traverse from one earth-berg to another, which would in itself be no easy task.

Half of the elements orbited the maelstrom in a clockwise direction, pulled by the force of one reality shard, while the other half orbited in a counter-clockwise direction under the influence of the other reality shard. The closer that one traveled toward the maelstrom, the faster and more chaotic things became as the opposing orbits led the elements to frequent and near total destruction of each other.

Wow, this is not going to be easy ...

Just as he reached the conclusion and turned to look for his companions, a clap of thunder shook the heavens, and before he could even react, the unexpectedly catastrophic sonic blast wave rippled through him, and all went black.

* * * *

"Friend ... here ... too?" the entity asked Jexi.

"Yes! Three!" Jexi replied excitedly.

"Only ... one ... hurt ... by ... Thunder ... Goddess," the entity said.

Jexi's complexion paled, and she inadvertently switched back to the common speech in a rush to convey her message. "Can you please show me to them?"

The air whisked her upward, and she immediately found herself traveling at a far faster speed than she had experienced even with the griffons during their steep dive, but she did not feel the same buffeting effect.

Within seconds, she reached the top of the hemisphere and saw Eldrin lying on top of the very center, blood oozing from his ears, nose, eyes, and mouth.

The air suddenly slowed and gently set her down near him. She immediately knelt down and placed her hand on his chest and a wave of relief washed over her as she discovered that he was still breathing.

"Oh thank God!" she gasped. *"Thank you, Etheriani."*

The entity spoke again, and Jexi's understanding of the language slowly stitched the message together in her mind. But when she completed the translation, she was convinced that she had not interpreted it correctly.

"I ... am ... at ... your ... will ... Thunder ... Goddess."

She had no time to consider, and instead of seeking clarification, she chose to ask another favor of the omnipresent air entity.

"Two friends I expect, may bring to me when arrive?"

* * * *

Lauriel had no sooner taken in her first deep breath and drew her strange surroundings into focus when she was suddenly catapulted up into the air like an arrow from her bow. She flailed wildly as the ground under her feet dropped away with nauseating speed, but the more that she thrashed about, the more she felt enveloped by the thick atmosphere.

Before she could even begin to consider the strange feeling, or how to extract herself from the seemingly deadly situation, the wind placed her on the very top of the barrier, right next to Jexi and Eldrin.

Seeing Eldrin's dire condition immediately refocused her and she took no time to consider what had just occurred.

"What happened!?" Lauriel exclaimed, her eyes immediately filling with tears.

"He's alive, just unconscious," Jexi replied.

Lauriel knelt down and immediately placed her hand on his chest as she began the most powerful healing spell that she could invoke. Soft blue light enveloped her hand, and Eldrin's eyes began to blink and refocus.

He looked up at Lauriel and smiled, but as soon as he tried to sit up, the smile turned into an obvious wince of pain. He laid back and placed the palms of his hands up to his head and began to rub his temples and eyes.

"What happened?" he groaned.

"Some type of primordial elemental thunderclap," Jexi quickly answered.

"Thunder … Goddess … Jexi," a voice whispered upon the wind.

Lauriel stood and spun around to look for the voice, but saw no obvious origin.

"Did you hear that?" Lauriel turned back to Jexi, her eyes wide like she had just heard a ghost in the night.

"Hear what?" Jexi asked.

"I heard it too, even with this all-encompassing ringing in my ears," Eldrin said as he slowly sat back up. Eldrin's face darkened. "And if I heard it, you certainly did too. What did you do, Jexi?"

"Me!? Why do you always jump to the conclusion that it was me?" Jexi retorted.

"Thunder … Goddess … Jexi," the voice whispered again.

Lauriel spun around again, looking everywhere for the voice.

"As I said … What did you do, 'Thunder Goddess Jexi?' And what is it that you summoned this time?" Eldrin questioned.

Seeing that her attempts to hide the fact that it was her spell that had almost killed him, Jexi abandoned her efforts at concealment and came clean. "It was just a minor cantrip!"

"Minor cantrip! It almost killed me!" Eldrin snapped.

Lauriel's eyes caught a glimpse of a small cloud forming near them. "Uh guys, there is something here," she warned.

The tone of her voice immediately ceased Eldrin and Jexi's discourse, and their eyes followed the direction of Lauriel's pointing finger.

"This is Etheriani, the primordial air entity that I have befriended. She is native here and means no harm," Jexi instructed.

The cloud continued to form, and the breathy whisper in the common language carried again upon the wind. "Thunder … Goddess … friends."

Eldrin and Lauriel observed Jexi whispering something strange and unintelligible into the wind.

"Yes Etheriani, friends no harm."

Jexi turned back to Eldrin and Lauriel. "It was her that I was attempting to befriend with the thunderclap cantrip. It obviously worked, but in the process, the elemental spell was somehow unexpectedly amplified at least one-hundredfold. So, whatever you do, do not use any elemental based spells here."

Eldrin slowly stood and stabilized himself with his staff. The look of ire that had settled upon his face relaxed as it gave way to reasoning. Jexi's act of attempted diplomacy was not careless, and there was no way that she could have anticipated the ramifications of her spell's effect.

Jexi continued, "Etheriani told me that you had been injured and after she brought me to you, I asked her to bring any others to us. Since you were not injured, Lauriel, I assume that you stepped through the barrier just after the spell's effects passed, and Etheriani immediately brought you to us as soon as you arrived."

The constant state of abstrusity that Lauriel had felt since the moment of her arrival began to subside as her strange and unexpected experiences finally gave way to a newfound clarity with Jexi's explanation.

But the cascading series of events that began with the existential dread in the pocket of incorporeality, to being carried off by a gust of wind to her seeming demise, to briefly thinking that Eldrin was dead, began to catch up with her and she was overcome by a flood of emotions. Her body suddenly felt numb, and she felt like she could not get a deep enough breath. She looked down at her hands and saw that they were uncharacteristically trembling.

A firm, steady hand took hold of hers, and when she looked back up, Eldrin was standing beside her.

And even though he himself had just experienced a brush with death, he had a calm reassurance on his face that immediately comforted her. She stepped forward into him, throwing her arms around him like she had not seen him for ages.

*   *   *   *

Jexi gave Eldrin and Lauriel several moments of respite before she spoke back up. "I guess Nyx is having a hard time with navigating the incorporeality."

But just after she finished her statement, the sound of a distant, bloodcurdling scream traveled up to them from somewhere below.

Lauriel immediately stepped back from Eldrin and drew her weapons, and Eldrin spun around toward the rapidly approaching noise.

"Friend ... bring," a breathy voice announced.

In the span of a few seconds, Nyx's upward movement through the air came into view above the plane of the hemisphere like a moon rapidly rising over the horizon. The sounds of her continuous scream became louder with each second of her approach.

The wind whisked her directly to the group and placed her down gently, but her legs were incapable of supporting her own weight and she collapsed to the surface of the barrier that the others stood upon. Her eyes were open wide in shock, and her face was so bone-white that it looked like a vampire had drained every drop of blood from her body.

"Nyx!" Lauriel exclaimed.

Lauriel knelt down beside her and propped her limp body up in her arms, embracing her tightly.

"Breathe, Nyx, you are safe here," Jexi encouraged as she knelt down and joined Lauriel in the embrace.

"I ... I th ... thought I was d ... dead ... Couldn't ... find my way. And then ... the wind," Nyx stammered.

"I understand completely. The same thing happened to me!" Lauriel replied empathetically.

Eldrin joined the others, and they continued to hold onto Nyx to help calm and reassure her.

They sat huddled together for several minutes, and Nyx found great comfort in their reunification. She had been severely shaken by the frightening experience, but their warm, reassuring embraces combined with their comforting words helped to chase away the intense fear that had firmly gripped her. The color in her face slowly returned, and along with it, her composure.

"I just don't know how much more of this quest my heart can take," Nyx fretted.

Lauriel stood and held out her hand to help Nyx to her feet.

"When the burden of all this begins to feel too great, I find solace in the fact that I have each of you, my family, right here with me. And in that thought alone I find the courage and reason to carry on against all odds."

Nyx looked up at Lauriel with tear-filled eyes and nodded. She took firm hold of her hand and stood, and as she did, she rose with a resolute determination to continue onward.

Thunder Goddess

Jexi and Eldrin studied the elemental chaos that orbited around the maelstrom for almost an hour as they attempted to identify any safe patterns or pathways to transition from one earth-berg to another, and determine what magic spells in their inventory might get them there. But each solution seemed to end in destruction as their chosen pieces inevitably obliterated themselves in violent collisions with other oppositely rotating objects, or were annihilated by fire, lightning, ice, or any combination of deadly elements as they neared the maelstrom.

They were just about to take a break from the seemingly impossible task, when Eldrin came the sudden realization that they faced another, even more discouraging problem.

He realized that the distances between each transition were far greater than what they initially appeared to be when he recognized that the maelstrom itself was actually two continent-sized cyclones that were attached at the very center. One, in an upward position, and the other in an exact mirrored position downward.

Eldrin shook his head dejectedly. "I just don't see how this is possible; even if we were able to find a safe path, we would run out of Fly spells before we even transitioned to the first earth-berg."

"What do you mean? It doesn't look that far," Lauriel said as she pointed to the nearest floating island.

"It's the same perspective as looking at the mountains from a faraway plain. They do not look large, or that far away, but in fact it can be quite the opposite," Eldrin explained.

Lauriel nodded in understanding. "But how do you know that same perspective exists here?" she continued to question.

"Look closely at the maelstrom. That is not some small whirlwind from a storm; it's a continent-sized double cyclone. And if we can see the entirety of it from here, we are a long, long way from it, which means that the island nearest to us is actually quite distant."

Nyx nodded and interjected with an idea, "Can the wind just take us over to it like it brought us up here? Not that I ever EVER want to do that again," she added.

Both Eldrin and Jexi looked at each other and began to laugh; they had considered every possible spell and method, but had been too tunnel visioned to even think of the most simple and obvious of solutions.

"Etheriani, are you able to take us to the maelstrom like you brought us together up here?" Jexi asked in the common speech so the others could understand.

"Forward … yes … but … destroy … closer … Etheriani … domain … here," Etheriani replied in broken common speech.

"Destroy?" Eldrin asked.

"Air … opposition … elements … and … hedged … no … air," the wind whispered back.

Jexi spoke again but switched to the Primordial speech to try and get a better understanding of the garbled warning.

"What is meant?"

"Etheriani … home … here … enemy … other … element … forward … Outsider … need … air … no … air … closer."

Jexi shook her head in understanding. *"Can you safely bring to nearest island? There?"* Jexi asked as she pointed to the earth-berg.

"Yes … Thunder … Goddess."

"Hang on, everyone, I think we are about to go on another ride!" Jexi warned.

The air around each of the companions began to thicken until they had the same strange feeling of complete submersion, and an instant later, they were whisked upward and outward toward the floating earth-berg.

"Hang on to what?" Nyx yelled, but her voice was carried off into the distance.

Within seconds they transitioned the entire length of the island and passed into the abyssal void at an incomprehensible speed. But as they moved toward the maelstrom and the earth-berg, a strange thing began to happen.

The air turned into a misty vapor as Etheriani drew in all of the elemental atmosphere that encircled the outer fringes of the Plane of Discordance into a singular, colossal entity as she coalesced into a primordial cloud form.

The companions' attention was drawn away from the targeted earth-berg and fully onto Etheriani as they marveled at the sheer size and magnificence of the entity that had fortunately befriended them.

*   *   *   *

Even at the speed of the wind, the transition to the next island took almost an hour, and Eldrin realized that he had been correct about his observations of distance. By the time they landed gently on the next earth-berg, Eldrin concluded that the span had likely been several hundred miles.

Etheriani spoke again, but instead of a whisper upon the wind, the fully consolidated Primordial sounded more like distant thunder.

"Closer … element … discord."

"I understand. Thank you, you help all outsiders, not only Thunder Goddess," Jexi replied. "I believe she means that she can only take us part of the way to the maelstrom and that once we get beyond that point, we may be without air," Jexi warned.

"Well, this just keeps getting better and better," Eldrin muttered under his breath.

But just as he was reaching the height of discouragement, a globe of water came into view as it orbited around the maelstrom in a much closer proximity, and it gave him an idea.

He watched its transition for several minutes, and observed many of the smaller pieces of earth slam into it, but they seemed to have little effect as it absorbed the impact and continued onward, expelling them randomly as it went.

"Etheriani … can you get us close to that water?"

"Difficult … but … Thunder … Goddess …commands," the colossal cloud rumbled.

Jexi smirked at Etheriani's answer. "Just remember that, brother …What are you thinking?"

Lauriel couldn't help but laugh. Even in the most inhospitable place under one of the most stressful conditions imaginable, Jexi not only kept her humor, but actually seemed to be enjoying the challenge.

Eldrin did not miss his opportunity to respond appropriately, "My apologies… Your Eminence."

"In answer to your question, before we came here, I prepared a Water Breathing spell that I can use on all of us. If we can make it to that globe, it looks like a relatively safe area where we could figure out our next move."

"Water … name … Aequoreae … friend … but … far," Etheriani advised Jexi.

"Can you take there once prepare?" Jexi asked.

"Etheriani … try."

Jexi nodded. "Well, that looks like our only move at this point; the rest is too chaotic to plan out every step. Etheriani will take us whenever you are ready."

Eldrin began to brief the others on his spell.

"Okay, once we get close, I will cast my water breathing spell on us. Once you enter the water, try to breathe normally. It is going to feel really weird, but we are already somewhat prepared for it from the way that the thick air felt."

Lauriel nodded, and Eldrin noticed that she was particularly focused on his instructions. He made a mental note to ask her about her experience in the pocket of incorporeality.

"Any questions?"

After a brief silence, Nyx spoke up. "I would just like to say that I REALLY don't like this place."

Lauriel smiled and nodded vigorously in agreement.

"*We are ready, Etheriani,*" Jexi stated.

At Jexi's notice, the primordial cloud colossus whisked them off of the earth-berg and proceeded toward the far-distant globe of water.

CHAPTER TWENTY-FOUR

Maelstrom

The companions had been traveling through the relatively benign outer perimeter of the void for nearly an hour when they felt Etheriani change course several times in rapid succession. Jexi felt the distinct emotion of fear emanating from her, and the thought of the colossal primordial entity being afraid of anything at all sent shivers of equal intensity down her own spine.

"Etheriani, what's wrong?"

"Fire ... name ... Pyronos ... domain ... enemy ... notice," Etheriani replied.

Jexi looked onward at the large ocean of liquid fire in the distance and pointed to it as she warned the others, "I think that fire-ocean is another living primordial, but one that is hostile!"

They were still hundreds of miles away from the elemental inferno and could already feel the intensity of the radiant heat.

"Ugh, I think you're right! I've been watching it and it is moving independently of everything else orbiting around the maelstrom. No matter what direction we go, it floats directly back into our path," Eldrin observed.

As they pressed onward, the fire-ocean continued to move in their direction, and by the time they closed to within a few hundred miles, it became apparent that they would not simply be able to bypass it.

The heat from the liquid inferno continued to intensify and so too did Etheriani's continuous thunder as she compressed and reformed into a slightly smaller, denser form. As she did, the misty vapors condensed around the companions, swaddling them in an even thicker blanket of protection from the increasing heat.

Once they were within about one hundred miles of the ocean, Etheriani slowed her movement to a near standstill.

"Pyronos ... too ... strong ... block ... way," Etheriani thundered in the common speech so all of the companions could understand.

Suddenly, a city sized mote of fire ejected out of the ocean and hurled rapidly toward them.

"Oh crap!" Eldrin exclaimed.

The companions watched helplessly from their front row seat as the giant ball of liquid fire careened toward them on a catastrophic and deadly collision course. Even with Etheriani's protective layer of dense, cool wind around them, they still felt the scorching heat intensify every second it drew nearer.

"We'll be dead long before it even hits us if we don't do something soon!" Nyx shouted over the sound of the continuous thunder.

Eldrin pulled the amulet out of his pocket, intending to use it to take the group back to the pocket of incorporeality as a last resort, but his heart sank when he realized that the magic had not yet recharged.

Etheriani suddenly veered to the right and headed directly toward a nearby floating glacier, and the massive ball of liquid fire followed. As they arrived, Etheriani shielded the companions directly behind the mountain of ice, and the intense heat the companions had felt just seconds before, suddenly switched to a bone chilling cold.

The thunderous rumbling intensified as Etheriani once again compressed herself even further so that she could hide behind the mountain of ice, but she was unable to fully conceal herself before the fire impacted the glacier.

The giant ball of flame slammed into the mountain of ice with meteoric force, and a cataclysmic conflict of elements ensued. The glacier fractured into an innumerable array of ice shards, and the intense heat of the liquid fire instantly vaporized a vast majority of them. But the rock-hard, icy core of the glacier was just large enough to withstand the initial onslaught and provided adequate shielding to save the companions from instantaneous cremation. The fire enveloped the remaining surfaces of the glacier, and a torrent of water and steam spilled into the void in all directions.

Jexi felt Etheriani's immediate and intense reaction of pain mixed with anger as the liquid fire splashed into the many parts of her that had remained exposed, burning large holes in her as they passed through her cloud-like form unabated. Thunder crashed throughout the heavens as she caught the water up in a wild tempest and used it against the remaining fire that clung stubbornly to the surfaces of the glacier.

Just as things looked like they were beginning to settle down and end in an elemental stalemate, three more motes of fire erupted out of the ocean, heading directly at them.

"There are no more large glaciers to hide behind!" Lauriel warned.

"Etheriani, back!" Jexi shouted.

Etheriani began a rapid retreat back toward the safety of the outer perimeter and was forced to flee for ten agonizing minutes before the terrifying balls of fire finally ended their pursuit and fell into the void. Once they had achieved a safe distance from Pyronos's threat range, Etheriani brought them to a halt.

"Way … blocked."

"Unfortunately, the book didn't mention anything about the dangers of spellcasting, friendly and hostile primordials, or how to get past one or more guarding the maelstrom. It's obvious that the author only observed and did not attempt any exploration," Eldrin explained, clearly frustrated by the reversal of progress, their lack of options, and the lack of knowledge on how to prepare for the strange plane of existence.

Jexi's eyes suddenly lit up. "That's it! I have been looking at spellcasting here all wrong!"

"How so?" Eldrin asked.

"Maybe instead of fearing the dangerous amplifying effect of elemental spells, if we are very careful, we can use it to our advantage."

Eldrin looked at Jexi and raised his eyebrows as he considered her statement.

"Remember the dragon's breath spell that I empowered the succubus with when we fought Malthrax?"

"Yes, of course."

"Well, unlike the deadly concussive thunder wave traveling outward in all directions, the icy dragon's breath is very directional, and as long as we are behind it, we should be okay!"

"That may very well work, but what about the range?" Eldrin questioned.

"I have plenty of different ice evocations that can travel a good distance, but nothing that would be effective a hundred miles away, even if it was enhanced a hundredfold. With the Dragon's Breath spell, you have to be right up close and personal."

"If I can cast it on Etheriani, she might be able to use it at a much greater distance. And if not, maybe she can use it as sort of a shield to stop the fire comets," Jexi contended.

Eldrin nodded. "Well, I think we have run out of other viable options."

Jexi looked at Nyx and Lauriel for acceptance, and they both simultaneously shrugged.

"That decision is between you two, but I do believe that the only way we are going to get there is through a combination of Etheriani and magical means," Lauriel affirmed.

Jexi nodded. "Okay then, here goes."

"Etheriani, I give to you, power of ice to fight Pyronos."

"Thunder ... Goddess ... ice ... too?"

"Yes ... Please proceed on path."

"Thunder ... Goddess ... commands," Etheriani said as she moved forward again.

* * * *

Jexi began her spellcasting as two large motes of fire erupted from Pyronos and began hurling toward them.

"Nas-thrax-aerthos ... Vasterix kai!"

Just as the temperature had dropped markedly when the companions were shielded by the glacier, the already dense atmosphere around them suddenly became frigid as the spell imparted into Etheriani.

"I hope you are right about this!" Nyx said through already chattering teeth.

"Etheriani, when half distance, exhale tempest at fire. If fire not stopped ... run," Jexi instructed.

Etheriani stopped her forward progress and waited for the flaming spheres as instructed, and each of the companions held their breath in anxious apprehension as the fire streaked toward them.

When the spheres reached the halfway point between the two primordials, she exhaled with the full fury of the entire planular firmament, and an icy elemental onslaught of apocalyptic proportions ensued.

To everyone's immediate relief, the massive blast of cold traveled outward and away, leaving them completely unharmed as it formed a billowing cloud of ice shards that sped forward at cyclone-force speeds.

Based off her observations of Malthrax's breath weapon, Jexi estimated that the icy blast was equivalent in size to at least twenty adult dragons breathing simultaneously. She could feel Etheriani's mixture of surprise, awe, and excitement, all of which mirrored her own feelings.

"Ice … Goddess … too!" Etheriani thundered.

"Well done, Etheriani!" Jexi replied.

Minutes later, the giant polar vortex storm clashed with the spheres of liquid fire, and the sheer volume of magically enhanced ice and cold proved too much for the fire attack to penetrate before they were extinguished by the relentless barrage.

"Okay, Etheriani, forward!" Jexi instructed.

With seemingly newfound confidence, Etheriani charged directly at Pyronos, successfully extinguishing several more attacks before closing in on him. As she exhaled for a fourth time, Pyronos made no attempt to counter, choosing instead to retreat far away from the angry tempest. And as he rapidly withdrew, Jexi felt yet another feeling from Etheriani—satisfaction. It reminded her of a meek child finally standing up to the schoolyard bully and punching him in the mouth, but it was a long-awaited retribution on a celestial scale.

"Yes!" Lauriel let out a cheer.

"Great job, Jexi! AND Etheriani!" Nyx added enthusiastically.

"Well done, 'Ice Goddess,' maybe your strange magic is worth something after all," Eldrin teased.

With their path to the maelstrom finally cleared of the belligerent enemy, Etheriani continued onward into the middle perimeter, and the companions moved toward their goal with renewed spirits.

*   *   *   *

Etheriani continued her lengthy press into the middle perimeter, and just as the companions had observed from their perch high atop the pocket of incorporeality, the speed and density of the elemental debris fields slowly but steadily continued to increase as they drew closer to the maelstrom.

Etheriani was able to easily maneuver around the numerous obstacles, but the closer they came, the more maneuvering she had to do, and the less efficient their journey became.

After several hours of bobbing and weaving, ducking and dodging, Nyx's voice rose over the thunder, "Look at that!"

Her eyes were wide with fright, and her mouth gaped open in disbelief as she pointed outward. The rest of the companions looked in the direction and saw the emerging source of her concern. A massive, cloud-like formation of rocks had just come into view from the back side of the maelstrom. The upper torso appeared in the form of a towering thunderhead, and two rock tornadoes formed the legs of the bottom torso. Two rock-composed arms of incomprehensible size and weight continuously swept up the rock debris from the collisions and fed the never-ending food supply into the insatiable storm.

Jexi spoke loud enough for her message to carry to Etheriani above the sound of the thunder, and even though they could not understand what she was saying in the Primordial speech, they could still feel her nervousness radiate from it.

"Is that enemy?"

"Terratholon … name … not … enemy … not … friend … not … bother … unless … bother."

Jexi immediately translated for the others, her voice trembling as she spoke, "Etheriani said that is Terratholon, an earth primordial, and there is no hope of getting away from him."

"What!?" Eldrin exclaimed.

"Oh crap!" Lauriel gasped.

"Well, what do we do now!?" Nyx questioned anxiously.

"Nyx, I think it is time to bend over and kiss your ass goodbye," Jexi replied.

A smile slowly drew across Eldrin's face, and he breathed a sigh of relief as he shook his head at Jexi.

Jexi burst into laughter.

"I'm just kidding, Etheriani says he is harmless as long as we leave him alone."

Lauriel also began to laugh at Jexi's ruse as Nyx shook her head and breathed a very obvious sigh of relief, clearly feeling foolish at falling for anything from Jexi.

For the next several hours, the companions sat transfixed as they watched him tirelessly carry out his continuous and depressingly futile mission to reform earthen terrain. Once he scooped enough rocks, he would compress them into large earth-bergs and launch them in random directions, hoping that one might successfully find its way out of the elemental chaos before being destroyed.

* * * *

Lauriel was the first to notice that the continuous sound of rolling thunder that Etheriani made as she moved was slowly but steadily increasing, and as she began to look around inquisitively, she noticed that Etheriani had noticeably shrunk in size. She turned around to look behind them and discovered that a trail of vapor was continuously leaching away from her like an immeasurably long tail of a comet.

The rumbling sound was so loud that she didn't even try to speak over it, choosing instead to nudge Jexi and point toward the phenomenon. Eldrin noticed the interaction and quickly used his spell that allowed them to communicate mind-to-mind.

Something about that doesn't look right, Lauriel observed.

Yeah, that is really odd, Jexi replied.

Etheriani, are you okay? Jexi asked.

"*Middle ... perimeter ... not ... mine ... hurt.*"

Jexi had been so focused on their goal of moving forward, that she had only considered that Etheriani's warnings about the elemental discord were meant for them. But as her previous interactions began to replay through her mind, they suddenly made sense: "Destroy ... closer ... Etheriani ...domain ... here, Air ... opposition ... elements ... and ... hedged ... no ... air, Etheriani ... home ... here."

Jexi's throat constricted, and she was overcome by a sudden wave of emotion when she realized that Etheriani had tried numerous times to communicate the issue to her, but faithfully and dutifully continued to follow her request and pressed onward even as she was slowly being ripped apart.

She's bleeding! Jexi exclaimed. *The farther she gets from her domain at the outer perimeter, the more she dies!*

Oh no! Nyx cried. *What can we do to help her?*

Do you think there is a way we can heal her? Lauriel asked.

It's worth a shot! Nyx replied.

Both Nyx and Lauriel tried their hand at healing the primordial but neither of their spells appeared to help her in any way.

Eldrin's logical mind raced rapidly for a solution, "Etheriani, can Aequoreae move toward you?"

"No ... Terratholon ... enemy ... Aequoreae ... not ... pass."

"Etheriani, please stop! We don't want to hurt you," Jexi shouted above the thunder.

Etheriani drew to another stop, hovering just past the halfway point to the inner perimeter.

"Outsiders ... not ... exist ... if ... no ... Etheriani ... help ... yes?"

"Yes, but there must be another way!" Jexi replied in an uncharacteristically distraught voice that was choked with raw emotion.

"Unknown ... other ... way," Etheriani thundered.

Jexi looked at Eldrin, tears filling her eyes.

He slowly shook his head. "I'm sorry, sister, I can't think of any other way to travel that far without air. Even if we tried to teleport, misjudging it by even a mile would be disastrous."

"Etheriani ... help ... outsiders ... and ... Thunder ... Ice ... Goddess."

Jexi felt that their ability to retrieve the shard on their own accord was almost impossible and would certainly fail without Etheriani's help. She was angry that their naiveté and lack of knowledge about traveling to the plane was having a very real and detrimental effect on such an innocent and fascinatingly gallant inhabitant.

But with no other apparent options to continue onward, she was forced to make the agonizing decision to accept her new selfless companion's offer to carry them forward even as it was slowly destroying her.

"Okay, Etheriani, I ask that you please help us, but 'Thunder Goddess' does not command it."

Etheriani once again began her push forward, and with every new mile of vapor that she left behind, Jexi felt like her own heart was slowly being sucked away with it. As the hours ticked by, the speed and density of the elemental chaos orbiting the maelstrom continued to multiply, and so too did the frequency of danger. Etheriani's movements became increasingly violent as she was forced to spend much of her time dodging and maneuvering around the elemental hazards.

By the time she neared the inner perimeter, the maelstrom had grown so large in their field of view that they could no longer see the top or bottom of it. The once small globe of water they were desperately trying to reach had also grown in perspective to the size of an entire ocean.

But their observations of the once unfathomably large living air primordial were the exact opposite. Etheriani had continued to shrink, now only the size of a small hill, a mere grain of sand on a vast beach in relation to the maelstrom.

The thundering had also increased and become so deafening that the companions were forced to use their hands for no other purpose than to continually cover their ears.

I have an idea! Lauriel suddenly exclaimed in the mind-to-mind communication, breaking the doleful silence that had descended upon the group. *Pyronos was able to attack and control the direction of the motes of fire when we were within about a hundred miles of him. If Aequoreae can do the same with a smaller globe of water, that would save Etheriani at least a couple hundred miles of travel through the inner perimeter. We could jump directly from her to the safety of the water, and Aequoreae might be able to move us directly into the maelstrom.*

Jexi's mournful glumness was immediately chased away and replaced by a look of hope and optimism. *That would work! That is a great idea!*

Eldrin nodded in agreement. *Yes, I think that's a great plan!*

You know, I have a spell I have really never used called Control Water. I always thought it was kind of useless, but in this situation, it may somehow be able to help! Nyx added.

What does it do? Eldrin asked.

Basically, I can control the movement of water to a certain degree, Nyx explained.

That may very well be exactly what we need! Eldrin exclaimed.

Jexi wasted no time communicating the plan to Etheriani, and as soon as she finished, a blinding flash of white light lit up the vast expanse as a massive bolt of lightning, the first they had seen from Etheriani amidst all of the continuous thunder, instantaneously arced across the void and struck Aequoreae. The jagged tendrils of light appeared to zig zag across the vast surface of the globe.

What are you doing!? Aequoreae not friend? Jexi asked Etheriani.

Friend … communicating … Thunder … Goddess … message.

No sooner had Etheriani replied when another bolt of lightning arced back from the globe of water to her. The companions could feel the sudden tingle of energy race throughout the cloud, but were otherwise unharmed.

Fascinating! They have their own mind-to-mind type of communication with the use of lighting! Jexi exclaimed as she relayed to the group what was transpiring.

Like a falling drop of rain, a mote of water separated from the globe and rapidly moved in their direction.

It's working! Lauriel exclaimed excitedly.

Source of Life

By the time that both Etheriani and the drop of water closed the distance between each other, Etheriani was only about ten times the size of Gorian's earth elemental form, and the many thousand gallon drops of water from Aequoreae was at least one hundred feet in diameter.

The thunder was so loud and distracting that Eldrin had to attempt his Water Breathing spell several times before he was finally able to concentrate enough to invoke the magic.

"Thank you, my friend!" Jexi shouted as they prepared for the transition to the water. Her voice was so completely drowned out by the thunder that not even her companions next to her could hear her, but Etheriani somehow heard the message.

"Etheriani … fulfillment … help … outsiders."

As the globe of water finally touched the surface of the vapor, the two elements appeared to hold each other in a long embrace, like two friends finally reuniting after a very long absence. Just before she exited, Jexi could feel Etheriani's strong feelings of longing to stay with the water.

The companions transitioned into the sphere and found an immediate reprieve from the roaring thunder, but it was quickly supplanted by the feeling of drowning as Lauriel, Nyx, and Jexi fought to hold their breath, even as Eldrin coaxed them to breathe normally. One by one, they finally succumbed to the urge, and just as Eldrin had described, the strange feeling of the cool water entered their lungs as they finally began to breathe in the life sustaining liquid.

After several minutes of getting used to the strange sensation, they were able to relax and even enjoy their effortless float in the crystal clear water of the protective globe.

Okay, we have experienced many weird things on this quest, but this has to be near the top of the scale! Nyx commented.

The others nodded in agreement.

It's so peaceful and serene! Lauriel observed.

Indeed! What a nice reprieve from the chaos! Eldrin replied.

Jexi's tone was more serious. *I hate to be the one to break up our only moment of tranquility, but we aren't moving anymore. Nyx, maybe you should try that Control Water spell of yours to make sure that we're not stuck again.*

Nyx nodded, and all eyes turned toward her.

* * * *

Much to Nyx's surprise, the entire sphere of water lurched forward under her control as soon as she finished the last word of her spell. Her face beamed with excitement as she moved the group rapidly toward the maelstrom with little effort.

It's working! she exclaimed.

But as they began to push into the thick debris field of the inner perimeter, the blissful ride soon became an increasingly difficult challenge.

Nyx nimbly maneuvered the globe around the larger objects, but the unavoidable smaller debris pelted them with such frequency that the surface of the sphere looked like a hailstorm hovering over a pond. The globe absorbed and protected the companions from each punishing strike, but with every impact, many gallons of water were lost as it splashed away from the sphere and into the void.

We are going to have to do something soon or we are not going to have any water left by the time we get there! Lauriel cautioned.

I have an idea, Eldrin said as he began to swim toward the outer surface. *I have a minor cantrip spell that may help, but I'm not sure how well. It creates a bit of frost, so depending on how much it is amplified, we might get a bit cold again.*

Eldrin held out his hand and spoke the simple phrase to invoke his spell. *"Xavathos Auronas"*

A beam of blue-white light sprang from his hand and raced to the surface of the sphere. And as the spell began to take effect, they stared in awe at the unexpectedly beautiful sight that it created.

A large, crystalline, snowflake-like structure crawled rapidly across the entire surface of the sphere until the myriad of angular, geometric shapes grew together as one. The structure continued to thicken and fill in until a five-foot-thick shell of hardened ice covered the entire surface.

Eldrin breathed a sigh of relief when the spell completed and the rock-hard shield immediately started deflecting the incoming debris.

If we could only concentrate our elemental magic like this outside of this plane! he marveled.

Jexi nodded. *No kidding! We wouldn't even need the Reality Shard!*

Over the next several hours, Nyx continued to maneuver the sphere through the relentless barrage, while both Eldrin and Jexi worked with their cold and heat cantrips to keep the core interior temperature habitable while renewing and maintaining the hard, icy exterior.

They were just beginning to learn and understand how to adjust their spells to the plane when the constant sound of dull thuds from the debris strikes suddenly ceased.

Nyx brought the orb to a halt, and an eerie silence settled upon them. The surface had been struck so many times that the thick spiderweb of cracks made it difficult to see clearly out of, so Eldrin began to slowly and cautiously melt the shield of ice. After nearly ten minutes, the last opaque layer melted back into the water, and a clearer picture of the world outside of their droplet came in to view.

Well, that is unexpected, Eldrin observed.

What in the world going on? Lauriel asked.

While the immeasurably large maelstrom in front of them continued far beyond their field of view, a nearly flat region of rocks, fire, water, and air bubbles extended outward in the same horizontal plane of the large gap that separated the two opposing cyclones. And in stark contrast to the elemental chaos that existed not far above and below it, not a single piece moved.

This is only a guess, but I think that the opposing forces of the two storms offset each other so completely here, that they cancel each other out and leave the elements trapped in the very center in some sort of strange equilibrium, Eldrin concluded.

Very odd indeed, Jexi added.

Should I continue onward? Nyx asked.

Yes, if you can stay very close to this field, we should be okay all the way to the gap, Eldrin advised.

I hope we're close. I have had to renew this spell many times, and I'm almost out, Nyx warned as she began to move the sphere forward again.

Eldrin pulled the amulet from his pocket and breathed a sigh of relief when he found that the magic had finally recharged.

He looked back up and placed his hand on Nyx's shoulder. *You are doing a great job, Nyx. I think we are about to cross the finish line!*

And what then? Lauriel asked.

Jexi shook her head and shrugged. *We haven't a clue.*

Reality Shards

Nyx had just used her final spell of water control when the companions completed the transition through the gap and moved into the inner core of the maelstrom. Much to their relief, they found that the inner core contained no debris whatsoever, and the calm stasis field at the very center remained intact.

A bright, singular point of light resembling a miniature star illuminated the interior from the very center eye of the storm, and Nyx cautiously moved the sphere toward it.

It wasn't until Nyx brought the globe to within just a few feet of the bright starlight that they finally beheld their long-awaited objective.

There they are! Lauriel exclaimed.

The two objects were shaped just like an icicle but with perfectly smooth surfaces. And like an icicle, both were translucent but had a distinct, purple hue. Each shard was slightly smaller than a magic rod, about eighteen inches from the bottom to the sharp tapered tip. One of the shards was in an upward facing position, and the other faced downward in an opposing, mirrored position. Starlight emanated from the very center of the two pointing tips, bathing everything in an otherworldly glow. The light passed through the shards, illuminating them and shooting concentrated beams of light through each end that traveled infinitely in opposite directions.

And now it is just a matter of capturing one of them, Eldrin said. He began to swim toward the surface, and the others followed.

I'll try my Mage Hand spell; I can move and grasp objects at a distance with it, Eldrin explained.

When he finished his spell, a spectral, floating hand appeared next to the reality shard.

He held out his own hand and made a motion of clenching it around the shard. The spectral hand followed his every move, but the instant that it touched the shard, it disappeared.

Woah! Eldrin blurted

What happened!? Lauriel asked.

The shard is spinning so fast that we can't even see that it is spinning! We can't just simply grab it and leave.

Eldrin and Jexi discussed their spell options for capturing the shard for several minutes, and with each unsuccessful attempt, both Eldrin's and Jexi's face looked increasingly troubled.

We have come this far; I just have to believe that we can figure this out, Nyx offered in encouragement.

The cube! Lauriel exclaimed.

What about the cube from Malthrax?

Eldrin nodded and immediately withdrew the cube of force from his backpack. The very sight of the device turned their stomachs.

Jexi, maybe both of us can use our Mage Hand spells to position the cube to capture a shard when it activates.

Jexi nodded.

Two floating spectral hands, one grasping the top of the cube, and one grasping the bottom, pushed the object through the water and into the void, stopping just inches away from the shard.

I don't mean to be overly dramatic, but the fate of the realms could very well depend on this working, Eldrin noted.

Nyx clasped her hands together, and her lips moved in silent prayer.

Eldrin uttered the command word for the device to activate, "*Velixium!*"

And just is it had ensnared Dante, it instantly captured one of the reality shards within the six walls of force.

You got it! Lauriel yelled in excitement.

Eldrin and Jexi quickly retrieved the now rectangular shaped cube into the water and brought it to rest in front of them.

A silence once again fell over the group as they looked onward at the beautiful object in awe, but the feelings soon turned to thoughtful reflection as they each contemplated the nearly implausible series of events that led them to the very spot.

Jexi finally broke the silence. *I'm not sure if I believe in providence, but I just don't see how everything that's happened could have been completely random. I mean, here we are in a globe of water, breathing it, in the center of Plane of Discordance, staring at a reality shard. No wonder the High Council of Wizards thought we were crazy. Yet throughout all of the dead ends, opposition, and selfless sacrifice of others, here we stand with it.*

The others simply nodded, finding any other words unnecessary. As their tears flowed freely into the water, they each joined hands and took several moments to absorb the magnitude of their accomplishment.

CHAPTER TWENTY-FIVE

Unexpected Alliances

ight, powdery snow had just begun to dance in the frigid evening air when the small contingent of soldiers arrived at the camp. Newly promoted Field Marshal Stephen Drägo stood at the door of his large command tent and stoically observed the new addition to the expansive encampment. He caught a brief glimpse of their red and white flag, and his face unwittingly darkened.

"Cembrionians… forty-nine of them," he said with tempered disdain.

A venerable, battle-worn dwarf shook his head in contempt as he chronicled the new arrivals onto the tally sheet at the large table. His impossibly weathered hand looked far too stiff and calloused to manipulate the delicate quill pen, but he appeared to be able to add the numbers to the document with a surprising degree of ease. His finely crafted dwarven war-axe leaned against the table next to him and his heavy, grizzly bear fur cloak was slung over the back of his chair. He wore a well-tailored leather jerkin that was adorned with a thick, gold chain livery collar that designated him as the Highlord Protector of the combined dwarven realms. He laid the quill down and looked up at the field marshal from his seated position at the table. His thick, white beard and bushy eyebrows hid any expression on his leathery face.

"I don't like it any more than you do, but I'll take what we can get," the old dwarven thane asserted.

The field marshal immediately nodded in agreement but seemed to ponder the statement while he continued to observe the encampment. "Dordolek, my old friend, who would have ever thought we would be sharing a war camp with our former enemies?"

"And sitting on the doorstep of Draxanarek'Vel waiting to join even more of them for a little guided tour of their realm!" Dordolek added with a chuckle.

The field marshal did not respond, seemingly lost in his own thoughts as he watched the dark clouds scuttle across the moon with increasing frequency. He absentmindedly stroked his thick, salt-and-pepper mustache, and his brow furrowed as he began to speak again. "This snowstorm will delay any others; let's hope it passes quickly. We have less than one-third of the numbers we had hoped for."

"Yes, too many have either fallen in battle or have been held back to protect their own. I find it ironic that I find myself hoping that Draxanarek'Vel still has a few legions," Dordolek said in a feeble attempt to sound reassuring.

The old dwarf stood from the table and donned his heavy cloak before clutching his axe in a viselike grip. "Well, that should be all for the night. I think I'll retire. We are approaching three legions of one thousand each. Two human and one dwarven." He patted the field marshal on the arm. "There will be more, Stephen. I just have to believe." He began to walk out and then quickly paused and turned back to face the field marshal. "Excuse me, sir… Field Marshal Drägo," he clarified with sudden formality as he saluted.

The field marshal returned the salute to the dwarf. "That is not necessary, my friend."

"Oh, but it very much is!" the dwarf counseled. "It is important that all of the troops, no matter where they are from, see the unquestionable chain of command."

The field marshal nodded in understanding. "I always cherish your wizened advice, my friend. This is new to all of us."

Timely Arrivals

The field marshal awoke suddenly from his troubled sleep.

Was that someone knocking? he thought to himself.

The howling wind battered the tent relentlessly in a seemingly determined struggle to move the foreign obstacle out of its way.

It must have just been the wind, he concluded.

The knock at the door came again, this time even louder. "Sir, we have significant arrivals!" the voice called, barely carrying above the tempest.

"Yes, come in," he answered loudly.

The door opened, and a soldier quickly stepped through the threshold. He was joined by a heavy gust of bone chilling wind and snow as they all entered the tent together before he was able to quickly close the door behind him.

He saluted and then began his hasty briefing. "I am sorry to disturb you, sir, but it appears that the elves have arrived."

"In this weather!? What time is it?" the field marshal questioned.

"About two hours after midnight, sir," the soldier replied.

"How many?"

"One legion of one thousand, sir. They are dangerously fatigued and suffering from the cold, but many of our men have mustered to help them set up camp."

"See to it that they get any food, warmth, or shelter that they may need. I will be there quickly," the field marshal instructed as he began to hurriedly dress in his heavy winter gear.

"Yes, sir!" the soldier said as he snapped to attention and saluted before quickly exiting.

*   *   *   *

The glacial cold air seemed to cut right through the field marshal's thick fur cloak as the tempestuous wind whipped around him. The heavy snowfall that accompanied it created a pervasive, textured veil that made it difficult to see even twenty feet ahead. But he knew the paths through his encampment well and quickly arrived to find a flurry of activity that rivaled that of the furious snowfall. He was immediately filled with awe at the esprit de corps that was on full display as the human and dwarven soldiers from all parts of Alynthi, many of them former belligerents, scrambled to help the elves set up their shelters and get them out of the elemental onslaught.

A stately, silver haired elf approached, and the sight of the elven leader's command presence made the field marshal question his own qualification to lead such a combined army. The elf's ageless gray eyes reflected the wisdom of a lifetime that transcended at least six human generations, and a confident ferocity that he had only seen once before in the Blademaster. The knowledge and experience that he brought to the field of battle was only rivaled by that of the venerable Dwarven Highlord Protector. He was a High Elf, slender and graceful, yet strong and resolute. He neither shivered from the cold, nor seemed to be in any haste.

He strode purposefully up to the field marshal and saluted, placing the palm of his right hand to the left side of his chest and then motioned outward. The gesture was foreign but well understood, and he quickly reciprocated. The battle warden's formal acknowledgement made him feel even more awkward and unworthy of his title and position.

The battle-hardened senior elven commander had been in the military service since before his great grandfather was born, and had survived and commanded more battles than he could in three lifetimes. But the humans had sent out the rallying call and had assembled an army twice the size of the others, and the field marshal stood unquestionably at the head.

"I am Elenduï Adayr, battle warden of the elven realms. I present to you one legion of the remnants of the combined High, Woodland, Moon, and Sun Elven armies, the latter traveling as far as two hundred and thirty miles in just under two weeks to answer the most dire call of our age."

The field marshal nodded approvingly, his respect and admiration of his counterpart readily apparent. He was thankful that they were allies and that he was not here to face him in battle. "Welcome, and well met; thank you for answering the call. We now stand at nearly four legions combined."

The battle warden's face was cold and unflinching, but the field marshal could feel his concern.

"Hopefully we are not the last," the elven commander stated coolly and then abruptly changed the conversation. "Is the Blademaster here with you?"

"She is not, though we expect her imminently," the field marshal replied

He could see the first visible hint of emotion briefly cross the smooth stone facade of the battle warden's face. It was the brief but unmistakable look of disappointment.

Convergence

The dawn of the next morning broke with a brilliant fiery red. The snowstorm had exited just as rapidly as it had arrived, leaving behind a pristine blanket of white snow that stretched outward from the encampment in all directions. The air was crisp, and the howling wind had died down to a gentle breeze.

Smoke from the many roaring fires rose high over the plain, and the troops huddled closely around the pockets of warmth as they began to devour their meager morning rations.

A gilded battle standard stood next to the command tent, proudly displaying the many campaign victory ribbons of the various human armies that were represented on the field. It was capped with a newly minted two-headed phoenix that had been hastily but masterfully created for the occasion.

It represented a fusion of the factious and often opposed human kingdoms, rising out of the ashes of their shattered towns and villages to join into one allied force. One head looked left, toward the western kingdoms, and the other to the right, toward the kingdoms in the east. The sharpened claws reached down toward the southern kingdoms while the crowns on the heads pointed to the north.

The stirring site of the standard overlooking the encampment with its war streamers lazily fluttering in the gentle morning wind was enough to inspire the mixed human army troops with a unified sense of camaraderie that transcended their combative histories with one another. But it was not only their standard that created such a remarkable display; two others now stood with it. The dwarven and elven standards shone with equal splendor, and the three of them together boldly proclaimed that a "triumviri" had been assembled. Never before had such a vast combination of human, elven, and dwarven soldiers been assembled into a single field army under one command.

The highlord protector entered the command tent and found his elven and human counterparts already assembled around the large table. The field marshal had been bringing the newly arrived battle warden up to speed on the troop status, capabilities, and battle plan. Four wooden pieces were placed on the table, each indicating a different legion of one thousand troops.

The field marshal paused and politely greeted his dwarven ally and waited until he took his seat at the table before he began again.

"It is difficult to prepare for a battle without having any idea of the enemy's numbers. We know that it takes at least four of our soldiers for every one of those creatures. Together, we have mustered the largest army ever assembled, yet we are not near the strength that we had hoped for. The survival of our realms hangs precariously upon the strength of this field."

The others nodded in agreement. He picked up two more of the carved wooden pieces and placed them on the map near the symbol indicating the near-unfathomably large gate to the underground realm of Draxanarek'Vel.

"One of the other problems we face is the fact that we have had no contact from the Dark Elves and therefore have no idea what strength remains within their realm to help fight the enemy. I had hoped for at least two legions from them."

He looked at the others and quietly awaited their council.

"I would plan on zero; you can never trust the treacherous Dark Elves, even at a time like this," the battle warden said with a rare moment of disgust plainly radiating on his face.

The highlord protector slid the two pieces backward, off of the field of battle. "I agree about planning on zero, but for different reasons. We have no idea how many of them are still alive; they all could have been decimated. I fear that is why they have not opened the great gate."

The battle warden was about to speak again when the sharp sound of a warning horn pierced the calmness of the morning, abruptly ending the conversation. The tumultuous sounds of thousands of troops hastily preparing for an unexpected engagement created a noisy and chaotic ruckus throughout the encampment.

The triumviri exited the tent and quickly spotted the source of the alarm. Another entire army, many thousands strong, had just entered the distant valley and was marching rapidly toward their position on the high plain.

The legions hastily assembled into battle formations. They could not distinguish the composition of the group, but could tell that it was no human, dwarven, or elven army.

One of the human soldiers quickly made his way to the field marshal with a copper telescoping spyglass. He raised it to his eye and began to identify the incoming troops to the others in short succinct statements.

"Orcs, about one legion in strength. Goblins, possibly two legions but hard to tell. About half a legion of hobgoblins with them, and ..."

He paused and brought the spyglass away from his eye as he blinked a few times before returning it.

His brow raised in questioning disbelief. "I see many minotaur, and even a few manticore." His last description sounded more like a question than an observation, as if he did not believe his own eyes.

"We must make ready for a difficult battle. Our old enemies have lured us into a trap! We are between their hammer and the anvil of Draxanarek'Vel, like sitting ducks on the open plain!" the highlord protector exclaimed.

"They could have been recruited by the unnatural creatures to join in some kind of sinister alliance," the battle warden said coldly.

The field marshal's blood ran cold as he listened to their council. It was wise and made perfect sense. *Could it be? Have my actions doomed us?* His mind raced as he began to second-guess his decisions. *I just have to believe that this is an answered call, not an attack*, he concluded.

"No ... they are here at my invite," the field marshal declared.

There was a sudden, complete silence near the command tent as the battle warden, highlord protector, and several of the senior officers that were in the area stared at the field marshal in shock and disbelief at the words that he had just spoken.

He continued before the others had a chance to interject or protest. "Although I did not hear any word back from them and assumed until now that the call went unanswered."

"What have you done? Why have you hidden this from us? We cannot trust these wretched brutes farther than we can throw them!" the highlord protector growled angrily.

"You have brought all manner of evil upon us," the battle warden added in a sharp reproach.

"This is not about good or evil, us or them, it is about all of our survival!" the field marshal retorted sternly. "And they are to be given the same mutual respect as all other troops here on this field," he commanded.

One of the human soldiers ran up to them, interrupting the heated exchange with an update, "Sir, four advanced riders approach and have stopped at the edge of the plain."

"My horse," the field marshal ordered.

"This is my doing, and I will go meet them," he declared without averting his gaze from the piercing stares of the highlord protector and battle warden.

He could tell that although they were genuinely upset by his actions, they were quickly reaching the conclusion that he had been right to reach out to them. They were wise and experienced enough to see the importance of the added numbers, even if they did not at all agree with the source, though they were still not fully convinced that it was not some carefully plotted sinister trap by all of their enemies.

The highlord protector and battle warden understood his reticence in telling them that they could be fighting alongside orcs and goblins. Just the thought of fighting as allies with the Dark Elves was almost too much for the elves to even consider joining.

"Well get my mount as well!" the legendarily cantankerous dwarf barked. "I'm coming with you; I can't let you go off and get yourself killed out there!"

The field marshal looked away in an effort to avoid even the slightest hint of a smile that desperately wanted to draw across his face. He did not want to risk infuriating the angry dwarf even more.

The blade warden simply looked at one of his attending soldiers and gave a very slight nod. The soldier instantly turned and ran to retrieve his battle mount.

Within minutes, the triumviri were seated upon their mounts and proceeding toward the other armies contingent. The field marshal sat upon the mightiest of warhorses, standing a full twenty-one hands tall.

The archetype equine was dark gray and had long, shiny, black hair on its mane and tail. Its head was held high as it pranced proudly forward with its ornate and highly protective full plate barding.

It was flanked by a golden caparison that had an exquisitely embroidered lion rampant design on each side, the unmistakable markings of the Golden Company.

Its powerful muscles rippled and twitched, anxiously awaiting the opportunity to charge at an unfortunate enemy.

The dwarven highlord protector rode a ram that was much smaller but no less impressive than the massive warhorse. The ram was not meant for long charges at enemies, but could buckle even the finest crafted plate armor with its thick, curled horns after just a few feet of movement. The ram was just like the dwarf, an obstinate and immovable juggernaut. He would not give up a single inch of ground no matter the challenge, and no matter the cost. Like the field marshal's horse, the short and stocky ram was protected by customized full plate barding.

The battle warden's mount was a light warhorse that was a size in between the ram and the field marshal's steed.

It was built just like the elves—slender and graceful. The elven horses were known for their speed, maneuverability, and high degree of sure footedness. The stallion was as pure white as the pristine snow upon the ground and had intelligent, sky-blue eyes that reflected its spirit and large personality. It was just as proud as the heavy warhorse next to it but did not prance like it did. Rather, it had a uniquely smooth gait that caused the rider very little motion, even at a full gallop. It afforded the deadly elven archer an unparalleled partner for their longbow. His barding was comprised of finely crafted elven chainmail and was overlaid with a deep royal blue silk caparison that was trimmed in a bright silver color.

With the formidable power and splendor of the remaining allied realms on full display, the triumviri rode out to meet the new arrivals.

The entire encampment watched the historic event taking place with silent trepidation.

Their perpetual enemy had emerged from their dark caves and shadowy realms to answer the clarion call to fight the common foe, but the long adversarial history of the two sides could not simply be erased.

The orcs, goblins, and hobgoblins had always appeared to the "civilized" realms to be a splintered group of brutish savages, but they were feared and respected for their ferocity in battle and tenacity for survival. As much as the humans, dwarves, and elves had tried to subdue the menace, the full display of their united tribes upon the field of battle was a testament to their effort in futility. Their enemy had not only survived against the constant and enduring threat from all of the other races that opposed them, but their warlike culture had also survived the terrible incursion of the vile creatures.

After what appeared to be a very brief exchange, the troops at the encampment saw the large orc make a gesture with his hand, and the sound of many drums began to carry upon the wind, signaling the advance of the enemy army.

The triumviri then turned and headed back toward the encampment with the new contingent following closely behind. Though it appeared they had agreed to unite for a common cause, the sight of so many of their enemies moving toward them was so unnerving that the remaining commanding officers began ordering their troops into defensive lines. Even in the dire circumstances, there would remain no trust between them.

War-Chief

As the triumviri reentered the camp with the new contingent, the field marshal led them toward the command tent. All eyes stared in shock and disbelief at the sight of their old, persistent enemy making their way through the encampment as tenuous allies. Their coming was in keeping with the chaos and confusion of the realms.

At the front of the contingent rode destruction incarnate; an orc war-chief of such enormous stature that even the hulking minotaur behind him was made to seem less imposing. When he dismounted from his warhorse-sized dire boar, he stood a monstrous seven feet tall. His broad shoulders and freakishly large muscles sent shivers down the spine of all those that observed him.

His coarse black hair was pulled back into a topknot, and his permanent scowl was accentuated by three piercings above his left eye. Two large tusk-like teeth protruded upward from his heavy-set jaw and ended in sharp filed points that rested against the dark, forest green skin of his cheeks.

Strapped to his back was a nightmarish weapon. It was by far the largest double headed greataxe that any of them had ever seen, and to their surprise, it was not some crude weapon, but something of fine craftsmanship. His armor was also of well-crafted make, consisting of thick, heavy plates that were accented with large spikes. The spikes on his pauldrons were adorned with the skewered skulls of his fallen humanoid victims. The armor appeared to be impossibly heavy, at least the weight of three sets of human full plate, but he seemed to be unencumbered by it in any way.

The field marshal began his formal introduction. "This is orc War-Chief Gorgath N'Kdzul, he is my counterpart—leader of their combined army. With him, hobgoblin Overlord Nillirk, minotaur Battlelord Kanmyr, and goblin Supreme Tyrant Schittikus."

The moment was formal, serious, and unnerving, but the officers could not help but chuckle at the goblin's title and name. The field marshal immediately shot them a sharp, disapproving glance, and the officers quickly regained their composure. "They are here as our invited guests, with separate but equal ranks as ours. Together, the seven of us will form a Council of War."

The orc took the battle standard that the hobgoblin was holding and walked over to where the other three standards stood. The obscene emblem had been festooned in trophies of vanquished human, dwarven, and elven foes.

With the strength of five men, he impaled it deeply into the frozen ground next to them and turned back to face them. The look of certain doom for his enemies was in the glare of his deep-set eyes. He spoke in a gruff but booming voice that traveled far beyond the area of the command tent. "Our realm is this also, and together we will kill."

The parallel primal struggle for survival struck a chord with the troops, and they were immediately impressed and inspired by his matter-of-fact confidence. They could see that he was not some dumb brute, but a battle-hardened conqueror. They suddenly felt ashamed of their predisposed prejudice and underestimation of a greatest of foe.

The orc war-chief let out a sudden harsh bellow that broke the poignant silence of the camp and, in a uniquely sublime moment, was joined by the entire encampment of soldiers.

They erupted into a cheer that grew into such a raucous roar, that it carried far into the valleys below.

CHAPTER TWENTY-SIX

The Great Gate

The chess board had been set, and the collective world held its breath with nervous anticipation of the looming battle for the survival of Alynthi. All available soldiers and militia that were able to join the ranks of the combined army had arrived and were assembled into an uneasy alliance. Almost seven thousand had gathered on the doorstep of Draxanarek'Vel to join with the underground realm in a last desperate offensive against their common foe.

The rumor of the companion's quest to retrieve a magical shard that had the ability to close the portal had spread prolifically and quickly became the last, best hope of the shattered realms. The encamped armies awaited their return with eager anticipation, but each passing day brought with it more apprehension and impatience. As the initial goodwill waned and old prejudices began to return, the field marshal and war-chief realized that a simple fist fight between their troops could quickly escalate into a blood bath of apocalyptic proportions, and they decided to separate their armies into two detached encampments.

The soldiers from both sides were becoming frustrated by the inaction as their homes, villages, and cities continued to burn.

They were eager to storm into Draxanarek'Vel, but the Dark Elves had not opened the great gate, and no amount of force could breach the monolithic structure that led to the underground kingdom. The impossibly solid barrier had taken the dwarven stone-craftsmen many decades to complete, and it would take just as many to tear down. Lauriel had been given the magic key by the Dark Queen herself and only she could open it from the exterior.

Swordsong Continues

On the fourth day after the arrival of the war-chief's army, four riders arrived at the edge of the plain late in the afternoon. Their rapid approach on horseback was noticed by the watchmen, but they were paid little attention. It was common for an occasional straggler to join, or messengers to arrive with news from the many distant lands that were represented. But as they got closer, it soon became apparent that they were no messengers or militia—the storied group of brave adventurers had finally arrived.

"Notify the triumviri!" the watchman captain yelled down excitedly from the crudely constructed watch tower.

By the time the companions had closed the distance to the encampment, word of their arrival had already spread, and a throng of soldiers were pressed tightly around the entrance, eager to get a glimpse of the fabled group that so much hope rested upon. The commotion caused many of the soldiers from the other encampment to spill into the mass gathering to observe the highly anticipated arrival for themselves.

Lauriel, Eldrin, Jexi, and Nyx arrived at the entrance of the field marshal's encampment to find a bizarrely mixed group of human, dwarven, elven, orc, goblin, hobgoblin, and minotaur soldiers staring wide eyed back at them as if some mythological creature had just descended from the heavens.

The sight of the mixed group was both astonishing and indescribably encouraging. Two armies had amassed with the sole mission of helping them fight their way to the portal. Jexi quietly choked back her tears of joy that Gorian had heeded her advice and was successful at convincing the field marshal to reach out to their enemies. She had not told anyone else of her plan that ultimately united the entire realm.

Lauriel was uncomfortable with all of the attention and the seemingly hallowed silence, but the captive audience had the opposite effect on Jexi. She quickly dismounted and began to address them.

"We're back, boys, did you miss us?"

Several of the soldiers who were already completely enthralled by the new red-headed seductress nodded their heads energetically.

"Yes!" one of the men blurted enthusiastically as his voice broke the silence. But the combination of the bewitched look on his face and his captivated stare told that it was clearly an unintentional outburst. He had not even realized that he had said anything out loud.

The other men laughed heartily at him, but he continued to be oblivious of all things.

Jexi walked up to him and closed his gaping mouth before kissing him on the cheek.

"Well at least someone did." She gave him a playful but painful slap before walking back to the center of the circle. The other soldiers erupted again into laughter at his expense, and the orcs seemed to find the gesture particularly amusing.

Lauriel shook her head and tried to contain her laughter as the rest of the party dismounted.

"We bring her to an encampment with thousands of men; we should have expected nothing less," she whispered to Eldrin.

Eldrin could not contain his chuckle.

Jexi continued to address the captivated crowd that she knew was now putty in her hands.

"In answer to the question that all of you are dying to know... yes, we have the shard!"

A great cheer erupted, and the crowd began to jubilantly celebrate. The exultation rippled outward throughout the encampment as the word of the good news quickly spread. The surreal sight of orcs hugging elves, and dwarves high-fiving goblins would never be adequately captured or described by any journal or historical manuscript, no matter how well skilled its author.

Only those that were present in that moment would believe the odd and unique event had occurred.

In completely uncharacteristic haste, the battle warden burst through the throng and stepped to the forefront. The crowd again drew silent as they respectfully awaited the triumviri's interaction with the companions. His normally cold gray eyes now danced with excitement as he began to directly address Lauriel.

"I am Battle Warden Elenduï Adayr, commander of the combined elven armies. You must be *Andúlarium* Valendril?"

The use of her formal title was a proper acknowledgement of her rare skill and achievement.

"I am. Well met, sir," she replied.

"I knew your grandfather well. He was one of the finest that I have ever met; and he was always so proud of you." He then motioned to the two scimitars at his side and switched to Elvish. *"Ni maith Andúlarium."*

Lauriel's eyes grew wide. He was only the fourth singing blade master that she had ever met. The mention of her grandfather caused a sudden sense of longing, as a pleasant memory of him sprung to the forefront of her mind.

But the moment was fleeting as the battle warden continued, "Is it true that Isilmwé, Blade of Power and greatest of all elven weapons, has returned, and that you are the Blademaster?"

Lauriel nodded in acknowledgement but did not immediately speak her answer. She instead drew the mundane scimitar from its scabbard and then allowed the artifact to take its true, unconcealed appearance.

The crowd around her gasped as they were suddenly bathed in the calming radiance of its cool white light. The blade warden's position and authority suddenly seemed profoundly diminished as the troops from both armies found themselves fixated on the otherworldly beautiful Blademaster, eagerly awaiting her next command. Many of the elves began to push their way to the front to glimpse the pinnacle display of bygone elven power.

She held out the weapon for the battle warden to observe, and the mere sight of the wondrous artifact and the Blademaster that confidently held it confirmed the tale of its resurgence more dramatically than any spoken word. He closed his eyes and breathed a long sigh of relief, as if a great weight had been lifted from his shoulders. He looked back up at Lauriel and his calm and collected composure had already returned.

"This gives me great hope, *Andúlarium*."

Lauriel met his gaze intently. "It is true, battle warden and *Andúlarium* Adayr. The Swordsong of Isilmwé continues, but although the blade is light, the weight of the responsibility is almost too much to bear."

Her statement struck a chord deep within him. He knew all too well the obligations that came with the title of *Andúlarium*, and he understood that the added burden of being the Blademaster would be crushing.

Before his interaction with her, he had not intended to swear any kind of oath. But he could not deny his sudden feeling of intense desire to help her on her quest and felt an overwhelming sense of conviction to publicly declare it.

"If my life or my scimitars can help to lighten this burden but a moment, they are yours, *Andúlarium*. And you shall have one thousand elves to help you and your companions carry this burden as well."

Lauriel was startled by his ardent vow. She had not anticipated nor prepared for any type of reception like she had just experienced and struggled through an unrehearsed reply.

"Thank you for your encouragement and your willingness to help us on our quest, Battle Warden Adayr. I can't tell you how much encouragement it gives me to have all of your support."

He nodded in satisfaction at her simple but sincere reply and finally turned his attention to the other companions. "Pardon my manners, but I have been eagerly awaiting confirmation of the rumors of a Blademaster. Welcome and well met to each of you as well; any companion of the *Andúlarium* is a companion of mine."

He motioned toward the tent on the small rise. "Please join us at the command tent, there is much to catch you up on."

Before proceeding, Lauriel turned to address the soldiers. She raised both swords and shouted so that everyone that had gathered could hear her. "This is now all of our quest, and I have no doubt that together, we can rid Alynthi of these vile creatures once and for all. Sleep well, my friends, for tomorrow we shall have our vengeance!"

Reunion

Seven thousand soldiers were still clapping and cheering wildly when the companions arrived at the command tent to find a familiar face standing at the entrance, eagerly awaiting their arrival.

"Captain Drägo!" Nyx exclaimed as she ran up to him and gave him the biggest bear hug that a halfling could muster, foregoing any formality or protocol.

He smiled and reciprocated the warm hug before addressing them. "Welcome my friends. You know how to make an entrance. I thought you would never get through the crowd." He stepped to the side and motioned for them to enter. "Please, join us."

The companions filed into the spacious tent but by the time that everyone had entered, it felt uncomfortably crowded. In yet another surreal sight that was quickly becoming the norm, the Council of War, a mixture of mortal enemies, stood together around the table. The field marshal walked to his place at the table and began to make introductions.

"My brave friends, I would like to introduce you to our Council."

He motioned around the rectangular table. "You have already met Battle Warden Elenduï; this is Highlord Protector Dordolek, War-Chief Gorgath, Overlord Nillirk, Battlelord Kanmyr, and Supreme Tyrant Schittikus."

"Schittikus?" Jexi interrupted.

Nyx began a muffled giggle that she had a difficult time suppressing.

The field marshal looked at her pleadingly and continued his introduction.

"Council, this is Warlock Jexi, Archmage Eldrin, High Priestess Nyx, and Blademaster Lauriel."

The companions each nodded in acknowledgement, and the field marshal immediately took his seat at the table, indicating that further introductions or pleasantries would have to wait.

"Now, let us get to the urgent business of your quest," he began "May we see the magical device that may close the portal?"

Lauriel nodded and removed her backpack. While she retrieved the object, Jexi briefly explained its esoteric existence.

"Reality shards were used by the Gods during the creation of the planes to anchor and stabilize them, bringing them into order and existence.

For some unknown reason, an extra was left in the Plane of Discordance, creating the chaos of the two realities that occupied that place. Placed into a dimensional portal, it should destabilize it enough to collapse it."

Lauriel held the rod-shaped object up for everyone to see. "This is the extra shard," she proclaimed triumphantly. She let go of the translucent purple object but it did not fall. To the Council's amazement, it continued to hover in the exact place that she had released it. The peculiar device slowly rotated on its long axis as if it was trying to bore a hole into some unseen dimension.

As it spun faster and faster, an extremely low-pitched hum began to emanate from it, causing a perceptible vibration throughout the room.

Eldrin explained its strange properties. "As the shard continues to spin, do not be alarmed if you see odd things appear around us. It is now actively opposing the other shard in this plane and beginning to create small rifts in our reality as it tries to establish its own."

Lauriel allowed it to continue to whirl until dark shadows began to skirt around the room in the same direction of the spin, randomly winking in and out of existence.

"This obviously should not be here; how long do we have until its presence here disturbs something that should not be disturbed?" the battle warden questioned. The obvious look of concern on his face caused an uneasiness throughout the entire room.

"You are correct, Battle Warden Adayr, it should not. It is trying to anchor itself, and given enough time, it would bifurcate our reality just like the Discordance. Thankfully, we can disrupt it, but only temporarily."

"I have seen enough of this devilish device. Let's get it the hell out of here," the dwarf exclaimed.

The orc had been eying it suspiciously and nodded in agreement.

Lauriel took the cube out of her backpack and tossed it to Eldrin.

"It seems luck was with us when we came across this extremely rare cube of force. We can capture the shard within, temporarily disrupting it. But it takes constant magic energy to keep the cube active. So much so, that I have to use all of my magic throughout the day to keep this trapped in its temporal prison."

Eldrin held the cube up to the shard and spoke the command word, "*Velixium.*"

He pressed the cube into the shard, and it passed effortlessly into it. The cube instantaneously grew into a long, narrow, rectangular shape that was just large enough to encapsulate the object. The shard slowed and the shadows ceased.

"If we did not have this, we could spare no extra second," Eldrin said in a final conclusion to their presentation.

He handed the cube back to Lauriel and she placed it into her backpack.

"And now we must get it there; that is our sole objective," the field marshal declared as he redirected the attention to the map at the large table.

"The entrance to Draxanarek'Vel is only an hour march from here to the valley below." He pointed to the place on the map.

"You may have noticed the large, extinct volcano that looms in the distance. The great gate rests within that mountain, but the Dark Elves have not opened it." He looked up at Lauriel. "Lauriel, I am under the understanding that you possess the key that will open it?"

She pulled out the silver spider necklace that she had been given and held it up for the group see. "I think so; this is what the Dark Queen gave me."

"Think so!" the orc exploded. "What you mean, 'think so'? We march here away from homes and tribes and you not even know if we get in?"

He slammed his fist down on the table, splintering a section of it and nearly knocking it over. The wooden pieces were catapulted into the air and flew across the room.

He was shocked that the small, little female elf did not seem at all intimidated by his outburst. He was accustomed to others cowering down from his violent displays of displeasure. She met his furious gaze unflinchingly and then answered him, "No, and we don't know if the shard will work either, but what other options do we have?"

Expecting the worst, the field marshal held his breath in anticipation of the war-chief's reaction toward the unsubmissive elf.

The massive orc glared at her but appeared to be considering her words. After a few tense moments, and in no small part to her calm confidence, Lauriel won his respect.

"How we get there?" he snorted.

The field marshal breathed a sigh of relief and picked up the wooden pieces while the others propped the table back up. He placed the first piece directly in front of the gate to Draxanarek'Vel. "The Golden Legion will form a spear tip formation and be made up of the combined human soldiers." He took the second piece and placed it just to the left and diagonally behind the first. "The elven army will be designated as the Silver Legion and form into a left echelon that further extends the left side of the spear tip formation."

He placed the third piece on the right side. "The dwarven army will be opposite, forming the right echelon as the Steel Legion." He took the last piece and placed it behind the first piece in the center. "The Bronze Legion will be comprised of the rest of the human armies but held in in the center of the spear formation as reserve, filling in any part of the spear formation that begins to falter." He looked back up at the companions. "Lauriel, you must stay in the center and protected as much as possible. We must do the heavy lifting to get you there."

Lauriel nodded in understanding, but Eldrin felt a tremendous uneasiness. Shying away from combat and staying out of harm's way while others fought for her was not in her nature.

The field marshal took four more pieces and placed them on the table next to the others and arranged them in the same formation. "War-Chief Gorgath, we could mirror this formation with your army, creating a two-pronged spear attack. The orcs designated as the Iron Legion, the goblins assigned as the Copper and Brass Legions, and the minotaur, hobgoblins and manticore formed into a mixed Legion named Granite."

The orc nodded in understanding but moved the pieces into a line against the mountain. "We not fight in fancy shapes; we smash lines and kill."

"Very well." The field marshal nodded. He knew that it was a pointless effort in futility to try and get them to fight in a way that they were not accustomed to.

He placed two final pieces on the table. "If we get any help from the Dark Elves, they will be the Onyx and Obsidian Legions."

He looked around the table. "Does anyone have anything to add or change? Comments or suggestions?"

Dordolek nodded. "That looks like a sound plan to me."

The others at the table nodded in agreement.

"Very well, we attack at first light," the field marshal stated.

The room suddenly became quiet as the reality of the situation loomed large in everyone's thoughts. The plans were made, the armies were assembled, and the only thing that remained was the conflict of the ages.

"There is one last thing," the battle warden's voice broke the thick silence. He picked up a backpack that had been sitting next to him and tossed it to Lauriel. "I have a gift for you from the High Queen of the Woodland Elven realms, Audrianna Rhyuviell."

Lauriel's eyes danced with excitement as she took the backpack and opened it. When she withdrew the contents, all of them gasped at the exquisite beauty and craftsmanship of the object that she held.

Dark, emerald green scales shimmered in the light of the many torches as she held up the unique armor piece that was unlike any that she had ever seen. It was a set of scale mail, but the scale armor pieces were made of no metal. Something about the scales looked strangely familiar to her but she could not immediately place them. Unlike the regular bulky and cumbersome mail armor that was traditionally formed into a loose-fitting hauberk, this armor had been carefully crafted for a female in the likeness of a form-fitted corset.

As she continued to inspect it inquisitively, the battle warden told the history and significance of the piece.

"It is the queen's personal armor, passed down to her through several generations. It is nearly as old as your sword, but as protective as the day it was forged. The master armor smith had to invent new ways to work with the difficult green dragon scales.

None now know of the technique that he used to shape each one, for his knowledge passed with him before any other dragon scales were obtained."

"Dragonscale armor," she gasped. With the revelation, she connected the familiarity of the look of the scales to those finest of scales that she had observed on Malthrax.

The battle warden continued, "The scales are as hard as adamantium plate but less than the weight of leather. I know that as *Andúlarium*, we do not use heavy or restrictive armor, but this was specifically crafted with that free-flowing purpose in mind. Wearing it causes no loss of speed, movement, or dexterity."

Lauriel stared in amazement at him and then the remarkably lightweight armor several times before Jexi finally ran out of patience.

"Well put the damn thing on, we all want to see it."

The group shared a collective moment of levity, and the field marshal offered her his private quarters next to the tent to use as a changing area.

When Lauriel reemerged just a few moments later, she looked like an avatar of the Goddess Kathele herself.

"Sweet mother of the gods," Eldrin muttered with all of the breath that remained in him. The battle warden seemed to agree with his statement, and even the orc nodded in approval of the dainty elf.

The sleek corset shape of the armor piece fit the contours of her body like it had been custom crafted specifically for her. Each protective area was covered by carefully shaped segments of overlapping scales. The smith had worked the smallest scales into uniformly sized pointed diamond shapes that were about the size of a fingernail.

The plackart area that protected the lower half of the front torso was formed with six prominent strips of the smallest scale pieces that had been placed into an arrangement that resembled her own, well-defined abdominal muscles. The protective bust area had been created with slightly larger pieces that the smith had added curvature to so that it would form snugly and comfortably around the breast. The largest scales, about the size of two thumbnails, had been formed into armored pauldrons. The scales rested upon a base layer of soft, supple leather that was comfortable yet snug against her skin.

She was shocked at the properties of the armor. It had the same lightweight feeling of a finely crafted set of leather armor but afforded her even greater mobility.

At the same time, it had the protective properties of a set of half plate armor. She raised her arms high and low, front to back, and the scales moved with her effortlessly.

"What spectacular craftsmanship!" Lauriel exclaimed.

"I must admit that if it were my size and not a gift from the queen, I would have been tempted to keep it for myself," the battle warden jested.

"Thank you for bringing this remarkable gift on such a journey, battle warden. I hope that I can live up to the queen's endorsement."

"Well, on that positive note, we have a long day tomorrow." the field marshal interjected. He turned to the companions. "I have had a tent for each of you placed up here with a few warm accommodations."

The Council of War stood up from the table and quietly exited the command tent to convey the final plan to their troops. They were followed by all of the companions with the exception of one.

"May I help you, Jexi?" the field marshal questioned.

"You may indeed," she said with a seductive smirk that immediately revealed her true intentions. "If this is to be my last night, then I intend to enjoy it," she said as she locked the door.

He raised his eyebrows and then walked to her. "The thought of you has filled my mind every day since we parted," he admitted candidly.

To his surprise, she leaned into him and whispered in his ear, "I too have shared this pleasant fantasy."

The field marshal met her gaze momentarily and then pulled her closer, kissing her passionately. She reciprocated and then pulled him to the table. With a quick spell and the wave of her hand, the contents went flying across the room.

He began to unbutton his jacket, but she stopped him.

"Leave it on. I like the uniform," she instructed.

Big Words

Eldrin took Lauriel by the hand and drew her into one of the available tents. His palms were sweaty, and she could immediately tell by his tense body language that he was extremely anxious.

"Eldrin, what's wrong?" she asked, her voice suddenly filled with concern.

Eldrin turned to face her and drew her close. "There is one thing that needs to be made right before the battle tomorrow, *Ælfen*."

Lauriel looked up at him questioningly. "And what is that?"

Eldrin paused and seemed to have trouble finding his words. "I have waited for the perfect time to express this, but with everything that has gone on, I have only realized that there will not be a perfect time, unfortunately." His rambling speech was uncharacteristically nervous. Eldrin shook his head in frustration and drew in a long, deep breath before he started again. "The thought of you fills my heart and mind with something that I have never before known or felt, and I don't know if you feel the same, but I cannot go into battle tomorrow without telling you how I truly feel. *Ælfen* ... I am one hundred percent, madly in love with you."

It was in that very moment that Lauriel finally broke free of the last vestiges of her past that plagued her.

No longer would she allow the fear of losing someone to shackle her heart and prevent her from getting too close. And although it scared her more than many of her enemies, she realized that she was ready to love him back with reckless abandon.

"I love you too!" she exclaimed. "I have wanted to tell you also!" she cried enthusiastically as her eyes filled with tears of joy.

Lauriel could see a wave of relief wash over Eldrin as his shoulders relaxed and he exhaled like he had been holding his breath for several minutes. Lauriel threw her arms around him and kissed him with a passion and excitement that surpassed even their first kiss. After several minutes of unbridled affection, she extracted herself from him and walked over to secure the tent flap.

"Jexi's not the only one that gets to have fun tonight," she said with an unmistakably seductive smirk on her face.

CHAPTER TWENTY-SEVEN

Dark Tide

The peaceful stillness of the pre-dawn morning stood in sharp contrast to the disquiet apprehension that had settled over the assembled legions. One thousand yards separated the two combined armies from the largest man-made structure in Alynthi, a colossal wall of stone that was almost incomprehensible in scale. Beyond it lay an enemy of completely unknown strength hidden somewhere within.

The immense gate dwarfed the seven thousand troops and made the two formations that stood before it appear small and insubstantial, like a single songbird perched in front of the large portcullis of a grand castle. Affixed to the very center of the great gate was a massive, circular stone of black obsidian.

Its smooth, polished surface exhibited a carefully crafted silver inlay of a spider, the well-known symbol of Draxanarek'Vel. It stood as a foreboding beacon and symbolic reminder of the beautiful but deadly Dark Elven realm that lay beyond.

Lauriel's heart pounded in her ears as she moved to the front of the Golden Legion formation with the "key" to the gate.

She had no idea what she was supposed to do with it or how the necklace even functioned, but felt the tremendous pressure of getting the gate to somehow open without delay.

The already frigid temperature had plummeted even further throughout the night, and the early exit away from the warmth of the encampment fires was already taking a toll on the troops. She knew that not even the imminent break of dawn would provide any relief from the cold, and the armies needed to either move or enter the mountain to stay warm.

As Lauriel neared the gate, a strange thing happened. The legs of the silver spider on her necklace began to twitch. She reflexively grabbed the necklace and yanked it off of her neck, tossing the spider to the ground.

To her shock, the spider grew rapidly, doubling in size every second until it reached the size of the Red Dragon Malthrax. Both her and the Golden Company troops at the front of the formation were forced to quickly scatter away to avoid being crushed. The gargantuan monstrosity of a silver-haired spider quickly scurried toward the gate, as if it recognized its long-lost home. It closed the distance in mere seconds, and when it reached the wall, it climbed up to the black obsidian stone and placed itself directly on top of the silver inlay, its head downward at the six o'clock position like it had found the center of its own web. To their amazement, the spider fit perfectly within the inlay. Each leg pressed into eight previously unseen holes in the disk, and once all of them were in position, the unmistakable sound of stone grinding upon stone began to echo throughout the valley. The circular stone disk rotated one hundred and eighty degrees until the head of the spider faced upward and no longer guarded the entrance.

An eerie silence fell over the valley as the grinding stopped and all of the troops waited nervously in anticipation of what would happen next. The silence seemed like an eternity but then, ever so slightly, the ground beneath their feet began to tremble.

Suddenly, a thunderous boom echoed throughout the valley, and a visible seam formed vertically in the middle of the wall.

Dust and loose rock debris tumbled from the stone gate, and the ground's trembling increased in intensity to a full, earthquake-like tremor. The seam widened until the wall was split into two giant pieces.

With an intense rumbling that sounded like the volcano itself had suddenly sprung back to life, both pieces of the wall slowly rotated backward into the mountain. As the colossal doors opened, warm air blasted forth from the darkness of the deep kingdom and tumbled across the field in a terrifying but welcome reprieve from the cold.

But when the rumbling ceased, no army of Dark Elves greeted them.

"They have scurried into their crevices and left us to fight their own battle," the battle warden said bitterly.

"Or there are none left to join," the highlord protector added dubiously.

"Signaller, sound the advance," the field marshal ordered.

A bright, clear trumpeting pierced the morning air, and a thunderous response from the war drums of the orcs' army answered. The two formations began advancing toward the entrance but had only spanned two hundred yards when they were brought to an abrupt halt by another rumble emanating from deep within the gaping maw of the mountain. The noise was much different than the sound of the grinding stone; it grew louder, and closer.

Dark, indiscernible shapes began to appear against the blackness from beyond and before they were recognized, thousands upon thousands of the abraxoth and gwillinix creatures spilled like a dark tide out of the opening and into the valley. From high above, the scene looked like a fire ant mount that had just been kicked.

"Oh shit ... We do not have enough," the field marshal quietly voiced.

CHAPTER TWENTY-EIGHT

Dread Lord

A dark sea of at least five thousand vile creatures poured from the mountain and crashed directly into the two army formations like a lethal tsunami. The Gold, Silver, and Iron Legions fought desperately to keep their lines from buckling under the staggering pressure, and the Copper Legion that was to be held in reserve had to be called up almost immediately.

"This is unsustainable! We need at least twenty legions for this position," the battle warden advised.

The highlord protector also weighed in, his voice grave. "We cannot stay here defensive, but any advance will lead to full encirclement and a quick death if they get behind us."

The field marshal nodded in agreement but was otherwise silent while his sharp, tactical mind raced for a winning solution.

The triumviri's urgent discussion was interrupted by the thunderous drums of the war chief's army. To their surprise, his troops surged back into the attackers with a counter charge of the same primal ferocity, but it quickly stalled as it devolved into furious hand-to-hand combat that was absent of any order or formation.

* * * *

Shortly after the engagement of the first wave, another wave of at least two thousand abraxoth and gwillinix spilled from the darkness of the mountain and charged across the field.

"We must do something!" Nyx cried in despair.

It had been everything that Eldrin could do to hold Lauriel back from charging into the foray, but when it became evident that morale was about to break, there was no stopping her.

With her scimitars drawn and her visibly concerned eyes fixed firmly on the rapidly collapsing spear tip formation, she calmly addressed Eldrin. "Eldrin … my love … I'm so sorry, but I just can't sit back and watch this fail."

"Lauriel!" Eldrin shouted, but it was too late. She began to charge toward the front. "Shit!" he exclaimed. He was still being forced to use his arcane magic to contain the shard in the cube of force, and his capacity to help her with his spells was very limited. "Jexi!" he shouted frantically. The tone and urgency of his voice immediately drew her attention, and she quickly picked up Lauriel's emerald green armor and glowing Moonblade charging toward the tumult.

"Crazy bitch!" she muttered in exasperation.

She pulled a small talisman necklace from a belt pouch and placed it around her neck. The strange, black, metal pendant appeared to have a sigil with numerous geometric shapes and runes inscribed into it. She then dropped her backpack and withdrew a black, leather book that had the very same symbol boldly emblazoned on the cover.

"Nyx, tell the triumviri not to be alarmed by what they see, and you in particular must stay far, far away from me."

Eldrin looked at the talisman and then the book in alarm. "Demonicon!? Where the hell did you get such a thing!?"

She dismissed his comment and opened the book to a specific page. She then pulled her dagger from her belt and drew the blade across her outstretched arm that held the book, letting her blood spill freely upon the ground in front of her.

A dark look of concern overtook Eldrin's already tense face. "You should not be summoning something that is banished from this realm, nor something that you cannot control!"

"What choice do we have?" Jexi snapped.

"I give it a fifty-fifty shot of it submitting to the summons or killing me—maybe better with the talisman; now go!"

Eldrin knew that any efforts to convince her otherwise would be futile, and he began to chase after Lauriel.

As soon as her companions were a safe distance from her, she began to read the summoning spell from the book that had been written in a strange language. *"Naz-Dath Incinktus, Orneth dax novos. Nin ha luxuvehenath argonos ..."*

The ground fractured into an open fissure where her blood had spilled, and a dark shadow formed above it.

* * * *

"Oh shit!" the field marshal exclaimed. He watched helplessly as Lauriel charged to the front of the formation and engaged the enemies. She was exceptionally skilled at fighting multiple opponents, but she had not been trained for the chaos of the battlefront. She was used to being able to easily dodge or parry attacks but quickly realized that there were simply too many enemy claws raking at her from every direction. Several attacks glanced off of her dragon scale armor, and her Divine Shield spell protected her from many others. She knew that it was only a matter of time until they scored a deadly hit against her.

She found that furious solo combat was not the answer; she needed the strength and teamwork of the military unit.

"Push forward!" she yelled in encouragement.

Her charge had not only inspired them, but her words were taken as an order of the highest rank. The command of the Blademaster rippled down the line, and the signallers switched to the flag that signaled the advance.

All four legions began a furious press forward, directly into the dark tide of enemies. The push also caused the war-chief's chaotic mass of violence and death to lurch forward with them. But as the formations moved, the highlord protector's previously expressed fear came to fruition; they were becoming fully encircled.

"We are about to be flanked with no way out of this!" he shouted in alarm.

"That might not be a bad thing after all! We may have better luck in the narrower caves of Draxanarek'Vel, at least our sides will be protected by the cave walls!" the field marshal exclaimed.

The battle warden nodded but was quick to address the reality of their situation. "My friends, there is no way out of this anyway; there is only forward."

* * * *

Jexi finished her spell, and an abomination of an old kind arose out of the shadows and unfurled its abhorrent wings. More terrifying than the enemy itself, entire allied units scattered to keep their distance.

His malevolent stare was enough to collapse the heart and will of men, and those unfortunate souls whose legs had failed them near his presence could only grovel for his mercy.

The Dread Lord, a most terrible of fiends, slowly turned to destroy the one that had dared disturb him from his lair in the pits of hell. But Jexi met his terrible gaze with one of equal doom.

The twelve-foot-tall demon looked her up and down and quickly spotted his own talisman around her neck.

"I was going to kill you quickly, but I see that you have stolen something that belongs to me. Now I will take my time, and you shall suffer terribly."

His dark and foreboding voice somehow emphasized the death and agony of the field of battle.

"I also have your name," Jexi declared as she slammed the demonicon shut.

"And because of that, I now command you to do my bidding, Dread Lord Kabruz'zt, Fiend Prince of the Seventh."

His eyes opened wide, and he burst into flames from his own uncontained rage. He drew a ghastly black mace that appeared to smolder like a glowing charcoal ember. It continuously belched acrid black smoke, and any unfortunate soul who inhaled it died the slow death of strangulation.

"You bitch!" he roared. His now booming voice echoed off the mountain and spread throughout the valley. It was so terrifying that the dying screams of those struck down in battle suddenly brought others comfort in knowing that they did not die by his hands.

"You have one minute of my time; what is your task?" he questioned.

"Help us to advance from here to the entrance of the cavern by ridding us of our enemies," Jexi replied.

He looked out across the field of battle and began a hellish laugh that made shivers run down her spine.

"My pleasure, witch, but the end justifies the means," he cryptically forewarned.

Before she could say another word, he charged toward the front, sadistically slaying everyone and everything in his path.

His first strike removed six souls from a mixture of the Gold and Copper Legions and his equally devastating second followed quickly after.

"Run!" Jexi screamed.

It was the first time Eldrin had ever seen her in a near panic. She had not anticipated that the summoning would have such negative and calamitous consequences.

She mistakenly thought that her subject had to obey her commands and submit to her control, but to her horror, she found that she was only partially correct.

He did have to briefly follow her command, but he was free to carry it out in any way that he saw fit, and a path of allied carnage soon followed.

Lauriel, move left! she could hear Eldrin's urgent warning in their mind-to-mind communication.

The field marshal's formation quickly broke down as the legions scrambled to move away from the Dread Lord, but there was no sudden collapse as even the abraxoth and gwillinix desperately scattered away from the presence of the dreadful entity.

Lauriel followed Eldrin's caution and moved to the left just as the demon surged to the front of the line. She had just made it out of his immediate reach when he passed by, but suddenly stopped, and his attention was unexpectedly drawn fully to her. He looked down, quickly picking her out of the frantic throng. His terrifying gaze was drawn to Nightfang, and the red glowing runes of the scimitar began to eerily mirror the glowing ember colors of the Dread Lord's own mace of death. She could see a recognition on his face that resembled the chance meeting of a long-lost friend, and she could clearly remember Eldrin's words echo through her mind: *"The runes and word of concealment are actually that of the Infernal tongue, a language that is only spoken in the hellish underworld!"*

He said nothing but nodded at her in acknowledgement before continuing forward with his annihilation.

She immediately understood his gesture to mean that, as wielder of the respected weapon, she would be spared the brutal death of the others. She fell in behind the fiend and ordered another push toward the gate.

* * * *

Nyx had just made it to the triumviri as fast as she could when Jexi's spell concluded and the Dread Lord rose from the shadow.

"What in the name of the abyss!" the field marshal exclaimed.

"It's okay, it is just Jexi's spell!" she panted, but she had not yet turned to behold the horror. When she saw the ashen, terror-stricken look on their faces and heard the diabolical laughter from the field, she knew that something terrible had happened.

She forced herself to turn around and as she did, she observed the single most deplorable blasphemy that she had ever seen.

"Oh, Jexi no!" she cried.

They all watched in horror as Jexi appeared to lose control of her subject and the formation quickly collapsed as he decimated everyone around him.

"What the hell do you mean it's just Jexi's spell?" the highlord protector bellowed. "It's killing everything!"

Her blood ran cold, and she fell to her knees while clutching her holy symbol. She begged for a quick departure of the malefic presence, and for mercy upon the departed souls that had been struck down by the damned.

They observed in stunned silence as Lauriel unexpectedly fell in behind the fiend and the formation suddenly reformed with her. The Dread Lord began to clear a deadly swath forward, and the vile creatures continued to scatter away from him like cockroaches from a light.

The wake of his destruction left a space for the stalled legions to begin a rapid advance toward the entrance of the cavern, and the entire field of battle surged forward.

In a tactically brilliant move, the war-chief's army used the momentum and chaos to disengage from their enemies and fall in immediately behind the field marshal's legions. The timing of the action could not have been more fortunate.

Just as the second wave of two thousand creatures arrived, the war-chief's merge was complete, and his remaining legions were in place to protect the rear flank. In an effort to complete a full encirclement and avoid the Dread Lord, the two thousand newly arriving creatures had swarmed around to the rear. But as they arrived, they were met by the unexpectedly stubborn resistance of the war-chief's army.

The demon pushed all the way to the entrance, completing the geas that Jexi had imposed upon him.

Now free of his unwelcome obligation, he immediately reappeared back in front of her. His hand was outstretched, and the talisman around her neck glowed red hot, melting into her skin like a hot knife through butter. She ripped it off of her neck and tossed it to him, but not before she had suffered a painful burn. She looked down and the imprint of the talisman had been branded on her.

The demon laughed sardonically. "May it be a constant reminder of your treachery."

With his talisman back in hand, he disappeared.

CHAPTER TWENTY-NINE

Service and Sacrifice

The combined armies had fought together valiantly but by the time they made it to the threshold of Draxanarek'Vel, less than half of their troop strength remained. Two thousand of the vile creatures had been killed, but the battle remained hopelessly pitched. All of the allied troops clearly understood that a push into the darkness of the underground kingdom was a one-way trip, yet not even a single goblin hesitated.

The massive gates that had swung inward into the cavernous mountainside created an immense, two-thousand-foot-wide by one-thousand-foot-long entrance corridor. The cavern extended beyond the gates and farther into the mountain for another one thousand feet where it narrowed into a single, one-hundred-foot-wide passage that began an abrupt descent into the heart of the underground realm.

The early morning light from the surface peeked into the giant opening like an unwelcome intruder, but it was not yet bright enough to illuminate the vast cavern.

As the army began their push into the mountain, the eyes of the surface dwellers adjusted to the darkness, and they found that the underground kingdom was illuminated by a soft, ambient, red glow from phosphorescent fungus that covered the walls and ceilings.

To the light-sensitive eyes of the Dark Elves, it was as bright as daylight.

The five thousand remaining abraxoth and gwillinix reestablished their pressing, three-hundred-and-sixty-degree offensive, and the forward momentum of the legions quickly faltered just as they reached the defensive bottleneck of the narrower passage.

Lauriel attempted to lead another push, but as desperately as the troops tried to carry out her orders, the strength and overwhelming numbers of the enemy were too great to overcome. The army had become trapped like a cork in a bottle, and no viable path to victory, or escape, remained.

As the circle of allied troops became smaller and smaller, Eldrin gathered the other companions together to arrange one last desperate salvo of magic. The triumviri drew their weapons and saluted each other in final farewell as they prepared to charge forward to die beside each of their own legions. But just before they did, something miraculous and terrifying happened.

In an instant, they were all enveloped in a pitch darkness so deep and disorienting, that they felt they may have been blinded. Even the dark vision of the elves and dwarves could not pierce the veil. The companions recognized it as the same magical darkness that had enshrouded Malthrax's lair.

From the depths of the blackness came a deep rumbling of stone on stone, and the ground beneath their feet shook again with earthquake-like tremors. Jexi immediately used a spell that allowed her to see in magical darkness, and as soon as it completed, she witnessed the Dark Elves beginning to execute their carefully planned trap.

As the great gates drew to a close at a surprisingly fast rate, Dark Elves poured into the cavern from the multitude of fissures and crevices that had been concealed behind the massive doors.

Over a long period of time, the Dark Elves had developed innate spell casting abilities that they learned to harness at a young age. It gave each of them the ability to cast two arcane spells—Darkness, and a Web spell that could trap their opponents in a thick, sticky spiderweb. By the time that the two-thousand-strong force finished entering the cavern, the entire rear half of the enemy army was blanketed in layer upon layer of adhesive web. Each strand was individually no match for the razor-sharp claws of the abraxoth, but they were covered in such thickness that the more they cut, the more they became entangled.

The Darkness spell had a very short duration, and when it suddenly lifted, the rest of the allied army observed the shocking scene that played out before them.

Multiple bright flashes of orange light illuminated the cavern and streaked toward the tangled mass as the last few remaining Dark Elf sorcerers unleashed a coordinated volley of spells. When the flaming bolts impacted the web, it ignited, and flames raced across the entire flammable surface. The ensuing firestorm was brief, but by the time that it had consumed the web, almost the entire rear section of the abraxoth and gwillinix army had been decimated.

Before the smoke even began to clear, the Dark Elven army charged into the remaining few and violently finished them off with a fury that only comes with exacting a long-awaited revenge. The hammer and anvil position that the highlord protector had feared on the plains had indeed taken place, but it was the Dark Elves that had been the hammer, and the allied army the anvil. With the enemy's second wave annihilated, the two forces joined together for another push to the portal.

Into the Depths

The sudden change in the tide of battle caught the front enemy force by surprise, and Lauriel wasted no time leading another furious charge.

She activated her Bracers of Blinding Strike and began to slice through the enemy with a speed and intensity that none of them had ever seen.

Combatants from the war-chief's army as well as the Dark Elves joined the front, eagerly following her without hesitation.

The renewed push was enough to move the stalled army forward again as the creatures fell backward down the relatively narrower corridor.

Eldrin decided that the time was at hand to cease his focus on containing the Reality Shard and unleash the full potential of his magic. He knew that if the battle continued for too long and the enemy had time to summon another wave of reinforcements through the portal, any chance of closing it would surely be lost. He could feel the magical energies emanating from it, and although he did not know where it was, he knew that it was not far away. The Dark Queen had intentionally provided them the key to the entrance that had the most direct route to the portal. He formed up with Nyx and Jexi, and together, they focused on advancing Lauriel through every offensive, defensive, warlock, arcane, and divine spell that they could muster.

Eldrin began the offensive with a powerful spell that reversed the gravity in a fifty-foot radius centered in the middle of the mass of enemies. Many dozens of the creatures flailed wildly in the air as they fell upward toward the ceiling and smashed into it with bone crushing force. The sound of multiple thuds from the heavy bodies impacting the solid stone like giant slabs of meat echoed throughout the cavern, carrying above the clamorous sounds of battle.

As soon as they all hit, the spell ended, and the dead bodies rained from the ceiling, falling back to the ground and pummeling many more of their troops that happened to be in the way.

Jexi targeted a separate area with a warlock spell of the most powerful order that she had affectionately named "Hell Fire." Wizard and sorcerer spells were universally ranked on a level system of first through ninth based off of the power and difficulty of the spell.

Since Jexi was the first warlock, she used the same, already established system, to rank her spells by level.

Very few users of magic ever reached the pinnacle ability of casting a single ninth level spell in their entire lives, even with the most fervent and studied practice of magic; but Jexi seemingly pulled it off on a whim.

A ten-foot-tall, circular wave of white-hot fire spread outward like a ripple in a pond, instantly incinerating all those in its deadly path of destruction. It reached its maximum fifty-foot radius just seconds later, and the conflagration ended before the ashes of the unceremoniously cremated creatures even finished falling to the ground. In six seconds, Eldrin and Jexi alone had cleared the field of almost one hundred enemies.

Eldrin did not recognize the warlock spell but felt the massive release of destructive arcane energy that could only come from a spell of the highest order. He looked at Jexi in shock, trying to understand her newfound, near-godlike abilities. As one of the highest-ranking wizards in his order, even he could not yet cast a spell of that level.

What the hell was that!? he asked in their telepathic communication.

When the gate opened, a barrier seemed to be removed from the magic that I can call upon. I feel limitless! she answered back excitedly.

Over the next minute of battle, Eldrin and Jexi each unleashed an onslaught of ten more of their most powerful offensive spells that targeted large swaths of the battlefield.

The other Dark Elf sorcerers enthusiastically joined in the destruction, expending every bit of their impressive destructive magic into the enemy as well. The ensuing carnage killed off fully half of the remaining front, leaving only about one thousand five hundred of the vile creatures remaining, but just like the magic users in the defense of the Tower of Nemerse, their magic waned.

Nyx had focused her divine magic solely on keeping Lauriel's health and stamina renewed, and the Blademaster had killed scores of enemies as a result.

The remaining allied force of four thousand continued their push down the corridor, making steady progress, but the vile creatures continued to fight fiercely and contested every inch of ground.

A cold chill traveled down Lauriel's spine when she felt the Reality Shard shatter its cubical prison like a fragile glass vase thrown at a brick wall.

The magic of the cube had waned to the point that it could no longer function, and without any renewed magic from Eldrin, it was destroyed by the Reality Shard.

Lauriel immediately disengaged so that she could grab the shard from her backpack before it began to spin beyond her control. With no cube of force to contain it, she knew she had to keep it from spinning as long as she could so that it would not begin to tear apart their reality as it attempted to establish its own. And in the quick moment that passed before she was able to retrieve it, it had already begun its rotation and was gaining speed. She immediately found that it was already difficult to hold on to and she had to continually fight the odd centrifugal force that kept trying to rotate her wrist and arm outward. The shard wanted to spin, and no matter what, it would eventually achieve its goal.

Seeing the Blademaster's sudden disengagement, the battle warden readied his scimitars.

"Friends, there is no more to command here; there is only forward," he said matter-of-factly.

The highlord protector gripped his axe eagerly. "Aye, it's now or never. Permission to charge these bastards, field marshal?"

The field marshal held out his sword and nodded without breaking his gaze over the battle. "It has been the honor of my life to stand at your side as peers. Triumviri ... luck in battle."

With the field marshal's dismissal of their command, they each charged to lead their troops forward. The battle warden quickly filled the position that Lauriel had assumed at the front. His blades rang pure with the deadly song as he rapidly sliced through the enemy.

Lauriel remembered the heartfelt words that he had spoken to her: *"If my life or my scimitars can help to lighten this burden but a moment, they are yours, Andúlarium."*

He was now carrying out his pledge, and Lauriel looked on with respect and admiration at the beautiful sight while she caught her breath and fought the Reality Shard for control.

Wretched Amalgamations

The corridors had many turns, splits, and junctions, and it quickly became apparent that without the Dark Elves leading them through the confusing labyrinth, the path to the portal would be almost impossible to find.

The allies had pushed the remaining enemy force deep down into the bowels of the kingdom, but every hundred feet of progress had come with a heavy toll. By the time that the Dark Elves advised the field marshal that the portal chamber was just around the corner, their combined strength had fallen to less than one total legion. Only two hundred and fifty abraxoths remained, but it was still more than enough to challenge the remnant of the fatigued allied armies.

The cavern is only about one hundred yards away, but something isn't right. It is becoming unnaturally cold, Eldrin advised the group in their mind-to-mind communication. *How is your magic, Jexi?* he asked.

I have expended almost every bit that I can. I only have a few low-level spells left, she replied.

Same here. I do still have the magic of my staff that I am holding in reserve though, Eldrin stated.

Good thinking. Before this is over, I'm afraid we are still going to need it, Jexi answered.

Nyx, how about you? Eldrin asked.

Running low also! Only a few spells left, Nyx replied.

I've only used the bracers once, and have used a few spells, but I can no longer use my weapons. I have to hang on to this blasted Reality Shard that is hell bent on spinning, and it is becoming more and more difficult by the moment, Lauriel chimed in preemptively, her frustration clearly evident.

The Reality Shard continued its determined pursuit to spin and had begun to exert so much force that Lauriel was forced to use both hands to maintain control of it. She knew that she would not be able to hold on for much longer and quickly made her way from the battlefront to the companions in order to get their assistance.

Nyx could see that she was greatly fatigued from both the fighting and the struggle against the object. In an attempt to buy a little more time, she used two of her last four spells to help Lauriel recover from her exhaustion and boost her strength.

"The spell only lasts a few minutes!" Nyx said.

Lauriel could feel the immediate surge of vitality and it was just enough augmentation to help her keep the shard in check for a little while longer.

With Lauriel effectively out of the vanguard, the battle warden, highlord protector, field marshal, and war-chief converged at the front and made the remaining vile creatures pay dearly for the pain and death they had dealt to their troops. They attacked with the same ferocity and vengeance that the Dark Elves had in the entrance corridor when they unleashed their trap on the enemy.

Rivulets of blood spilled from their weapons as they led their troops through the stubborn opposition, pushing them backward and down the final distance of the corridor. All remaining soldiers of every represented race fought with unbridled enthusiasm as they began to sense that victory was finally within their grasp.

But their hearts sank when they rounded the corner and found what awaited their arrival.

The corridor opened up into another immense cavern. A shimmering, fifty-foot diameter circle of bright blue light swirled like a two-dimensional whirlpool against the backdrop of the rear wall.

The vortex slowly rotated in a mesmerizing clockwise motion that faded to black as it reached the center. It was framed by a faintly glowing circular archway that appeared to be embedded into the solid stone wall. Eldrin could feel the strange, sinister power emanating from it and immediately understood what drove the Dark Elves' curiosity.

But it was what lay guarding the portal that dashed any hopes of victory—or survival.

"Well, shit!" Jexi exclaimed, summing up succinctly the feelings of her companions.

Immediately to the left and right side of the portal were two monstrosities that eagerly awaited the opportunity to annihilate anyone or anything that drew near. Wholly foreign and unlike any creature found in Alynthi, the guardians possessed a multitude of deadly options to kill scores of enemies and protect the gateway from whence they had been summoned.

Their deadly form most closely resembled a wretched amalgamation of a Blue Dragon, giant snake, and monstrous centipede. Their giant, serpentine shaped bodies were reared up into an intimidating and aggressive striking position that towered over everything else in the room.

They were protected by a full covering of thick, glossy, Blue Dragon scales, but the scales were only part of their armored defense. Beginning at the nape of their necks and running along the top side of their long bodies, an additional layer of six-inch-thick hardened carapace segments provided enough protection to stop even a siege ballista.

Two rows of large spines ran on each side of the spiked centerline and ended in a deadly array of large caudal spines that bedecked their eagerly flicking tails.

The creatures had the ability to move like a serpent but had numerous pairs of centipede-like appendages that propelled them forward, making them dangerously mobile. The limbs became larger and more developed as they ran upward toward the head; and by the time they reached the upper portion of the body, they had formed multiple pairs of fully functional dragon-like arms. Each pair of arms possessed deadly claws that could be used to either rake at numerous enemies or grapple them in an inescapable bond.

Their heads resembled the likeness of a dragon, and were flanked by two large prominent horns that swept back toward their bodies.

Their row of sharp, bone-white teeth, indicative of a voracious predator, were intermittently hidden by the cold frost that billowed from their open maws. Not unlike the legendary breath weapon of a White Dragon, the abominations could breathe an icy blast over a large area that was so cold, their victims could be frozen solidly into place by even a glancing hit.

But one of the most unsettling things about the creatures was not their host of available methods to strike down their prey—it was their cold and emotionless eyes. Free of any pupils familiar to their reptilian or draconic features, only a blue glow emanated from their sockets. It matched the color and intensity of the portal and told the story of their only purpose—to kill.

Nyx made a feeble attempt at humor to bolster her companions' nadir morale. "Have any more of those demons available?"

Eldrin's head bowed in readily apparent despair and anguish.

Two hundred additional abraxoth and gwillinix reinforcements had just entered the realm and were joined by the remaining one hundred and fifty that had been engaged in the fighting retreat.

Instead of immediately attacking, they cautiously formed a defensive formation in front of the portal, ensuring no possibility of any enemy drawing any closer to it.

Retributive Strike

With only five hundred allied troops remaining, everyone knew that there was no way to push their way past the host of defenders with brute force. A tear rolled down Eldrin's cheek, and his voice quivered as he spoke to the companions.

"My friends, my love, I'm sorry that it has come to this, but I don't see any other choice."

Lauriel looked at him with alarm and tried to grab his arm as if she were attempting to keep him from doing something foolish, but her hand was drawn immediately back to the difficult task of holding onto the shard. She vigorously shook her head, and tears began to run down her cheeks.

"Eldrin ..."

He interrupted her with a brief kiss and placed his hand upon her cheek to comfort her. When he pulled back and looked at her, she saw in his eyes a startlingly intense focus, one that was free of any doubt or question.

"When I clear the pathway to the portal, you will only have seconds before the enemy regroups," he calmly instructed.

"Brother, NO! Give us a second to figure this out!" Jexi pleaded as unchecked tears streamed down her face as well.

"PLEASE DON'T LEAVE ME! I CAN'T LOSE YOU TOO!" Lauriel sobbed in anguish.

Eldrin knew that the spell he intended to use would not work with the shard on him, or he would have carried the burden without hesitation.

He also knew that every second that ticked by only strengthened the enemy, and his next action was not one of foolishness, but very much calculated.

In an instant, he used his last remaining spell energy to cast the same Dimensional Step spell that Jexi had used to escape Malthrax's attack. But instead of using it to escape from the danger, Eldrin appeared right in the middle of it, less than twenty feet away from the portal. The enemy did not even have the opportunity to realize that he was standing among them before he executed his final action.

* * * *

Eldrin used his powerful staff sparingly, only occasionally supplementing his own prepared spells with the release of its destructive magic. The immensely powerful and unique artifact contained within it a well of arcane energy that was enough to cast seven separate high level Fireball spells.

After use, the staff would slowly recharge its lost arcane energy over several days, and Eldrin had ensured that it had reached its maximum capacity before they had even begun the journey to Draxanarek'Vel.

He had made the decision to unrestrictedly use the staff when they had become encircled with no hope of escape, but just as he held it up to cast the first fireball, the Dark Elves had joined with their deadly trap that helped to turn the tide.

The magically bonded wielder of the artifact had one additional option afforded to them; they could say a command word that would allow the willful destruction of the priceless object.

But to do so would result in the immediate and simultaneous release of all of the stored energy, creating a catastrophic explosion that was several orders of magnitude more powerful than even Jexi's ninth level Hell Fire spell.

"Daronos," Eldrin uttered the command word as he cracked the staff over his knee without hesitation.

A bright flash temporarily blinded everyone in the room as the magical energy released in a deafening detonation that shook a vast portion of the underground kingdom. The blast wave spread outward for one hundred feet in all directions, vaporizing everything in its path. Beyond the initial wave, the force of the concussion leveled anything not firmly affixed to the ground for an additional one hundred feet. When both allied and enemy eyes adjusted, nearly three hundred of the enemy troops had been obliterated, and a further fifty had been knocked prone. The explosion had even knocked the monstrous amalgamations back and away from flanking the portal. Several of their dragon scales and segmented carapace armor pieces had been ripped away by the force, and dozens of their centipede-like appendages had either been blown off, or hung uselessly at their sides.

Only a crater remained in the solid rock where Eldrin had been standing, but just as he had advised, a gaping hole now stood where the enemy army had established their defensive blockade in front of the portal.

Lauriel had no time to even consider the horror of what had just occurred.

She activated her bracers and sprinted the four hundred feet that lay between her and the portal.

"For the Blademaster!" the battle warden cried as he charged toward the enemy in an attempt to help keep her path clear.

A palpable wave of malevolent rage could be felt carrying on the air as the remaining fifty abraxoth raced to close the gap, and the other fifty that had been knocked down stood back up in a hurried frenzy to protect the portal.

Lauriel had made it two hundred feet when the first few abraxoths began to draw near from the rapidly closing flanks. She attempted to nimbly maneuver away from them, but the force that the Reality Shard was exerting upon her kept her from any quick changes in direction. She realized that she only had one option before the inevitable merge, and that was to slow down just enough to let the blade warden catch up to her and remove the threat.

Just as the vile creatures were about to close to within striking range of their defenseless target, the fellow *Andúlarium* made it to her and engaged all four of them using the same Surge of Violence attack she had learned from Adamar. Their blood splattered against her in several separate wide arcs as she gained distance from them while he skillfully kept them off of her. Any that turned away from him to pursue her faced a flurry of murderous blades to their backs.

His attacks bought her the needed time and space to continue forward, but it came at great cost. While he was tied up with the engagement, six more abraxoth reinforcements arrived with the sole purpose of bringing an end to the high-value target. When the brief but vicious battle concluded, the battle warden had fallen in a befittingly heroic last stand. Lauriel could not see the death blows, but she knew full well by the sounds of the battle that he had fully committed himself to a selfless act of sacrifice in order to buy time for her.

With less than one hundred feet between her and the portal, the guardian amalgamations moved forward to block her advance. Her mind raced to determine any viable options to get past them.

She knew that she would be well within their striking range before she would be able to span the remaining distance.

Nyx could see the rapidly devolving situation and knew that Lauriel would require more than skilled fighters, fancy footwork, or destructive magic to get to the portal. It would take no less than the rest of the divine magic she could muster for her to have even the slightest chance.

Her eyes locked on to a suitable subject, and she cast her spell on the closest abraxoth to Lauriel, one that was approaching from the left flank and had closed to within thirty feet of her.

Nyx was suddenly standing where the abraxoth had been, and the vile creature looked around in confusion at his sudden new perspective of the field of battle. Her spell had swapped places with him and placed her very close to Lauriel. For her last remaining spell to work on someone other than herself, she had to physically touch the target with the divine energy. She began to sprint toward Lauriel, and her short legs carried her forward as rapidly as they could. To her amazement, the other abraxoths that had been only a few feet behind her did not pursue.

Lauriel's brow furrowed as she instantly recognized the sound of a dragon sharply inhaling as the amalgamations prepared to use their breath weapon. She knew that, while holding the Reality Shard, it would not be possible for her to tumble out of the way of the deadly wave of energy aimed in her direction, and she had already resigned herself to the fact that she would most likely not survive the attack. But she was determined to get the shard as close as she could in hopes that someone would pick up the dropped baton and cross the finish line.

A light and rapid pitter patter of someone small approaching from her left side caught her attention. She glanced over her shoulder and could see Nyx charging toward her at a full sprint.

"NYX, GET BACK!" she yelled in warning just as both of the portal guardians unleashed their breath weapons.

But Nyx had also recognized the telltale sound of the impending attack and pushed onward with steely determination, closing the remaining ten feet just as the dual cone shaped blasts of grave cold raced toward them.

With all of her strength, she gave one final push and dove at Lauriel just before the icy fury washed over them. As she made contact, she felt her spell discharge into Lauriel, and a jubilant look of relief and satisfaction drew across her face.

Lauriel reactively winced and closed her eyes as the white cloud of death engulfed her, but to her surprise, she felt no sudden cold or pain, and when she looked back up to see what had happened, she saw that she had been safely cocooned in a clear, shimmering bubble of protection.

As the thick and obscuring frost quickly lifted, she looked around to thank Nyx for saving her life, but Nyx was no longer near her. She couldn't understand how she had disappeared from her side so quickly, and she rapidly scanned the room again for her. It wasn't until she looked down at the ground and saw several solidly frozen chunks that her mind began to rapidly stitch together the missing pieces of the puzzle.

Nyx had used her last and newest spell, a short-lived globe of invulnerability that afforded Lauriel the protection she needed to survive the blast and continue her progress toward the portal. In doing so, she was completely exposed to the full fury of the two shockingly powerful dragon-like Cones of Cold. The bi-directional direct hits were enough to freeze her solid, and the momentum of her run and diving contact with Lauriel caused her frozen body to shatter like an ice sculpture pushed off of a pedestal.

Lauriel could only stare in shock and horror. Tears burst from her eyes as her mind could no longer contain the burden.

It had been everything she could do to hold herself together and remain focused when she had lost Eldrin, but to lose two of her closest companions within seconds of each other proved too much.

She stood motionless, one hundred feet away from the portal.

The divine magic that protected her began to wane, and the remaining abraxoths that had held back in order to stay out of the way of the breath weapons began to charge.

Her thoughts were interrupted by the familiar haunting vision of a little elven girl peeking through the shredded grapevines, too petrified to move. But this time, it was followed by a clear memory of the words that her Goddess had spoken to her: *"That was not your fight, not yet anyway."*

That same little elven girl's eyes narrowed with singular focus, and her jaw clenched in ardent resolve.

"This time, it IS my fight!" she yelled.

Her strong, athletic legs propelled her forward and she reached her full sprinting speed within seconds. The serpentine-like creatures struck at her several times, but their deadly attacks only glanced off of the globe of invulnerability. In a fortunate stroke of luck, or foresight on Eldrin's part, his Retributive Strike had blown off or broken the arms and tails of the creatures, denying them any ability to grapple or use their deadly weapon-like tail attack.

The protective globe wore off just as she closed to within twenty feet, but her augmented speed from the magic of her bracers was enough to help her cover the remaining distance before the wretched amalgamations could strike again.

With all of her remaining strength and determination, she extended the reality shard in front of her just as she hit the portal at full speed, and the instant the tip of the shard pierced the swirling blue vortex, a great rending sound, like that of lightning splitting a tree, echoed throughout the cavern.

The portal absorbed the unwelcome intruder and immediately began to collapse inward upon itself, causing strange vibrations and force to ripple and pulse throughout the cavern.

When the collapse finally reached the darkened center, the portal winked out of existence and the strange vibrations suddenly ceased.

At the exact location where the Reality Shard had hit, the solid rock cavern wall was sundered from floor to ceiling, and the strange circular archway that had contained the portal crumbled to the cavern floor.

CHAPTER THIRTY

Warlock

When the last death blow was struck, there was no victory cheer from any of the remaining soldiers. The corpses of elves, orcs, dwarves, goblins, humans, minotaur, and hobgoblins littered the ground in a bloody trail of death and carnage that stretched all the way back to the floor of the valley. Nine thousand had put away their differences to join together in a final fight, and less than one hundred remained.

Jexi sat on the blood-soaked floor of the cavern and cradled the field marshal gently in her arms. The highlord protector and war-chief knelt beside her, their hands placed gently upon their comrade in silent respect. All remaining soldiers from every unit had knelt around them in a show of revered recognition and gratitude.

She carefully wiped the blood off of his face as unchecked tears ran down her own. The mortally wounded soldier struggled for each breath, but he met her anguished gaze with one of peaceful serenity. It was a look that told of victory, that the great burden that had been placed upon his shoulders had finally been lifted.

He attempted to raise his hand to her face in an effort to comfort her but was far too weak to complete the minor task.

Even in his grave condition, his thoughts were still on helping others.

Jexi grabbed his hand in hers and helped him hold it to her cheek. As he began to speak, she had to lean in close to his lips so that she could hear his feeble words.

"I'm so thankful … that I got to gaze upon your face … one last time … My only regret in this life … is that I do not have more time with you."

Jexi's eyes stung, and her heart physically ached. She turned her lips to his and gently kissed him. It was a genuine kiss, full of compassion and love, different than any other meaningless or lustful kiss that she had become accustomed to from another.

"You are a good man, Stephen; loyal, dedicated, compassionate, honest, and a man with great honor. You will be remembered not only for leading us to victory in this terrible battle, but for all of those wonderful attributes. I too wish with all my heart that we had more time together." Her voice trailed off as her throat clenched so tightly that she couldn't speak another word.

He drew another ragged breath and tried to pull her closer, once again trying to comfort her in his arms.

"I suppose … that is the best compliment … that one could ever get … In the end … if one is remembered with those qualities … and can die in the arms of a good woman … then they have been truly bles …"

His words trailed off, and he let out one last peaceful exhale. The gleam in his eyes dulled, and his muscles relaxed as they finally found a long-awaited tranquil rest.

The war-chief placed his massive arm around Jexi's shoulder. With his other hand, he gently closed the eyes of the field marshal.

"A good man indeed, the finest I have met," he declared.

The highlord protector was too overcome by emotion to speak. Tears ran down his weathered cheeks, and he wept bitterly for his friend.

* * * *

Many hours had passed when Jexi finally stood back up, and when she did, she stood as the lone representative of the heroes and companions whose difficult quest had made it possible to rid Alynthi of the baneful nemesis. She had not only lost her brother and her friends, but she had also lost her power. When the portal collapsed, the strange power she'd learned to draw upon immediately ceased. Her spells and unique "warlock" magic no longer functioned.

Homecoming

The field marshal's body arrived back in Silenus with full military honor. He was carried on a specially prepared catafalque that had been decorated with the exclusive golden cloth used only for the Golden Company capes. The four battle standards of the human, elven, dwarven, and orc armies adorned each corner in a prominent and dramatic display of respect by all troops of every race that served under his command. Roses and olive branches bedecked the platform as a constant stream of well-wishers lovingly placed them on it as the parade went by.

By the time the funeral procession had finally made it to the wide-open gates of his hometown of Silenus, it had grown from the few surviving troops from the Battle of Draxanarek'Vel, to a several-hundred-yard cavalcade attended by all remaining soldiers from every settlement, township, city, and kingdom throughout the land. A massive crowd had gathered to welcome home their brave heroes and pay respects to the fallen. But it was not just the citizens of Silenus that packed the streets.

A crowd that represented every race throughout Alynthi, many of which had made long pilgrimages to attend the memorial celebrations, were in attendance. On this day, any differences had been put aside, and no enemies remained.

When the procession finally breached the main gate, the great bells of the tower began to ring steadily, and the captive crowd fell silent as the impressive column made their way toward the inner ward of the castle.

A dark gray riderless warhorse with polished barding and golden caparison was led in the front by the two remaining members of the Golden Company. Its head was held high, but a sadness was in its eyes as it continually searched for its missing companion that it took so much pride in carrying. All those that gazed upon the display wept at the poignant reminder of the cost of victory.

In a symbolic display that military order still existed, the dwarven highlord protector, orc war-chief, and Dark Elven commander followed in the next position. Behind them came the most honorable position of the escort, the catafalque bearers. It was filled only by a rotation of the ninety-six surviving soldiers of the Battle of Draxanarek'Vel. Sixteen at a time would bear the field marshal while the remainder formed a ceremonial guard around him. Jexi humbly accepted the troops' request for her to perform the role of lead sentinel guard.

As the procession reached the inner ward and stopped in the very center, the duke and duchess stepped forward to assist with the body as it was carefully placed on a platform that had been constructed for the event.

The fallen soldier had been dressed in a polished set of parade plate armor, and his sword lay in final rest upon his chest. His stately appearance was enough to inspire even after his death.

The duke and duchess personally thanked each surviving member of the battle before making their way to the balcony to address the large crowd.

When they emerged, the large inner castle ward was filled to capacity.

The duke began his unscripted address.

"This war has brought pain and suffering on an unimaginable scale. It has affected almost every family throughout the whole of Alynthi.

But if there is ever a silver lining to this tragedy, it is that never before have we put aside our differences and come together for one purpose like we have done now.

"Look around you, good people of Silenus. You stand now in solidarity with representatives from every race and kingdom. Let that spirit of cooperation and harmony continue to be a shining beacon as we all stand back up together, dust ourselves off, and rebuild our lives and lands in a new age of tranquility.

"Today, and in the coming days, we shall bury, mourn, and honor the fallen. And we start by celebrating the life and service of Field Marshal Stephen Drägo."

The duke took a knee and bowed his head. The crowd followed the moving gesture, and a blanket of thick silence settled across the expanse.

After many moments, many of which were spent in effort to regain his composure, the duke stood once again and finished his address.

"In the days ahead, three moons from now, we will put away our sorrows and celebrate our journey through the darkness, ushering in with open arms the golden days that now lie before us."

A New Dawn

And so it was that all returned to their own homelands and began the long and difficult task of picking up the pieces of their shattered realms and rebuilding their lives. Some returned to only broken remnants of their lands, while others found that theirs had largely escaped the hammer's fall.

Three new moons had passed, and the people of Silenus had given their best efforts to repair the ugly scars of war and make all things ready within the city.

The first day of spring had finally arrived, and like the buds of a tree springing forth from the darkness of a bleak winter, thousands had arrived through the open gates for the highly anticipated celebration.

Dark Elves from Draxanarek'Vel, orcs from their realm of Kaldorak, and elves from their many fair lands were all alike greeted with kindness as their arrival processions passed through the flower laden streets.

Kanarus and other griffons ringed the ramparts, free from harassment or danger. Stories of their heroic deeds were told to the wide-eyed children who stared at them in wonder.

There was great cheering, singing, and joyous celebration throughout all of the open places of the city, and music from all manners of wind, string, and percussion instruments filled the air.

Golden victory streamers fluttered in the gentle spring wind from each open window, from the high points of every tower and from all of the castle turrets.

In the center ward, the dwarves had sent their best stonemasons to build a breathtakingly beautiful rotunda directly on the spot where the field marshal had been buried. Upon each column had been affixed a perfect stone carving of each of the different armies' battle standards. The top had been adorned with the gilded two-headed phoenix that had been the adopted symbol of the combined human armies, but it no longer stood only for the human race. It now stood as a unifying symbol of all peoples of Alynthi, rising out of the ashes of the east and west, north and south.

In the center of the rotunda knelt a female half-elf clad in a black, flowing raiment, her long red hair spilling in waves from the concealing hood of her robe. Her hand gently caressed the smooth stone cheek of the embedded sculpture that had been carved in the perfect likeness of the field marshal in his final rest.

"Jexi?" a familiar voice called.

She turned toward the caller and pulled back her hood as she attempted a cordial smile, but her red, tear-filled eyes gave away her sentiments.

"Duchess Faelyn," Jexi said as she nodded in acknowledgement and quickly wiped away her tears.

"Ahh, it is you! I missed you after the memorial, and I have not seen you around to thank you for everything you have done," the duchess said.

"Thank you, Duchess Faelyn, but no thanks are necessary. I was merely one of the many pieces of the chessboard. I apologize for my absence, but I needed to get away for a while to clear my head."

"I understand, but I know the hand that you played in making all of this possible. You were not merely one chess piece, Jexi, but an inextricable part of setting all of this in the proper motion. Without your insistence to rally our enemies, all of this would be lost," the duchess said as she gestured around the inner bailey.

Jexi looked around at the lively crowd, and the heartwarming sight brought a smile to her face and a small cheer to her heart. Children laughed and played in the streets, free of worry or harm, and complete strangers danced with each other in unbridled joy. It didn't remove her pain, but helped to dull the sharp dagger as deep down she knew that their costly quest had been worth it. She smiled again at the thought that, given the chance, she knew her companions would do it all over again without hesitation.

The duchess continued, "There is yet another reason I seek you, Jexi."

Jexi looked at the Duchess questioningly.

The duchess handed Jexi a small satchel. "Before his departure, Eldrin had asked me to give you these items in the event that he did not return and you did."

Jexi's eyes opened wide, and she opened the small leather bag. In it she found three items. A thick, heavy book titled, *Codex of the Planes*, another much smaller book bearing the title *Retributive Strike*, and the Amulet of the Planes.

Her jaw dropped, but before she was able to speak, a little girl burst out of the crowd.

"MISS JEXI!" the little girl squealed with delight. Her arms waved wildly, and she dropped her two "sword" sticks as she ran over to Jexi and leapt into her awaiting arms.

"Mira! It's so good to see you," Jexi said as she embraced her warmly.

"Thank you for saving all of us! But where are your friends? Where is Miss Lauriel?"

"She has traveled far, far away, my dear—and I am going to find her."

THE END OF BOOK ONE

The Epic of Alynthi

Part 2

The realms unite with no grudge old,
they gather in final stand.
The heroes return with power untold,
and greatest of skill at hand.

Through land and sea and day and night,
as beasts and men collide.
A battle so great that all would fight,
with nowhere left to hide.

And charge they do in final flight,
for those they all hold dear.
Their swords and spells gleam pure and bright,
as end of all draws near.

Through courage and great sacrifice,
the gallant do prevail.
The bells now toll the heavy price,
yet sing the victory tale.

Made in the USA
Coppell, TX
09 December 2021

67817984R00261